“THINKI

NOW, ARE YOU?”

His voice was so low, and dangerous, Ashley felt a tremor go through her body.

But now was the time to get things straight between the two of them; so she quickly, eagerly, nodded her head several times. And at the same time as her head was bobbing like a cork on the ocean, she was saying, in a rush of words, “Oh, yes, Garick. Of course I am. I’m so sorry I put you in this position, but I was desperate. I couldn’t bear the thought of having any of those men paw me.”

“But you didn’t mind the idea of *me* pawing you?” Garick asked.

Ashley paused with her mouth open, her golden-hazel eyes wide with consternation. It was a tricky question. If she said yes, it might hurt his male pride, and she would be in even more trouble than she already was. But if she said no....

Other *Leisure Books* by Jackie Casto:

DREAMS OF DESTINY
DAUGHTER OF DESTINY

The New Frontier

JACKIE CASTO

LEISURE BOOKS NEW YORK CITY

This book is dedicated to all who have faced the loss of the familiar and the uncertainty of the future with faith, courage, kindness, and hope. To all who light candles instead of cursing the darkness.

A LEISURE BOOK®

January 1992

Published by

Dorchester Publishing Co., Inc.
276 Fifth Avenue
New York, NY 10001

Printed in the United States of America.

The New Frontier

Chapter One

New York City
2052 A.D.

The small, preprogrammed view screen in her tiny dormitory room clicked on, and an announcer began reporting on that morning's air quality in the city. Ashley Bronwyn turned over in the narrow bed that took up almost half her quarters, and opened golden-hazel eyes still bleary with sleep.

According to the announcer, she wouldn't need to wear nose plugs today, because a night breeze from the Atlantic Ocean had dispersed enough of the nauseating miasma from the giant food factories to make breathing less unpleasant than normal. That was the good news.

The bad news came a moment later as the announcer reported that today the Census Bureau, where Ashley was employed, would begin tabulating the latest raw census data. The director of the Bureau was hopeful the numbers would show a down trend in the population of the United Americas.

Sure, Ashley thought as she sat up and swung her legs over the side of the bed. *And when I go downstairs for breakfast, I'm going to find that the Easter Bunny came during the night and left thousands of real eggs for the residents of this dormitory to feast on as well. If the director can hope, so can I.*

Since individual water use was strictly monitored and Ashley couldn't afford the heavy fines which were levied on abusers, she turned on the taps in her miniscule shower just long enough to wet herself. She then turned them off and used as little of her dwindling supply of ersatz soap as possible to lather her body.

As she washed, she reflected on how depressing her day's work was likely to be. She didn't want to learn that the population of the United Americas had jumped again over the preceding six months. But since that was more than likely exactly what she would learn, and since her job paid enough for her to have a private room rather than being crowded in with three or four other people, she would do her best to input the ominous census figures into her computer as quickly and accurately as possible.

True, her job was a boring, make-work occupation which could have been done more efficiently by other sophisticated technology, and it was a far cry from the teaching job Ashley had hoped for after graduating from New York University the year before with a doctorate in history. The government had long since discovered that when efficiency was pitted against the government's promise of employment for every adult citizen in the northern and southern hemispheres of the United Americas, it was safer to provide the jobs and let efficiency go by the wayside. But as the population exploded, the government's promise was getting more difficult to keep, and Ashley performed her duties to the very best of her ability in order to keep the job she didn't like, but was grateful to have.

After rinsing off, she smeared a sun-blocking lotion on her body that would protect her skin from the dangerous sun rays that shot through the almost-nonexistent ozone layer. Then she dressed in one of her two shabby, secondhand gray tunics, combed her long auburn hair which badly needed a cut she couldn't afford, grabbed her carryall, and hurried down a seemingly endless hall to the stairs. It was seven floors down to the dormitory dining room. But Ashley felt lucky to be on the seventh floor in the vast building which housed thousands of tiny dormitory rooms just like hers, because the carrier shafts were as often out of order as usable.

As she neared the dining room and became aware of the rising level of noise from the hundreds of voices raised in conversation, she automatically blanked her mind to the cacophony. She had learned the technique almost from birth in order to ward off a nervous breakdown. The mental institutions in the city were filled with people who couldn't cope with overcrowding and noise.

Inside the dining room, she skillfully dodged other breakfasters on her way to a conveyer belt, where she noted wryly that there had been no visit by the Easter Bunny the previous night. All that was visible, as usual, was a long line of bowls containing glops of synthetic food. Grabbing one of the bowls, she again dodged her fellow dormitory residents and squeezed into a place at one of the long tables.

Though Ashley waved at friends from time to time as she ate, everyone who knew her was aware she didn't like trying to converse over the dining-room noise in the morning. So aside from waving, they left her alone—as alone as anyone could be in a room of perhaps a thousand people, all of whom seemed to be talking at once.

A bare five minutes after collecting her breakfast, Ashley returned her now-empty bowl to another conveyor belt and headed for the exit. Outside, she shoved her way onto a crowded pedway and stoically endured the indignity and discomfort of being squeezed on all sides by complete strangers until she came to her stop.

Hopping off the pedway, she shoved her way through the crowds streaming into the government building which housed the Census Bureau. Inside, she placed her credit disk into a slot among hundreds of other slots on one vast wall, then hopped onto another pedway that went past numerous identical cubicles. Only the small directional signs placed at intersections allowed anyone to find the way to his or her own particular cubicle, but Ashley had worked long enough at the Census Bureau to find her way without difficulty.

Fifteen minutes later, her fingers were flying over her computer's keyboard, inputting the latest census data, while her expression showed her concern at the numbers. Despite the decade-old law restricting couples deemed unsuitable for reproduction from having children at all, and restricting suitable couples to having only one child, the population of the United Americas had jumped alarmingly again over the past six months.

On one level, Ashley hated the reproduction law as much as most of the rest of the population did. Not only was it tragic for the couples denied permission to have children, but she knew the decision-making bureaucrats gave priority to people just like themselves to reproduce rather than using scientific objectivity. The governing council of the People's Revolutionary Party—PRP, an illegal, secret political group which had been courting Ashley this past year and whose meetings she occasionally attended—maintained that a couple's politics played a bigger role in whether they were selected to have children than anything else.

On a purely practical level, Ashley understood the need for population control. The synthetic food industry couldn't feed all the people now, much less a growing population. And unemployment was rising so rapidly that if she hadn't met a member of the governing council of PRP, she would be among the unemployed. Masquerading as a loyal bureaucrat for the Census Bureau during the day and fomenting plans for an overthrow of the government at night, the man had been in a position to recommend her for her present job.

No, Ashley amended grimly, *I wouldn't be unemployed. I'd probably have starved or frozen to death by now.*

A year ago, fresh from getting her degree, but with no opportunity to use her education because all the teaching jobs at the university and elsewhere were taken, Ashley had been on the verge of eviction from her cramped dormitory room for nonpayment of rent. Had that happened, she would not only have been exposed to the rigors of a New York winter without shelter—unless she could have somehow squeezed a place for herself in one of the already overcrowded tunnels that had once housed subways—and without adequate clothing, but she would also have faced starvation. Food was available only in the dormitory dining rooms.

When she had been at her lowest point, she had met the council member. In return for securing her a job, he had asked only for her attendance at a few PRP meetings, and her serious consideration of joining the group. His harmless proposal made her cast aside her fear of the internal police and she agreed. With the choice between an arrest, which might never happen, and starvation, which had been imminent, her options had been nonexistent. Of course she had never intended to become a member of PRP, because she considered the council's views appalling.

Hard on the heels of that last thought, the buzzer on her terminal sounded, and Ashley frowned in puzzlement. That buzzer, signaling that her inputting wasn't at an acceptable rate of speed, was sounding altogether too frequently this morning, and yet she knew her speed was more than adequate.

Uneasily, she began to wonder if the PRP council's contention was true. Did the government, in the interest of eliminating superfluous employees while purporting to provide full employment, tamper with the computers to make it appear as if certain employees were incompetent, thereby providing an excuse to discharge them from their jobs?

But surely, Ashley thought an instant later, the PRP council member wouldn't let her be discharged for false reasons? Unless, she thought, alarmed, he was tired of waiting for her to join the PRP and was giving her a warning to make up her mind or else.

Or perhaps he didn't like the content of the guest speech she was to give at the meeting that night, Ashley thought worriedly. When she had submitted it to him as required, he hadn't said anything negative, but the look on his face hadn't been at all encouraging either. That wasn't surprising. Her speech had criticized him, gently and tactfully, and the other council members for the extreme disruptive measures they wanted to adopt.

Ashley had debated the wisdom of preparing an honest speech instead of saying what she was sure the council wanted to hear. But the discussions at the meetings she had attended had seemed to be open and tolerant, and she disagreed so strongly with the council's proposed solution to overpopulation and society's dwindling resources that her conscience would no longer allow her to remain silent.

In her view, the council's desire for all-out war between the northern hemisphere of the United Americas against the southern hemisphere was not an acceptable solution. True, the southern Americas, mostly for religious reasons, were much more resistant to population control than the northern Americas. But in Ashley's view, education, not war, was the solution to the problem.

And though she didn't like the present government's recent repressive measures to suppress dissension any more than the council did, she didn't trust the council to be any less repressive once they took control. She knew the council hoped to assume power in the chaotic aftermath of their proposed war. As far as Ashley could tell, they had no real concept of even *how* to govern, which was why they occasionally asked her to give a guest speech on history. They were searching for a role model.

Therefore, her speech that night would begin with a gentle chastisement of the council's seeming refusal to take sufficiently into account the unspeakable suffering war would impose on humanity, as well as the unacceptable amount of material resources it would consume. She would point out the dangers of assuming power in the chaotic aftermath of a war without having a well thought-out, workable alternative to the present government firmly in mind. And, finally, she was going to advocate that if they ever succeeded in gaining control—which she seriously doubted would ever happen—they should adopt a true democracy, rather than the one in name only which presently existed, and the dictatorship she suspected attracted the council far more.

The buzzer on Ashley's terminal sounded again, interrupting her thoughts, and bringing a grim frown to her face. Then, to her dismay, her screen went blank for a second before displaying an ominous message.

"SPEED RATE UNACCEPTABLE. REPEAT, UNACCEPTABLE.
CHECK WITH YOUR SUPERVISOR."

Ashley had no choice other than to follow the instructions. Her computer keyboard had automatically locked following the message. As she reached over and dialed her supervisor on the videophone, she was anxious, but not truly frightened, for her supervisor was the PRP council member who had helped her get her job in the first place.

Prudence argued that she be as formally respectful as any other subordinate as Supervisor Agee's face filled the small screen on the phone. No one knew that she and Agee had any dealings with one another outside the office, and such viewphone conversations were occasionally monitored. But before Ashley could even greet Agee, he shocked her with the tone and content of his words.

"Well, well," he mocked in a sneering tone. "You're not up to par anymore are you, Bronwyn?"

Puzzled and alarmed, Ashley fought to keep her tone neutral. "I apologize, Supervisor Agee," she said. "And I promise to do better. In fact, I don't really understand why—"

"Spare me the promises!" Agee snapped. "It's too late for them. Since you obviously don't care about performing an adequate day's duty for a day's credit, I'm sure we can find someone to take your place who will. Collect your credit disk and report immediately to Central Citizens Employment, Bronwyn. Your employment here is terminated as of now."

Stunned, Ashley would have protested, but Agee didn't give her time. He abruptly disconnected the call.

"No!" Ashley cried at the now blank screen. But she didn't try to dial Supervisor Agee again. She knew her phone wouldn't work any more than her computer would.

Shaken, she leaned back in her chair and took several deep breaths to calm her anger and her fear and to allow herself to think about what had just happened. Had Agee fired her because he'd been ordered to by his superiors, or had he done it because he didn't like her speech?

But there was no point in speculating. She wouldn't know the answer to that question until she saw Agee at the PRP meeting tonight. But since he had told her to report to Central Citizens Employment—a superfluous instruction, since that was her only option—and had seemed to stress that she should do so immediately, she hoped that he had been ordered to fire her, and that he had already taken steps to assure that she would find another job. She knew he had contacts at Central Citizens Employment; that was how he had arranged to get her hired by the Census Bureau a year earlier.

Feeling somewhat calmer, Ashley stood up, pulled her shabby gray tunic down around her hips, and picked up the carryall containing her pitifully few personal belongings. Straightening her shoulders, she pushed her long swath of silky auburn hair away from her face and stepped out of her cubicle onto the moving pedway. Near the building's exit, she hopped off the pedway and went to the vast row of slots on one wall to pick up her credit disk from the slot where she'd deposited it earlier that morning.

Before she stepped outside the huge government building, she glanced at the disk and shook her head in worried discouragement. It was up to date, including payment for this morning's work, and the balance was barely enough to last her a week. She could only hope that Agee meant to help her get another job or else she was in real trouble. The job market was even tighter than when she'd been last unemployed.

Outside the building, Ashley shoved her way onto

the crowded pedway to the employment office. Crammed between two men who showed no remorse over the fact that she could barely breathe, she stoically endured the ride until she got as close to the employment office as possible, and then she hopped off the pedway. A short while later, she stepped into the up shaft of the huge government building that housed the employment office, said "Ninety" in a clear voice, and was wafted to that floor.

As she settled herself into an empty booth in a long line of occupied ones, the dark cubicle behind the protective glass barrier lit up. The barrier was to protect the job counselor from any rage an unhappy applicant might display. Ashley's heart lifted as she found herself staring into the cold, stern features of Case Officer Karl Karlton. She'd had him a year ago when she'd been looking for work, and though he was pompous, officious, and about as sympathetic toward job applicants as predators were toward their prey, she was sure he was one of Agee's contacts.

"Citizen number?" he demanded.

Ashley gave it, wondering if all job counselors were like him—leeched of any spark of human kindness by the power they wielded over other people's lives, arrogantly smug because they had employment when others didn't.

"Ashley Bronwyn," he pronounced in a bored tone as the number he'd punched into his computer brought up Ashley's complete history on the screen. And then his eyes narrowed for an instant, and when he looked at Ashley again, there was no longer any boredom in his manner. Instead, there was suspicion and cold distaste.

Ashley couldn't see Karlton's screen, so she had no idea what he had read to bring such an unpleasant expression to his puffy features.

"So you were terminated from the Census Bureau?" he sneered.

Of course the information that she'd been fired and why had immediately been inserted into her file, but Ashley also hoped Agee had already alerted Karlton to give her preference in finding another job. So why was he behaving so nastily? Was he just covering his tracks as well as Agee's? Giving anyone job preference was a felony, of course, so that must be it, Ashley decided. And she had to go along with his act.

"They claimed my speed rate was unacceptable," she replied. "But I think there was something wrong with my terminal, because my speed test scores have always been among the highest—"

Karlton interrupted. "You young people today seem to think the government owes you any job you want. What's the matter? Didn't you like the job? Did the census work not live up to your grand, university-engendered expectations?"

Ashley bit her tongue against a scathing reply. She already knew Karlton was prejudiced against university-educated applicants. He had made that clear the last time he interviewed her, explaining proudly that he had been trained specifically for his present position right after receiving a basic education.

"I'm not so young that I can't appreciate almost any job that pays my living expenses," she replied, keeping her tone level. "I'm a realist. I know how scarce jobs are, and I did not lose my last one simply because I didn't like it. In fact, as I started to tell you, I think I was terminated unjustly, because—"

"That's something you overeducated spoiled brats are good at," he interrupted again, his tone and his expression sourer than before. "Excuses. Excuses, and overly inflated opinions of your so-called intelligence, and making trouble."

Ashley frowned. People in Karlton's line of work almost never had pleasant dispositions, of course, but it seemed to her he was behaving with a good deal more nastiness than was called for, even though he had to protect himself and Agee.

"I'm not making an excuse," she responded coolly. "I'm giving you an explanation. I think my termi—"

"Forget it," he cut her off a third time. And now the cold distaste in his brown eyes was even more pronounced. "What do I care what you think? Anyway, I've got a place to send you right now, so there's no point in listening to you whine."

"You do?"

Ashley was immensely relieved. She had begun to worry that Agee hadn't alerted Karlton to help her, that he was so angry about the speech, and impatient because of her refusal to join the PRP that he would let her fend for herself this time.

"Oh, yes," Karlton said. "It's perfect for someone like you."

His tone made Ashley angry. He'd made it sound as though someone like her didn't deserve any job at all, but if she had to have one, she deserved the lowest form of employment available.

"Report to this address immediately," Karlton said, slipping a card under the glass barrier to Ashley.

She looked at the card, but it showed no name, only an address. "But what sort of work is it?" She glanced back up at Karlton.

"They'll tell you when you get there," he said, impatient now. "Just make sure you report there today."

"But—"

Karlton's expression became hostile as he interrupted her again. "Take it or leave it. It's that or nothing. You show up there today, or don't bother coming back here looking for something else tomorrow. Got it?"

Ashley thought she did get it. Karlton must need more time to find her a good job, so he was employing an old trick to make it appear as if he wasn't giving her any special treatment. And probably he had a quota of people to send to this address anyway. One of the more unpleasant government bureaucracies was probably having trouble keeping employees—and it had to be a *very* unpleasant bureaucracy to lose employees in this day and age—which meant Ashley wasn't going to want to work there either. But if she didn't at least show up and make a show of being interested in the jobs offered, she would be denied another employment interview. Without an interview, she would have no chance of getting the good job she hoped Karlton would eventually find for her.

Though she was indeed grateful, it was beyond her to thank someone as thoroughly repulsive as Karlton. So she picked up the card and got to her feet.

"Good luck," Karlton smirked, his tone implying that she was going to need it.

"I'm sure I'll be back here tomorrow," Ashley retorted.

"Don't count on it," Karlton responded, smiling a broad, nasty smile. "I've never had anybody who went to that address come back."

Ashley paused, momentarily alarmed by that last remark. Then she dismissed it as merely an indication of Karlton's inherent nastiness. Pivoting on her heel, she strode to the down shaft, floated down ninety floors, exited the building, and took a pedway that led to the address he had given her.

Despite the fact that it wasn't rush hour, the city's pedway corridors, flanked by huge buildings blocking the sunlight and plastered with murals admonishing conservation, and the pedway itself, were, as usual, crowded. Every time someone forced himself or herself onto the moving ribbon, Ashley felt in danger of being suffocated.

Ashley recalled from her studies in history that at one time, people had travelled such long distances in individual vehicles or busses through these corridors, or under them in subway trains. When Ashley had read that, she had experienced a feeling of sharp regret that she lived in the present and not the past before overpopulation had strained the earth's resources and automobiles and subway trains could no longer be built, repaired, or fueled.

Today, her discouraged state of mind, the unusual length of her journey, and the ever-increasing rudeness of her fellow passengers increased that feeling of regret more than ever. Her one consolation was that her destination was near the entrance to the subway tunnel where the PRP would meet tonight, and she would have had to make this trip anyway later in the evening. After she reported for the interview and rejected whatever loathsome job was available, she would simply arrive for the meeting early.

The building located at the address for the interview was unusually small and bore no sign identifying the offices inside, which only increased Ashley's certainty that it was one of those bureaucracies everyone hated. Then a dart of alarm shot through her breast. She wondered if it housed a branch of the internal police who spied on the populace. The more people became dissatisfied with their lives, the more they were spied upon in order to stop any dangerous rebellions from getting under way. Ashley, on general principles as well as from a very personal need to hide her involvement with an illegal political organization, had no desire even to talk to anyone who worked for the internal police, much less interview for a job with them.

Looking at the building, she felt so discouraged about her own plight, as well as that of her fellow human beings, that she actually found herself wondering if she should, after all, take a job with the internal police. True, she would hate every moment of it, and would constantly risk exposure as well. But on the other hand, perhaps she could manipulate the computers and head off the arrests of people who had been forced, as she had, to court imprisonment or death by associating with an illegal organization that helped obtain employment which was the only way to stave off starvation. Perhaps she could even head off her own arrest should her association with the PRP ever be suspected.

But until she discovered which bureaucracy she would be dealing with, Ashley reserved judgment.

Inside the doors, she headed for an information desk to her right where a man was seated. Ashley's feeling that an arm of the internal police was in the building increased when she looked at him. He was too tall, too muscular, and looked too self-confidently assured to be a normal downtrodden, undernourished New Yorker.

"Yes?" he said as he raised his ruddy face from studying his computer terminal screen.

Ashley noted that his blue eyes widened with pleasurable surprise when he focused on her face and figure, and she gritted her teeth. She hated the way some men judged her merely on her appearance, and not on her mind, her skills, her character, and her personality.

"My name is Ashley Bronwyn," she introduced herself, her voice stiff. "I was sent here by the Central Citizens Employment Agency."

An extraordinary thing happened then. Not only did a twinkle appear in the man's vivid blue eyes, but he smiled at her. He had an attractive smile, but Ashley was too startled by his smiling at all to return his friendly expression. Smiles didn't come easily to people's faces these days, much less when strangers first met and certainly not to the faces of members of the internal police.

"Oh, yes, Ashley Bronwyn," he said with affable courtesy as he got to his feet. "The employment office alerted us to expect you. My name is Krell Garold, and if you'll follow me, I'll take you where you need to go."

Ashley followed the man down a hallway fronted by closed doors which had no names on them, only numbers. When they were almost at the end of the hallway, Garold stopped in front of a door on his right, opened it, and gestured her inside.

Ashley passed him, took a few steps inside, then stopped, surprised. She was in a medical infirmary. Turning, she gave Garold an inquiring look.

"A medical exam is the first thing on the agenda," he explained, his deep voice still pleasant, his smile still in place. "If you're not healthy, there's no point in going on with the interview."

Ashley frowned, wondering what being healthy had to do with anything. One didn't have to be robust to operate a computer, which was all she was trained to do other than teach history. But if this really was a branch of the internal police, perhaps all employees had to be physically fit to subdue a poor downtrodden citizen deemed worthy of arrest.

With muted grimness, she said, "I'm healthy."

"I'm sure you are," Garold said genially. "In fact, I fervently hope you are," he added, his seemingly perpetual smile broadening. "But we have to check. Ah," he added as a white-coated man appeared from an office on the far side of the room. "This is Doctor Grainger. He'll conduct your exam."

Smaller, darker, and more taciturn than Garold, the doctor nodded at Ashley, then turned his attention to Garold. "Come back in an hour. I'll know by then."

Garold nodded, smiled at Ashley again, then left the room.

"You will please undress," Doctor Grainger said

without preamble. "There are robes in the drawer of the examining couch. Put one on. I'll be back in a few minutes."

Ashley made a face at his back as he returned to his office and shut the door. Then she did as she was told, thinking she would at least get something out of this odious experience. It was almost impossible to see a doctor these days, and she hadn't had a physical since entering the university years ago.

Awhile later, Ashley was feeling somewhat dazed by the speed and thoroughness of the examination. Doctor Grainger had drawn some of her blood and placed it in an all-purpose diagnostic machine. Then he had taken a skin sample for a genetic exam and placed it in another machine. He had passed a portable scanning machine over her body to study her internal organs, given her an eye and hearing test, and prodded and poked her everywhere. And as his hands and eyes did their jobs, he asked questions.

What was Ashley's medical history, as well as that of her parents'?

Ashley had never known her father. Her mother had been artificially inseminated before the reproduction law had been passed. But her parents' medical histories were both on file at Central Registry, as was her own.

"All of that is in the central computer registry," she informed Doctor Grainger, "but I've never had a serious illness, and as far as I know, my parents were healthy as well."

What was her sexual experience? was his next question.

Ashley thought the question peculiar, but decided

it must have to do with her general health and answered truthfully that her sexual experience was nonexistent. She had never been in love and had never felt interested in any of the men she'd met at the university to want to experiment.

There were various other questions she thought odd, and then Dr. Grainger, telling her to stay where she was, stopped examining her, and turned to check the results of her blood and genetic tests. After that, he moved to a computer and called up various files, which he studied so long that Ashley grew impatient.

When he finally turned off the computer, Ashley sat up on the examining couch, pulling the scanty robe more closely around her. "Well?" she asked, trying not to sound as impatient as she felt.

When Doctor Grainger turned his head and looked at her, there was something in his dark eyes that caused a chill of uneasiness to trace Ashley's back. But when he spoke, the uneasiness turned to puzzlement.

"You're extremely healthy," he said. "You'll be able to carry your share of physical work and produce strong, healthy children. Ah," he quickly amended his statement, "that is, if you're ever selected to have children."

Ashley frowned. It sounded as if the type of work he meant was manual. But there were few jobs these days that required manual labor and those that did were taken by people a great deal more robust than she was. And what did bearing children have to do with anything? And why had he used the plural when everyone who was approved to bear children was restricted to having only one child?

"What—" She started to ask some questions of her own, but Doctor Grainger cut her off.

"Get dressed. Garold will be back for you in a few minutes." And he disappeared back into his office before Ashley could detain him.

Irritable now, Ashley put on her gray tunic and was about to beard the doctor in his den when the door to the corridor opened, and Krell Garold stepped into the room.

"All done?" he said, flashing his charming smile. "Good. Just stay put a minute while I talk to the doctor."

"Wait . . . I want to ask . . ." Ashley started to say, but for a big man, Garold moved fast. He disappeared into the doctor's office and shut the door.

Ashley normally disapproved of eavesdropping, but in this case, she was certain Garold and the doctor were discussing her, and she felt she was entitled to hear what they said. She moved silently across the room and hovered near the office door. She heard Doctor Grainger say, "Yes, physically and genetically she's fine, and her emotional profile in her dossier bodes fairly well for her making a successful adjustment. But it may take some doing for her to overcome the biases her mother implanted in her mind and emotions when she was young. God help her if she can't, but that's not our worry."

Ashley frowned, wondering uneasily what it was she was supposed to adjust to and what her mother's biases had to do with making such an adjustment.

"But she seemed to do all right in the mixed environment at the university," Doctor Grainger went on, "and she's an innovator, an independent thinker, and highly intelligent, so there's at least some hope she'll rise above her early training. The only thing that really disappoints me is that while she's dabbled in some studies that might be of use, she doesn't have a full degree in any of the skills that are badly needed."

"It can't be helped," Garold responded. "Since your examination ruled out any physical reason not to take her, the government says we have to, and since, as you say, she is intelligent, she should be able to learn whatever is necessary for her to know. Later on, when conditions allow, maybe she can use her history education to teach the information we can't be bothered with learning right now. And the best thing is that morale will be boosted enormously when she appears on the scene. In case you're too wrapped up in your stethoscopes and test tubes to notice, she's a real beauty."

Ashley barely heard the part about morale being boosted and her beauty. She was too stunned with happiness at hearing that she might one day be allowed to teach history.

"Oh, I noticed her beauty, Garold," Doctor Grainger said with a dry lack of enthusiasm, "but that beauty could just as well be a problem as a morale booster, at least for a while. Think of the jealousy and strife she might provoke until she makes her final choice."

Ashley was puzzled again. What did her beauty have to do with anything? Why should it be a problem? And what choice was Doctor Grainger talking about?

"Maybe so, but once she has chosen, the psycho-programming will take care of all that," Garold responded unconcernedly.

Psycho-programming? A chill of uneasiness rippled through Ashley.

"Yes, I'll admit the programming hasn't failed us yet," Doctor Grainger replied, "but there is still the risk that she might cause problems for a while. But maybe she'll choose quickly, and, anyway, as you say," he added resignedly, "we don't have any choice now. She fulfills our quota and just in time, considering our tight schedule. So that's it. It's decided."

Doctor Grainger's voice was coming closer to the door, and fearing that he might open it, Ashley quickly moved away before she could hear anything else.

From across the room, she stood frowning at the doctor's office door, confused by the men's conversation. But one thing was clear. Whatever job it was she was being tested for, it had sounded as though she wasn't going to have any choice about taking it, and that didn't sit well. Of course, she could file a complaint with the Civil Rights Department, but that was just a waste of time. The only rights that department enforced were those of the government.

Her thoughts were interrupted as Doctor Grainger and Krell Garold emerged from the office. The doctor immediately headed toward a nearby table and Garold, still smiling, headed for Ashley.

"You'll be glad to know you're in splendid physical shape," he said.

"That's nice to hear," Ashley responded stiffly. "But what I'd really like to hear is why it matters whether I'm in good physical shape or not. Sitting in front of a computer doesn't require one to be an athlete, and computer work is what I've been doing for the past year."

Garold glanced at Doctor Grainger, who was now coming toward them.

"Well, you see . . ." Garold said as he moved closer to Ashley, ". . . you're not going to be doing computer work anymore."

To Ashley's astonishment, Garold then slipped his fingers around her wrist. Alarmed, she tried to pull away, saying, "But what if computer work is what I *prefer* to do?"

Instead of letting her go, Garold tightened his hold. "I'm afraid," he said, "that it doesn't matter what you want. What you want ceased to matter when you got yourself mixed up with the People's Revolutionary Party."

At that, Ashley felt a surge of panic knot her stomach. Since it was known that she had had dealings with an illegal political organization, she would either be sentenced to prison or executed, and it was rumored that most judges these days opted for execution as an aid to population control.

She had only one alternative and that was to run. But not to her dormitory. They would find her there. She would either have to live on the streets or hide underground, and either way, she would ultimately starve. But she'd rather die of starvation a free woman than be imprisoned or executed, and she attempted to jerk her arm from Garold's grip and run for her life.

But Garold wasn't taken off guard. He spun her

around into an arm lock and immobilized her.

As Doctor Grainger approached with a needle gun in his hand, Ashley screamed, "No!" and tried to struggle, but she couldn't move.

"What's going to happen to you now is preferable to the alternative, Ashley," Garold said calmly as though she were about to be inoculated against a childhood disease. "You're going to a better life than you have any prospect of enjoying in the future here on earth."

Doctor Grainger took hold of her arm, and an instant later, as Ashley felt the sting of the needle in her arm, she realized that Garold's words meant she was about to die and go to heaven. Far from inoculating her against disease, Doctor Grainger was injecting her with a lethal drug.

Ashley opened her mouth to cry out a final, futile protest. But before she could make a sound, everything went black.

Garick Deveron, Jim Jacobs, and Bud Saunders were exiting the room they'd used to change clothes, commenting on how good it felt to be back in their own attire, when Krell Garold opened the door of the infirmary and looked up and down the hall. When he saw Garick, Jim, and Bud, he motioned them toward him.

"Which one of you wants to carry this one to the hover?" he asked as he led them to the examining couch.

Garick, slightly ahead of the others, at first gazed down at the woman on the couch with impersonal curiosity. After a moment's inspection, however, his gaze was no longer quite so aloof. Nor was Bud's reaction.

"Wow!" he said admiringly from beside Garick. "What a beauty!"

Garick couldn't have agreed more with Bud's comment. He'd always been partial to auburn hair and the sort of creamy silken skin that usually went with it. And the woman's face was undoubtedly lovely. But it was the delicate vulnerability he imagined he saw etching the lovely features that pulled at Garick's heart more than conventional prettiness ever could. Too, though her body was small and slender, it suggested a hidden, secret sensuality that challenged Garick in a way he'd never experienced before.

It was rare for Garick to respond to any woman as quickly and as intensely as he felt himself responding to this one, and his personal circumstances deemed it wise for him to back off rather than explore where his unusual reactions might take him.

Nevertheless, he said, "I'll carry her."

"Good," Garold answered. "Here," he added, extending a sheaf of papers toward Garick. "This is the scoop on her. You know what to do with it."

Garick nodded, took the papers, folded them, and stuck them in his pocket. Then he took hold of the woman's arms, raised her limp body to a sitting position, and shifted her over his shoulder in a fireman's grip.

"Let's go," Jim said. "We're running late."

Garick didn't comment, and frowned. His response to the contact between his body and the woman's was even more electrifying than his response had been to the sight of her. Indeed, though his reactions made no sense, he felt acutely interested on several different levels in the woman he carried. He was even beginning to feel connected to her in some mysterious way that he wanted to ignore, but couldn't.

When they reached the hover, Garick felt an odd, unexplainable sense of loss when he had to put the woman down on the deck so he could sit in one of the seats and belt himself in. But it wasn't until he pulled her documents out of his pocket and read them with intense interest that he realized how very out of character he was behaving.

The realization didn't stop him from continuing to read the documentation to the end. It did, however, make him very thoughtful once the papers were back in his pocket.

Chapter Two

Each time Ashley awoke for a short, groggy period of consciousness, she discovered something new. First, she discovered she was strapped down in a narrow bed, and above the bed was a flat rectangular surface jutting out from a wall. Next, she saw two bare legs dangling over the side of that surface above her and realized a man was sitting there; the legs were too muscular and hairy to belong to a woman. And finally, when she was completely awake, though still slightly woozy, she noticed a low hum, a vibration, in her body . . . or her bed . . . or somewhere.

Frowning in confusion, she looked blearily at what she could see of the very small, dull gray room. It wasn't that much different from her dormitory room except that it was uglier and smaller, and had no table, view screen, or bathroom. There was only a small sink in one corner and a short distance from the sink, a metal tubing extending from the wall.

This can't be heaven, she thought, shaking her head weakly. *Please God, You wouldn't let heaven be this dreary, would You?*

She decided she definitely wasn't in heaven, not only because of the ugly surroundings, but because of her need to use the bathroom and surely one didn't have to do that after dying. So where was she? The only possible answer was prison, and Ashley moaned in despair.

In reaction to her moan, the owner of the two legs dangling to her right jumped down from the overhead bunk and an instant later, to her amazement, Ashley found herself looking at the powerfully muscled body of a total stranger who wore only the skimpiest of briefs.

The almost-nude stranger bent and peered into the bunk enclosure at her face. When he saw she was awake, he smiled and said, "Ah, so you've joined the living at last."

He sounded and looked too cheerful to be a prison inmate, but Ashley was too shaken to try to figure out why he was greeting his fate with so much grace. True, she was appalled at the realization that she'd apparently been assigned a cell mate of the opposite sex, but first things first. She wanted to know where this prison was.

"Where are we?" she demanded. She then frowned, puzzled. She sounded to her own ears as though she hadn't spoken for days, but it seemed to her as though she had just been needle-gunned a few minutes earlier.

"Aboard the *Mayflower VII,*" the man replied, holding out his hand to shake. "I'm Jim Jacobs. We're going to be bunkmates for the trip. Welcome to our community, Ashley."

Bunkmates? Trip? Community? Ashley stared at his hand, blinking in alarmed confusion. Nothing this man had said made any sense to her. If they were on a trip, then this must not be a prison. Was the *Mayflower VII* a ship then? Were they merely on the way to prison? But why had Jim Jacobs welcomed her to "our community," making it sound as though prison was some kind of pleasant retreat?

After a moment, when she didn't take his hand, Jim withdrew it and replaced it on his knee, but he didn't seem offended. He was still smiling.

"I guess you're still a little dopey, right?" he said. "Those drugs they use on you deportees are pretty powerful. But now that you're awake, you'll be okay soon."

Ashley felt more confused than ever. "Deportees?" she croaked, her tone baffled. Why would the government call their political prisoners "deportees"? The term had to be a euphemism, because the government didn't deport native citizens for political crimes. And, anyway, why would another country take in outcasts from the United Americas when there wasn't a place left on the planet that wasn't already too overcrowded and resource poor to support its own population?

Jim grimaced, looking as though he'd spoken out of turn. "Listen," he said, "I could explain things to you, but the orientation people like to do that sort of thing themselves. There will be a meeting for you new people in a little while, and you'll learn everything you need to know then. So why don't we forget the questions for now and concentrate on getting you on your feet, all right?"

Jim's words only made Ashley's mind boil with more questions, but she decided getting on her feet might be the wisest thing to do. If her situation was as bad as she feared, she would have to be physically mobile as soon as possible in order to attempt an escape.

She nodded and Jim reached over to unstrap her from her bunk, pulled back the sheet covering her, and helped her sit up.

When she discovered that she was clad in a short, very sheer sleeping shift that was definitely not part of her own wardrobe, Ashley was further baffled as well as embarrassed. Who had undressed her, and where had the shift come from? But she had something else more urgent to think about and she muttered, "I need to go to the bathroom."

"All right. The receptacle pulls down from the wall over there. Let's see if you can walk, and if not, I'll carry you."

Jim more or less hauled Ashley out of her bunk, and though she would normally have kept her distance from any almost-naked male, she had to cling to her cell mate to keep from falling. She felt dizzy and weak. Thankfully, however, Jim didn't seem to react lustfully to having a scantily dressed female in his arms.

"Want me to carry you over there?" he asked sympathetically.

"Just help me walk," she said. "And once I'm

there, would you give me some privacy?"

"I'll turn my back." He then half dragged her over to one wall, pulled down the receptacle, helped her sit down, and turned away.

Merely turning his back wasn't exactly what Ashley had had in mind, but if they were prisoners, they might be locked in this cabin, and he therefore couldn't leave to give her some privacy.

She also didn't give much credence to Jim's words of "community" and "deportee." For all she knew, he could be a government agent planted to gain her trust and obtain information from her.

When she was done, she stood up and was relieved to discover she didn't feel as weak as she had.

"Now what do I do?" she asked, forlorn.

Jim turned and strode over to her. After pushing a button that flushed the receptacle clean, he tilted it up into its wall recess, then led her to the sink in the corner.

"Can you wash by yourself, or do you want me to help you?" he asked as he reached up to a cupboard above the sink and extracted a cloth.

"I'll do it," Ashley hastily responded, taking the cloth from him.

He said nothing more, turning his back again as she used the cloth to give herself a sketchy sponge bath. She kept a wary eye on Jim to make sure he didn't peek as she adjusted her sleeping shift to reach the more private parts of her body. But she was beginning to get the impression that even if he'd been facing her, Jim wouldn't have displayed any interest in her body. *Maybe,* she thought hopefully, *he isn't heterosexual.*

When she was done washing, she adjusted her

sleeping shift to cover her, then asked, "Where are my clothes?"

"Yours are gone," Jim said with a shrug as he knelt by her bunk. "The stewards always throw that kind of clothing away." He pulled open a drawer that was fitted under Ashley's bunk, extracted something, then stood and handed it to her. "You'll wear these aboard ship," he explained. "They're one size fits all, so you shouldn't have any trouble with the fit."

What he'd given her turned out to be a one-piece, armless and legless white undergarment and a soft, gold-colored, tie-belted wraparound overtunic that fell mid-thigh on Ashley. Compared to her usual gray tunics, the outfit was lovely. But Ashley wasn't in the mood to be pleased about anything at the moment, not even the happy exchange of her dull clothing for something better.

"What about you?" she asked, eyeing his barely clad body obliquely. "Don't you wear clothes?"

"Sure." He shrugged and went through the same routine again. Only this time, the drawer was under his bunk, and the garment was a one-piece, dark blue bodysuit. "I'll turn my back again while you dress," he said, turning around and stepping into his bodysuit.

Profoundly grateful for his sensitivity, Ashley slipped off her shift and began dressing. "Does everybody in this . . . this community . . . have to share a cabin with someone of the opposite sex?" she asked.

Jim obviously knew what was on her mind, and he hastened to reassure her. "You don't have to worry about my making a pass at you, Ashley," he said matter-of-factly. "I'm married."

"You are?" So much for Ashley's hope that he

might not be heterosexual. Despite his words, she wasn't all that convinced that she didn't have to worry. Just because a man was married didn't mean he was a *faithful* husband.

"Yes."

"Where is your wife?"

"She's not aboard. She's back home."

"Not aboard the *Mayflower VII?*" Ashley asked.

"Right."

"The *Mayflower's* a ship? We're on the ocean? Where's home?"

Ashley was growing more and more anxious. How was she going to escape if they were in the middle of an ocean? And if she couldn't escape, what awaited her when the ship docked?

Jim didn't answer her questions. He shook his head and said, "Don't ask that sort of thing, Ashley. As I told you, everything will be explained to you in a little while. Are you dressed yet?"

"Yes."

He turned around and smiled. "You look nice," he said with perfunctory politeness. "Are you hungry?"

Thinking about it, Ashley discovered she was very hungry. In fact, her stomach was growling so ferociously, she wondered just how long it had been since she'd last eaten.

"How long have I been drugged?" she asked.

"A couple of days. You didn't answer me, Ashley. Are you hungry?"

"Yes."

"Then, come on. We'll go to the galley and eat." He stepped to the hatch and it swooshed open.

So they weren't locked in after all, Ashley thought

with relief as she followed him out into a corridor, looking around her with anxious curiosity. But there was nothing to see other than a long hallway with closed hatches.

Jim led the way to the end of the corridor, where another door opened, revealing a room with round empty tables scattered throughout and curious-looking equipment on all the walls.

Jim walked to one wall, looking back at Ashley over his shoulder. "What'll you have to eat?"

"What is there?" she responded, puzzled by the question. Surely, there wouldn't be anything available other than synthetic glop.

"Name it."

Sure, Ashley thought disbelievingly. But there was no harm in dreaming, so she named a meal she hadn't had in years. "How about eggs over easy, bacon, toast, orange juice, and coffee?"

To Ashley's amazement, Jim said, "That sounds good. I think I'll have the same thing." He faced the wall and punched some buttons.

A panel at the back of the counter slid open, and a tray slid from the recess behind the panel to the flat counter under the buttons. Then, to Ashley's astonishment, an aroma reached her nostrils that made her salivate. She walked quickly to the counter to stare down in disbelief at a plate of two perfectly fried eggs, three strips of bacon, and two slices of toasted bread. A glass of orange juice and a pot of coffee were also on the tray.

Her expression made Jim smile. "Yeah, it's the real thing," he assured her. "Been a long time since you saw something like that, I'll bet."

Numbly, still staring at the feast in front of her, Ashley nodded.

Jim's smile broadened. "Well, I know you'll enjoy it then. Why don't you carry your tray to a table? I'll get my own food and join you."

Feeling as though she were dreaming, Ashley took her food to a table where a round container in the center of it held utensils. After retrieving a fork, she was prepared to eat quickly, before the mirage in front of her disappeared, when Jim joined her.

"Hold on," he said. "I'll ask the blessing."

Reluctantly, Ashley put her fork down and bowed her head. And it was only as Jim said the "Amen" after his short blessing that she realized she should feel grateful that apparently he was a religious man. Maybe that and his being married meant he wouldn't try to rape her while they were bunking together.

Ha! she thought gloomily an instant later. *Everybody knows what prison inmates are like. If you really want to indulge in some useless wishful thinking, Ashley, then how about pretending that all your meals in prison will be as good as this one and that your treatment there will be wonderfully humane?*

But she was too much of a realist to pretend any such thing. One good meal did not necessarily signify anything meaningful at all except maybe that the government tried to keep its prisoners pacified until they were safely behind unbreachable bars or were facing a firing squad.

A moment later, however, as she chewed the first delicious bites, Ashley was almost ready to die in peace if that was to be her fate. At least, she would have had the pleasure of tasting real food again before she went to meet her Maker.

Jim watched her with a faint smile on his lips. "Good, huh?"

"Better than good," Ashley said around her next bite. "Ambrosia."

Jim's smile broadened before he dug into his own breakfast.

After she'd cleaned her plate and was sipping her last cup of coffee, Ashley felt better able to try getting a little more information out of Jim. But before she could ask her first question, the door to the galley whooshed open, and two men, both dressed in a fashion that made Ashley blink in disbelief, came through the hatch.

The men wore all black—black turtlenecked shirts, black leather jackets, and black leather pants—and everything clung to their marvelous physiques in a perfect fit. If Ashley hadn't just eaten a meal that hadn't been available in her dormitory for a long while, she wouldn't even have entertained the idea that their clothing could be real leather. There weren't enough animals left on earth to provide real leather anymore. Clothing was all synthetic nowadays. But she was convinced that what she saw was the real thing.

Under the leather, the almost intimidatingly perfect body of the first man was broad-shouldered, narrow-hipped, and long-legged, and the man's walk was graceful. But even as Ashley was objectively admitting that the effect of the skintight black clothing on such a beautiful body was stunning, she also noted that there was an aura of thinly veiled raw aggressiveness about the man that caused a prickle of nervous tension to run down her spine.

She then looked up from his body to his face, and

suddenly, her breath froze in her throat. He had thick, dark hair, and his face was tanned, hard, primitively compelling. His was the face of an undoubtedly attractive, but certainly dangerous, barbarian. While Jim didn't look like any prison inmate Ashley had ever pictured, this man did, and she could only thank God that it was Jim who was her bunkmate, and not this undoubtedly uncivilized savage.

Ashley's eyes focused on a long, white scar at one corner of the barbarian's mouth, and she wondered if he'd gotten the scar in a brutal prison fight. Then she glanced at his mouth and found it so rawly sensual, almost cruel, that she doubted even a sexually experienced woman would be comfortable looking at it. Since Ashley was sexually inexperienced, it made her feel downright threatened. She quickly moved her eyes to the man's nose. She decided that while it might once have been straight, it must have been broken at some point, no doubt in another brutal prison fight, and now its slight crookedness suited the rest of his face perfectly.

But it was the pair of deceptively lazy, piercingly intelligent, cool gray eyes that really disturbed Ashley. Those eyes assessed her with a thoroughness that made her feel stripped naked, while revealing nothing of what the man was thinking. And then, to her heartfelt relief, the gray eyes passed on to Jim. The coolness in his eyes thawed so slightly, that Ashley would have missed it if she hadn't been staring at the man so intently she'd lost track of everything and everybody else in the room.

"Jim," he said, nodding at Ashley's companion.

"Garick." Jim nodded back. Then he glanced at Ashley. "This is Ashley Bronwyn. That's Garick Deveron, Ashley. And behind him is Bud Saunders. The two of them are scouts. Bud's also a chemist."

Scouts? The term didn't make sense to Ashley, except in a historical sense. But she didn't have time to wonder about it before Garick Deveron, from his position before the food counter where he'd already punched in his order, looked at her again over his very broad shoulder. He stared directly into her eyes, and there was something so primitive in his gaze that Ashley froze.

Through sheer will power, she forced herself not to look away. She thought anyone who came under Garick Deveron's direct gaze must immediately begin to start totaling up his or her deficiencies in looks, character, and intelligence. Thankfully, however, the assessment didn't last long because his food appeared.

As he turned away to pick up his plate and cup, Ashley went limp inside. She hoped, too fervently to satisfy her sense of self-respect, that he and his companion, who was now punching in his own food order, would sit as far away from her as possible. Preferably out of her line of vision. Instead, Garick sat directly across from her, beside Jim. Ashley was grateful that she'd already eaten because she knew she couldn't have gotten a bite down her throat as it had closed up from anxiety.

She was trying to relax so that she could ask some questions, when Jim thwarted her purpose.

"Careful what you say," he murmured to Garick. "She hasn't been through orientation yet."

Garick glanced at her, the faintest tinge of amusement in his gaze, then looked at his plate and began eating.

Ashley glared at Jim who smiled back at her. It seemed nothing ever daunted his perpetual good humor.

"You drew this gorgeous beauty to bunk with?"

Bud Saunders had arrived at the table now and he indicated Ashley with a tilt of his head while addressing his smiling question to Jim.

"Yep." Jim nodded, smiling as well.

"Think your psycho-programming will hold?" Bud teased, grinning now.

"Barely." Jim's smile broadened. "But even if it begins to fail, I've got Mary to answer to when we get home, and the thought of explaining things to her should keep me in line."

"Too bad." Bud shook his head, his blue eyes sparkling mischievously. "But if you're worried, I'll be glad to trade places with you."

Jim snorted. "Nice try, Bud," he drawled. "But you know the rules. If Ashley wants to bunk with you sometime, she'll have to do the asking."

"Shucks. I'd hoped you'd forgotten."

"Not likely." Jim shook his head.

Ashley was looking from one to the other of them in alarmed puzzlement. She didn't understand much of what had been said, and the mention of psycho-programming made her uneasy.

Garick looked up from his plate, noticed her expression, and the scar at the side of his mouth crinkled very slightly for a bare instant, before it settled back into its normal position.

Ashley stared at him, wondering if that slight movement passed for a smile where he was concerned. Then she tried to dismiss the man from her mind. It made her distinctly uncomfortable even to think about him. Besides, she had other things to think about. She was tired of having people talk over her head. She looked at Jim.

"Now, look, Jim—" she started to say.

He interrupted. "You finished eating?"

"Yes, but—"

"Then I'll take you to the orientation room in a minute. It's a little early, but you shouldn't have to wait too long to get your questions answered."

Deciding it was futile for her to protest, Ashley, acting compulsively, then made the mistake of looking at Garick again, expecting him to have his head down.

He didn't. He was staring at her breasts in a way that brought a blush of anger to Ashley's cheeks and a vague fear to her heart. She had thought she had gotten over reacting badly to the way men leered at her body, but there was something about Garick Deveron's look that brought back all the old feelings she had experienced when she'd left her all-female dormitory and entered the coed environment at the university. Then the gray eyes moved to her face, and she had the odd feeling he knew exactly what she was thinking, that he had the power to stare into the back of her skull and pick over her every thought and feeling at his leisure.

But that couldn't be true, and Ashley couldn't tolerate the feelings he had managed to arouse in her any longer. She reacted to Garick's stare with a sudden, inappropriate anger that surprised even herself.

"Stop that!" she blurted out.

He raised one finely shaped black eyebrow and said nothing. But Ashley saw a gleam she couldn't really identify appear momentarily in his gray eyes. She suspected, however, that what she saw was amusement at her expense, and she grew even angrier.

"Just stop it!" she repeated.

Again, he didn't say a word. And Ashley could no longer see any hint of amusement in his eyes. Rather, there was a calculating assessment there that confused her.

Since Jim and Bud were obviously as confused by her behavior as she was by Garick's, she felt embarrassed. She got to her feet, turned on her heel, walked to the galley hatch, and stepped through as it opened. Once outside in the corridor, however, she paused. Without Jim, she didn't know where to go, and he hadn't followed her.

Then she was sure she felt Garick's gray eyes burning a hole in her back, and her nerves were too frazzled to stand any more of him, so she turned abruptly to her right, and stepped forward two paces. When another door opened in front of her, she blindly stepped through it.

She heard Jim yell, "Ashley, no!" But then the door closed behind her, and his voice was cut off. And the next instant, she found herself staring through a huge pane of thick glass at black emptiness, twinkling stars, and down and to the left, the slowly spinning blue-and-white globe of earth itself.

It took Ashley's numbed mind a moment to make

sense of the data her eyes were feeding her brain and to combine it with what Jim had told her since she'd awoken. She put all the pieces together just as the door behind her opened again, and Jim urgently said her name.

She didn't answer him. She couldn't. She was in the process of fainting.

Garick quickly pushed past Jim and knelt beside Ashley, placing his fingers against the pulse in her neck.

Having read her dossier, he knew he'd behaved foolishly, looking at her the way he had. But, damn it, she'd affected him exactly as she had when he'd first seen her, first touched her. And how could a man be expected to fake being impervious to her feminine appeal? Besides, Bud had been more overt in his attraction to Ashley than he had, and she hadn't reacted to Bud's teasing badly. Of course, he had a good idea she hadn't understood half of what Bud was saying either.

"She's only fainted, Garick," Jim said, resigned. "And who wouldn't under the circumstances?"

"We'd better take her to sick bay anyway," Garick said, trying not to sound as overprotective as he felt.

"If you think it's necessary," Jim agreed, obviously surprised by Garick's concern.

"Just to be safe," Garick said as he gathered Ashley into his arms and got to his feet. "Come on."

Bud had joined them by now, and the three of them made their way to sick bay. But neither of the other two men could have told by the expression on Garick's face how much pleasure he felt having

Ashley in his arms again. His eyes and features showed nothing other than blank impassivity.

When Ashley regained consciousness, she was lying on a table in the ship's infirmary and a white-coated stranger was bending over her. Jim, Garick, and Bud stood in the room, also, but they were out of Ashley's line of vision. But then, she was too consumed with rage to see much of anything other than the calm, disgustingly complacent face above her.

Abruptly, she reached up and grabbed the lapels of the stranger's white coat, pulling his face down to hers until she was almost nose to nose with him. His brown eyes widened, but he didn't pull away.

"Are we in space?" she demanded, her tone fierce.

"Yes," he said, eyeing her uneasily. "We're on our way to New Frontier. It's a planet in the . . ."

"Hold it, Johnson," Jim spoke up from behind Ashley. "She hasn't been to orienta—"

He broke off what he was saying because Ashley let go of the medic's lapels, swung her right fist, and socked him as hard as she could.

Blood spurted from the medic's nose, and he voiced a curse and jumped back. At the same time, Jim quickly stepped forward and grabbed Ashley's wrists. She fought in earnest then, but Jim held her as easily as if she were a small child, and calmly said over his shoulder to the medic, "Give her something to calm her down. Don't make it strong enough to put her out because she's due in orientation in a little while. Just give her enough to keep her from hurting herself."

"Or somebody else," Garick's amused drawl came from the corner of the room.

Ashley froze at the sound of his voice. What was he doing in here? And then, she became aware of Bud.

"Ah, hell," Bud responded to Garick's comment, his tone as amused as Garick's. "She's too little to hurt anybody else." But then he glanced at the medic, who was holding a gauze pad to his nose as he fetched a needle gun from a nearby cupboard. "At least, not much," Bud amended, staring respectfully at the blood on the gauze.

Their amusement and the presence of the two scouts in the infirmary enraged Ashley further. But struggling with a man as large and fit as Jim was about as effective as having a fistfight with a block of granite, and Ashley wasn't completely physically recovered from being drugged. So when the medic placed the needle gun against the vein in her arm and injected her with a tranquilizer, she was already slumped back against the table, panting and defeated. But Jim continued to hold her wrists.

As the tranquilizer took affect, she was treated to more comments of a personal nature, spoken as though she wasn't there, from Jim, Garick, and Bud. Though her rage still burned, it was muted now.

"You can see why they decided on deportation instead of execution in her case," Jim said, his voice containing a certain proprietorial pride, as though she somehow now belonged to him.

"You bet," Bud responded as he came to the side of the examining couch and stared down at Ashley with admiration. "She's got the right spirit. Too bad she's so little though. A fighting spirit can get you in trouble if you don't have anything to back it up with."

Jim, holding Ashley's wrists in a lighter grip now that he could see her eyes clouding from the tranquilizer, shrugged unconcernedly. "We can teach her some judo. She may need it to protect herself when the fellows on New Frontier get a look at her."

Bud snorted. "If you ask me, she's going to need more than that. It may take a laser gun."

"Better make sure she's not mad before you let her near a laser," Garick's lazy drawl echoed in Ashley's ears, making her tense. "Otherwise, she may shoot everybody in sight."

"And you'll be my first target," Ashley said without thinking.

And a moment later, when she did think about her words, she frowned, wondering why she felt so hostile toward Garick Deveron. He wasn't to blame for her predicament. And he hadn't looked at her any more lasciviously than many other men had. So why had she reacted differently to him than she had trained herself to react over the years since first attending the university? Was it simply that she thought of him as barbarous enough to act on what he had so obviously been thinking, even if she was unwilling to oblige him?

Garick came into view then, and his expression didn't help her peace of mind. He gestured for Jim to release her and to move away. When Jim complied, Garick leaned over her, placing his arms on either side of her body. Suddenly, his gray eyes filled all of Ashley's universe. Her throat went dry with the fear she had felt once, long ago, for all men, but had never tried, nor had even wanted, to find reasons for.

"This isn't New York, Ashley," he said softly, but commandingly, "and neither is where you're going. Out here, friends count for something. Sometimes, they're all you've got. So I suggest you adjust your attitude and start making some. You can begin by apologizing to Johnson for bloodying his nose."

At that moment, though Garick had managed to arouse Ashley's self-protective instinct, she wouldn't have apologized to the President of the United Americas for treason, even if such an apology would have saved her from execution. Not when it was Garick Deveron who wanted her to do it.

She couldn't verbalize her defiance, for fear her voice would shake and destroy her pride. Therefore, through a fierce act of will, Ashley held Garick's gray gaze and said nothing. She let her silence and her look speak for her.

When he realized she wasn't going to comply, Garick smiled a smile as intimidating as everything else about him. Then he leaned down and whispered in her ear. His masculine smell, and the feel of his breath against her skin, made a strange tremor rush through Ashley.

"You will do it, you know—sooner or later. And, remember, Ashley," he added softly. "You can run from what I make you feel, but you can't hide from it indefinitely, because I'm not going to let you."

He straightened, gave her one last look that shook her to her toes, then left the infirmary. Bud, after shaking his head at her, followed Garick, leaving only Jim and the medic and Ashley in the room.

Before Ashley could even begin to try to sort out what Garick had meant by his comments, her body started shaking, which made her furious. She quickly sat up and swung her legs over the side of the examining couch. Then she fixed her eyes on the medic, who still held the gauze pad to his nose.

"I apologize for hurting you," she said, her voice shaking so badly, she was doubly grateful she hadn't responded to Garick's demand. "But if you tell *him*" —she jerked her head toward the closed hatch through which Garick had disappeared—"that I apologized to you, I'll hit you again."

She jumped down from the couch, and fortunately, Jim moved forward to catch her or she would have landed on her face. The tranquilizer had weakened her legs, and she clung to him for a moment until she felt able to stand on her own. Then she tilted her head back and glared up into his face.

"Where's this orientation?" she spat.

"I'll take you there," Jim said, his tone as calm as ever.

"Good! Let's go!"

And though it took every fiber of her will, she walked under her own power to the conference cabin to hear why she'd ended up on a spaceship, where exactly it was taking her, and how others intended for her to live the rest of her life.

Garick settled himself on a couch seat in the view lounge, tilted it back, and fixed his eyes on the huge view screen displaying the blackness of space, twinkling stars, and occasionally, the spinning globe of earth. But he wasn't thinking about space; he'd seen it several times before. He was thinking about how Ashley Bronwyn had once again had a strange effect on him, strange enough that he hadn't acted toward her the way he'd planned to. Instead, he'd behaved and spoken spontaneously.

As he idly reviewed in his mind what had taken place during the last half-hour, and most especially his remarks to her while she'd been lying on the infirmary couch, he found his own behavior curious. And, of course, if he ended up choosing one particular option concerning her that had crossed his mind his behavior would probably be the wrong approach this early in the game.

But then, Ashley's effect on him since the moment he'd laid eyes on her was curious—curious and interesting and highly unusual. So much so that he wondered if, contrary to his lifelong habit of being as much in control of his words, his actions, and his purposes as possible, he was really going to have all that much choice about what finally did happen between him and Ashley. He also wondered if going with his instincts was all that bad an idea. Maybe his instincts knew better how to handle her than his conscious mind did.

At that point, a full-blown smile curled the white scar at the corner of Garick's mouth, indicating that his attitude toward such a new, unexpected loss of control was more positive than negative.

He found that attitude more curious, interesting, and unusual than any of his other reactions concerning Ashley Bronwyn.

Chapter Three

"I am Counselor Vanion. Welcome to the *Mayflower VII.*"

The woman who stood at the head of the conference table was handsome, middle-aged, and assured. She, also, to Ashley's experienced, cynical eyes, looked exactly like one of the high-level bureaucrats on earth who got to *be* a high-level bureaucrat at least partly because of an ability to tell boldfaced lies without blinking an eye.

As Ashley glanced around at the dozen or so dazed, confused women who sat around the table with her, she didn't think they looked in any shape to detect, much less question, any lies they might be told. She clenched her jaw, grateful she at least had had some warning of what was to come. She was even grateful for the tranquilizer she'd been given, for it would help control her anger, which would allow her to think clearly.

"The *Mayflower VII,*" Counselor Vanion continued, her gaze calm, her tone as soothingly matter-of-fact as though she were announcing that she enjoyed the smell of roses, "is a spaceship, and it is carrying you to a planet discovered several years ago called New Frontier."

Counselor Vanion paused, and for a half-minute, there was complete silence in the cabin. Then it was shattered as some of the women screamed, some cursed, and some burst into tears. There were also a few, like Ashley, who sat quietly, saying nothing. However, while the other silent ones looked as though they had gone into a severe state of shock, Ashley stared at Counselor Vanion, her eyes steady, her jaw clenched in stubborn anger.

The counselor stood patiently waiting, and then, in a firm, strong voice, she ordered, "Silence!"

Being the type of woman people automatically obeyed, she got immediate results. The noise died away and the women sat frozen in their chairs, their expressions displaying varying degrees of horrified disbelief and denial.

"I will not mince words," Counselor Vanion said, her tone very stern now. "All of you are guilty of crimes meriting imprisonment or execution. But because it takes a certain amount of spirit and ingenuity and toughness to commit the sort of crimes you have, you have been chosen for another fate. To assure that the human race survives whatever happens on our native planet."

Ashley glanced at the other women and saw that

Counselor Vanion's last sentence had gotten their attention with a vengeance. Now *everybody*, except for she and Counselor Vanion, looked as though they were in shock.

"I assure you," the counselor went on, "that I am not exaggerating. Conditions on earth are deteriorating much faster than any of you realize. It is not at all certain that human life *can* survive there, at least not indefinitely. Topsoil, clean water, mineral and food resources are becoming too depleted to feed and support a population that continues to grow past sane limits. Mass starvation, catastrophic outbreaks of disease, and even world war are on the horizon. And while such disastrous solutions to the problem of overpopulation could eventually result in a much smaller population, there may not, by that time, be enough resources left to support even the small number of people who may survive. Therefore, you women should be grateful that instead of being punished as you deserve for your crimes against the government, you will not only live, but you will make a vital contribution to humanity."

Ashley didn't feel grateful. She didn't know what the other women had done. Perhaps something as pitiful as stealing a little food out of desperation. But in her case, she didn't think attending a few meetings of people with whom she didn't even agree, simply out of a desire to obtain work and survive, merited either imprisonment or execution. Neither did she believe that things were as hopeless on earth as Counselor Vanion made it sound. She thought it was just a spiel to make the deportees accept their situation with more docility than they otherwise might.

Tired of feeling helpless and of being addressed in an accusing tone, and still feeling very, very angry, she spoke up. "Why have we never heard of New Frontier?" she asked, her tone sharp. "I thought all space exploration stopped a long time ago when the resources on earth began to run out. Was that just another government lie, like the one where it promised everyone in the United Americas a job?"

The counselor turned her calm dark eyes in Ashley's direction. "Yes, it was a lie," she admitted with no apparent remorse or embarrassment. "Space exploration never stopped. It didn't stop because our scientists have known for a long time that our planet is dying and the government decided an alternative to earth had to be found to avoid the prospect of the human race becoming extinct. And the reason no one was told that space exploration was continuing is because there would certainly have been widespread protests against spending what resources are left for such an endeavor. Humans are good at thinking in the short term instead of looking to the future."

"But if they knew a new planet capable of supporting human life had been found, those protests might diminish," Ashley countered.

Counselor Vanion smiled faintly. "Ah, but if the existence of such a planet became widely known," she replied, "an entirely different protest might erupt. If the populace learned there was a new planet capable of supporting human life opening up for settlement, a planet where they could get away from the environmental degradation and the hardships and the hopelessness they're experiencing on earth, millions of them might *demand* to be allowed to go there. And since we do not have a sufficient number of spaceships available to transport more than a few people at a time, their demands could not be met, and anarchy might result."

"If you think so many people would be anxious to go to this new planet, then build more ships," Ashley suggested caustically. "If you're right that the public would *demand* to emigrate, they'd be glad to see the remaining resources spent so wisely."

She didn't, for a moment, believe the counselor's explanations. She was convinced this New Frontier was a prison planet, and that she and her companions would be forced into slavery. But from the looks on the faces of some of the other women, they were beginning to buy Counselor Vanion's propaganda, which made Ashley grit her teeth at their gullibility.

"Earth simply no longer has the resources available to do that," Counselor Vanion said. "And even if we could transport a larger number of people than we already are, we couldn't transport enough tools and supplies to support a large population on New Frontier. One day, when the planet is further developed, it is hoped that new ships can be manufactured right on New Frontier. But none of that is possible at the present time."

Ashley snorted her scepticism. "Sure. You know as well as I do that no matter how difficult it gets on earth, there will never be a great number of people who will be anxious to leave it. It's home. And space is dangerous. And New Frontier is probably a Godforsaken wilderness where only cavemen and animals can survive. So why don't you tell us why we're really being sent there?"

"Ah, but so was every new frontier on earth a wilderness before mankind tamed it," Counselor Vanion pointed out, her black eyes sparkling as though she were enjoying this debate with Ashley. "And the people who did the taming were often rebels like you people—tough, innovative survivors. And that's exactly why you've been chosen to be sent to New Frontier, to do what you've shown you're better equipped to do than more conservative people—survive."

"And keep us from causing any more trouble on earth!" Ashley snapped. Then, as she looked around the table, something occurred to her that made her frown. "Anyway, the people who tamed the frontiers on earth weren't usually women," she added. "At least not at first. They were men. And while I wouldn't expect that to be true these days, I would at least expect an equal mixture of men and women to be at this table. So why are there no men here?"

At that, the sparkle in Counselor Vanion's eyes increased. "There were men at this table at one time," she answered. "In the beginning, when people were first sent to New Frontier."

She paused, waiting, and Ashley, from her studies in history, plucked a memory from her mind that brought a look of consternation to her face. Abruptly, she sat straighter.

"You can't be serious," she said to the counselor, shaking her head, horrified.

Counselor Vanion raised her dark eyebrows. "I beg your pardon?" she responded with a bland, and completely false, lack of understanding.

"You can't be sending us there to be—" Ashley

choked, unable to get the words out. The concept was so foreign, so revolting to her, that she didn't want to hear that her conclusion was correct.

But Counselor Vanion nodded. "As brides. You women," she continued, looking at the other women now instead of at Ashley, "are being sent to New Frontier to marry the single men who are already there."

There was a collective gasp from the women at the table. But none of them, other than Ashley, responded with words.

"That's barbaric!" she cried. "Women on earth have worked long and hard for equality, and now that we've finally gotten it, you're telling us that we're being sent to this unholy wilderness to end up as chattel for men?"

"Nonsense!" Counselor Vanion said sternly. "The wives who are already on New Frontier are far happier than any you've ever met on earth. They're not treated as chattel. They're highly valued. And they have complete freedom to pick the men they want as husbands. The women do the choosing, not the men."

For the moment, Ashley was too shocked to respond, and the counselor continued her explanation. "When you arrive on New Frontier, each of you will have six months to get to know all the single men. You may live and sleep with any of them who piques your interest on a temporary basis so that your final choice will be an informed one. Furthermore, once you choose a husband, you are assured of your man's fidelity. All of the men on New Frontier are subjected to a form of psycho-programming that makes it impossible for them to be unfaithful to their wives. And once a woman is married, it will no longer be possible for the single men to think of her in sexual terms. The psycho-programming bonds a husband to his wife mentally, emotionally, spiritually, and physically, and the bond lasts until one or the other of them dies."

Ashley stared at Counselor Vanion, enraged. "That's barbaric, too," she said. "That's mind control!"

"It may sound barbaric to you," Counselor Vanion responded crisply, "but to us, it's merely practical. There are so few women on New Frontier, we can't have men fighting over them and disrupting the peace of the whole community when everyone needs to be spending his or her energy in more positive ways."

She then turned away from Ashley and concentrated on the other women. "And there is one more benefit on New Frontier that I haven't mentioned yet," she said with a warm smile. "There are no limits to the number of children you are allowed to have. None at all, other than those nature may impose on you."

The other women gasped, and then a rush of excited murmurs began. As Ashley looked at her companions' reaction to Counselor Vanion's statement, she knew she was likely to be the only one of the deportees who would object any longer to being kidnapped and sent to outer space as a modern-day version of mail-order brides. The other women's faces now reflected hope and growing acceptance instead of shock or resistance.

Counselor Vanion then returned her attention to

Ashley, and her expression was both amused and empathetic. "You'll one day come to accept it, too," she murmured softly.

"Never." Ashley shook her head, her voice bitter.

The counselor smiled. "You're old enough to have learned never to say 'never,' Ashley Bronwyn," she said matter-of-factly. "And if you're as intelligent as your dossier says you are, you also must know it's better to light a candle than to curse the darkness, especially when the darkness is only in your imagination. One day, you'll realize that being sent to New Frontier is the best thing that could ever have happened to you. Or are you so worn down by the conditions on earth that you prefer death by execution instead of deportation to a place where you'll have the opportunity to live like humans once lived on our home planet—with plenty of space, more than enough food, the opportunity to bear children without asking anyone's permission?"

"My so-called crime didn't merit a death sentence," Ashley stated flatly. "I was merely trying to survive. And any government worth the name wouldn't have sentenced me to death for what I did."

Counselor Vanion responded with amusement in her voice. "But the government didn't sentence you to death," she pointed out. "They sentenced you, in effect, to life. And keep in mind that the same government you're so bitter toward has worked tirelessly and diverted badly needed resources to insure that you and many others do live." Then she added with dry chastisement, "Grow up, Ashley. Nothing is ever all black, nor all white."

"If *something* isn't all white, then what's the point of survival anyway?" Ashley responded bleakly.

The counselor cocked her head, then diverted her attention to the other women around the table.

"We'll be jumping into hyperspace in approximately two hours," she informed them. "There's time before then to give you a tour of the ship. After all, you'll be on this vessel for several weeks, so you might as well settle in. And during the trip, if any of you begin to feel too disoriented to function because of your altered circumstances, I'll be available to help you. This is all a very big shock, and it's only natural to experience adverse emotional reactions at first. But, believe me, that negative reaction and disorientation will pass."

Ashley was the last one out of the cabin, and before she stepped through the hatch to join the rest of the women on their "tour," Counselor Vanion came up beside her and detained her with a light touch on her arm.

When Ashley turned to her, her gaze flat and unfriendly, the counselor gave her a gravely indulgent look and shook her head.

"You're one of the few people who recovered from the shock quickly enough to challenge me during orientation, Ashley," she said, her voice so quiet no one else could hear her. "And that fact leads me to believe that you're either going to be a tremendous asset to the colony on New Frontier, or that we made a big mistake in choosing you. Either way, I suspect that sooner or later, you're going to be a lot of trouble for everyone. So let me give you a word of advice."

Ashley stared at her, unyielding.

"Though New Frontier functions as a loose democracy, it is not without laws. They can just as well execute you there as they could on earth," Counselor

Vanion warned in a subdued tone. "So you're going to have to make up your mind whether to survive, or whether to die for no better reason than misguided pride and petulant selfishness. I sincerely hope you do choose to survive. You owe it to those children who will carry your excellent genes—and to some man whose loneliness goes deeper than you can imagine."

She turned and left, and Ashley stared after her, unsure if she was capable of taking the counselor's advice. Only time would tell.

Most of her companions covered their eyes against the blinding colors on the view screen, which displayed the effects of jumping at hyperspeed through space. But Ashley, after noting the phenomenon with unabashed wonder and a certain amount of apprehension for a few moments, diverted her attention to a more important matter. How was she going to avoid sleeping with numerous barbarians before being forced to marry one of them and endure his phony psycho-programmed fidelity for the rest of her life?

Ashley's excellent mind had sorted out everything she'd learned and she viewed the information on two separate levels. On an intellectual level, she understood the government's actions toward her and others like her. There was historical precedent for it. Many of Australia's first European settlers had been convicts and history had shown it was often the rebellious who had the courage and the grit to tackle the unknown and make adjustments that suited the territory. Less imaginative, more conforming citizens usually preferred the status quo . . . or to bring it with them if they had to change location, whether their way of life was appropriate to the new location or not.

But while Ashley's mind accepted the logic of what the government had done to her, her emotions were in chaotic rebellion. She felt afraid and disoriented. But she covered those reactions by concentrating on her deep-seated fury at having her freedom taken away from her so summarily, so irretrievably. No one could escape from a planet in outer space, so no matter what, she could never go home again.

True, earth's economics hadn't allowed her much real freedom either, but at least she hadn't faced the prospect of losing her autonomy in such a personal matter as marriage. Counselor Vanion could dress things up all she wanted by stressing that the women chose their mates. But the fact remained that a marriage was in Ashley's future whether she found anybody on New Frontier she wanted for a husband or not. Since she'd never found a man on earth she wanted, she was positive there wouldn't be one on New Frontier either. The future she faced made Ashley feel sick to her stomach.

Her unconscious scowl lightened momentarily as she realized that New Frontier was probably large enough to allow her to disappear before she had to choose a husband. The scowl returned, however, at the realization that she wouldn't have a clue as to how to survive after disappearing.

Though the logical part of Ashley's mind knew already that she was well and truly trapped, her emotions couldn't accept the truth. But, finally, grim reality won out and she thought instead of finding at least a partially acceptable solution to a problem that wouldn't disappear. One fact stood out. There was no way she could endure having to sleep with numerous men, so she must somehow find a husband right away, and that man must be someone who would be as little bother to her as possible.

At that point, she remembered Garick Deveron and Bud Saunders. Jim had said they were scouts. Ashley wasn't sure exactly what scouts did on New Frontier, but she presumed they did what scouts had done in the past on earth—explore. And explorers, she thought with a sudden lift of her heart, would be away from home a lot, wouldn't they?

Ashley refused to consider marrying Garick, however. Just looking at him frightened her and damaged her faith in her own courage. He had such an aura of untamed ruthlessness that she could envision him beating a wife—or worse. And even if his barbarism didn't extend quite that far, she had no desire to spend the periods when he was home enduring the gaze of those dangerous gray eyes and suffering his no doubt aggressively demanding nature in bed.

On the other hand, Bud Saunders seemed a very pleasant, likable man whom she doubted would hurt a fly. He didn't appeal to her sexually, of course. No man ever had. But she could at least envision eventually liking him as a friend, and she thought he might be malleable enough so that she could avoid having sex with him too often. And, hopefully, his trips home wouldn't occur more than she could tolerate.

Her grim decision made, Ashley immediately got up from her couch and went in search of Bud.

She found him in the galley. Unfortunately, he was sitting with one of the other deportees, and he looked too flirtatiously involved to be interrupted.

Gritting her teeth with frustration, Ashley went to sit down with Jim.

"How are you doing?" he asked quietly, his glance at her gently sympathetic.

"Surviving," Ashley responded shortly.

"Do you want something to eat?"

"Not just now. I'd rather hear about New Frontier."

"Didn't they give you a brochure?"

"Yes, but I'll save it to read later. I'd rather hear about the place from someone who has been there. And by the way," she added, frowning in puzzlement, "what were you doing on earth?"

"I'm part of the government on New Frontier, and I periodically have to meet with the bureaucrats on earth who oversee the colony to give them reports on our status. And in any case," he added, "someone has to make sure they send the kind of tools and supplies back with us that we really need, instead of some bureaucrat's usually inaccurate guess about what we should have."

Ashley understood and nodded. Then she asked, "Why did Garick and Bud return to earth?"

"There were some things to be handled that I didn't have time for, and no one else could be spared to take care of them. Scouting is necessary, but it can be put off for a while. Planting crops at the right time can't."

Ashley then got back to business. "So tell me about New Frontier," she prodded Jim. "What's it like?"

"Like earth must have been before we humans overpopulated, overused, and overexploited it." Jim smiled. "It's pristine . . . beautifully untouched."

Ashley's expression grew a little wistful. "I've seen artists' reproductions of what earth must have been like once," she said. "But it's hard to relate to them, considering what it's like now."

Jim nodded. "You're in for a treat," he promised, "not only because of the environment, but because of the people. Garick was right when he told you we have to depend on each other there. It's not like New York, where overcrowding has made everyone surly, nasty, and suspicious of one another. We treat each other with respect and kindness. It's all for one, and one for all."

Ashley wasn't sure whether to believe Jim. But he was making her feel minimally better about her destination. Very minimally.

"Of course, some things are different," he went on. "The animal life will no doubt seem curious to you at first. For instance, we have the equivalent of horses, and they're our main mode of transportation. What aircraft we have is mostly used for transferring farm machinery from place to place in order to grow more crops, and we have very few ground vehicles as yet. But our so-called horses are more like a cross between an earth horse and an earth deer, and they have personalities and characters all their own. If you don't make a friend of a femura, you don't ride it."

"Femura?" Ashley repeated.

"That's what we call them. And we have other domestic animals that look and behave differently from those on earth, too. But the animals we've found there so far are either useful or harmless. We haven't come across anything dangerous yet."

"No predators?" Ashley asked, frowning. From the zoology she'd studied, that didn't make sense. What kept the other animals from getting so numerous that they overgrazed their habitat?

"No predators. At least, not that we've found yet."

"Where do people live?" Ashley inquired.

"Some live in our one town, Plymouth," Jim answered, "but most live on outlying farms and ranches. If you've ever studied early American history, we operate the way people used to when most people made their living through agriculture or ranching."

Ashley nodded. She'd studied that period.

"The ones who live away from town are the ones who really need wives," Jim went on. "It's lonely out there on your own. I had to live like that until my Mary came, and let me tell you, having her with me has made a world of difference to my emotional happiness."

"I imagine so," Ashley agreed, her tone neutral. But she was wondering if Jim would be as happy with his Mary as he obviously was if he hadn't had to undergo psycho-programming. "Do you have children?"

"Not yet, but we plan to start a family when I get home," Jim replied, his smile soft, anticipatory.

"How—" Ashley stopped and cleared her throat. "How exactly does this mating business work on New Frontier?" She slid a glance Bud's way. To her dismay, he looked smitten with the blonde and she with him. Damn it! Ashley hadn't counted on competition this early.

"Didn't they tell you in orientation?"

"Sort of, but . . ." Ashley cleared her throat again. "Well, the thing is, Jim, I'm rather inexperienced. I've never been in love and I've never . . . ah . . . been to bed with—" She stopped. The look in Jim's eyes was incredulous.

"Never?" he asked wonderingly. "You're a virgin?"

Ashley gave him a disgruntled look. "What's wrong with that?" she asked crossly. "Friendship is the strongest emotion I've ever felt for any man I've ever met, and why would I want to make love with a friend?"

"Do you think you're frigid?" Jim inquired, sounding worried.

Ashley gritted her teeth, then snapped, "How would I know? And, anyway, what does it matter if I am?" she added caustically. "Once I choose some poor sod and his artificial devotion clicks in, he has to love me whether I like having sex with him or not."

Jim frowned. "You think the psycho-programming makes our feelings artificial?"

"Of course!"

Jim shook his head. "The hell it does," he said, a trifle indignant. "I'm in love with my Mary and she's in love with me. And that's the way it is for all the married couples on New Frontier." He hesitated, then added, less indignantly, "But if you've never been in love, I guess you can't understand—not until you fall in love yourself."

"That's not likely to happen," Ashley said, more or less as a vow rather than a statement.

Jim smiled. "Don't be too sure. The men on New Frontier are a lot different than the ones on earth."

"Well, they're certainly bigger," Ashley agreed,

eyeing Bud across the room. Her gaze was more critical than approving. "I guess that has to do with diet."

"Among other things," Jim responded drily. "Hard work builds muscles, too."

Ashley sighed, suddenly feeling more forlorn than angry. The thought of being mauled by any of the oversized New Frontier men was anything but a happy one for her.

"Look, Ashley," Jim said, "we have a very small population on New Frontier, and we have to get along. When you consider the prospect of the one mechanic in our community getting his head bashed in by the one botanist over a woman, it's a matter of survival. And sexual taboos have never worked very satisfactorily. The psycho-programming is just a way of ensuring that adultery doesn't hurt the whole society. But there's still freedom before a marriage takes place. You can marry whomever you love."

"I know, I know," Ashley said absently. "I understand the logic. It's just the idea of mind control that turns me off."

"You'll change your mind once you see it in operation," Jim said, sounding convinced that he was right.

Ashley had a thought. "But the women aren't psycho-programmed, too, are they?" she asked, alarmed by the thought.

"No, but they can't stray if a man won't play," Jim said matter-of-factly. "And once a woman is mated, she's off limits to other men, single or married."

"Oh. Well, that's good. I guess."

At that moment, Ashley forgot about her conversation with Jim, for the simple reason that Garick Deveron had entered the galley. Ashley watched his broad back warily as he got his food, and then, to her dismay, he sat down beside Jim.

"Excuse me," she said, standing up. "I'm going to get something to eat." She walked away, avoiding looking directly at Garick's sardonic, too-knowing expression, which Ashley was afraid meant he suspected how he affected her.

As she was collecting a bowl of stew, a small loaf of bread, and a glass of real milk, she was wishing she hadn't used the excuse of being hungry to avoid Garick. She should have just left the galley. But she *was* hungry, she thought resentfully as the odor of the stew wafted to her nostrils, and she couldn't get in the habit of running from Garick like a scared rabbit. For all she knew, that would just encourage him to act more like the barbarian toward her than he already did.

Ashley was vaguely aware that her logic wasn't precisely on target in accusing Garick of acting like a barbarian; in fact, she couldn't think of a single thing he'd done to justify that description. But his face and body did. True, he was by no means ugly. It was just that he looked so . . . dangerous.

Determined to restore her self-respect by at least acting courageously, she carried her food back to the table and sat down across from Garick. She gave him one cold, defiant glance, then concentrated on eating. She was just swallowing a rather large bite when Jim, whom she would have sworn was not the type to betray anybody, betrayed her.

"Did Johnson tell you Ashley apologized to him for

bloodying his nose after you left the sick bay today?" he asked Garick in a casual fashion.

Ashley choked slightly, and then her head shot up and she directed a ferocious glare in Jim's direction. Out of the corner of her eye, however, she saw that Garick was smiling a satisfied smile, and she wanted to hit him as hard as she'd hit the medic earlier.

"No, he didn't," Garick replied with serene self-confidence. "But I knew she would."

Ashley immediately switched her glare to him. "You knew no such thing," she said indignantly.

He held her gaze, his gray eyes displaying amused certainty. "Sure I did," he drawled. And before she could protest further, he added, "You act tough, but you aren't. When you hit Johnson, you acted spontaneously. And then you were sorry."

"I was not!"

"Then why did you apologize to him?" The tone was a challenge.

"Because . . . because it's the civilized thing to do."

"Sure," he responded with a shrug of his broad shoulders that dismissed her explanation completely.

Ashley clenched her jaw and decided to ignore him. She bent her head over her stew and crammed some of it into her mouth.

"Ashley's concerned about the psycho-programming," Jim said, infuriating Ashley further. She didn't want Garick to know her private feelings. "I guess it's because she says she's never been in love . . . never—"

"Jim." Her voice was low, but it fairly reeked with a warning for him to shut up.

Jim glanced at her, surprised. Then he went on. "Anyway, I told her it's not as bad as she thinks." Then he paused and shook his head and grimaced. "Sorry," he said to Garick. "I guess you don't understand either since you're not psycho-programmed yourself."

Ashley's head swivelled of its own accord to stare at Garick. For some reason, though she hated the idea of psycho-programming, the knowledge that Garick had somehow managed to set himself above the rules made her even more indignant than the psycho-programming itself.

"Why not?" she asked, her tone accusing.

"Why not what?" he responded, his drawl unperturbed.

"Why aren't you psycho-programmed?"

"Because so far, there's been no prospect of my marrying anyone," he said, his gaze very steady on hers, "so there hasn't been any point to it."

"Why not?"

He smiled just enough to crinkle the scar at the corner of his mouth a little. "Why not what?" he repeated, mockingly this time.

"Why hasn't there been a prospect of your marrying someone?"

Ashley was beginning to feel slightly foolish for delving into Garick's private life. But she intended to stick to her guns instead of backing down from Garick Deveron, which, for some reason, was becoming ever more important to her peace of mind.

Jim, with a puzzled frown, started to say something, but Garick held up a hand to stop him. He gave him a warning look that made Jim look even more puzzled, but which effectively shut him up.

"Because, like you," Garick said softly, "I've never been in love and haven't expected to be. Also, I'm away from Plymouth most of the time, so a wife wouldn't get much satisfaction out of me. Nor me from her. I get all the . . ." He hesitated, then smiled in a way that made a peculiar tremor ripple through Ashley before he went on. "All the *companionship* I need from the women who arrive as brides, before they choose their husbands. So I really don't need a wife, do I?"

Ashley hesitated, thinking she was stupid to continue questioning him. Nevertheless, her mouth opened and she blurted, "Did none of those women you slept—" She blushed and abruptly changed what she'd been about to say. "Did no woman ever choose you for a husband?"

"No."

"Why not?"

"Because I told them not to," Garick responded simply.

Ashley understood completely. Where Garick Deveron was concerned, she thought any woman whom he warned off would weigh the consequences of going against his wishes with the utmost seriousness. As a matter of fact, she thought that only a woman who didn't value her life very much would choose to defy his wishes. But that conclusion only made Ashley more determined than ever not to let him intimidate her, lest she lose all respect for herself.

She looked away from Garick and glanced with relief at Bud, thankful that there were two scouts, leaving her with an acceptable alternative to Garick. But Bud and his female companion were now gazing into one another's eyes as though the secrets of the universe were to be found in their separate skulls.

Surely they couldn't already be in love, Ashley thought worriedly, frowning now. It was too soon for that. And if Garick dallied with the mail-order—space-order, rather—brides, surely Bud did too. So just because he was flirting with the woman in a way that made it seem as though he'd fallen in love didn't mean he and the blonde were at the stage of making a commitment to one another. Maybe tomorrow he'd be flirting with some other woman.

As Ashley continued to eat, she certainly hoped she'd see Bud with an entirely different woman—preferably herself.

Jim and Garick discussed things that made no sense to her. And when she was done with her meal, she stood up, nodded at Jim more than at Garick, and left the galley behind in favor of lying in her bunk and reading the pamphlet she'd been given on New Frontier.

She fell asleep in the middle of it, only awakening when Jim came into the cabin to go to bed. But she kept her eyes closed because she didn't want to talk to him. She was still angry with him for disclosing her private comments to Garick.

Jim shucked out of his bodysuit, climbed into the upper bunk, then leaned over the edge to peer at Ashley.

"You awake?" he whispered loudly enough to wake the dead.

Ashley stifled a sigh and opened her eyes. "I am

now," she responded, her tone dry.

Jim smiled. "Good. I wanted to tell you Garick's not as bad as you think he is."

"I didn't say I thought he was bad," Ashley said stiffly.

"No, but every time you look at him, it shows what you think," Jim answered. "And, I guess, considering the type of men you're used to, it's not surprising that you find him a little rough around the edges. But he has to be tough, Ashley. Scouting is dangerous."

"There's a difference between rough and tough, Jim," Ashley said.

Jim looked puzzled. "Maybe so," he said doubtfully, "but he's not rough around married women. My Mary thinks he's wonderful. Well, actually, most women think he's wonderful, even if some of them are a little scared of him at first."

"I'm not scared of him," Ashley lied.

"No, you don't seem to be," Jim agreed. "And I guess in some ways that's not a bad thing, so long as you're not so openly hostile toward him that you make other people uncomfortable. I have to admit, it's kind of interesting to see him finally come up against a woman who doesn't melt at his feet."

"I have no intention of melting at his feet!" Ashley snapped. "Nor at any other man's feet."

Jim chuckled. "Wait until you fall in love."

"I'm not going to fall in love."

"Sure. Well, good night, Ashley. See you in the morning."

"Good night, Jim."

But Ashley spent most of the rest of the night tossing, turning, and thinking rather than sleeping.

And surprisingly, a lot of her thinking had to do with why she was so sure she would never fall in love. She'd never sorted the matter out clearly in her own mind before.

Maybe it was because she'd never had a father, never had much contact with men at all until she'd entered the university. She and her mother had lived in an all-female dormitory, and she'd attended the all-female elementary and high schools located in the dormitory. In fact, though she and the other girls had occasionally been taken on excursions in the city, until Ashley had entered the university, her whole life had centered around her self-contained, all-female dormitory.

Too, her mother hadn't liked men. Ashley didn't know why for her mother had never explained her reasons. But Ashley couldn't remember a single comment her mother had ever made about the opposite sex that wasn't either dismissive, contemptuous, or hostile.

Considering her background, her life at the coed university had at first been somewhat of a shock to Ashley. And though some of the girls, who had been as sheltered as she, had gone hog wild over the men they were discovering for the first time, Ashley had withdrawn into herself, assessing the situation, assessing the character of the males she met.

The young men seemed to have only one thing on their minds, and because of her striking good looks, Ashley had been a favorite target for their propositions. But their sexual attention had frightened her in a way she'd never understood, and since she couldn't bear to acknowledge that she was frightened, she had told herself she didn't like being valued only for her looks. Without really thinking about it more deeply than that, she had rejected all of the men's advances and concentrated on her studies.

As time passed, she had gotten to know some of the men better. There had been quite a few among her fellow students and among her professors, whom Ashley had come genuinely to like. As a result, she had come to view males as human beings, not as some alien race to be completely avoided. However, none of those males she liked had stirred more than feelings of friendship within her. She hadn't been sexually attracted to any of them. But perhaps it was only that she hadn't met the *right* man yet that had her convinced she would never fall in love?

Ashley didn't know the answer to that question. She only knew she resented being *forced* to marry anyone. And though she would be allowed to select her mate, that didn't mitigate the fact that being forced to marry at all was barbaric. What if none of the single men on New Frontier turned out to be that right man whom she could love? How could she bear being trapped in the same domicile, trapped into sexual intimacy, with a man she didn't love? The very thought made her shudder.

Ashley then decided her original plan was the best one. She must somehow find a man to marry who would be absent most of the time and whom she could at least like when he was around. It wasn't a perfect solution, but it was the best chance for maintaining a semblance of freedom she could think of.

With renewed determination, Ashley decided that

she would begin the very next day to see if Bud was serious about the woman she'd seen him with in the galley. If he was, Ashley knew she couldn't in all good conscience interfere with true love. But if he wasn't, she intended to do her best to attract his interest and keep him in reserve in case that right man wasn't available on New Frontier.

Deep down, Ashley hoped she did find a man to love on New Frontier. Loving the husband she was going to be forced to pick was far preferable to liking him. But given her history with the opposite sex, she couldn't count on that happening, and so she didn't count on it at all.

Garick lay in his bunk with a small smile on his lips, thinking about what Ashley had unknowingly revealed at dinner that evening about her inner feelings, as well as how out of touch with her own feelings she truly was. He also thought about what he was sure she was planning to do to avoid dealing with those feelings which she didn't understand and could barely tolerate.

Unlike Ashley, Garick understood her feelings perfectly and was encouraged by them, as well as moving closer and closer to a decision to exploit them.

But "exploit," he amended his thinking, was too strong a word. After all, if he acted on what he was thinking, the result would be as much to Ashley's benefit as it would be a source of satisfaction for him. Otherwise, being such a babe in the woods, she might do something so foolish she would end up ruining her whole future.

At that point, Bud entered the cabin, a silly smile on his face.

"You look like the cat that ate the canary," Garick remarked with lazy interest. "Have you been naughty?"

"I'll say," Bud said, his smile broadening. But then he sobered and added, "But it's not really like that with Sheila, Garick. This time, it's different, more serious."

"Ah," Garick murmured with satisfaction. The one problem concerning Ashley he'd thought he'd have to deal with had just been solved. Not to mention that his friend, Bud, had just had a narrow escape from what Garick was sure would have been a total mismatch.

"What did that 'ah' mean?" Bud asked, looking at him in puzzled surprise.

Garick then surprised Bud again. Though he seldom laughed outright, he did so then. And when the laughter died down, he glanced at Bud with totally uncharacteristic mischief in his gray gaze.

"Let's just say that if this Sheila turns out to be your true love, you found her in the nick of time," he said with comradely lightness. And before Bud could ask any questions, Garick turned away and murmured "Good night" with such finality that Bud had no choice other than to drop the conversation.

Chapter Four

Feeling almost as tired as she had when she'd retired for the night, Ashley awoke to the sound of loud snoring from the upper bunk. Then, realizing that she was still thinking in terms of day and night aboard a ship traveling through the black void of space, she shook her head, feeling momentarily disoriented.

Quietly, she got up, washed, combed her hair, donned her clothing, then eased out of the cabin to go to the galley.

She was enjoying her second cup of coffee when Bud strolled in. Seeing him, Ashley's mood brightened considerably. It was a good sign that she hadn't had to seek him out. And it was an even better sign when he gave her a quick, friendly smile. Her returning smile was nothing short of radiant.

Bud looked a little startled by the intensity of her

smile, then asked, "Mind if I join you?"

"Not at all. In fact, I'd love it."

Her enthusiastic response startled Bud again, and Ashley looked down at her cup, wondering if she was overdoing it. She'd never flirted with a man in her life, but wasn't showing eagerness to be in a particular man's company the way other females did it? However, Ashley realized that observing someone else do something wasn't quite the same as doing it oneself, so she decided to tone things down a little until she got more comfortable with this flirting business. She didn't want to come on so strongly that she scared Bud away.

When Bud settled into a chair across from her with his coffee, Ashley adopted an expression she hoped was friendly and encouraging, without being fatuous.

But before she could say anything, he spoke. "Have you accepted what's happened to you now that you've had a chance to sleep on it? Are you getting used to the idea?"

Ashley hadn't really, but she didn't see any point in sounding as disgruntled with her fate as she felt. After all, there was nothing she could do to change the basic situation. It was only some of the details she was going to try to twist to her own satisfaction.

"More or less," she said evasively.

"Good. I know it was a shock, but trust me, Ashley. You'll have a good life on New Frontier. You'll be glad you're there eventually."

Ashley smiled, then said, "Tell me what you do there, Bud. Jim said you were a scout. What exactly does a scout do?"

"Explore. Actually," he added, "I'm more the exploration team chemist than a full-fledged scout like Garick. I do water-and-soil tests on our trips. Have you seen a map of New Frontier?"

"Yes, there's one in the pamphlet they gave me."

Bud drew his own planetary map out of his pocket and spread it out on the table, pointing with his finger at one small area. "That's where our only town, Plymouth, lies," he explained. "It's surrounded by farms and ranches. But as our population grows, we're going to spread out. Garick and I—Garick's the chief scout," he added as an aside, "—and a few others—a botanist, a geologist, and so forth—spend our time exploring and mapping the planet in detail, showing where the land is suitable for agriculture, what minerals there are that we can use. Things like that."

Ashley nodded. "So you're away from Plymouth a lot?" she asked casually.

"Most of the time," Bud agreed. "That's why I haven't married so far. We all have land and a house allotted to us, but I've never had time to plant crops even if I could be sure I'd be there at harvest time. And those of us on the team who are male don't think it would be fair to leave a woman to try to run a farm or ranch on her own. She couldn't handle it."

Want to bet? Ashley thought with a combination of muted resentment of Bud's chauvinism and relief that his continuous absence was exactly what she had wanted to hear.

Aloud, she said, "Even though men do? Jim said he ran his ranch on his own until he got married."

Bud shook his head, smiling at her with indulgence. "It's hard physical labor, Ashley. Men have the build for it. Women don't."

"I think you might be surprised what women can do, Bud," Ashley said, taking care to keep her tone neutral. "I've studied early American history, and there were many times when women ran farms and ranches on their own. They *developed* the brawn to do it."

Bud inspected Ashley's slight, slender body, then shook his head. "Some might," he agreed. "But I can't see you doing it. You're just too small."

"But I'm determined," Ashley pointed out. "I have a strong will. And sometimes that's more important than brawn."

"Not on New Frontier," said Bud.

Ashley took a deep breath to stifle her impatience, then said, "But what if I were married to someone like you, Bud?" She tried not to see how his eyes widened at that suggestion. "You make a salary, don't you? So all I would really have to do is cultivate a kitchen garden, right? I wouldn't have to handle a big farm."

Bud didn't say anything immediately, and Ashley couldn't look at him. Indeed, she could feel her face flushing with embarrassed heat. She hadn't meant to hint quite so broadly that she was interested in him as a husband. Not yet.

Finally, Bud started to say, "Ashley, I'm not sure if you mean what it sounds like you—"

At that moment, the door to the galley opened, and when Bud looked up and saw Garick step across the threshold, he shut up.

Ashley was furious at the interruption, and she glared at Garick. He saw her expression, glanced at Bud, and the scar at the corner of his mouth crinkled ever so slightly while his gray eyes indicated he saw more than Ashley wanted him to. She quickly looked down at her cup, hoping she was wrong. Surely, Garick could have no idea what she had planned.

"Morning, folks," he said, with a wry drawl.

"Morning, Garick," Bud replied.

Ashley said nothing.

Garick got himself a cup of coffee, and then, without asking permission, he joined them at the table.

Ashley could barely keep from glaring at him again, but somehow she managed to maintain a bland expression, while she silently prayed Garick wouldn't stay long. But if he did, she would just tackle Bud later.

"What are we talking about?" Garick inquired deceptively mild and innocent.

"I was just telling Ashley a little about New Frontier," Bud said.

"I see." Garick nodded his head. "Did you tell her about the calderas?"

Frowning, Ashley looked up. "Calderas?" she asked, puzzled.

"They're New Frontier's version of cattle," Bud explained. "Only they don't look much like cows. But they taste good, and their coats are luxury items. Garick and I just sold some of them on earth. Only we couldn't say they're actually what they are, of course, and I believe the government stores call them new mink. That's why Garick and I went to earth, to sell some of New Frontier's products. Nobody else could be spared to make the trip."

Ashley blinked at him. She'd never been able to

afford such a coat herself, of course, but she'd seen them in the few luxury stores the high-level bureaucrats patronized and which low-salaried people like her were allowed to browse in. They were gorgeous garments—multicolored, water-repellent, wonderfully warm, and yet as light as a feather.

"Those come from New Frontier?" she asked, astonished.

Bud nodded. "They're one of our few exports right now, because they're almost weightless and easy to transport. But calderas don't give milk like cows on earth do—or used to, rather. We use garellas for that. They're sort of like a goat and they feed on anything. Only they don't look like earth goats any more than calderas really look like earth cows."

Ashley opened her mouth, then shut it again. What could she say? It was all too new, too disorienting.

"You'll get used to things," Bud said comfortingly. "It won't take long before you're riding a femura like a real cowgirl, milking garellas, and roasting caldera over an open fire."

Ashley couldn't help it. As she pictured what Bud had suggested, she burst out laughing.

When her laughter died down, she saw that Bud was grinning broadly at her, but Garick wasn't. He had a look in his eyes she couldn't interpret. It wasn't hostile, and it wasn't friendly. It was simply . . . odd. And though she had a sense that his response to the sound of her laughter had been more positive than negative, his gaze made her uncomfortable.

Bud turned to Garick. "I've been telling Ashley about our work, too," he said.

"About the fact that we're away from Plymouth for

long periods of time?" Garick said, his eyes resting on Ashley so perceptively that she again uneasily felt that he knew what she was up to. But that was silly. How could he suspect her plan?

Bud nodded, and his face flushed slightly. Ashley was dismayed by how transparent he was. If Garick hadn't already guessed her plan, Bud's expression might give it away.

"Yes, I told her earlier that we're away so much of the time that it makes marriage difficult," Garick said.

Ashley had the distinct impression that he was amused and she forced herself to return his look with a nonchalance she was far from feeling. "What if either of you fall in love?" she asked.

"We haven't so far," he drawled.

Ashley turned to Bud. "Is that right, Bud? Have you never been in love?"

Bud hesitated, then said quietly, "Well, Garick's right. I haven't been in the past. But though it's really too soon to be sure, I think I am now."

Ashley caught her breath, hoping against hope Bud wasn't going to say what she feared he would.

"With one of the new deportees," Bud went on, looking at Ashley with kind regret and with obvious apprehension that what he was saying might hurt her. "I met her last eve, and we just sort of clicked. I think it was love at first sight."

Oh, hell! Ashley thought, dismayed. But seeing how uncomfortable Bud looked, she had to relieve his mind about her own feelings. So she gave him a sweet smile and said, "Congratulations, Bud. I'm very happy for you. Do you think you'll end up marrying her?"

Bud nodded, smiling. "We're already talking about it. She says she doesn't mind that I'll be away a lot until New Frontier is fully mapped and explored. She's a potter, so she can keep busy making things for our own use and to trade for other things while I'm away. And once I don't have to go on exploration trips anymore, I can stay home full time and we can make a go of my farm together."

To Ashley's surprise, Garick smiled broadly and said, "Sounds like I'll be wishing you happy marriage soon, Bud. Congratulations."

Ashley hadn't seen Garick smile before, and the effect was stunning, changing his aura of barbarism to something a great deal more appealing. In fact, his smile was so appealing that for a long moment, Ashley couldn't look away from it. Then she became aware that Garick was watching her stare at his smile, his expression enigmatic, and she quickly turned her gaze toward Bud again.

"You'll have to introduce me to your prospective bride soon, Bud," she said. "I didn't meet anybody at orientation yesterday, but from what I saw of her when the two of you were sitting together last night, I think you have very good taste."

Bud looked pleased. "I think I do, too."

Ashley then got to her feet. "Well, I'm going to do a little exploring of my own now. We only got a cursory tour of the ship yesterday, and I'm curious about it. See you later."

She left the galley, feeling Garick's gaze boring into her back again, and drew a breath of relief when the door closed behind her. And then, grimacing with forlorn disappointment that her first plan had failed, she began to tour the ship and tried to devise a new plan.

His eyes on Ashley's tempting derriere as she walked out of the galley, Garick was unaware that he was grinning until Bud commented on it.

"What's amusing you?" he asked.

Garick got his grin under control and shrugged. "I was just thinking how one's best plans often go awry," he said mildly. "But you can tell a lot about a person by the way he or she reacts to having a plan bite the dust."

"Are you talking about some plan of your own?" Bud asked, puzzled.

"Only in a manner of speaking," Garick responded mysteriously. "All plans hinge, at least to some extent, on the success or failure of the plans of other people."

Bud looked more puzzled than ever.

"It isn't anything you need to worry about, Bud," Garick said with a dismissive smile. "You're out of it now."

"Out of what?"

"Out of coffee. Want another cup? I'll get you some when I get mine."

Garick got to his feet, went to the counter, and deftly changed the subject upon his return.

As the days passed, Ashley had no luck coming up with a new plan and was finally reduced to hoping some single man on New Frontier would, against all odds, take her heart by storm. She also hoped that would happen very quickly after her arrival on New

Frontier. She had no intention of sleeping with any man other than the one she eventually chose for a husband, and the longer it took to find a mate, the longer she would have to dodge a horde of lusty bachelors.

Since there was nothing further Ashley could do until she arrived on the planet, she spent her time learning about the practical things that would help her adjust to her new life. She studied agriculture in the ship's garden and mechanics in its repair shop and picked Jim's brain clean every time they were together.

He didn't mind. They were friends now. He accepted her without judgment and without criticism, except for her attitude toward Garick.

As they were walking to the galley one day, he said worriedly, "Listen, Ashley, if Garick's there, let's sit somewhere else for a change. I'm not in the mood for the tension you two create every time you're near one another. I've already got a headache from drinking too much beer last night."

Ashley was annoyed that Jim made it sound as though she were as much at fault as Garick for the tension, when it was always Garick who made remarks which aroused her temper.

"If it were up to me, I'd never sit with Garick, Jim. It's always he who comes to our table, not the other way around."

"Yeah," Jim responded gloomily. "And damned if I know why he does it. If he was the kind of man who took women seriously, I'd say he was interested in you, but since he never puts the moves on you, I guess he just sits with us out of habit."

Ashley frowned at Jim. "Jim, he sits with us because he likes *you*," she said. "Surely, you know that."

Jim glanced down at her, the expression in his blue eyes doubtful. "Oh, I know he likes me," he agreed. "We go back a long way together. But he's never been *this* chummy with me before."

Ashley shrugged. "Well, he can't sit with Bud. Bud's always with Sheila. So that leaves us."

"And about a dozen women who would give their eyeteeth not only to have him sit with them, but to go back to their cabins with them later," Jim muttered under his breath.

Ashley heard his comment, and for some reason, it irritated her.

"Maybe he's decided to be celibate," she said, her tone surly now.

"Garick?" Jim gave a short laugh and shook his head. "I don't think so. He likes sex as much as any man."

"But if he doesn't love any of the women he has sex with," Ashley suggested, "maybe it's like having dessert after a meal. He can take it or leave it."

"Maybe." Jim shrugged but the look in his eyes said he didn't believe that.

They entered the galley, and Ashley was disappointed that Garick wasn't already there so she and Jim could sit elsewhere. But maybe they'd be finished eating before he arrived, she consoled herself. She didn't like the tension Garick provoked in her any more than Jim did, but so far, she thought she'd done an admirable job of responding civilly to his insinuations. She didn't answer back nearly as bitingly as she would have if their skirmishes didn't always make Jim so uncomfortable.

When she and Jim were seated, Jim continued their previous conversation. "Anyway," he said glumly, "it's a good thing Garick's away from Plymouth as much as he is. The kind of sparks you two set off together can affect everybody else . . . Make people choose sides. And we don't need that kind of tension in our community. We have to get along."

His comments made Ashley doubly glad that she had so far refrained from reacting to Garick's baiting as heatedly as she wanted to. Since New Frontier was going to be her home and its people her only friends for the rest of her life, she didn't want to gain a reputation as a troublemaker. Nor, even if she did feel an occasional strong desire to sock Garick Deveron right on that stubborn, rock solid jaw of his, did she want to damage his relationships with his friends on New Frontier.

It was at the end of that thought that Garick came into the galley. Ashley's reaction was her usual one. Looking at his lithe body and primitively handsome face, and especially his eyes, stirred up something inside her she had so far failed to identify and shied away from even thinking about. Listening to his voice, which she had to admit was a very attractive one, always made her feel tense. But she was sure that was only because that voice uttered comments which always made her want to hit him.

As Garick carried his food to the table, Ashley, sighing inwardly, made up her mind, as usual, to control her temper while she endured his company. Garick's first words, however, tested her resolve.

"I saw you working in the machine shop yesterday," he drawled. And without looking at her, he added, "Next time, turn the wrench the other way. You might find it tightens what you want to tighten instead of wasting a lot of energy accomplishing nothing."

Ashley's temper immediately seethed, but before she could snap a retort at him, Jim answered for her.

"Hey, she's doing better than a lot of the women," he said, his tone mild. "And since she's never had to do anything but punch a button for whatever she's wanted up until now, I'd say she's adapting wonderfully."

Though grateful for Jim's defense, she would rather have defended herself—preferably physically. However, since she knew she would get the worst of it in a physical fight with Garick, despite Jim's giving her some rudimentary training in judo recently, a muted verbal attack was her only option.

"And how good were you with wrenches before you were taught the proper way to use them?" she asked, slightly surly.

He looked at her, and she wished he hadn't. Almost every time he gazed at her, his gray eyes seemed to be enjoying some private joke—at her expense, naturally.

"I'm not an expert at using them now," he said in a dismissive way. "I don't have to be. But you should be."

"I don't see why," Ashley said, barely managing to speak without clenching her teeth.

He shrugged. "Because you'll probably end up on some ranch or farm where either you or your husband have to do your own repair work or it doesn't get done. And surely, you don't want to be a burden to your husband by being incompetent at such things, do you?"

"What does it matter whether I'm a burden or not?" Ashley responded, her tone getting more sour with each word. "With all that psycho-programming going for me, I could be a complete idiot and my husband would still have to love me."

Garick eyed her, his gaze, as usual, enigmatic. "And are you the type of woman who would take advantage of some poor guy's psycho-programming to get a free ride?" he asked.

Ashley wasn't, but Garick's words made her temper slip upward another notch, while her usual self-control began to slip to an all-time low. "Sure," she said, her voice now verging on open hostility. "Why not? I didn't have any choice about going to New Frontier, and I'm not going to have any real choice about whom I marry. Considering that there won't be all that many single men to choose from, I'm probably not going to want any of the men who are available. So why shouldn't I just pick out the most accommodating wretch of the whole bunch, and in exchange for giving him a child a year, let him work himself to death providing me with bed, board, and mechanical maintenance? I may just let him nurse the babies and change the diapers as well!"

"Ashley, cut it out," Jim interjected. He turned to Garick, who was staring at Ashley enigmatically, but was also now subtly dangerous. "She doesn't mean that, Garick," he said with irritation. "If she did, she wouldn't be studying twelve hours a day to learn what she'll need to survive on New Frontier. You just rub her the wrong way, and she's getting back at you."

At that, Ashley's control stopped slipping and disappeared entirely. "The hell I am!" She threw her napkin down on the table and got to her feet, her glare directed full strength into Garick's gray eyes. "I'm a lazy leech, a flaming parasite, an incompetent mechanic, and morally deficient to boot. Right, Mr. Deveron? And since that's the case, I must mean every word I just said!"

She then turned on her heel, stormed out of the galley, and headed for the only area of the ship where she was likely to find any safe release for her temper —the gym.

She still had fire in her eyes, and was seething with anger, and breathing hard when she entered the gym and headed for the punching bag. She just wished she had some paint and enough artistic skill to reproduce Garick Deveron's image on its leather surface.

She had drawn back her arm to slam the first punch into the bag when someone caught her wrist from behind. Furious, she pivoted on her heel and found herself facing the living image of the source of her anger.

"You want to hit something?" Garick said, his eyes holding hers with amusement. "Hit me."

"You'd just duck and hit me back!" she responded, her tone scathing. "I'm sure you've had a lot more practice at physical brutality than I have!"

Though Ashley now knew that Garick wasn't a prison inmate, she still had trouble viewing him as anything other than a barbarian, and she could easily picture him having brutal fistfights with anyone who displeased him. In fact, one of the reasons she was so determined to stand up to him was because deep down, she was actually scared to death of him.

"Then I'll teach you how to do it right and maybe, if you're smart enough to learn, you'll get part of the satisfaction you think you want, even if it won't be what you're really looking for," he proposed. "Otherwise, go throw yourself on your bunk and have a good cry."

Ashley didn't understand Garick's reference to "what she was really looking for," but she understood all too well the implied insult in his reference to her crying.

"I *never* cry," she said in a frigid tone. "And I doubt if you even know how to teach," she added for good measure.

"Try me."

"With pleasure," she lied.

"Take off your tunic."

"What?"

"You don't want to rip it while we're fighting, do you?"

He was shrugging out of his black leather jacket, and since it would have been cowardly to back down, Ashley quickly untied the belt of her tunic and took it off. Then she stood facing Garick in her white bodyshirt, her heart beating at a furious pace. She was, on one level, terrified. But she would have died rather than let Garick know that.

He gave her long, shapely legs the briefest of glances, then said, "Now try to hit me." And when Ashley hesitated, he added drily, "I won't hit you back."

The blow never landed, of course. As her arm was in motion, her fist aimed at his chin, he reached up, deftly grabbed her wrist, spun her arm as well as her body so that her back was to him, and she was immediately immobilized.

As he held her with her back tightly pressed against his body, his cheek over her shoulder pressed against hers, he asked, "Want to learn how to do that to me?"

The humor in his voice deflated some of Ashley's fear and replaced it with anger. "No," she said, panting a little. "I want to learn how to deck you."

He laughed softly, and the low sound, as well as the touch of his cheek against hers and the feel of his breath against her skin, suddenly made Ashley's stomach clench against a sensation she'd never experienced before. She didn't know what that feeling meant. She only knew, to her decided puzzlement, that it wasn't unpleasant. Far from it.

"Then pay attention," Garick said, distracting Ashley from thinking about the flutterings in her stomach. An instant later, he spun her out of his hold and began to teach her more about judo.

He worked with her for about half an hour. He turned out to be a better teacher than Ashley would have ever given him credit for and she learned more about judo than she'd known before. While some of her fear of him was dissipated because he was careful not to hurt her, she never did get to deck him. She did, however, experience more of the strange, pleasant sensations in her stomach every time he put his strong warm hands on her bare arms and legs, and each time he pressed his hard body tightly against hers. And with those exciting feelings came a certain breathlessness as well as a flush of heat to her body that confused Ashley enormously.

"Maybe you can deck me next time," Garick said casually when the so-called lesson was over and he was reaching down to pluck his black leather jacket off the gym floor. "If that's what you still want to do," he added mysteriously in a tone of voice that implied he was laughing at her.

As usual, the idea of his ridiculing her sparked her temper. "Sure," she retorted. "When you let that happen, I'll know you're in the first stages of a mental breakdown. You're the last of the male chauvinist pigs."

He threw the black leather jacket over one broad shoulder and shrugged, while a faint smile crinkled the scar at the corner of his mouth.

"Maybe so," he agreed mildly. "I've always thought there was a good reason why God made men and women different. Earth women just seemed to have decided a long time ago not to accept His design."

"But New Frontier women do?" Ashley snorted.

"New Frontier women are everything a woman should be," Garick said, baiting her now.

Ashley almost snapped back a retort, but something about his tone, as opposed to all the other times he'd baited her, made her hesitate. She stared at Garick, frowning thoughtfully. She had wondered before if his taunting her was deliberate. If for some reason, he *wanted* her to lose her temper with him. But she had always dismissed the idea because she'd never been able to figure out why he would want to do such a thing. And she still couldn't fathom what his motive might be for wanting her angry.

Seeing her expression, he smiled one of his rare, genuine, absolutely stunning smiles, and Ashley reacted by catching her breath while her eyes fastened on his mouth with an almost hypnotic fascination.

"Think about it," he said, his voice roughly soft and, if Ashley had been experienced enough to believe what her ears were telling her, almost caressing. "One day, you'll figure it all out. But if you can't, I'll let you in on the secret before too much longer—when you're ready to hear it."

Then he walked away, leaving Ashley feeling weary, frustrated, and thoroughly, maddeningly confused.

Garick's smile faded to a grimace of pure male frustration as he headed for his cabin to get control of his aroused state and to sponge off his sweat.

Sometimes, when he was away from Ashley, he found it hard to believe she could really be as dense about the games men and women played with one another as she seemed to be. But each time he was in her company, she rose to the bait which he used to keep her aware of him—even if her awareness was hostile at this stage—with such beautiful spontaneity that his doubts disappeared.

However, if he was any judge of women, her hostility might be changing to something else. For she had certainly responded to the physical teasing he'd been tossing her way during the past half-hour. At least her body had responded, even if she hadn't seemed to realize what those responses implied.

It was a tricky stage in Garick's plan, and he knew he needed to handle things just right the next time he saw Ashley. Perhaps, in the interest of letting her body lead the rest of her, he should offer to teach her more judo soon. But there was a problem with that tactic. He wasn't sure if he could tolerate looking at her in that skimpy bodysuit and touching her as intimately as judo required without blowing his whole plan sky high and kissing her senseless. And if he ever kissed her, he was very much afraid he wouldn't stop there even if she asked him to.

Garick was normally a patient, controlled man, and he had never in his life contemplated seducing a woman faster than the pace she wanted to set. But he didn't react to Ashley with his customary controlled patience. Yet, if there was one thing he knew for certain, it was that forcing the pace with her would be exactly the wrong thing to do. So perhaps what he should do was begin to ease off on the verbal taunting and start pouring on the charm instead? If that worked, *then* he could offer to teach her more judo and maybe by that time her head would have caught up with what he was pretty sure her body already knew.

Garick sighed with resignation, wishing he wasn't so caught up in the challenge of seducing Ashley Bronwyn. There were at least half a dozen other women aboard ship who had indicated they would present no challenge at all if he turned his interest in their direction.

But, hell no, he thought with wry self-mockery. He didn't want an easy affair. Apparently, judging by the single-minded way he was pursuing his objective, he wanted an affair with a woman who would no doubt swear on a stack of Bibles at this very moment that she'd rather face a firing squad than sleep with him.

Little liar, Garick thought, hoping he was right.

Chapter Five

After their judo lesson, Ashley began avoiding Garick. She didn't think about her reasons other than to acknowledge that she felt out of control of her emotions and reactions. She varied her meal times—more often eating alone than with Jim—spent even longer hours studying information about New Frontier, and checked corridors before entering them, heading the other way if she saw Garick.

But she couldn't elude him all the time, and when she did see him, she often caught herself surreptitiously staring at his rugged face and taut male body with a wistful sadness. She told herself her sadness was due to too much tension between them for them ever to be friends. For when she was able to be objective, she had to admit that there was something about Garick when he was relaxed and in a good mood that would have made her want him for a friend. But he made her feel in ways she couldn't remember ever feeling before and that made friendship between them impossible.

Besides, she had plenty of other friends. She got along well with Jim and Bud and most of the other women. However, where once she had wanted to know all she could learn about the mating rules on New Frontier, that changed the closer the ship came to the new planet. Now, whenever Jim or Bud or anyone else even hinted about the courtships that would be expected of her, she grew snappish and changed the subject. Even thinking, much less talking, about having to spend time with men who would court her with the expectation that at some point she would go to bed with them, made her furiously resentful.

Of course, she had absolutely no intention of fulfilling any such expectations. No, if she were lucky, she and her future husband would fall in love at first sight like Bud and Sheila had, and she would be spared any courtships at all other than the one that really mattered. But she knew that was unrealistic and that she would have to go through the motions of courtship for a short while. But she intended to avoid any physical intimacy until she had chosen a tolerable marriage partner whether she loved him or not.

When the ship was at last close enough to New Frontier to see it as a tiny dot in the distance, Ashley couldn't stay away from the view screen. And as the planet grew larger and larger on the screen, she gazed with mingled fascination and dread at its jewellike colors set amidst the blackness of eternal space.

The planet's sun sparked its northern white polar

cap into emitting shimmering beacons of light, but the southern pole was a different story. It was covered with a reddish cloud cover, and north of that was a stark, desolate area, which was topped with a swath of green.

"Why is the southern pole's cloud cover red?" she asked Bud one day after he'd settled into the seat beside her in the viewing area.

"We don't know much about that area yet," he answered. "Haven't had time to make a thorough survey. But the red is because there are active volcanoes at the southern pole. That desolate area above it was recently volcanic and has now cooled. The green is jungle." He drew Ashley's attention to an area where the green color faded to a less intense shade. "That's grazing land for calderas," he explained, "and above it is farmland. Plymouth is situated right in the middle of the farmland."

Ashley noticed he was smiling with anticipation, and his next words confirmed his mood. "It's a beautiful planet, Ashley. Primitive and untouched and in some places really wild. But there's no crowding, no pollution, and no oppressive government. We have a loose democracy. And I'm positive that once you've been with us for a while, you're going to bless the day you were dragooned into joining us."

"Maybe so," Ashley said quietly. But she knew she would have liked New Frontier a lot better if marriage hadn't been a requirement for any female who stepped on its surface.

Garick sat some distance behind Ashley and Bud watching them talk, his feelings shifting from disgruntled frustration, to reluctant resignation, to something resembling pity. Time was growing too short to put his plan into effect, but there was little he could do to change things. Every time he got near enough to Ashley to speak to her, which was seldom, she bolted and he had no chance at all to try to charm her. In fact, he was positive that she went to a great deal of trouble to avoid him.

But, hell, he wasn't going to chase her down and force her to endure his attentions, even if he did feel sorry about the shock he suspected she was going to get once she disembarked and fully realized what awaited her. Jim and Bud had told him they'd tried to talk to her about the arrival procedure, but she always got snappish and avoided the subject. Garick was positive Ashley was in the habit of evading situations she didn't want to accept, and he had an uneasy feeling that that mind set had prevented her from understanding the rules that applied when new women arrived on New Frontier.

Well, if she won't listen to Jim or Bud, it's certain she won't listen to me, Garick thought grimly as Ashley turned her head, and his eyes traced her delicate profile, smooth cheek, and slender neck. *So there's nothing I can do other than let her be thrown to the wolves like a lamb to the slaughter. I could ease things for her if she'd let me, but since she won't, she'll just have to take what comes and deal with it the best she can. But, damn it, if she only knew what awaited her, she would have been running toward me all this time, not avoiding me like the plague.*

As that last thought surfaced, Garick momentarily wondered if Ashley had hurt his male ego more than made any sense. True, he wasn't used to any woman running *from* him; in fact, he couldn't remember ever having to pursue any woman he'd ever wanted—not for very long anyway. But he knew Ashley's early history, so surely he wasn't letting his pride be hurt because someone who'd been indoctrinated as unwholesomely as she had been was proving to be the exception to the rule.

You probably misjudged her reactions to you during the judo lesson anyway and she's as cold as a loaf of day-old bread that's been left outside through a winter night, he told himself in an attempt to ease the flare of desire that rose inside him as Ashley stood up and stretched and his eyes traced the line of her breasts and the curve of her buttocks. *So forget her. You're probably lucky she didn't give you a chance to teach her a few things. Because if you reacted to her in bed the way you've been reacting to her since you first set eyes on her, and she's truly frigid, nothing could have come of the affair but a whole lot of grief you don't need.*

On that note, he made himself get up and leave the view room. He was not a man to dwell on lost possibilities when there were half a dozen definite prospects scattered around the rest of the ship. But for some reason, before he found one of the "definites," he lost interest and ended up in the gym for some strenuous exercise instead.

It took several shuttle trips from the *Mayflower* to transport all the people and cargo to New Frontier. Jim, Garick, and Bud departed on an early shuttle, Ashley and the other women later.

Ashley was the first to step onto the ramp that had been let down from the shuttle's hatch to the surface of New Frontier. As she stood there so, she had a sudden uneasy feeling it had been a mistake not to let Bud or Jim tell her exactly what to expect. But what did it matter anyway? she thought, dismissing the feeling. She had her own agenda and was only going to pretend to follow the rules.

Her first glimpse of her new home was somewhat of a disappointment. The shuttle had landed on a meadow which was surrounded by trees, and the grass was scorched and burned around the shuttle, while it was tough and brown elsewhere.

Turning her eyes from the scenery to the end of the ramp, Ashley saw that there was a crowd of people—mostly male—clustered there and every male gaze was focused intently on her. Swallowing a burst of nervousness, she took two steps forward, then stopped when a bearded, widely grinning giant of a man clad in a crudely styled caldera coat bounded toward her. Since there were other women crowding behind her, there was nowhere for Ashley to go to escape the man and nothing she could do when he grabbed her under the arms, swung her around, then plopped her back down on her feet. But he didn't release her as he turned to roar at the other men, who were still waiting at the foot of the ramp.

"Well, there's not much of her, boys, but what there is is nice and tasty!"

As Ashley stared up at the man's face, her mouth open in astonished alarm. He proceeded to prove that she was tasty by dipping his head and planting a smacking kiss on her lips. Ashley didn't have time to recoil from his rather gamey breath before he raised his head, then carried her down the ramp like a sack of meal, and handed her over to another man. He then rushed up the ramp to fetch the next woman.

Within a few moments, Ashley was almost hysterical as man after yelling, laughing man grabbed her, hugged her, kissed her, slapped her bottom, and passed her on. While being clutched to yet another hairy chest with a fervency that threatened to crack her ribs, she looked desperately over her current greeter's huge shoulder, looking for a familiar face—looking for rescue!

She almost cried out in relief when she spotted Jim. He had a pretty, buxom woman clinging to his arm, and he was striding toward her in a purposeful manner that gave her hope that he understood she couldn't take much more of this. The man who was crushing her ribs was also now nibbling her neck!

Sure enough, when Jim reached her, he good-naturedly pried her out of the grip of the hairy man who had begun to fondle her bottom. Jim picked her up, swung her around, and deposited her by the side of the woman who had been clinging to his arm. As he turned back to the surging crowd of lusty men and started roaring at them to show a few manners, the woman beside Ashley wrapped an arm around her shoulders.

"Don't worry, dear," she said with a cheerful smile. "They'll settle down in a little bit. They just get all worked up when a new batch of women arrive and it takes awhile for them to remember to behave civilized."

Jim was at their side now, introducing Ashley to the woman who held her and who was, as Ashley had already guessed, his wife, Mary.

"It's nice to meet you," Ashley responded automatically. And then she quickly added, "How soon can you take me to my quarters? I'd like to spend some time alone. The way those men"—she gestured at the men milling around, eyeing her as though she were a tasty meal offered after months of starvation—"greeted me has rather shattered my nerves."

Mary looked at her in shocked surprise. "But, Ashley, my dear, you don't have any private quarters. In a few minutes, you'll choose your first lover and go home with him. And you'll go from him to another man and then another and another until you've decided whom to marry." She then frowned at Jim. "Didn't you tell Ashley what to expect?" she asked incredulously.

Jim grimaced and shook his head. "I tried to, but she wouldn't let me." But at Mary's stern look, he sighed, and added, "Well, actually, I didn't try very hard once I'd figured out you'd blow your top, Ashley. I thought I'd let you have the bliss of ignorance until you absolutely had to face the truth. The fact is, the more men you sleep with, the better. These men are starved for female companionship, and the kindest thing you can do is spread yourself around as much as possible while you're looking for a mate. Everyone would be most grateful if you took your time. And, actually, it doesn't matter whether you feel like being kind or not, because short of choosing a husband right away, you don't have any choice in the matter. You're going home with some man tonight and you're going to have to sleep with him, and that's the way it's going to be until you choose a husband, so you might as well accept the situation with good grace."

Mary clucked her tongue at her husband and turned back to Ashley, who now had a look of absolute horror on her face.

"No," Ashley said, desperate. "It can't be like that."

But Mary was already nodding. "Those are the rules," she said, a note of sympathy in her voice. "We can't disappoint these men, Ashley. They've been waiting for this for months. We'd start a riot if we tried to do things any differently than what is expected."

"Sorry, Ashley," Jim chimed in. "Just try to make the best of it."

Ashley felt sick. Her hope that she might experience love at first sight had already crumbled when she'd been passed around among the single men. Not one of them had elicited anything in her heart other than panicky distaste. And her backup plan to take her time and keep her suitors at a polite distance while she looked for a man she could tolerate marrying had just crumbled before Jim's explanation.

Anything was preferable to having sex with any of the hairy, smelly men Ashley had met so far. But unless there was a man she hadn't seen yet, apparently she was stuck with the horrible prospect of sleeping with not just one of the bachelors but perhaps all of them!

Wildly, she looked around her, trying to spot a new face, hoping against hope that there was someone she'd missed. Surely, there had to be somebody here whom she could bear to sleep with! They couldn't all be as bad as the ones she'd already met!

Jim was walking away from Ashley and Mary, yelling at the men. "Come on, you hairy sons of garellas! Let's get organized here. Form a line so the women can get a good look at you and start choosing their companions for the night."

At that, the men practically stampeded into a wavering line, where they stood grinning, winking, and beaming at the new women who were gathering together in a group.

"Go on, Ashley." Mary pushed her forward toward the other women. "If you're not quick, the best ones will be taken before you make up your mind. Now, if it were me, I'd choose that little fellow with the mustache on the end. He's shy and will likely be more gentle than some of the others. Besides, he's the smallest man we have, and if, as I suspect, this is your first time, you might be able to handle him, even as little as you are, while some of these others will just eat you up."

Ashley stared at the man, but despite his size, he looked every bit as rapaciously lusty as all the other men, and every bit as crude. She couldn't bear the thought of him touching her.

"But this isn't even decent," she protested to Mary. "And Jim seemed to imply that the people here are religious!"

"We are," Mary said a little indignantly. "But sometimes," she added in a calmer tone, "the rules have to be bent a little in the interest of practicality and reality. You can't expect men who have been without women as long as these men have to settle for hand holding and chaste kisses."

Ashley grasped at a straw. "Psycho-programming," she murmured distractedly. "What about the psycho-programming, Mary? I thought—"

"That's *after* you're married, Ashley," Mary interrupted firmly. "Once you're married, none of these men will think of you in a sexual way. But until then, you're fair game."

Which was another good reason for getting married as quickly as possible, Ashley thought and again, she scanned the crowd in a desperate fashion. But there wasn't a single man in the crowd of males waiting to be chosen whom she thought she could even let touch her, much less marry.

She was at the edge of despair, ready to run from the meadow and take her chances in the wilderness, when someone off to her right moved away from the crowd. She focused on a familiar face—Garick Deveron's.

Ashley froze, her mind racing. She thought Garick was probably as much of a barbarian at heart as any of these other men, but at least he bathed and was clean-shaven, and he would be away a lot. When he'd taught her judo that time, she hadn't flinched from his touch as she knew she would from the other men here. And at least she *knew* him.

Ashley was almost past the ability to think rationally by now, but she did recall that Garick didn't want to marry. In fact, she wasn't at all sure he wouldn't kill any woman who proposed to him. However, at the moment, death seemed preferable to what the night might hold. Anyway, if she could somehow get hold of a laser to protect herself from Garick until he left for his next exploration trip, she would at least have time to think of another plan to save herself before he came back.

Mary was about to leave her with the other women

when Ashley grabbed her arm. She had to be certain before she did the unthinkable.

"Mary, if I propose to one of these men, do they have to accept? Can anybody turn me down?"

Mary's pretty brown eyes opened in surprise. "Why, no, Ashley. If you propose to a man, he has to accept. That's the rule. But surely you haven't already chosen someone to *marry?* I'd advise against it if you have. You can't possibly know someone until you live and sleep with him, and, believe me, if you choose the wrong man, you'll regret it. There's no divorce on New Frontier, so I strongly suggest you wait until you find someone you're sure you love."

Ashley assumed the ban on divorce was because of the psycho-programming. But Garick wasn't psycho-programmed, she remembered, so maybe it wouldn't apply to him. If that were so, she thought with a great sense of relief, and if she could just hold him off from killing her long enough to explain that she would be delighted to divorce him later, then maybe he wouldn't kill her at all!

At that moment, Ashley saw another of the women in her group—a very pretty woman—eyeing Garick speculatively, and a dart of panic shot through her breast. Maybe this woman didn't know that Garick's reaction to a proposal of marriage was likely to be violent. And maybe Garick, against all odds, might change his mind if a marriage proposal came from a woman as pretty as the one who was eyeing him. In either case, it behooved Ashley to get her bid in first. She whipped around to find Jim, who seemed to be the ringmaster of this fiasco!

He stood in the clear space between the line of

single men and the group of women and said, "All right, in just a moment, we'll start the choosing. But first, I want to say . . ."

Ashley didn't hear whatever it was Jim wanted to say. She had turned to make sure Garick was still where she'd last seen him. And to her horror, he wasn't in the line of men who were waiting to be chosen by the women. He was walking away toward the line of trees that circled the clearing!

Panic-stricken, Ashley turned her head back to Jim and called his name very, very loudly.

Jim paused and looked at her in puzzlement.

"I've already chosen, Jim!" she yelled. "I've chosen a husband!"

Jim's eyes widened in astonishment. "Now wait a minute, Ashley," he started to say. "You'd better think twice before—"

"I can't wait, Jim!" Ashley yelped. "I choose Garick! Garick Deveron! I want *him* to be my husband!"

A hush settled over the crowd and the men in the line looked shocked, then crestfallen, then speculative. Jim looked appalled. And Garick . . . Ashley didn't want to look at him, but she had to make sure he'd heard her and to see if his reaction was as bad as she feared it would be.

He had obviously heard her because he'd stopped walking. But he hadn't turned around yet, and he didn't turn around for a long while.

Garick was walking away from the choosing for several reasons. He knew the other single men were becoming resentful of his always being one of the first men chosen, so that some of them had to wait longer to have their chance at a woman. And their resentment would be even more intense this time if he was chosen first. Considering that he'd been on the ship with the new women, the men would assume he'd had most of them already.

He also wasn't particularly interested in any of the women brought back from earth other than Ashley, and the way she'd been avoiding him, he didn't think there was a chance in hell that she would select him as her first lover.

And finally, he was walking away because he didn't really want to watch Ashley choose a man, especially when he'd already glimpsed enough of her reaction to feel a deep sense of pity for her. This part of her introduction to New Frontier was exactly what he'd wanted to ease for her, as well, of course, as satisfy the desire she had aroused in him. But it was too late now. Ashley would have to resign herself to her fate, and he would have to accept that he would never experience making love to her.

Then Garick heard Ashley yell to Jim that she wanted to marry him and he stopped, momentarily taken off guard. But his surprised shock didn't last a minute before he realized why she'd chosen him. Quickly, his surprise changed to angry resentment. An affair was one thing, but he had no business marrying knowing what his future held. Besides, as much as he sympathized with Ashley's position, he didn't want her choosing him so she wouldn't have to sleep with anybody else, which he knew was exactly what she was doing. If she was going to choose him, let it be because she wanted *him*, damn it!

But Garick knew Ashley didn't want him. He knew she didn't want any man. And as he slowly turned around, he was trying to decide how to refuse her proposal. He didn't want to humiliate her, but neither did he want to leave any doubt that his rejection was final.

But then he saw her face, and suddenly, he wasn't certain that he could refuse Ashley no matter why she'd proposed to him, and despite what might lie in his future.

By the time Garick slowly started to turn toward her, Ashley's nerves were stretched so tight, she was afraid she was going to faint. But she didn't, for Garick's face didn't show the dangerous fury she'd dreaded. It was as blank as an empty sheet of paper. If her life had depended on it, which it very well might, Ashley couldn't have guessed what he was thinking. Then he started walking toward Jim, who looked wary, as though he thought a war was about to break out.

Ashley was so tense that she knew her muscles were going to ache for days after this experience—assuming she would live past tonight.

Garick walked so unhurriedly that Ashley wanted to scream at him to move faster. And when he arrived at Jim's side, he stood silently for such a long time that she became worried he was going to rebel against the rules and refuse her proposal, causing an uproar in the whole community and humiliating her in the process. But after what seemed forever, he finally bent his head to Jim's and they talked quietly, so quietly that no one else could hear what was said.

Then both men looked up, and Ashley thought Jim looked tremendously relieved. Garick still looked blank.

"All right," Jim said, turning his gaze to Ashley and eyeing her in a way that was not entirely friendly. "Garick accepts."

A groan of disappointment rose from the line of men, and Ashley closed her eyes, weak with gratitude. Of course, Garick had had no real choice but to accept, but he'd had her worried there for a while, and his delay in answering was also humiliating. But Ashley didn't care about the humiliation. She was simply relieved to her soul that he'd said yes.

"When's the wedding to be?" Bud Saunders yelled from somewhere off to the side. He hadn't joined the line of waiting men either, and he had Sheila under his arm. "Maybe we can make it a double."

The men groaned again at learning they had lost another woman.

Ashley opened her eyes abruptly, but it was beyond her to look at Garick, who stood right in her line of vision. Instead, she looked down at the ground, thinking hard. It had never occurred to her that she could delay the wedding! And if she could, until Garick left on one of his trips, and keep delaying it again and again until. . . .

"Right after the choosing!" Jim yelled back at Bud. "We'll all go to the town hall and get you and Garick married off to your women and celebrate a little, and then everybody can go home."

"Good deal!" Bud yelled back.

Ashley gritted her teeth at Jim's answer, and at last looked up at Garick, thinking if she could get him alone long enough to propose the idea of a delay, he would surely accept. But he was staring at her in a way that scared the idea of a private conversation with him right out of her head. He looked too dangerous to tackle until she could gather enough courage to do it exactly right—preferably with a weapon in her hand with which to protect herself.

Then he walked toward her, and with every step he took, Ashley's body tensed a little bit more. When he finally reached her side and slipped an arm around her waist, his touch made her jump almost a foot off the ground.

He bent his head toward her, and Ashley leaned away from his face, and closed her eyes. She didn't want to see the expression in his. And then she felt his mouth close briefly over hers, and her eyes flew open in astonishment. Garick's eyes were open as well, but again, she couldn't tell what he was thinking. However, she took courage from the fact that he didn't look like he meant to kill her yet. But that was probably only because they were surrounded by witnesses. Later, when they were alone, was the time to really start worrying.

Garick's kiss brought a cheer from the men, and Ashley dazedly wondered if the psycho-programming had already kicked in. Either that, or these men were exceptionally good-natured, considering that their hopes where Ashley was concerned had just bitten the dust.

Garick raised his head in the middle of the cheer, and when he turned away so that she didn't have to look directly at his face, Ashley somehow found her voice.

"Listen, Garick," she said, uncaring for once that her voice was trembling, "we have to talk. If you'll just cooperate, we can—"

He interrupted her. "Let's get on with the choosing," he called to Jim. "It's getting late and I'm sure everybody's eager to get home."

The men cheered again, so loudly this time that Ashley knew she wouldn't be heard if she tried to talk to Garick again. In any case, he didn't give her a chance. He left her and headed toward Bud and Sheila.

Ashley didn't know what to do. Since she was no longer a chooser, she didn't belong with the other women anymore, so she finally moved off to the side and stood beside Mary, who gave her a look that was both admiring and incredulous.

"My goodness," she said for Ashley's ears alone. "How did you ever get the courage to do that?"

Ashley took a deep breath and shrugged. "I'll never know," she said with flat honesty. "I'm just glad it's over and I won't have to do it again . . . ever."

Mary shook her head in awe. "You could have knocked me over with a feather when Garick accepted," she said wonderingly.

Ashley glanced at her, feeling belatedly guilty about having forced Garick to agree to marry her when she knew he didn't want to get married, especially not to her.

"Well," she said glumly, "he didn't have any choice in the matter, did he?"

Mary looked startled and started to reply, but one of the women had just chosen a man, and the other men's roar of disappointment made conversation impossible. In any case, Garick came up behind Ashley and took her arm. She jumped again.

When the roar died down, he said, "Come on, Ashley . . . Mary. Let's go ahead to the town hall and get things started. Bud and Sheila will go with us."

"Good idea," Mary agreed cheerfully.

As the five of them walked toward a line of trees, Ashley remained silent, thinking about how she could get Garick alone before it was too late and propose that they delay their marriage indefinitely. But though her purpose was clear, she was surprised to find that her mind kept slipping from practicalities to Garick's kiss. She'd been very upset from it, but not so upset that she couldn't remember that it hadn't been nearly as unpleasant as she'd always thought kissing would be.

But kissing was a world away from having sex. And Garick might be barbarian enough to want sex with her before he killed her. But there had to be a way, Ashley told herself firmly, that she could avoid both rape and her own murder and free both herself and Garick from the bonds of marriage as well.

Garick glanced at Ashley's face and as usual, had a good idea what she was thinking.

Hell, he thought sourly. *Now she's trying to decide how she can get out of sleeping with* me. *She's also probably trying to think of some way to get out of the marriage entirely, which is exactly what I ought to let her do.*

But there would be long-term negative consequences for Ashley if Garick let her back out of the marriage now, which was another reason why he had wanted to have an affair with her aboard ship. He had wanted to keep her from doing what she'd just done, or else something worse like refusing to observe the rules at all, in which case her future on New Frontier would have been destroyed before it ever had a chance to begin.

As Garick contemplated letting Ashley renege on the marriage, he discovered his softheartedness in accepting Ashley's proposal in the first place had trapped him into the position of continuing to protect her. Loyalty was his watchword. And though Ashley was not yet his wife, their official betrothal had activated his sense of loyalty in spite of his having good reasons to ignore that facet of his character.

All right, he thought with resigned grimness. *I'll go through with this marriage, and if it turns out she's frigid, I'll make the best of it for as long as I'm on New Frontier so as not to upset the rest of the community. Then I'll leave her behind when I have to go explore any new planets which are discovered. She'll probably cry for joy as she waves good-bye to me because she'll not only be free of me, but, if I don't divorce her, she'll be free from ever having to marry anybody else.*

But what, Garick thought an instant later, if Ashley turned out to be frigid, and no new planets were found for years? True, he would be gone so much of the time exploring New Frontier that it wouldn't matter for a while. But when it was fully explored and he had to stay home awaiting a new planet to be discovered, the marriage would then be as much a prison for him as for her because he couldn't be psycho-programmed to make things more bearable.

I'll wait to find out if she's frigid and if anything can

be done to get her over it, he thought disgruntledly. *And if there's no hope, then I'll invoke my special status to petition for a divorce regardless of whether it upsets the community. And maybe if I explain her problem to the court, they'll make an exception to the rule about remarriage and will let her stay single.*

But what if she wasn't frigid? What if in reality she was as good in bed as she was in his fantasies? And what if he fell in love with her?

That possibility raised questions Garick couldn't answer. But he frowned as he realized that if Ashley learned too soon that his special status meant they were one of the few couples on the planet who had any chance of obtaining a divorce, she'd go straight for the divorce to avoid having to go to bed with him. Then they'd never have a chance to find out if their marriage could work, and Garick thought any marriage, even one that was starting off for all the wrong reasons like his and Ashley's, deserved at least a fighting chance.

Well, she's not likely to find out for a while about my status, he thought irritably, *and maybe by the time she does, I'll know about our chances for making it together. In any case, unless I want to see her life here ruined before it even has a chance to get started, I'm stuck with keeping my word and going through with this marriage.*

So despite his misgivings, Garick continued walking toward the town hall. At this point, however, the only thing for which he was truly grateful was that he wouldn't have to worry about Ashley getting pregnant for a while. All of the women who came to New Frontier had birth-control implants as a result of the mandatory childbearing restrictions in the United

Americas. Those implants also served the purpose of preventing pregnancies on New Frontier during the period when the women slept with the single men. Only after they married did the women have children, making the paternal parentage of the children clear, which was best for everyone.

But Garick was grateful that Ashley wouldn't get pregnant for another reason. Before fathering any children, he wanted to know if he'd married an ice maiden or if, with the right handling, she might be as sensuous as he hoped she was and therefore, their marriage had a chance to survive.

After all, divorcing a frigid wife or leaving her behind was one thing, but leaving his child was something else entirely.

Chapter Six

The town hall was a rectangular wooden structure, and its builders had obviously cared more about utility than architectural splendor. It looked similar to the rough log cabins Ashley had seen reproduced in history books, only bigger. Inside, it was a long empty space except for some roughhewn wooden benches. At the far end was a raised platform like a stage, with rooms on either side of it, and at the back, where Ashley and the others had entered, were a kitchen and a bathroom.

Mary took Sheila's and Ashley's arms and, with one on either side of her, started walking toward the stage. "Come with me. We'll get you dressed in something pretty for your weddings."

"Wait, Mary," Ashley said, trying to hang back as she looked over her shoulder at Garick. "I want to talk to Garick."

But Garick gave her a hard look. "Go on, Ashley," he said in a voice few people would have dared argue with. "Don't shame me."

Ashley blinked at him in confusion. What did he mean about shaming him? Surely, she had already shamed him by forcing him to marry her. But if he'd just give her a chance to explain that it was fine with her if he wanted to delay the wedding for all eternity, maybe he'd stop looking so dangerous.

Mary distracted her from Garick by whispering in her ear, and her tone was rather fierce.

"Do as he says, Ashley," she said. "If you show the least hesitation now, people will suspect you were trying to get out of sleeping with the other men when you asked Garick to marry you, and, believe me, you don't want them to suspect that. Not only will it be an insult to Garick, but also to our men, and your reputation will be so damaged by such selfish trickery that you'll be an outcast for the rest of your life. You'll spend the rest of your days a lonely misfit whom no one will have anything to do with, and you'll never get the chance to marry anyone else—nor have any children!"

Ashley looked at Mary in dismay. As Mary dragged her to one of the rooms off the stage and led her and Sheila into it, Ashley anxiously mulled her options.

True, the prospect of never having to marry was decidedly appealing. But being ostracized and denied the chance ever to have children wasn't appealing at all. There had never been any point to thinking about having children on earth, but now that the opportunity was available, she found that she wanted to have children someday.

And though she had to marry to have children,

being married to Garick Deveron, providing he refrained from murdering her during their honeymoon, was a far more acceptable prospect than any other she had faced this day. At least, Garick kept himself clean and smelled a great deal better than any of the men who had handled her after she'd debarked from the shuttle. And he was physically fit and intelligent, so his genes were likely very good. And when it came time to start a child, he would be less repulsive to have sex with than anybody else she'd seen here. That was if he wanted to have sex with her, which, Ashley realized, brightening, was not as much of a certainty as she had assumed. Probably, he was so angry at having to marry her that he wouldn't even want to touch her until he decided he wanted a child. And maybe she might not have to have sex with him for a long time. And her first decision to marry a scout still made sense. Garick *would* be gone a lot. And finally, he had asked her not to shame him, which was a reasonable request when she had trapped him into marriage in the first place. Surely, she owed him that much.

"We keep a couple of spider silk gowns here," Mary explained as she went to a cupboard on one wall, "for marriages and plays and things like that. Nobody has time to make pretty clothes, even if it made any sense to, which it doesn't because we're usually doing work that requires sturdy, functional clothing."

Mary pulled out two long, flowing dresses from the cupboard, one white, the other black. Since Sheila's blond coloring was better suited to the black dress, Ashley and Sheila glanced at one another, nodded, and reached for the dress that suited them.

The dresses were cut exactly alike—immodestly.

And when Ashley had taken off her clothes and donned the white gown, she blushed as she looked down and saw the thinness of the material and how much of her breasts the low-cut neck displayed. At the thought of wearing such a garment in front of a whole cluster of single men, she balked.

"I think I'll wear my bodysuit under this," she said to Mary.

"Why?" Mary frowned at her.

"Well . . . it's so thin . . . and it's cut so low . . . and all those men—"

Mary shook her head impatiently. "They won't bother you, Ashley. The psycho-programming clicked in the moment you and Garick elected to marry. The dress is for Garick, not anyone else. Don't disappoint him."

Ashley stifled a sigh. She thought Garick wouldn't be disappointed if she wore a death shroud instead of a pretty dress. After all, it would take less time to bury her after he killed her if she was already dressed for her funeral. But if Mary wanted to persist in treating this marriage as normal, perhaps it would be just as well to go along with the illusion. For if, against all odds, Garick didn't kill her, and if he then, in the interest of community harmony, elected to maintain the fiction that their marriage was normal, she didn't want to make him any angrier than he already was by letting anyone else know the truth.

"Stay here," Mary ordered as she went to the door of the dressing room. "I'll go get everything ready, then come get you when it's time for the ceremony."

When she was gone, Ashley looked at Sheila, whose expression was dreamy, contented, anticipatory. The last time Ashley had looked at Bud's face, his expression had been the same, but she had learned he was psycho-programmed so that wasn't surprising. Garick's expression, however, hadn't looked anything but blank, and Ashley could only guess at how much savage anger his face concealed.

Abruptly, Ashley felt a surge of guilt weaken her resolve. If she reneged, it might shame Garick a little, but at least he'd be free. And surely, *he* wouldn't be blamed and ostracized for her sin. And one day, he might meet somebody he really did want to marry. So what right did she have to. . . .

The door to the dressing room opened and Garick, dressed in his skin-hugging black bodyshirt, black leather jacket and trousers, crossed the threshold. But he had added an addition to his wardrobe that made Ashley blanch. On his hip was a holster, holding a laser gun!

As he smiled and nodded at Sheila, Ashley swallowed the fear rising in her throat. Did he mean to kill her now—*before* the ceremony? Surely, not even men as rough and ready as those who resided on New Frontier wore weapons to their own weddings unless they intended to use them?

"Ashley," he said, as he looked away from Sheila and rested his gray eyes on his bride-to-be, skimming her body lightly before his unrevealing gaze caught and held hers. "I want a word with you. Come here so we can talk in private."

Oh, God, Ashley thought as she reluctantly followed him to one corner of the room. *Please make him give me time to tell him I won't go through with this if he'll let me live. . . .*

Garick interrupted her prayer by taking hold of her

elbows in a grip that made her wince. And now his expression was no longer bland. His eyes blazed a warning at her.

"Thinking of backing out now, are you?" he asked. His voice was so low and dangerous Ashley felt a tremor go through her body.

But now was the time to get things straight between the two of them; so she quickly, eagerly, nodded her head several times. And at the same time as her head was bobbing like a cork on the ocean, she was saying, in a rush of words, "Oh, yes, Garick. Of course I am. I'm so sorry I put you in this position, but I was desperate. I couldn't bear the thought of having any of those men paw me."

"But you didn't mind the idea of *me* pawing you?" Garick asked.

Ashley paused with her mouth open, her golden-hazel eyes wide with consternation. It was a tricky question. If she said yes, it might hurt his male pride, and she would be in even more trouble than she already was. But if she said no. . . .

She gulped, and then, her pleading eyes locked on Garick's she said, "Well, actually, I thought you'd try to kill me for forcing you to marry me, and I was going to try to find some way to defend myself until you left for your next trip. I hadn't gotten that much further along in my planning before I asked you to marry me. But now that I've had a little time to think, I want you to know that it's all up to you. If you really hate the idea of marrying me, I'll let you off the hook and take my medicine."

And then, because she couldn't yet accept that the rules of behavior she had known all her life on earth didn't apply on New Frontier, she began desperately to try to twist reality into something she could handle.

"Maybe being ostracized won't be all that bad," she said with pathetic hopefulness. "Maybe after a while, people will forget what I did and begin to accept me into the community after all." And then she took a deep breath and finished with the bald truth. "And, anyway, anything is better than having to sleep with all those men."

Garick had stayed silent during her explanation, but with every word she spoke, his gray eyes had shown more and more incredulity. When Ashley at last fell silent, he shook his head as though to clear it. "You didn't answer my question, Ashley. Do you find the idea of sex with me less repulsive than with any of the other men?"

Ashley bit her lip, reluctant to answer. Telling Garick the truth would be hard on his pride. But he didn't look as though he would settle for anything other than an honest answer.

"Yes, it is less repulsive to think about where you're concerned." She nodded, hoping he wouldn't delve into her reasons.

"Why?"

Oh, hell, she thought crossly. *Why does he have to be so curious?*

But again, he didn't look as though he were going to let her get away with avoiding a truthful answer, so she took a deep breath and gathered her courage.

"Well," she said, trying to avoid his gaze now, and not succeeding because he reached up and took her chin in his hands to hold her head steady, "at least, you're clean. And you hate me, so you probably won't want to do it very often, if at all. And if you do want to in order to have children, I think probably you have excellent genes, so our children should . . . be . . ." She faltered, trying hard to discern what Garick was thinking. But his eyes and face were now blank again.

"Anyway," she quickly got back to the most important point she wanted to make, "it doesn't matter, because I'd rather be alive and ostracized than dead. So like I said, if you want to call this off—"

He interrupted her. "And insult every single man on New Frontier by letting them know you found them so repulsive you'd do anything to get out of sleeping with them?" His tone was hard and angry now. "Not to mention that you'd deprive the community of the contributions you could make if you're an accepted member of it, but won't be able to make if you're ostracized."

Ashley frowned. "Why would being ostracized mean that I can't contribute?"

"Because children are the biggest contribution someone like you can make to the community, Ashley, and if you're ostracized, you can't have any children, can you? We will have brought you all this way for nothing."

Insulted by Garick's implication that the only contribution she could make was as a mother, and by the implied insult that the community would have been better off transporting someone else, Ashley scowled.

"You mean I'm only useful as a brood mare?" she snapped.

"I didn't say that. You did." But his eyes said it for him.

"Well, I can't see why you'd want to produce children with someone who has nothing to offer other than a fruitful womb!" Ashley said, her tone scathing.

Garick shrugged. "I didn't propose to you," he reminded her. "You proposed to me." And before Ashley could utter a blistering retort, he added in a voice that chilled her, "And since you did, you're going to go through with it. If you were afraid I was going to kill you before, just try getting out of this marriage now. You do that, and you'd better head for the hills to hide. Or maybe I'll just let you run and let the lack of food and shelter and your ignorance kill you for me."

He let her go, pivoted, walked to the door, and left the room.

Ashley glared after him, no longer feeling the slightest bit guilty that she was forcing him into marriage. In fact, she thought she just might, on the few occasions he was likely to be home from his exploration trips, make his life hell on New Frontier.

Garick walked outside the town hall to find some privacy, then leaned against the wooden structure, shaking his head in anger. When he thought about the pathetic look on Ashley's face when she'd offered to let him off the hook and accept ostracism as her punishment, it tore his heart. And her futile hope that she could break the rules and still be accepted into the community eventually was an obvious indication that she either wasn't thinking straight, or that her emotions couldn't accept what her brain told her. Either way, what man with any compassion in his soul could let her ruin the rest of her life?

On the other hand, when Garick remembered some of the other things Ashley had said, his compassion turned to furious resentment.

"What the hell am I getting myself into?" he muttered under his breath. "The woman actually thought I'd kill her for asking me to marry her! What kind of idiotic ideas has she got in her head about the sort of man I am anyway? No wonder she doesn't want to sleep with me! I'm surprised she got up the courage to ask me to marry her at all!"

But, of course, Garick reflected with clenched jaw, the only reason Ashley wanted to marry him in the first place was to save herself from having to sleep with anybody else.

"And if she has to sleep with me," he muttered out loud again, "she'll suffer it because I bathe and have good genes! And what was I doing talking about her contributing to the community by having children anyway when I'll be damned if I'll have children with a woman who jumps every time I touch her! I should let her stew in her own juices and be done with it! If she has any juices to stew in, that is, which I very much doubt!"

But at that last thought, Garick hesitated, his groin tightening with desire as he thought about the way Ashley looked in the sheer white community wedding dress. How could a woman look so incredibly sexy and yet be frigid? he wondered, feeling baffled as well as sexually frustrated. But after a moment, he remembered the day he had taught Ashley judo. And after thinking very hard about her reaction to him, he began to feel a little better about the situation his cursed soft heart had gotten him into. If Ashley hadn't been at least slightly aroused by his touch, and by the way he'd held her against his body, he'd eat a whole caldera raw, skin and all!

And, by God, he thought fiercely, *if I can't build on what she felt that day and thaw her enough to make this idiotic marriage at least partially worthwhile, I deserve the life of misery I'm going to have married to that frigid spitfire for as long as I have to be!*

With that, Garick's decision to allow the marriage to proceed was reaffirmed, and he straightened, firmed his jaw, and headed back into the town hall to meet his fate.

Jim Jacobs, the mayor of Plymouth, was also the community's lay preacher and therefore officiated at marriages. And that was the only thing that made the ceremony bearable for Ashley. If anyone else had tried to wring promises of love, loyalty, and devotion for life toward Garick Deveron from her, she couldn't have gotten the words out.

It also helped that she and Sheila got to say their vows simultaneously. The first time the two of them were required to make a response of "I do," Ashley mouthed the words. But it didn't work, because Jim, gently but firmly, ordered her to speak up and then repeated the question. But at least, Ashley's "I do's" were muffled by Sheila's.

And then Jim announced that the husbands could kiss their brides, and Ashley stiffened. She stood with her arms at her sides, as Garick turned her toward him and lowered his head. But at feeling the rigidness of her body, he raised one long finger to her neck as though he meant to caress her bare skin. As a matter of fact, some of his fingers did caress her skin. But one of them also pressed a certain nerve, and the next instant, Ashley felt her knees go weak and she automatically grabbed Garick around the waist to keep from falling.

"That's better," he murmured against her lips as his gray gaze bored warningly into hers. "Now, open your mouth or my next touch won't be so gentle."

Ashley opened her mouth. Garick's closed over it, and he slipped his tongue between her lips.

Startled by the unexpected invasion, Ashley would have drawn back, but Garick's hand was still on her neck, only now he had slipped his fingers under her hair, and he held her so that she couldn't move her head. Resigned to the inevitable, Ashley closed her eyes and endured the kiss.

She had to bear it for quite a while, because Garick took his time. And as his mouth and tongue stroked and teased, gentle one instant, demanding the next, and his free arm pressed her tightly against his body, her endurance changed to what Ashley would have sworn couldn't be pleasure, but which felt as if it could pass for it.

Her body remained pliant, despite the fact that Garick obviously wasn't going to press the nerve in her neck again. And toward the end of the kiss, though Ashley didn't realize it, she began to squeeze her arms around his waist and to press herself hard against his body.

Her consciousness returned when Garick finally raised his head, and she saw that his smile was both satisfied, and if she wasn't mistaken, relieved. Then she became aware that their audience was cheering, whistling, stamping their feet, and calling encouragement to *her* to kiss *Garick* again.

Before she could do more than open her eyes wide in horrified embarrassment, Garick turned her to face the long length of the room and the cheering throng for whom she had apparently provided such rich entertainment. Then he moved behind her, put his hands on her waist, lifted her bodily down from the stage, and jumped down himself. Bud and Sheila had already descended from the stage, and suddenly, music from somewhere burst out, and Garick twirled Ashley into a wild dance.

The music was far more primitive than Ashley thought it should be for a wedding. It had a pounding drumbeat that affected her as strongly as Garick's kiss had, so that she was hard pressed to recall that she shouldn't want him to hold her so close, nor should she enjoy the way his body slid sinuously against her breasts and hips.

Fortunately, however, the newlyweds were only required to dance one dance together. Then they were ushered to a long table set with strange food where the four of them were seated in places of honor and had laden plates of food placed in front of them.

Not that Ashley ate any of the strange food. Instead, most of her time was spent being introduced to strangers, smiling at strangers, talking to strangers, and occasionally getting up to dance with strangers, all of whom were so tall that she soon developed a crick in her neck.

But finally, the celebration started winding down, probably because those single men who'd been chosen by the new women for a night's delight were anxious to get home and began slipping away. Bud and Sheila were also obviously eager to get on with their honeymoon, and at some point, Ashley noticed they had disappeared from the hall.

As the crowd in the town hall got thinner and thinner, Ashley felt worn out, dazed, and vaguely apprehensive about being alone with Garick. She still wasn't certain he didn't intend to kill her. She turned to him where he sat beside her at the table.

"Where will we stay tonight?" she asked, looking at his chin rather than into his eyes.

"Why, we'll be going to *our* home, of course, Ashley," he drawled, a tinge of amusement in his voice. "New Frontier isn't set up with honeymoon hotels yet."

"I didn't know you had a home," Ashley answered, disgruntled by Garick's remarks and his tone. "I assumed you stayed in a bachelor dormitory or something."

"There is a dormitory here where single men can stay until they've built a home on the land allotted to them. But I don't like crowds, so I built my own home some time ago."

Ashley wondered if his remark about not liking crowds was a dig at her, but before she could say anything, another couple came to the table to congratulate them before they left.

"Valerie . . . John . . ." Garick nodded at them, a pleasant smile on his lips. "I hope you enjoyed yourselves."

John was a bluff, good-natured, hearty type with a booming voice. "Wouldn't have missed it for anything," he practically roared. "Never thought I'd see the day when you'd accept a proposal, Garick, but I guess Ashley's beauty swept you off your feet."

Ashley was dwelling in a fog of fatigue and disorientation by now, but John's words made her frown in confusion. John had made it sound as though Garick had had a choice in accepting her proposal, but that couldn't have been what he meant. He must have meant that Garick had scared every other woman who had wanted to propose to him into changing her mind.

"Yes, well, it happens to everybody sooner or later, doesn't it?" Garick replied.

His tone sounded more vague than enthusiastic to Ashley's weary ears, but that didn't surprise her. She was merely grateful that he hadn't sounded as nasty about the whole thing as she knew he could if he put his mind to it.

Then Ashley became aware that Valerie, who was presumably John's wife, had been staring at her with a petulant look of jealousy on her face. Valerie switched her limpid blue gaze to Garick, and her expression then softened into a look that Ashley thought made her resemble a picture she'd seen of a caldera—a lovesick caldera with a facial affliction.

"When are you leaving on your next exploration trip, Garick?" she cooed at Ashley's new husband.

He shrugged. "When I get ready." His tone was no more than polite.

"Will you be with us for the Discovery Day celebration?" Valerie persisted.

"Judging by that wedding kiss he and Ashley exchanged, even if he's here," John broke in, his tone slyly meaningful, "he'll likely rather stay at home with his new bride and honeymoon than come into town and mix with the rest of us. Right, Garick?"

Ashley noticed that John's words brought a baleful glare to Valerie's blue eyes, but John grabbed her arm and turned her toward the door. "Let's go home, wife," he said boisterously. "Speaking of honeymoons, this wedding has put me in an amorous mood and I want to do something about it."

Ashley was positive that sharing an amorous night with Garick rather than her husband was what Valerie really wanted. When the two were out of earshot, she glared at her new husband and said sarcastically, "A former flame?"

"A friend." He shrugged, and the scar at the corner of his mouth crinkled slightly.

"Yes, I can see how friendly she feels toward you," Ashley muttered.

"Everyone is friendly here on New Frontier," Garick responded, his tone neutral, "and all my friends will soon be yours. You should be grateful for that, since it could all have worked out very differently for you."

Ashley didn't answer. She wasn't in the mood to feel grateful to Garick for rescuing her from ostracism.

"Do you need to use the bathroom before we leave?" he then asked.

A dart of maidenly alarm shot through Ashley's breast at the thought of soon being home alone with Garick. But then she remembered that her wedding night, unlike most, was likely to pass with her maidenhood remaining intact, and she relaxed.

"Yes, I do," she said, getting to her feet.

"I'll meet you at the door in a few minutes."

Mary was in the small restroom, and when Ashley entered, she said, with a smile, "Are you and Garick getting ready to leave?"

Ashley nodded tiredly.

"Yes, it is quite a distance to Garick's home, so you should be getting started," Mary commented. "Remember to leave the dress you're wearing in the room where we keep it."

Ashley, too weary to talk, again nodded and entered the privacy booth.

But as she used the facility, Mary continued to talk to her, raising her voice a little. "You're a very lucky girl, you know, Ashley."

"Oh?" Ashley didn't feel lucky. She felt threatened and depressed.

"Yes. There have been a lot of women who have wanted to marry Garick in the past, but—"

But before she could finish, a pounding sounded on the door, and Jim's voice echoed through the room. "Mary, let's go home!" he yelled. "I've been away a long time, and I want to be alone with you!"

"Yes, darling," Mary called out. "Good night, Ashley," she said as she opened the door to join her husband. "Happy wedding night!"

Ha! Ashley thought gloomily. *I'll be lucky if I survive my wedding night, much less enjoy it.*

Then she frowned, puzzled. If it was known that other women had wanted to marry Garick, how did the community feel about his intimidating those women into refusing to ask him? Wasn't that breaking the rules? Or didn't it matter as much to them when it was a man who didn't want to marry instead of a woman? If that was the case, it was damned unfair, and Ashley, for the first time in her life, wished she'd been born male!

A few minutes later, she was in the small room to the side of the stage, shrugging out of the communal wedding dress. She hoped her fear that Garick might be planning to arrange a convenient accident for her tonight was groundless. She felt too tired to put up much of a defense. But maybe he would wait until later during their so-called honeymoon to try to get rid of her. Surely, he couldn't be obvious about it as New Frontier must have laws against murder. But an accident could happen to anyone, and she couldn't really blame him if. . . .

At that moment, while she was completely naked and reaching for her bodysuit, the door opened and Garick entered the room. Ashley snatched up her bodysuit, held it in front of her, and glared at him.

"Do you have no manners at all?" she hissed, noting with resentment the way his eyes were inspecting her body. True, she couldn't detect much to be afraid of in his look, but she didn't want him looking at her at all. "I'm not dressed! What are you doing here anyway? Why aren't you waiting for me at the exit?"

"When you didn't show up when you were supposed to, I thought maybe you'd run like a scared rabbit for the hills," he drawled. "Besides, you can't be all that modest after spending weeks running around half-naked in front of Jim."

"Jim is married . . . programmed," Ashley snapped.

"Well, I'm not programmed, but I *am* your husband now," Garick said drily. "And that development was all your idea, remember? So get your clothes on and let's go. I'm tired and I want to get home."

He left the room, and Ashley was relieved that he was tired. Maybe he'd leave plotting her accidental death for another day. And if he had bedding her in mind before he killed her, which she hoped he didn't, he'd leave that for another time as well.

Quickly, she dressed and met Garick at the exit. They were almost the last to depart. Outside, she was startled to discover it wasn't dark yet. Then she saw a cart hitched to two animals that could only be femuras.

"Are we going to ride in that?" she asked, staring admiringly at the femuras. She had thought the pictures she'd seen of them lovely, but the reality of their beauty was even better. They had absolutely gorgeous eyes, the eyes of deer. Wanting to pet them, she headed their way, but Garick grabbed her arm and redirected her to the cart.

"They bite if they don't like you, and since they don't know you yet, we don't know if they're going to like you," Garick said. "Climb in."

"They'll like me," Ashley protested. "Animals always like me."

"On earth maybe," Garick said as he climbed in beside her, "though there are so few animals there, I wonder how you ever came in contact with any. But this is New Frontier. So we'll wait and introduce you to femuras in the proper way."

"I studied veterinary medicine once," Ashley said as Garick flicked the reins and the femuras started off. "That's where I came in contact with some animals."

"Did you learn enough veterinary medicine to be of any use here?" Garick asked.

"Not really. I didn't like what veterinary medics had to do to the animals. So I transferred to zoology. But I didn't get my degree in that either. I settled on history, and meant to teach it, but there weren't any teaching positions open for me when I graduated."

"Too bad," Garick said.

Ashley wasn't sure if he meant it was too bad she hadn't gotten a degree in something that would be more useful on New Frontier than history, or if it was too bad she hadn't been able to teach. But assuming how hostile he felt toward her, she thought he'd meant the former.

Disgruntled, she studied the countryside. Odd-looking trees lined the dirt road, and beyond the trees, she thought she saw pastures. But though she asked Garick a couple of questions, he sounded distracted when he answered, and in truth, Ashley was too tired to appreciate the environment of New Frontier. All she really cared about was finding a bed and getting some sleep.

That was the last thought she had before she dozed off, unaware that she had slumped against Garick's side with her head resting against his shoulder.

When Ashley leaned against him, Garick smiled with satisfaction. Her response to his wedding kiss had made him feel a great deal better about their marriage. Any woman who kissed back like that couldn't possibly be frigid. And now she was actually seeking physical contact with him, which must mean the kiss had had an even greater impact on her than he'd realized. This was a fantastic development, since his seeing her naked had aroused him so much that he wanted her in bed more than ever.

Then he made the mistake of looking down at her face, and his smile disappeared. Hell, she wasn't seeking contact with him. She was leaning against him because she was so bored with his company she'd fallen asleep!

Scowling, Garick started to turn away, but before he did, he noticed how vulnerable Ashley looked when she was asleep—like a tired little girl who'd had a very hard day. And as he thought about what Ashley's day had been like—indeed what her life must have been like on earth, and what she'd endured these past several weeks—his expression softened.

He remembered then that she'd told him she never cried, and his heart twisted with a combination of pity, anger, and protectiveness. Surely, if anybody had good reasons to cry, Ashley had had many of them, especially lately, and most especially today.

But she had never cried and wrung her hands in helpless despair, no matter what her situation. On earth, she had done what she had to to survive. When she'd awoken and discovered she had been kidnapped and placed aboard a spaceship, she'd reacted with anger, which would have been Garick's reaction. Then she had tried to find the best way not only to survive in her new situation, but to prosper, which would also have been Garick's response.

And today, though Garick knew she'd been almost sick with panic at learning what was expected of her, she had again acted decisively to take control of her destiny, rather than meekly accepting the cards she'd been dealt. Garick realized with a certain amount of disgruntlement, tinged with incredulity that she had also acted with a great deal of courage considering that she had expected him to kill her for proposing to him.

Still, he had had good reason to refuse Ashley's proposal. He still wasn't sure why he had let his softer side prevail in making his decision rather than using his head, as was his custom. There was also every possibility that he might come to regret his decision. But he could have done worse than end up with a beautiful, intelligent, strong-willed, and courageous wife who also stirred his ardor as strongly as Ashley did.

But all the beauty, intelligence, character, and courage in the world weren't enough to sustain their marriage if he couldn't stir Ashley's passion to match his own, and there was the rub.

True, their wedding kiss had given Garick reason to hope that he could, but it remained to be seen if he was merely engaging in wishful thinking. Yet he was not a man who had much use for wishful thinking, and his formidable patience had been stretched to its limits already during the trip from earth. He also knew that if he gave Ashley much time to think, she would find some way to thwart him and might actually come up with a good plan to accomplish that. So Garick decided it was time he took firm charge of one particular aspect of their relationship which might determine its outcome and the sooner the better.

He wouldn't force her. He wanted to seduce her. In fact, he couldn't even contemplate hurting her, but neither would he let her run from him. And, if he was right that Ashley was capable of enjoying her sensuality then he would not allow her to continue to deny it.

That wouldn't be fair to her, Garick concluded with a tiny bit of self-righteous justification.

Nor, he admitted with a great deal more wry honesty an instant later, would it be the least bit fair to him.

Chapter Seven

Ashley didn't awaken when Garick stopped the cart. She did, however, as he took her shoulders in his hands and sat her upright on the seat. As she wavered slightly, dazed and confused, he said, "Wait." He climbed down from the cart then reached up. He lifted her from the seat and carried her to the dark bulk of a house which Ashley could barely see. It was now totally dark.

Far from resenting his carrying her, Ashley was grateful for the warmth of his body. The night air was chilly. Besides, she hadn't been held like this since childhood, and in her half-awake state, it felt comforting to have someone big and strong take care of her, even if it only lasted for a few minutes.

Garick mounted three steps to a porch, walked to the door, and threw it open. Before he crossed the threshold, Ashley mumbled sleepily, and with some amazement in her voice, "You didn't lock your door? But you've been gone a long time."

"We don't have to lock our doors on New Frontier, Ashley," he said. "It's not like earth. Nobody here is a thief."

Ashley felt a stirring of guilt. After all, she'd taken Garick's freedom from him, and that made her, in a sense, a thief.

"You don't have to carry me anymore," she said, slightly shamed now. "I can walk."

"Ah, but the bridegroom is supposed to carry the bride over the threshold," Garick responded. Then he entered his home, with Ashley still in his arms.

It was dark in the house, and Ashley couldn't see Garick's face clearly. But the way he continued to hold her was beginning to make her nervous.

When she was about to tell him again that he could put her down, he spoke, "I'm waiting, Ashley."

"For what?"

"It's customary for a bride to kiss her husband after he carries her over the threshold."

She froze for a second, then said, "I don't remember that being a custom."

"Maybe it isn't on earth, but it is here. And I'm still waiting."

"Garick, you know this marriage isn't—"

"Just do it, Ashley," he interrupted. "And fast. I need to take care of the femuras. They wander off if they're not hobbled or enclosed in a barn, and I don't want to have to chase them down."

The prospect of getting rid of him for a while spurred Ashley into obedience. She needed time to get her wits about her.

She raised her head, aimed for Garick's cheek, and started to plant a kiss there. But she missed Garick's cheek entirely because he turned his head and her mouth ended up on his. When she leaned back to make the kiss brief, and to end her sudden breathlessness, he bent forward, and as he had during their wedding kiss, he slipped his tongue between her lips.

Ashley froze, but then, as she had at their wedding, she forgot that she shouldn't enjoy Garick's kisses. Acting from sheer instinct, she slid her hand to the back of his neck, opened her mouth wider, and kissed him with a fervor that she knew, in some distant corner of her brain, she would later regret. But she wasn't interested in that for the time being. She was only interested in the pleasure she felt.

After a moment, Garick broke the kiss, and to Ashley's horrified surprise, a small sound of disappointment issued from her throat. She clamped her lips shut, bent her head, and closed her eyes, wishing for about the thousandth time that she could control her reactions to Garick.

He then set her on her feet and she thought he was going to release her. Instead, he cupped her cheek with his hand, tilted her face up to his, and slanted his mouth over hers again. Only this time, his kiss was fiercer, more demanding, and he wrapped both arms around her, with one hand on the small of her back, and crushed her so tightly against his body she could barely breathe.

After a few seconds of muted alarm, Ashley forgot she couldn't breathe. She forgot everything other than the kiss, and she began kissing Garick back as feverishly as he was kissing her. And soon, she was trying to press her hips even closer to that part of him which was growing harder by the second and was provoking a delicious sensation in her stomach.

When Garick broke the kiss, Ashley made another sound of regret, only this time it was more of a moan than a small gasp. But when he placed his mouth on her neck and gently suckled her skin, the sound changed to a groan of pleasure.

Then she gasped with fright. Something outside made a horrible noise that made the hair on the back of her neck stand straight up. Stiffening, she pushed Garick away.

"What was that?" she demanded, her voice shaking both from alarm and arousal.

Garick took a deep breath. When he answered, his voice was deep and husky, and a primitive instinct in Ashley reacted to the tone with desire.

"It's the femuras," he said. "They want to feed."

"What do they eat?" Ashley asked. From the sound she'd heard, she wouldn't have been surprised to learn they were carnivores, and human flesh was their favorite meal.

"Grass and grain," Garick answered, his voice still rough. He backed away from her, removed something from his pocket, and reached up to his left.

Ashley heard a striking sound, saw Garick fiddle with something on the wall, and shortly, the room was bathed in soft light. The sight of her new husband's face, even more dangerous-looking because of the shadows flickering over it, made Ashley quickly turn her eyes to the flame.

"You light your homes with natural gas?" she asked, struggling for a normal tone of voice and missing it by a mile.

"It's the only fuel we've been able to find in abundance so far," Garick answered. "We use it for cooking and heating as well."

"Oh. I see." Ashley could feel his eyes on her face, but she was confused and alarmed at her reaction to his kisses, and she couldn't look at him.

Garick hesitated for a second, then said, "I'll go take care of the femuras. Make yourself at home. This house is yours now as well as mine. I'll be back soon."

He walked out the door, closing it behind him, and Ashley's whole body slumped in relief. She couldn't imagine what had gotten into her, responding to Garick's kisses the way she had, but judging by how aroused her response had made him, she wouldn't be the least surprised if when he came back, he expected her to give him more than just kisses. And Ashley didn't think having sex with Garick was a good idea at all—not until they got things really straight between them. There were things she needed to think about before she. . . .

At that point, she covered her face with her hands and whimpered. But her whimpering shamed her, making her feel like a coward. Angry at herself, she quickly uncovered her face and looked around. If there were two bedrooms, perhaps she could tell which one was Garick's, run to the other one, dive into bed, and pretend to be asleep. Hopefully, he wouldn't try to wake her up and. . . .

She shut off the thought and moved fast. There wasn't much ground to cover because the house was small, with one main room, which was furnished with a wooden couch and two wooden chairs that looked homemade; a kitchen, which she barely peeked into; a bathroom—and only one bedroom.

Damn! she thought, when she realized there was only one bed in the house. There was also the couch in the living room, of course, but it was bare wood and was too short to serve as a bed for Garick. Even if it wasn't excrutiatingly uncomfortable, she didn't want to sleep on it either.

All right, Ashley admonished herself. *Steady. You can still pretend to be asleep.*

Darting into the bedroom, she shut the door, which also shut out the light and left her in darkness except for the moonlight shining through the two windows in the room. Then she quickly untied and tossed aside her tunic, left her white bodysuit on, and dived beneath the caldera coverlet on top of the rudely constructed wooden bed. To her surprise, she found that under the coverlet was a squishy pouchlike rectangle, which was also covered with caldera skins. After patting it a couple of times, she realized it must be stuffed with feathers. Then her hand froze as she heard the outer door of the house open.

Rapidly scooting as far to the other side of the bed as she could without falling off, and leaving enough space behind her for two men the size of Garick, she put her head down, rolled into a ball, and shut her eyes. She concentrated on slowing her heartbeat and breathing in order to give the impression she was asleep.

It was a few minutes before the bedroom door opened, and when it did, all Ashley's efforts to calm herself were in vain. Immediately, her heart rate picked up, and it was all she could do to keep her breathing inaudible. She heard Garick strike a match, and a second later, through her closed eyelids, she saw light.

She almost forgot herself and frowned. She had hoped Garick would leave the light off and be unable to get a good look at her. She wasn't sure she was very convincing at pretending to be asleep, and she doubted if those gray eyes of his missed much.

"Ashley?" He said her name, softly, questioningly.

Ashley barely stopped herself from tensing her body. But, somehow, she managed to remain very still and continue to pretend to be asleep.

To her relief, Garick moved away. She heard his movements, and deducted that he was undressing and hanging his clothes away in the cupboard on the other side of the room, which worried her. She hoped he didn't sleep nude!

Soon, the light that filtered through her eyelids disappeared, and she relaxed a little, relieved that Garick couldn't see her anymore. But she tensed again when she felt him sit on the bed, turn, and lie down.

Ashley was so nervous that she knew if he touched her, it would be like tapping the taut surface of a drum. His hand would probably bounce right off the surface of her body. But maybe he wouldn't touch her. Maybe he would just go to sleep and. . . .

He not only touched her, which made her eyes fly open and provoked an involuntary gasp which she would have given anything to recall, he hauled her back against the full length of his very warm, very naked body.

"Don't!" she yelped, stiffening.

"Shhh," he said against her ear. "I know you're inexperienced, Ashley. I know you're frightened. Try to relax and it'll be easier. I'll be as gentle as possible. And I promise I'll make you like it."

Ashley stiffened even more. Obviously, Garick didn't mean to delay. He meant to consummate the marriage this very night—unless she could talk him out of it.

"Let's wait until we've talked, figured everything out!" she burst out, sounding as panicked as she felt. "Anyway, we're both too tired. We need our rest."

She felt his mouth move in a smile against her cheek as he murmured, "I think not." More alarmingly, she felt his hand move up her ribs, close on her breast, and gently squeeze it. She froze. Then as his thumb moved over her nipple, an involuntary shudder, the result of fear, tension, and—though she didn't want to admit it—pleasure, shook her body, reducing some of her anxiety.

"Why—" She had to stop and clear her throat. "Why must we do this tonight?" she asked, her voice quavering.

"Because there's no point in waiting," Garick answered. "And because I want it. You will too if you give it a chance."

His mouth was directly beside her ear, and he spoke softly, huskily. It wasn't an unpleasant sound by any means, and when he then touched his tongue to Ashley's earlobe, another shudder went through her body.

"Yes," she managed another protest, trying to speak reasonably, logically, persuasively, "there is a point to waiting. We don't really know one another all that well for one thing. And we didn't get married because we wanted to. I forced you into it to save myself and—"

"Shh. It doesn't matter why we got married. It's done. And it isn't going to be as hard for you as you think, Ashley, not after I show you all the pleasure we can give one another in addition to kissing. You like kissing me, don't you?"

Ashley had no intention of admitting she did. In fact, she intended to tell a bald-faced lie and swear she didn't like kissing at all. But she made the mistake of looking at Garick over her shoulder. She could barely see his face in the shadows, which was fine with her. If she couldn't see him clearly, then he probably couldn't see her clearly either and it would be easier to get away with lying.

Just as she opened her mouth to speak, Garick covered her lips with his own and shut off her words. And while he was kissing her, he turned her stiff, resisting body toward him, forcing her gently onto her back. After that, he half-covered her upper body with his powerful torso, trapped her legs by placing one of his over them, and continued to kiss her for a long while, using his mouth and tongue the way he had when he'd managed to make her like his kisses earlier. Only this time, he also stroked her breast, adding enormously to the pleasure of his kisses.

Despite the pleasure she felt, Ashley forced herself to lie still. She knew Garick was waiting for her to respond the way she had the other times he'd kissed her, but she was determined not to. She decided they were going to talk, because that was the only chance she had to avoid sex. If she could talk persuasively enough, there was at least a chance Garick would wait. And if she couldn't, maybe she could simply wear him out and he'd fall asleep.

On some level, Ashley remained determined not to respond to Garick's kisses even after her lips softened and her tongue began to twine with his, even after her arms somehow ended up circling his neck, even after she began to move with unconscious sensuality against his body. She stayed determined even after she became completely caught up in the delicious tremors his stroking hand on her breast sent cascading through her whole body.

Then Garick moved his hand to her stomach, and she was disappointed. But when he began to rub her, gently pressing inward, the pleasure returned. However, when he slid his hand lower to her thighs, and she felt his fingers slide between her legs, she regained some will power, tensed and clenched her legs tightly together.

She tore her mouth from his and gasped, "No . . . no . . . That's enough for now. Let's stop and talk—or something."

Garick kissed her again, briefly, then murmured, "I just want to unsnap your bodysuit and help you take it off."

Ashley started to protest, but she never got the chance because Garick's mouth sealed her lips. When he stopped kissing her, she had to take a breath before she could say anything, and he spoke before she could get any words out.

"Aren't you getting too warm, Ashley?" he whispered in a deep, soft tone that weakened her defenses. He followed his words with two more drugging kisses, then added, "I am. I'm beginning to sweat. Aren't you?"

The next kiss was very long and exquisitely sensual, and when Garick again raised his head, Ashley felt too dazed and weak to think of any more protests.

"It won't be that much different than being half-naked in front of Jim," Garick murmured softly. "You got used to that aboard ship, didn't you? And you and I are married, so it doesn't matter if I see all of you. Besides, it's dark in here."

Of course, the present situation was a lot different than sharing a cabin with a safely psycho-programmed Jim. But for some reason, Ashley couldn't find the will to point out the difference. Besides, she did feel hot. The caldera coverlet was probably wonderfully warm when there was snow on the ground, but it was beginning to smother her. In any case, Garick didn't wait for her to reply. He kissed her again.

When he finally released her mouth, Ashley managed to gasp, "All right. But I'll do it. You don't need to help."

She could see better in the darkness now, and she noticed his smile of satisfaction as he moved away from her, allowing her to pull off her bodysuit. But she felt such an immediate sense of loss when he moved his weight off her, she was distracted from feeling resentful at his smile. What she felt instead was an urgent desire to have him back where he'd been.

Quickly, she moved her hands between her legs. She had to unsnap the bodysuit before she could pull it over her head. But as she fumbled at the snaps, she discovered she was all thumbs. And the movements of her own fingers on that part of her body made the sensations that Garick had aroused in her intensify, making her even more awkward.

"Having trouble?" he asked softly. "Want me to help?"

Ashley had lifted her head and shoulders slightly to unsnap the bodysuit, and now she gave up and flopped down on her back. It was beyond her to speak, so she nodded instead.

It seemed to her that Garick had even more trouble unsnapping the bodysuit than she had. He took a long time about it. But what he was doing felt so good that Ashley didn't care; in fact, she wished he would spend the rest of the night getting her bodysuit unsnapped.

He didn't, however. As soon as she started instinctively moving her hips to intensify the feeling of his fingers between her legs, he quickly unsnapped the fastenings.

"Lift your hips," he said, his voice huskier than ever.

Ashley did as she was told and he pushed the bodysuit up.

"Sit up," he said.

Ashley did, and he pulled the bodysuit over her head, then tossed it over his shoulder onto the floor.

"Now lie down," he said seductively, robbing Ashley of every scrap of free will she had left.

He slid on top of her and pressed her down into the pouch. His weight created a fiery ripple in her stomach and between her legs, and she automatically slipped her arms around him and began to stroke his back and hips with her hands. His skin felt warm and smooth, and his muscles felt marvelous.

"Open your mouth," he murmured, low, commanding. "Kiss me the way you know I want you to."

She lifted her head slightly and met his descending mouth with her own. She kissed him not only the way he wanted her to, but the way she wanted to kiss him as well, which was perhaps not surprising, since he was the one who had taught her to kiss in the first place.

The kisses continued, growing more heated each time, until he slid down her body to kiss her throat, her shoulders, and finally, her breasts.

It was at that point that Ashley lost all control. She became a stranger to inhibition and a slave to desire, obeying without question any and every instruction Garick gave, responding to everything he did with new passionate shudders.

Even when she knew he was about to enter her, and that when he did, it would hurt, she opened her legs for him without hesitation.

He rose onto his knees and pulled her legs around his body. Then he put his large hands on her hips, lifted her, pushed forward until the tip of his manhood was at the opening he would soon enter, and then he paused.

"Don't pull away when it starts to hurt," he murmured with rough softness. "It won't hurt for long, and then I'll make it feel good again."

Though Ashley didn't know why she trusted his words, she accepted them without protest, without question. And then he plunged forward and the pain came so quickly that, though a small scream left her lips, she didn't have time to pull away. He was suddenly inside her and then he stretched out on top of her, pinning her to the bed, so that she couldn't pull away. Quickly, she wrapped her arms around his shoulders and tightened her legs around his hips to keep him still.

"Please . . . don't move!" she begged, a sob in her voice. "It hurts."

"I know," he whispered, his voice sounding ragged. "I know, baby. We'll rest a minute. And then I'll take you the rest of the way."

"The rest of the way?" Ashley asked the question automatically. She was in pain, and that was all she was concentrating on.

"There's more pleasure to come, Ashley," he murmured. "More than you realize. The best of it all."

Ashley blinked the tears out of her eyes, doubtful. Of course, she'd read about orgasms, and she knew that was what he meant. But she didn't see how she could stop hurting enough to have one.

"H—how?" she stammered.

"We start over," he whispered against her ear, and then he nipped the lobe with his teeth.

Ashley was frowning when he kissed her and stroked her breast again. But before long, to her relieved astonishment, she began to forget her pain and again to feel the pleasure Garick's mouth and hands had brought her before.

He waited until she moved her hips. Then he moved his, gently and carefully at first, and then more urgently as her body language demanded it.

"Harder," Ashley gasped. "Faster." She was caught up in seeking that pinnacle she somehow knew was just out of reach, impatient with Garick's gentleness. She wanted him to sweep her over the edge.

Her words released him, and he was as forceful and demanding as she needed him to be. And the pinnacle came closer and closer until she topped it at last. Her whole body spasmed with such intense pleasure, she never wanted it to end.

Feeling her release, Garick let go as well, and his hard movements merged with Ashley's, adding to her pleasure. She clung to him with all her strength, and tried to make the feeling last. But finally, gradually, it subsided, and Garick slumped atop her, his body heavy, comforting, slick with sweat.

He stayed there a long while until both his and Ashley's breathing had quieted, and their hearts had settled into a normal rhythm. Finally, he lifted himself on his elbows, lowered his head, gave her a long, slow kiss that was both possessive and approving. Then raising his head, he stared into her eyes.

"I told you I'd make you like it," he murmured softly. "Now, you tell me how much."

Ashley swallowed. She was suddenly feeling shy, slightly embarrassed. "As much as you did," she finally said, her voice low.

He shook his head, letting her know her reply wasn't good enough.

Ashley frowned. "All right," she said, pouting now. "It was . . . a lot less horrible than I thought it was going to be."

He shook his head again, and the scar was crinkling at the corner of his mouth.

Ashley clamped her jaws shut and gritted her teeth.

"I'm not moving off you until you tell me," Garick warned. "And it better be what I want to hear."

Ashley sighed, feeling weary enough to sleep for a

month. But, obviously, she wasn't going to sleep at all until Garick got what he wanted.

"It was wonderful," she said, her tone level.

"More enthusiasm, please."

She hit his shoulder with her fist, but he was immovable. Accepting defeat, Ashley wrapped her arms around his shoulders, pulled him closer, tucked her face in the curve of his neck, and whispered, "It was the best thing that's ever happened to me and I want it to happen again."

Garick's reply was a soft, pleased chuckle, followed by, "I know you do. And don't worry, it will. Probably first thing tomorrow morning."

Then he slid to his side, pulled her into the curve of his body, and yawned.

Ashley waited a moment, but he didn't say anything else. "You didn't tell me how it was for you," she prodded.

"If I hadn't liked it, I wouldn't want it again, would I? Since I do and soon, that ought to answer your question."

Ashley shook her head, letting him know that wasn't good enough.

A smile in his voice, Garick then whispered, "Let's just say this marriage has more to offer than I thought it would. And as long as you make me as happy in bed as you just did, I won't kill you for making me marry you."

Ashley shook her head again, frowning now, but that was all she got out of him. Too weary to persist, she let her eyes close, and within a few moments, she was deeply asleep.

* * *

Garick waited until he was positive Ashley slept, then gathered her even closer, pleased with the way her body fit in the curve of his. It felt right to lie with her like this. And the lovemaking had felt right as well. It had been well worth the wait, better than he had ever suspected it would be, given Ashley's inexperience. In fact, the only thing marring his present contentment was that he found it very odd that he felt so much satisfaction with his married state.

Maybe you're just more inclined toward domesticity than you ever suspected, he told himself with wry self-mockery. And shortly afterward, he also told himself it was too soon to be feeling as relieved and satisfied as he was. He and Ashley had barely started together, and only a fool would try to predict how their marriage would actually develop, especially when one of the partners was as volatile a woman as Ashley Bronwyn.

Ashley Deveron, Garick corrected himself, feeling slightly disoriented. But his disorientation wasn't unwarranted, he decided, as he had begun this day with no intention of changing his status as a bachelor any time in the near future, if ever. Yet he was ending it a more contented married man than made any sense since his new wife, if asked, would probably swear she didn't love him and if given the opportunity, would probably jump at the chance to get out of the marriage.

Did all this contentment mean he was falling in love with Ashley? he wondered drowsily.

Hell, he answered himself as he closed his eyes. *Who knows? But as long as she's loyal to me, I'll be loyal to her.*

When he awoke the next morning, he badly wanted to make good on his promise to make love to Ashley again. But she was sleeping so deeply, he didn't have the heart to wake her. Instead, he got up, dressed, and began to catch up on the chores that had been neglected while he'd been away.

Chapter Eight

There were no coverings on the windows, and sunlight bathed the bedroom, making Ashley uncomfortably warm under the caldera coverlet. She kicked it aside without opening her eyes, wanting to continue sleeping. But the sunlight filtering through her eyelids made sleep impossible, and she finally blinked her eyes open and stared in confusion for a moment at the unfamiliar vista outside the window.

Then reality hit, and she tensed. Garick had said he would probably want sex again when they awoke. But in the clear light of day, with her body aching from the previous night's exertions, she had difficulty accepting that she had actually *enjoyed* her first sexual experience.

It was somehow humiliating to Ashley that she had been so easily seduced, especially by a man whom her mother after one look would have immediately classified as a savage. Ashley knew Garick well enough now that she wouldn't have gone quite that far with her own description of him, but she still considered him only half-civilized at best, and he still frightened her.

True, he hadn't raped her the night before; in fact, he had been quite patient and gentle. But a truly civilized man wouldn't have insisted on having sex with her at all since they didn't love each other, even though they were married and the marriage had been her idea. But once they'd had a chance to talk, maybe they could do something about the situation. Mary had said there was no divorce on New Frontier. But since Garick wasn't psycho-programmed, there had to be a way around the rules if he would just be reasonable and agree to help both of them regain their freedom.

She didn't hear anything, and there was no movement behind her. Nevertheless Ashley moved very quietly and cautiously as she turned her head and looked over her shoulder at the other side of the bed.

Garick wasn't there! Breathing a sigh of relief, Ashley turned onto her back, wincing slightly as the movement exascerbated her soreness. She frowned. So much for Garick's supposed eagerness to have sex with her again, she thought sourly. Obviously, her mother had been right when she'd said that men would lie like dogs to get what they wanted from women.

But remembering that Garick had already *had* what he'd wanted from her when he'd said he would want it again, Ashley shook her head in confusion.

But then she remembered that her mother had also said that most men would lie just for the sake of lying, and her frown deepened.

Scooting to Garick's side of the bed, she got to her feet and looked at the bare wooden floor where Garick had thrown her bodysuit the night before. It wasn't there. Then she went to the cupboard against the far wall and opened its doors. The cupboard was full of Garick's clothes, but her bodysuit and tunic weren't there. And the bag containing the rest of the clothing she'd been provided aboard the *Mayflower* was nowhere to be seen either.

Shaking her head in frustration, Ashley pulled a caldera robe of Garick's off a peg and wrapped it around her. It was far too big, but at least it was a covering and she was grateful for it as she went to the bedroom door and opened it a crack.

She couldn't see Garick in the main room, so she slipped out of the bedroom and hurried quickly into the bathroom. She shut the door firmly behind her, wishing it had a lock.

The shower was made of crudely bubbled glass, and Ashley assumed that meant the community had a glass-making factory somewhere. It also had a tank with a chain on one wall, and the tank had a spigot leading from it.

Ashley slipped out of the caldera robe, stepped inside the shower, pulled the chain, then gasped and jumped back, letting go of the chain. The water was ice cold! Also, since the water flow had stopped when she'd let go of the chain, one obviously had to wet one's body, soap, then rinse off. There would be no steady flow of water, much less any hot water. But she was used to that. Clean water, as well as fuel to heat it, had begun to be so scarce on earth, she'd had to shower the same way there.

Still, it was the fastest shower Ashley had ever taken, and when she stepped out of the glass enclosure, she was blue with cold. Since there were no towels or hot air blower, she wrapped the caldera robe around herself again and went to the sink, where there were two toothbrushes. Ashley felt one of them. It was wet, so it must be Garick's. The other one was dry, however, so she used it vigorously.

Her toilet completed, Ashley felt more prepared to face Garick, so she threw the bathroom door open and walked boldly out into the main room.

Garick was seated on the wooden couch with something in his hands. He looked up as Ashley entered the room, but before he could say anything, Ashley identified what he held. It was his laser gun and it was pointed, more or less, in her direction! Her worst fears had come true! Now that Garick had had sex with her, he meant to kill her!

She screamed and darted back into the bathroom. There was a window, and if she could get it open and dive through it, she could hide in the trees and try to get away!

She was tugging frantically at the window, and not succeeding in moving it upward even an inch, when the door opened behind her. Ashley swung around, held her hands up in a warding-off gesture, and yelped, "Don't kill me! Please, Garick! I don't want to die!"

Then she noticed he didn't have the laser, and her plea died in her throat as she raised her terrified eyes to his face.

Garick shook his head, his expression both incredulous and long-suffering. "I was merely checking my laser, Ashley," he drawled. "I'm not allowed to take it to earth when I go, so I was making sure it was in good operating condition now that I'm back. And I swear," he added drily, "that unless you keep behaving like an idiot, I won't use it on you."

As Ashley realized she'd been in no danger, her fear turned to fury. She stamped her bare foot and glared at Garick. "Well, how was I supposed to know!" she cried. "You can't deny you wanted to kill me when I proposed to you! And I figured that now that you've had your revenge by forcing me to have sex with you, you were ready to get rid of me!"

Garick emitted a long, drawn-out sigh, the kind of sigh a genius might direct toward a moron. So naturally, from Ashley's point of view, it was thoroughly insulting.

"Don't you dare sigh at me!" she stormed at him.

But he sighed again exactly the same way and then took her completely off guard.

"Ashley, I'm hungry," he said. "Are you?"

Ashley hesitated for a moment, glaring at him, and then she nodded sharply.

"Then come out of here and fix us some breakfast."

He turned on his heel and left her standing where she was.

Ashley frowned thunderously, wondering why he assumed she was going to cook for him. She wasn't his slave! And, besides, she'd never cooked a meal in her life and wouldn't even know where to begin.

She stomped out of the bathroom. Garick was again sitting on the wooden couch, with his laser gun in his hands.

Ashley paused. While she nervously eyed the laser, she decided it might, perhaps, be wise to voice her refusal to fix breakfast in a slightly less ascerbic tone than she'd planned to use. But what came out of her mouth when she finally spoke had nothing to do with breakfast.

"Where are my clothes?"

Garick nodded to his left, where Ashley's carryall bag sat on the floor. She just hadn't noticed it when she'd come out of the bedroom.

"Oh. But what about the bodysuit and tunic I had on last night?"

"Outside soaking in the wash barrel with my dirty clothes."

"Wash barrel?"

"Except in winter, we wash our clothing outside." Garick raised his head and eyed her in a way that made her pull his caldera robe tighter around her nude body. "But you don't need to dress, Ashley," he added, his tone suddenly a rustle of silk over a rasp of rough purpose. "We're on our honeymoon, remember? So after you fix our breakfast, we'll be going back to be—"

Ashley rushed into speech before he could finish what she knew he was about to say. "I'm going to the kitchen!" She turned around so fast, she almost tripped over her own feet. As she almost ran toward the kitchen, she asked, "What do you want to eat for breakfast?"

If she'd looked over her shoulder, she would have seen a gleam of laughter in Garick's eyes. But when he answered, there was no trace of laughter in his voice.

"I collected eggs and milked the garella this morning," he answered, raising his voice as Ashley disappeared out of sight into the kitchen. "And Mary packed some food in the cart to bring home with us last night. It's in there on the counter. All you really have to do is cook the eggs and slice the grain bread and pour us some milk. Or if you prefer tea, there are some tea leaves in one of the cabinets."

"Fine!" Ashley called back absently. She was looking around at the equipment in the kitchen in bewilderment. She'd always taken her meals in a dormitory dining room and didn't know the purpose of most of the gadgets. Slowly, she walked around the small room, touching and poking, trying to deduce how to use the odd-looking machinery.

On the counter was a basket of raw eggs. They were larger than any eggs she'd seen on earth before they'd disappeared from her dormitory dining room's menu. And they were salmon-colored rather than white or brown. Touching one of them with her finger, she discovered it was warm as though it had just been laid, which made her wrinkle her nose. She wondered how long one was supposed to boil an egg. Deciding to worry about that later, she continued her tour of the kitchen.

Against one wall was a large appliance that Ashley decided must be an old-fashioned stove. It didn't look exactly like the ones she'd seen pictures of in history books, but it was close. When she approached it, she saw four circular wells on top which had holes in them, and decided the holes must be where the heat came out. But she didn't know how to make the heat start. There were five dials on the front of the stove, and she stared at them, puzzled. They had no directions printed beside them.

Ashley reached out and turned one of the dials. Immediately, she heard a hissing noise issue from one of the circular wells and she suddenly remembered Garick saying people here cooked and heated with natural gas, as well as used it to light their homes. But how did one light the gas? she wondered.

"Here," Garick said from behind her, making her jump a foot.

She swung her head around and glared at him, then realized he was extending a match toward her. Stifling her impulse to snap at him for sneaking up on her, she snatched the match from his hand. But then she looked at it uncertainly. She'd never used a match before.

"Strike it against the side of the stove," Garick said, his voice level. "Then light the gas."

Though there was really no inflection in Garick's voice, Ashley suspected he thought she was stupid for not knowing that and she reacted defensively.

"I knew that!" she lied, glaring at him again before she turned and scratched the match hard against the side of the stove. It promptly broke in half without lighting.

Garick handed her another match, saying, "You might want to lighten your touch a little."

His tone had more inflection this time; it was drier. But Ashley decided to ignore him and she took the match and struck it more gently this time. It still didn't light. Gritting her teeth, she tried again, and finally, the end of it burst into flame. She then extended it toward the hissing well, only to jump back in alarm as the gas ignited with a whoosh.

"It helps if you light the match *before* you turn on the gas," Garick commented.

Since his advice came too late, Ashley didn't appreciate it. After checking to make sure he didn't have his laser with him, she said, rather snappishly, "Look . . . I'll figure things out. Just leave me alone, all right?"

His face expressionless, he shrugged and returned to the main room.

Ashley then explored the cupboards, found a metal pan, filled it with water, and dropped three of the eggs in the water, which promptly spilled over. She poured out some of the water, then set the pan on the flame on the stove.

That done, she found tea leaves in a wooden box and hesitated. It seemed to her it would save time and water if she made the tea in the same water in which the eggs were cooking, so she dumped some of the tea leaves into it, then frowned, wondering if she'd used enough. It seemed to her better to err on the side of generosity than to make the tea too weak, so she dumped in more leaves—about half the box—before replacing the box in the cupboard.

After that, she sliced some bread, set the table with dishes and a pitcher of milk, and dipped the eggs out of the pan into a bowl. She poured the tea into cups and then, feeling pleased at how quickly she had learned to cook, and thinking she had done a lovely job of arranging everything on the table, she called Garick to come eat.

It seemed to her he approached the table rather warily and looked somewhat relieved when everything looked normal.

As she sat down across from him, she said, with a

tinge of smugness, "I told you I could do it by myself."

He didn't reply. He was picking up one of the eggs, looking at it with a frown. It was no longer salmon-colored. It was black. Hesitantly, he cracked it against his plate and immediately, a thin stream of matter spilled over his fingers. Then he looked up at her, the look in his gray eyes unreadable.

Though Ashley was disappointed with herself because it was evident she hadn't cooked the eggs long enough, she didn't intend to behave as though she'd made a mistake.

"Well, my goodness, Garick," she said indignantly, "how was I supposed to know how long to cook them? I thought they'd be hard by now."

He picked up a napkin and as he was wiping his fingers, he said, with obvious restraint, "You could have asked how long to cook them, and I would have told you. But never mind. I'll just eat bread and drink—" He stopped as he saw how black the tea was. Then he cleared his throat and finished, "Milk."

It was evident to Ashley he didn't think she'd done any better with the tea than she had with the eggs, and her mood deteriorated rapidly.

"You could at least taste the tea," she suggested, her tone verging on sulleness.

Garick sighed resignedly. "All right," he said reluctantly as he picked up his cup. "I'll try it."

After barely tasting, it, he grimaced. "I think perhaps you might want to use fewer tea leaves next time. And there's something else odd about the taste." He glanced at her face. "Did you put something else in the water?"

Ashley's mood took another downward tilt toward angry defensiveness.

"I cooked it in the same water with the eggs," she grated, throwing her napkin down. "And now I suppose you're going to tell me I shouldn't have?"

Garick hesitated. "It isn't normal to, no," he then responded, shaking his head. "It spoils the taste."

Ashley's temper shot upward, bringing color into her cheeks and a dangerous sparkle into her golden-hazel eyes.

"If you don't like the way I cook," she said through gritted teeth, "then you do the cooking from now on! Who said it was my job anyway?"

"It's customary here for women to do the cooking," Garick informed her. "Our society is based on the norms and customs of the past on earth, not on the present ones."

He studied her in a way that Ashley didn't like at all. She remembered what he'd said to her aboard ship about New Frontier women being perfect. He'd also, of course, implied that earth women were somehow deficient, and from the way he was looking at her, she was sure he found her most deficient of all.

"Is that so?" she snapped. "Well, I've studied earth's history, and I don't recall women having to sleep with every single man in a community before she chose a husband! It's a barbaric, indecent rule, and if it weren't one of the rules here, you wouldn't have to be sitting across from me eating my rotten cooking!"

Garick shrugged, and his eyes never left her face. "I've studied history as well. And it seems to me, a lot of women who started out as bar girls and whores when there were still frontiers on earth ended up as respectable wives."

At that thinly veiled insult, Ashley's temper exploded. Blindly, she reached for one of the eggs in the bowl, picked it up, and let it fly straight at Garick's face.

Garick's reflexes were better than she could have wished for. He quickly leaned to the side and the egg sailed past him and hit the wall behind his head with a resounding splat. As its runny interior streamed down the wall, he moved even faster, coming to his feet and circling the table as Ashley was reaching for the remaining egg.

Grasping her wrist before she could get a good grip on the egg, he pulled her up from her chair, and Ashley suddenly lost control. She fought him wildly, venting all the rage that had been building in her for weeks, perhaps even for years, against the first solid, if inappropriate, target she'd ever had.

But Garick employed the same maneuver he'd used on her when he'd taught her judo aboard the *Mayflower*. He spun her around until her back was to him and her arms were trapped.

"Let me go!" she yelled, her fury past containment now.

"No," Garick answered calmly. "Stop struggling, Ashley, before you hurt yourself. It won't do you any good anyway. I can hold you like this all day if necessary."

He sounded so calm, so implacable, and Ashley felt so frustrated at being deprived of her target, that after one last attempt to struggle out of Garick's hold on her, she did something that was, to her, unforgiveable. She burst into tears.

Ashley hadn't cried in so long, her tears took her more by surprise than they did Garick. Furthermore, she was crying so hard, she was hardly even aware of Garick turning her around, holding her tightly in his arms, and stroking her back comfortingly. She leaned against his body, buried her head against his shoulder, and cried her heart out. Cried until she felt so weak, she could barely stand and started to slip down his body.

At that point, Garick lifted her into his arms and carried her into the bedroom. He put her on the bed and settled down beside her. He held her again until the last few sobs and shudders had left her drained, exhausted, and unable to do anything other than lie in Garick's arms.

Finally, when she thought she could speak without blubbering, she murmured in a small, tired voice, "I'm sorry. That shouldn't have happened. And I don't know why it did. I never cry."

She felt Garick's mouth move in a smile against her temple, and she thought he didn't believe her.

"Well, I don't!" she protested. But she was so physically and emotionally exhausted, her protest was too weak to be convincing.

Garick's reply, when it came, took her by surprise. "Then it's about time you did," he said quietly. "You've held those tears back for too long."

Ashley somehow found the strength to move her head back a little, so she could see Garick's face. She was puzzled, confused. He looked calm and compassionate.

"Ashley, you've been living in a desperate situation

for years, crammed among too many people, with too little to eat and always one step away from disaster. Then you were drugged, kidnapped, and woke up on a spaceship to learn you were never going home again. Next, you were told you had to sleep with a bunch of strangers and eventually marry someone, whether you wanted to or not, and whether you found someone you actually loved or not. You deserve to cry," Garick finished, his tone wryly accepting. "Anyone would who has been through what you have."

Ashley didn't answer as she continued to study Garick's face and held back a sob. It was the first time she could ever remember him looking and sounding kind and understanding instead of too dangerous to trust.

"But . . . but . . . I *never* cry," was all she could find to say.

"Why not?"

Ashley hesitated, then gave a weary shrug. "My mother didn't like it. She gave me hell when I was little if I cried. She said it showed weakness."

The scar at the corner of Garick's mouth tightened almost imperceptibly. But his voice was level when he asked his next question. "What else did she tell you when you were a child—about men, for instance?"

"She said they were all scum," Ashley said matter-of-factly. Then, too tired to hold her head back any longer, she moved it to a more comfortable position on Garick's shoulder.

"And did you believe her?" Garick asked.

"Of course. At least, I did until I went to the

university. That was the first time I was ever around any men."

"And what did you think of men then?"

Ashley shrugged. "A lot of them were just like Mother said they were," she answered. "But some weren't. I liked them."

"But not as lovers?"

Ashley shook her head. "I never met a man who made me feel—" She stopped, frowning as she remembered how Garick had made her feel the previous night. But that wasn't love, of course. That was just lust.

To her discomfort, he seemed to read her mind. "The way I made you feel last night?" he said, matter-of-factly.

Unwilling to speak, she barely nodded.

"Then isn't it fortunate that you picked me to marry," he said, his voice still nonchalant. "Since you had to marry, it's nice that you don't find me sexually repulsive, isn't it?"

She hesitated, then barely nodded again, then once more found the strength to tilt her head back so she could see Garick's face and he could see hers. In light of his present kindness, she wanted him to understand how guilty she felt about depriving him of his freedom.

"I'm sorry I forced you to marry me, Garick," she said, low, her tone miserable. "It wasn't fair of me. And though Mary said there isn't any divorce here on New Frontier, surely there are exceptions to the rule. So if you want to try to get a divorce, I'll help you. I'll say everything was all my fault so you won't be blamed and—"

"Mary was right," Garick interrupted. "There is no divorce on New Frontier."

Ashley frowned, shaking her head. "But surely that rule only applies to people who have been psycho-programmed!" she protested. "I can understand how hard it would be for someone who's been brain-washed into regarding his spouse as absolutely essential to his happiness to have her torn from him. But you and I are not psycho-programmed, so—"

"There are no exceptions to the law," Garick interrupted again.

He wasn't looking at her now, but out the window over her shoulder, the expression in his eyes unreadable.

"Maybe it's just never come up before," Ashley tried again. "But you and I could test the rule, and even if we fail, at least we'll have tried."

Garick shook his head, still not looking at her. "There's no point to that. Everyone would resent what we were trying to do. It would be unsettling to the whole community. So forget it, Ashley. I'm not going to try to get out of this marriage as long as I'm on New Frontier. And you don't have to feel guilty about it. I'm all right."

Garick's attempt to make her feel better made Ashley feel like the scum her mother had always said men were. She was sure he was looking away because he didn't want her to see that he felt trapped.

Unthinkingly, she put her hand on Garick's cheek, her touch softly consoling as she turned his face toward hers. Then she held his eyes with her own as she said, "Then I'm more sorry than I can say, Garick, to have done this to you. Thank goodness you'll be gone a lot, so you won't have to spend much time with me. And when you come home, if you want a place where you can live your own life, then perhaps we can build another house and—"

Garick broke in, and his eyes, which had begun to display a softness Ashley had never seen in them before, were suddenly cool. "Are you telling me you won't mind if I sleep with other women?"

Ashley hesitated. She was dismayed to find that, for some reason, she was reluctant to say the words she was certain Garick wanted to hear. But she didn't understand why. Why should she care if he slept with other women?

"If that's—" She stopped, averted her eyes from Garick's, cleared her throat, and tried again to get the difficult words out. "If that's . . . what you want."

She felt his eyes on her face, studying, probing, assessing. And then he said, "That's adultery, Ashley. And while adultery may be practiced on earth, it's not accepted here."

Immediately, Ashley felt a strong sense of relief. But she quickly stifled it. It was unworthily, unforgivably selfish of her to be glad that Garick couldn't have sex with another woman.

"Oh," she said, exerting every effort to keep her tone neutral. "I see."

"*Do* you?" Garick drawled. He put his hand on her chin and forced her to look at him. "Do you understand that since I can't sleep with any other woman now, kindness and fairness and duty dictate that *you* take care of my sexual needs?"

Garick's eyes were no longer cool. In fact, his gaze was growing heated, lazily sensual.

Ashley swallowed as a battle between her mind and her heart erupted. Garick's recent kindness to her, and the way he was looking at her now, were making her more amenable to the idea of having sex with him again than she'd been this morning. And the sudden awareness of his body so near hers, reminded her that she had actually enjoyed having sex with him the night before. Too, he was right that it was only fair that she should fulfill his sexual needs since it was her fault he couldn't have sex with anyone else.

But it was very difficult for Ashley to adjust to the new feelings swelling inside her because they were so at odds with a lifetime of thinking that she couldn't feel this way. And it was even more difficult for her to say what she knew was required of her at the moment. Gathering her will power, she forced herself to say, "I suppose you're right. I guess it is only fair . . . to . . . to—"

She stopped and swallowed again because Garick was moving closer to her. His mouth was a bare inch from hers now, and she remembered how much she enjoyed his kisses. His hand on the small of her back was pressing her closer and closer to his taut loins, which awoke the memory of other things he'd done to her the night before that had felt even better than his kisses.

But she didn't think it was in her best interests to let Garick know she was beginning to want him to kiss her—and, if she had to be perfectly honest with herself, even to want more than just kisses. True, he had behaved more humanely toward her than he had before. But if he thought she liked having sex with him and wasn't just doing her duty as his wife, he would have power over her which he might use in ways she wouldn't like at all.

"To what?" he murmured in that deep, soft voice that meant he was becoming aroused, and which heated Ashley's senses.

She had to think a couple of seconds before she realized he was referring to what she'd been about to say earlier, that it was only fair she take care of his sexual needs.

Ashley hesitated, then voiced the words in her head, even if they didn't quite accurately reflect what was going on in her body. "To perform my wifely duty toward you."

Damn it! she thought crossly. Even to her own ears, her voice sounded slightly breathless now, and if she couldn't control it, Garick would realize how he was affecting her.

"To *what?*" He sounded mocking, disbelieving.

He was so close now, Ashley could feel his breath on her mouth. And to keep from giving him the humiliating answer she knew he wanted to hear, she murmured, "If you like, I'll do my duty now."

She quickly moved her head and pressed her lips to his to keep him from asking any more questions. But she hadn't planned to slip her tongue between his lips. It just happened. And it felt so good, she didn't want to stop. Instead, she kissed Garick more fervently, and her body strained closer to his.

She couldn't believe it when he drew back, breaking the kiss and putting distance between them, and she glared at him.

"To *what?*" he repeated.

His gaze was heated, but it was steady, denoting an

unwillingness to kiss her again until she'd answered his question. And his voice was low and pleasingly husky to her ears, but it was also demanding, intolerant of any attempt she might make to lie. And to Ashley's frustration, she realized if she didn't answer him, he was perfectly capable of getting up from the bed and refusing to let her kiss him anymore.

The battle inside her didn't last as long this time. She wanted the kissing and, yes, damn it, what would inevitably follow the kissing, too badly to let her pride get in the way of the pleasure she was beginning to envision all too vividly.

"I . . . Well, I *sort* of enjoy it, too," she hedged, hoping it was enough to satisfy him.

It wasn't.

"Sort of?" Garick mocked. "From the way you behaved last night, 'sort of' is a rather weak description of how much you like it, isn't it?"

Ashley glared at him but not very hard. "Well, if you think that, why do you insist I *say* it?" she asked crossly.

Garick leaned closer and kissed the corner of her mouth. But when she turned her head to capture his lips with her own, he moved his mouth to her ear. In a sensuous tone that brought a flicker of heat roiling through Ashley's stomach, he murmured "Because it excites me to hear you say you want me. And it's part of having sex, Ashley. The words are almost as important as the actions."

Ashley closed her eyes, understanding what he meant because his sensuous whispers, and the heat of his breath against her skin, were increasing her excitement. But she was still reluctant to make herself as vulnerable as he apparently wanted her to be, so she continued to hesitate. He nibbled at her earlobe, then suckled her throat, and he pushed aside the caldera robe and began to rub her stomach, pressing in with his warm fingers.

As a shudder went through Ashley's body, he returned his mouth to her ear. And his hand continued to stroke her skin, leaving lightning trails of delicious sensation wherever he touched her.

"Say it, Ashley," he murmured, his voice soft, sensual velvet. "Ask me to have sex with you." He paused a second, then added, "Will it make it easier for you if I say it first?"

Ashley quickly nodded, her head trembling slightly.

He smiled, then whispered, "I want you, Ashley. I want you wild for me, the way you were last night. I want you wet and ready for me, then I want you under me, and I want you to touch me. Take hold of me . . ." He reached for her hand and placed it against his hard shaft. He was clothed, but Ashley could feel the heat and hardness of him, and as he moved her hand, showing her how to stroke him, he added, "And I want you to put me inside you."

His voice was a low rasp of desire now, and that tone, as well as the way he was making her touch him, were Ashley's downfall. She wanted to feel the hard, pulsing heat of him without his clothing in the way. She wanted him inside her. And she was ready to tell him anything he wanted to hear to have what she wanted. And he made it easier for her by at last giving her a real kiss.

As his tongue entered her mouth, Ashley closed her

lips around it, suckled it, then gave him hers. And everything that followed came more easily to her than she would ever have thought only twenty-four hours earlier.

Garick drew back slightly and whispered, "Are you ready to tell me what I want to hear now? Do you want to have sex with me? If you do, say so. Take your time. Say it plainly. Be descriptive."

Ashley stared up into his gray eyes, seduced by the heat in them, unaware that her own golden-hazel eyes displayed as much heat as his.

"Yes," she murmured, her voice sensually husky now. "I want you to make love to me." She wasn't aware that she had substituted the words "make love" for "have sex." And she didn't notice the slight sharpness, the thoughtfulness, that came into Garick's eyes as a result of her unthinking substitution. "I want you to kiss me . . . touch me . . ." She took his hand and placed it on her breast. "I want you inside me, Garick. I want to give you—"

That was as far as she got before Garick's mouth seized hers. His kiss was hard, devouring, exactly what Ashley wanted it to be, and she reacted by pulling him on top of her. But he was still dressed, and she wanted to feel his bare warm skin against her own. So she began tearing at his clothes.

Garick sat up and pulled his bodyshirt over his head. Ashley lay where she was, disappointed over the lack of contact with him, but immeasurably pleased by the way his body looked. It had been too dark the night before for her to see him naked. Where once she'd found his body threatening, now she found his masculine contours absolutely beautiful.

He was powerfully built, but everything was in proportion, and she wanted to touch him everywhere—his chest and the silky black hair in the center of it, his strong back and thighs, his erect manhood, everything.

When he lowered himself beside her, she told him how beautiful she found him. She whispered other things as well, things that made the heat in his eyes turn to a scorching flame and the way he touched her turned possessive and demanding.

She didn't mind his demands. She gloried in them. Their mating was fierce, and so unexpectedly satisfying to Ashley in an emotional as well as a physical way. Immediately after she'd reached her climax, she discovered that this time, instead of being intent on her own pleasure, she also seemed to be one with Garick in other ways. She began to feel very, very vulnerable.

As Garick lay atop her while their breathing eased, Ashley's eyes were wide open, staring over his shoulder with shocked dismay. She didn't want anyone, especially someone as inherently ruthless as she believed Garick to be, to have so much power over her. But how could she hide from Garick how much she enjoyed their lovemaking?

The answer was that she couldn't. He knew too well how to make her body tell the truth her mind didn't want to reveal. But perhaps she could hide the other things he was beginning to make her feel.

Garick slid to her side, and Ashley put her head on his shoulder, and stretched her arm across his bare chest, her thigh over his. She didn't want to lose contact with him yet. And then, realizing what she was doing, she decided she had to say something to cloak what her body revealed.

"Garick," she whispered.

"What?" he mumbled sleepily.

"I meant it when I said I was sorry I deprived you of your freedom. But though I know it's selfish of me, I'm not sorry it was *you* I forced into marriage. Because you're right. It *is* fortunate that if I had to marry at all, I don't find you as sexually repulsive as any of the other men here. Otherwise, this whole situation would be unbearable."

She wasn't looking at his face, but she knew he smiled, and she found his reaction odd. Why should he smile at being trapped into a marriage he didn't want with a woman who said she could only tolerate being married to him because he happened to be good in bed? He couldn't possibly know she was beginning to feel other things for him besides sexual desire, he couldn't even suspect such a thing. She wouldn't allow it.

"Things will work out for the best, Ashley," he said softly. "Now rest a bit. Take a nap. We have things to do when we wake up."

Ashley wondered what they had to do, but she was suddenly too tired to think, too weary to do anything but sleep.

When Garick was sure Ashley slept, he turned on his side and stared down at her face, his gaze thoughtfully speculative.

For such an intelligent woman, Ashley, he thought with dry amusement, *you're a hell of a bad liar. The question is, who are you lying to most, me or yourself?*

Are you really only glad you married me because I'm good in bed? I'm beginning to wonder about that. And I'm beginning to wonder if, since I've made you feel one thing you didn't want to, I can also make you feel more. If I can make you tell me one thing you didn't want to, can I make you tell me more?

As Garick gazed down at Ashley, taking pleasure in her beauty, feeling possessive of her, he remembered that he had done some lying of his own. He had made her believe there was no way their marriage could be dissolved. Sure, it was true that it would upset the community should Ashley and he get a divorce, but because of his special status it wasn't impossible, despite what he'd said.

But if Ashley knew that, she would try to bolt before they'd had a chance to see if their marriage could work. Garick realized he was already beginning to hope, and hope pretty strongly, that it would.

His lie didn't make Garick feel as guilty as it should have or as it normally would have. He had always been scrupulously honest before Ashley had come into his life. But since the moment he'd met her, he'd been thinking one way, while behaving another.

Maybe I knew, Garick thought a little grimly, *at least on some level, even from the beginning, that the stakes were high enough to justify a little deviousness.*

Gazing at Ashley once more, he thought, *But I think I'll let both of us get away with lies a little longer until something happens that backs us into a corner and each of us has to put up or shut up. And that, my beautiful little spitfire, will be a day neither of us is likely ever to forget.*

His smile broadening slightly, he nuzzled Ashley's

hair, kissed her temple, and settled down to rest. But he continued to think, and eventually, his thinking paid off. He figured out the perfect way to thwart what he was sure would be next on Ashley's agenda —separating the two of them for a while so she wouldn't have to deal with what he hoped he was beginning to make her feel.

Well, if nothing else comes of this marriage, sweetheart, he thought with dry realism, *I'm going to make sure you at least come out of it free of your mother's strangle hold on your emotions. If I'm not exactly the right man for you, I think I'm close enough to leave you better off than I found you in terms of living a full, happy life.*

Which was all to the good, Garick thought more soberly a moment later, if he didn't have to pay for Ashley's ability to be happy with a loss of his own future contentment. He didn't want to fall in love with her, only to discover that she couldn't love him.

Thinking about the reasons Ashley might not be able to love him, besides all the nonsense her mother had planted in her mind for too many years, Garick remembered how frightened Ashley had looked when she'd come into the living room and found him with his laser in his hands.

But surely, she couldn't still believe he would kill her, he thought, frowning with incredulity. Sure, he'd joked about it a couple of times, but anyone with an ounce of perception could have told he was joking. And why had she ever believed he was capable of killing her in the first place?

Garick shook his head slightly. He couldn't really accept that Ashley might have erroneous ideas about his character. She must have been exaggerating to make a point, the way one sometimes did in an argument in order to put the other person at a disadvantage. That was the only explanation that made sense. He couldn't think of a single thing he'd ever done to make her view him as some kind of barbaric relic from the distant past who preferred violence to reason.

In any case, in view of his most recent plan, they would have time to get to know each other thoroughly. She would discover his true character, while both of them found out if they were compatible enough to sustain their marriage. And while they were learning about each other, he thought, with an anticipatory grin, he would make sure they explored the way in which they already knew they were compatible to the fullest extent possible.

Chapter Nine

"Wake up, Ashley. We have to go into Plymouth."

Ashley felt Garick gently shaking her shoulder and opened her eyes. He was standing by the bed, dressed, and he straightened when he saw that she was awake.

"Come on. Get dressed. Put on something that has legs to it because you'll be riding a femura into town. You need to learn how. I'll fix breakfast while you're dressing."

He left the room, and Ashley yawned, then got up.

A few minutes later, after washing and dressing in a full-length bodysuit, she sat down at the kitchen table across from Garick and rather glumly watched him bite into an egg that was cooked this time.

He glanced at her, noted her expression, and said, "These eggs are bigger than the ones on earth. You have to boil them about fifteen minutes."

"I never knew how long you had to boil earth eggs," she confessed. "I don't know how to cook anything, Garick. I never had to cook before. I always ate in a dormitory dining room."

"Don't worry about it," he said. "I'll teach you and help out until you get the hang of it."

Obviously, Garick intended that his wife would follow New Frontier's customs and do all the cooking once she learned how. But Ashley was no longer in the mood to argue the point, at least for now, so she reached for an egg. She found the shell very hard, and the taste rather odd, but it wasn't as bad as she'd feared it might be. The grain bread and milk, as well, were oddly flavored, but they satisfied her hunger. And the tea, which was just the right strength, completed her invigoration.

After he finished eating, Garick stood up. "If you don't mind cleaning up in here," he said casually, "I'll go saddle the femuras."

Ashley quickly looked up at him nervously. She didn't want to try to ride and fail, the way she'd failed with her cooking.

Garick smiled at her encouragingly. "You have to learn to ride, Ashley," he said. "It's quicker than traveling by cart, and it's the only way besides walking to get around. I told you, we have very few ground vehicles, and our hover aircraft is used to transport heavy machinery, not people, except in an emergency, of course."

"All right." Ashley nodded.

He left. Since he'd asked politely and prepared breakfast—and because she felt guilty when she saw that he had wiped the egg she'd thrown at him off the wall himself—Ashley didn't mind tidying the kitchen. When she was done, she went out on the front porch and looked around.

There was a dirt lane to the house leading from the tree-lined dirt road they'd traveled from Plymouth, and the area around the house was level and carpeted with brown grass. Ashley didn't know what season it was, but she assumed it was spring. She could see some new blue-green growth coming up through the brown grass, and some blue-green sprigs which were probably flowers poking through the soil alongside the house.

Garick came around the corner, leading two saddled femuras, and Ashley, at seeing their beautiful eyes, involuntarily smiled.

"You should do that more often," Garick said as he brought the two animals to a halt in front of the porch. His eyes were on her mouth.

Ashley was confused. "Do what?"

"Smile." Then he quickly added, "Come here."

Ashley descended the steps and approached him.

"I want you to look into your femura's eyes, and let her study you for a while," Garick said, tilting his head toward the femura on his left. "You have to establish trust with a femura before one of them will let you get on his or her back. Otherwise, they'll pull so many tricks on you, it isn't worth the trouble to keep trying to ride."

Ashley smiled again. "What do you think makes them decide a human is trustworthy?"

Garick, his eyes again on her mouth, shook his head. "No one's been able to figure that one out. But it seems they have personalities just like humans do, so some like one type of human, others like another. I'm hoping this one likes you, though. Otherwise, we'll have to keep trying to find you a femura that does."

Ashley walked to the femura's head and stared with open pleasure into the animal's liquid brown eyes. The femura stared back at her, giving the impression of conducting an intelligent, thoughtful inspection. Ashley then raised a hand to stroke the animal's furry muzzle.

"Ashley, be careful," Garick voiced a warning. "They bite."

But instead of biting Ashley, the femura stretched her mouth into an almost human grin, let out a crooning whinny, then turned her head and nuzzled Ashley's palm.

Chuckling delightedly, Ashley rubbed her cheek against the femura's velvet muzzle and scratched her under her chin, which brought another crooning sound from the animal's throat.

Still smiling, Ashley drew back to look at Garick. "I think she's accepted me, don't you?"

But Garick didn't answer for a moment. He was staring at her in an intent manner. His eyes traveled over her slender, seductively curved body, which her tight, one-piece suit displayed to advantage, then roved from her auburn hair, to her smooth complexion, to her golden-hazel eyes. His visual journey ended at her mouth.

Breathless from his perusal, Ashley's smile faltered and she bit her lip.

At that point, Garick seemed to collect himself, and

he nodded. "Yes, she's accepted you. The next step is to get on her back. Come here." He moved to the femura's left side and Ashley joined him. "Put your left foot in the stirrup and swing your other leg over her back," he instructed.

Ashley complied, and when she was perched on the femura's back, Garick handed her a pair of leather reins.

"Grip with your knees and hold tightly to the reins," he said. "You get her started by kicking her gently with your heels, and you turn her the way you want to go by tugging on the reins in the right direction. When she's moving, try to adjust to her rhythm and move with it." He hesitated and smiled mischievously. Looking directly into Ashley's eyes, he added, his tone low and meaningful, "You know how to adjust to a rhythm, Ashley. You did it beautifully with me last night and this morning."

Ashley quickly looked away as a feeling of warm embarrassment infused her body.

Garick laughed softly and walked away to mount his own femura. When he was astride, he said, "Come on. We'll keep the pace slow until you get used to riding."

Ashley nodded, and after Garick touched his heels to his mount's side, turned him with the reins, and started off down the lane to the main road, she followed. Immediately, she wished the saddle had a pommel to hold onto. She didn't feel at all secure. But her femura seemed to accommodate herself to Ashley's presence on her back, and after they turned onto the main road and rode for a few minutes, Ashley felt more comfortable.

"Ready to go a little faster?" Garick asked.

Ashley nodded, and Garick picked up the pace. And soon, as she got more used to the feel of the animal's bulk between her legs, she experienced a delightful sense of freedom. There was a slight breeze, and as it blew through her hair and caressed her face, she enjoyed the ride more and more.

There wasn't much to see around her, however. Just the tree-lined road and flat, grassy land stretching away on either side of it.

"What kind of trees are these alongside the road?" she asked Garick.

"I don't know their scientific name. We just call them flat leaves," he answered. "Not very original or creative, I know, but descriptive."

"Why are we going to Plymouth?" Ashley then asked.

"We need supplies."

"For the house?"

"For our trip," he corrected her, speaking casually and lifting a hand to swat away a large insect with irridescent wings that hovered around his face.

Confused, Ashley looked at him in puzzlement. "For *our* trip?"

Garick turned his head to look at her, his eyes steady. "Our exploration trip."

If Ashley had known how to stop her femura, she would have from sheer astonishment. But Garick hadn't told her how one made a femura stop. "You—you're taking *me* on—?"

Garick broke in. "You said you'd studied some zoology, didn't you?"

"Well, yes, but I'm not a qualified—"

Garick interrupted her again. "I was told last night that the zoologist who normally accompanies us is ill, so you're going to have to take her place."

"But . . . but . . ."

"You won't be expected to be an authority," Garick went on. "But I imagine you can handle taking blood and tissue samples, making drawings of any new animal species we find, and taking notes about their behavior. Right?"

"Well, yes . . . but . . ."

"I wouldn't ask it of you, but there's no one else available, and there's little you could do to fill your time while I'm gone anyway," Garick continued.

"I could put in a kitchen garden," Ashley said, her tone sharp. She was disgruntled that he thought she was so bereft of skills to do anything of much use while he was gone.

Garick shook his head. "The farmers and ranchers give those of us on the exploration team a tithe of what they produce. We don't need a garden."

Ashley frowned. "But I *want* to make a garden," she said. "I've been looking forward to it." *And I've been looking forward to being on my own for a while, too,* she added silently, if not quite as fervently as she would have before the preceding night and morning.

Garick looked at her again, and now his eyes were unyielding. "Individual wants don't yet count for much here, Ashley. We all do what's needed for the whole community."

Obviously not wanting to talk about it anymore, he picked up the pace, pulling ahead of her, and Ashley had no choice but to try to keep up. It wasn't easy. She was soon clinging for dear life to the reins and squeezing her knees against her femura's sides as tightly as possible to keep her seat.

The buildings in Plymouth were all constructed of wood, and their design made Ashley certain the architects had taken their inspiration from films about the opening of the early-American Western frontier. And perhaps that was appropriate, she thought as she glanced down at the hard-packed dirt street and pictured what it would be like after a rain. After all, this was a frontier, too, and the environment made it suitable for agriculture and ranching, so why not adopt a pattern that had worked in the past?

Garick had pulled his femura to a stop in front of one of the buildings and dismounted. As he tied his femura's reins to a railing, Ashley was grateful that when she instinctively pulled back on her own reins out of fear that her femura was going to crash into that same railing, the animal slowed and stopped instead.

Vowing to remember that pulling back on the reins stopped a femura, she climbed down, discovering in the process that her thigh muscles and bottom ached.

Garick looked at the way she was grimacing and smiled. "I forgot to tell you it takes awhile to toughen up the right body parts to make riding for very long comfortable," he said.

"How long does it take to toughen up?" Ashley asked as she walked stiffly to the railing, her femura's reins in her hand.

"It depends." Garick shrugged, then changed the subject. "Let me show you how to tie those reins. If you don't do it right, that femura will take off for the wide open spaces, and we'll have to chase her down."

He demonstrated how to tie the reins, then took Ashley's elbow and escorted her into the building, which was fronted by two large open doors. Once inside, Ashley discovered the place was a warehouse. There were countless boxes stacked in rows against the walls with aisles between them.

Before they'd taken a dozen steps, a voice belonging to someone Ashley couldn't see hailed them. "Yo . . . Who's here?"

"It's me, Burnie," Garick called out.

"Yo, Garick!" the voice responded. "How's the new bridegroom?"

An instant later, a short, rotund little man came out of a side aisle, his pudgy face stretched in a beaming smile.

"Hello, Burnie," Garick said, extending his hand to shake the other man's. "We missed you at the wedding."

Ashley wondered how Garick had known this man wasn't at the wedding. Then she realized he must know everyone on New Frontier.

"Sorry to have missed it," Burnie shook his head regretfully, "but I had to stow the cargo that arrived on the *Mayflower*. However," he added, his brown eyes twinkling merrily, "I've heard all about it already. I understand that if it weren't for the psychoprogramming, there might have been a riot when your little bride opted to propose to you instead of giving our randy single fellows their chance at her. And everybody has been speculating like mad why you ac—"

Garick cut in. "Acted as pleased as I felt that so beautiful a woman as Ashley chose me over all the other handsome devils here on New Frontier?" he said, his tone mild. "Wouldn't any single man on the planet have acted the same?"

Ashley frowned at him, wondering why he was being so gallant, pretending that he'd been pleased when she'd proposed to him. Then she saw that Burnie was buying Garick's act, and she decided it was simply Garick's way of promoting community harmony. Apparently, he'd been serious when he'd said that it would upset everybody if it were common knowledge that one of their marriages didn't fit the norm. She supposed that because the population was so small, everything that happened to anybody here happened, in a sense, to everyone.

"And speaking of my bride," Garick was continuing, "let me introduce the two of you properly." Ashley and Burnie shook hands, and then Garick said, "Ashley needs a complete camping outfit, Burnie. She'll be taking Sandra's place on the scouting team's trip south. Can you fix her up?"

"Of course." Burnie eyed Ashley curiously. "So you're a zoologist, Ashley?" he asked as he led the way toward a section of the warehouse.

Before Ashley could answer for herself, Garick spoke, "She's had extensive training in the field."

"Well, I wouldn't say ex—" Ashley started to correct him, but Garick interrupted again.

"She'll need sturdy clothing as well as the usual camping gear, Burnie. That stuff they issue the deportees on the ship won't do."

At the casual way Garick used the word

"deportee," Ashley almost winced. She felt a twinge of discomfort every time someone described her that way. But then she realized that probably most of the people on New Frontier had been deported from earth, and she relaxed a little.

"It's too bad about Sandra," Burnie said as he pulled a caldera-skin sleeping bag off a shelf. "It worries all of us. She's the first person to experience a serious illness here, and of course that reminds us all of our own mortality." Then he smiled, winked at Garick and Ashley, and added, "But it's an ill wind that blows no one any good. At least Sandra's illness means the two of you will have a real honeymoon, even if it will be spent in the company of other people and in the wild instead of at home."

"Yes," Garick said, "it will be nice to have the time together and to be able to show Ashley more of the planet. Of course, it would be even nicer if we were going to be alone, but we should be able to snatch some private time once in awhile."

Ashley was surprised by Garick's answer, until she remembered that he was set on fooling everyone into believing he was a happy bridegroom.

Burnie chuckled and nodded. "If I know you, Garick, you'll make sure of it."

Ashley didn't find that particular remark very pleasing, and she glanced at Garick disgruntledly. But he wasn't looking at her. He was now helping Burnie collect her camping gear.

In a short while, the two men had gathered everything Garick thought Ashley would need, and he said, "These are fine, Burnie. Send them by cart to the staging hut, will you? We need to go to Sandra's now so she can brief Ashley and loan her some field equipment."

"Sure thing, Garick. When do you plan to leave?"

Garick hesitated, then said, "Well, considering that Bud got married yesterday, too, and would probably appreciate a little honeymoon time of his own, I think we'll give him a couple of days with Sheila."

"Generous of you," Burnie said, his tone sincere.

Ashley didn't think it was so generous, but she didn't have time to say anything about it. Garick put his arm around her waist, looked down at her, smiled like a happily married groom, and said, "Ready to go, darling?"

Ashley blinked at him in surprise, then recovered in time to play her part. "Of course, dear," she responded with only the barest hint of dry mockery underneath her sweet, loving tone.

After she and Garick said their farewells and left the warehouse, she asked, "Garick, don't you think Bud will resent such a short honeymoon? After all, you're taking me along, and—"

"Bud will think I've gone soft in the head, but he'll take what he gets and think he's lucky," Garick interrupted wrily. "We don't operate here like they do on earth, Ashley. We don't take vacations, have few holidays, and we only have half a day off on the Sabbath to attend services. We have to work too hard to survive to waste much time on leisure."

"Oh." Ashley would have thought it a grim scenario if she hadn't already noticed that no one she'd met on New Frontier so far acted as though they minded such a regimen. Instead, they were some of the most cheerful people she'd ever met.

Outside, again to Ashley's surprise, instead of leaving her to mount her femura by herself, Garick helped her. And she looked down at him in a thoughtful way.

"Garick," she said as he went to mount his own femura.

"Yes?" He turned back to look at her.

"Do we really need to—to pretend quite so fervently that ours is a love match instead of—" She stopped because she was curiously reluctant to spell out the real nature of their marriage—and because Garick's intense gray gaze made her unaccountably nervous.

"I mean . . . all these endearments . . ." she faltered. "Don't you resent having to address me as though you really—" She stopped again.

"We'll do what's necessary to make people comfortable, Ashley," he said, his tone level, unyielding. "And we *won't* do anything to test whether the men's psycho-programming will fail under certain circumstances. Don't worry about how I feel. I'll take care of that."

He approached his femura, then swung into the saddle with an easy grace that Ashley admired. But as she turned her femura to follow him down the street, her mind slid away from thinking about how masculinely appealing Garick looked. Had Garick meant that there was a possibility that the men's psycho-programming *might* fail under certain circumstances? Did he mean that if they realized she and Garick weren't truly in love and committed to one another, they might regard her as fair game again?

The very thought made her shudder. As she and Garick rode out of town in the opposite direction from the way they'd entered it, she decided that if publicly displaying wifely affection to her husband would help her remain safe from other men's attentions, she would throw herself into the act with all her heart.

As they entered the countryside north of town, the landscape changed to rolling, freshly tilled farmland interspersed with small wooded hillocks. Looking up, Ashley noted that the cerulean sky, except where dotted with fluffy white clouds, had a clarity which she'd never seen on earth. But then the earth's sky was loaded with pollutants.

Thinking about earth's degraded environment saddened Ashley, for all her fellow humans would never have a chance to come to New Frontier and see what God had intended nature to be like. Only those who had lived long enough to remember how earth had once looked could really know what they were missing. Pictures and films could suggest, but they couldn't provide the real sensual enjoyment of nature at her best.

Suddenly, for the first time, Ashley realized how lucky she had been to be deported and sent here. It was almost as though she had been rewarded for the activities the government had interpreted as criminal, rather than being punished. But as she breathed deeply of the soft, scented air and reacted with a deep, peaceful serenity to her surroundings, she still wished many others could be this lucky.

Then she frowned. The presence of too many people would eventually change this pristine environment to an approximation of present-day earth's —unless humans could finally, voluntarily, agree to control their population and manage their environment wisely.

"Why are you frowning?" Garick asked from beside her.

Ashley told him, and he nodded. "Yes, right now on New Frontier, people are encouraged to have as many children as they can feed and love because they're needed. But at some point in the future, how far ahead I don't know, it may be that the same population controls that are in effect on earth will have to be imposed here."

Ashley shook her head, her gaze troubled. "And then what? Do we just keep trying to find new planets to take the place of the ones we ruin through overpopulation and a lack of regard for the environment? Won't there come a time when we run out of planets? It shouldn't be like that, Garick. Can't we ever learn what's in our own best interests?"

"We have to a certain extent," Garick responded. "Some of the lessons learned on earth are being put into operation here. Look at those fields, for instance. They're tilled to prevent as much as possible the loss of topsoil, and the trees are left to help out in that regard. But you're right. We can afford to do that now. However, when the population increases to a certain level, I suppose farmers may decide to cut down the trees and till in such a way as to get the highest yield possible."

"And when there are too many people here, whatever government is in power will implement population controls again," Ashley went on. "And that's just asking for trouble, giving any government the power to decide who can and who can't have children, or how many children anyone can have. Some parents may be excellent parents to a dozen children, while other parents may not be able to handle even one child responsibly. And yet, if the government doesn't choose, who does? Most people want children out of the biological instinct to reproduce, without knowing what kind of parents they'll be. I wish there were some way to determine who should be a parent. And I wish that people were intelligent enough to control their instincts when they see that there's no room or resources for an unlimited number of children."

She was getting depressed, starting to feel the same profound sense of pity for her fellow humans that she had often felt on earth. They never seemed to understand what was in their best interests until it was too late. And as a result of that inability, they often suffered profoundly.

After a penetrating glance at her face, Garick asked, "What sort of parent was your mother?"

The question made Ashley frown thoughtfully. "When I was small, I thought she was a wonderful parent," she mused. "But after attending the university and taking some psychology courses, I began to understand that she had some blind spots—biases, prejudices—that were a little warped. I don't know why she was that way. She didn't talk to me about her past much. But I have the feeling something must have happened to her in her childhood or later that hurt her very badly."

"Is she dead?"

Ashley nodded. "She was killed in a pedway accident my first year at the university."

Garick was silent a moment, then asked, "And what

sort of parent do you think you'll be?"

Ashley thought about it. The prospect of her ever having children had been so remote on earth that she hadn't dwelled much on being a parent. But once her five-year birth-control implant ran out, which would happen in about another year, the prospect would be very real. However, all she knew for the present was that she looked forward to having children—not whether she would be a good parent.

"I think I'll be all right," she answered Garick's question. "But who knows exactly how good a parent they'll be until they're responsible for a child's upbringing?" She paused, then added, "What sort of parents did you have? What was your upbringing like? And where were you born?"

"My parents were part of the team who discovered this planet," he said. "I was born here. But then we all went back to earth until we had enough people and had made sufficient preparations to start a colony. That took years, during which time I got my education. But I always knew I'd come back here. And if I never have to go back to earth, it will suit me fine."

"Are your parents still alive?"

He shook his head. "They were killed in an explosion aboard the *Mayflower V* when they were returning after a trip to earth."

"Did you have a good relationship with them?"

He smiled with fond remembrance. "Yes, I did. Then he pointed to the right and said, "That's Sandra's place."

Ashley saw a log house set back from the road. Behind it were two or three outbuildings and several enclosed pens, which Ashley thought must contain animals. But they were too far away for her to tell what sort of animals might be penned there.

A few moments later, they rode up to the house and dismounted, after which Ashley remembered to tie her reins securely to the rail.

Garick knocked on the wooden door, but to Ashley's surprise, he didn't wait for anyone to open it. He turned the knob and stepped inside. When Ashley followed him, she understood why he hadn't waited to be admitted. The woman he was greeting with a kiss on her cheek was sitting in an old-fashioned, homemade rocking chair in front of one of the windows, and she was obviously too ill to answer her door. Sandra's brown face was carved with lines of suffering, and her whole demeanor was one of exhausted endurance.

"Sandra, this is my wife, Ashley," Garick introduced the two women.

"How do you do, Ashley." Sandra nodded at her.

Ashley responded to the greeting, inspecting Sandra with concern. While she looked gaunt now, she had obviously once been a large, robust woman. Her hair was short and dark, framing her face in an untidy aureole. Only the dark, almond-shaped eyes retained the glimmer of an indomitable spirit.

Garick was explaining that Ashley would take Sandra's place on the expedition south, and then he said, "If you don't mind, Sandra, I'll leave Ashley with you while I go see to your animals."

"Thank you, Garick. The Fergusons have been helping out, but if you'll just fill the water and feed troughs, I'd appreciate it. Of course, I may have to let them all go soon," she added sadly. "I can't take care of them myself anymore, and I can't keep having others take responsibility for them."

"Don't be in a hurry to do that," Garick said firmly. "You'll beat this illness yet, and you won't want to have to start over when you do."

Sandra smiled, obviously grateful for Garick's encouragement.

Garick turned to Ashley then, moving close to her. "I'll be back when I've finished outside, sweetheart," he said as he put his hands on her waist. Then he bent down and kissed her exactly the way any doting new husband would kiss his bride farewell, even though their separation would be brief. And Ashley kissed him back with an enjoyment that had little to do with acting a role. Though she fervently wished it weren't true, she was beginning to crave Garick's kisses.

Ashley could tolerate wanting Garick's kisses better than she could tolerate the emotions his kisses aroused within her. One was a burgeoning longing for something more solid between them than mere sexual compatibility. But since she wasn't sure Garick would ever feel more for her than lust, she didn't welcome the strange new emotions—far from it. As Garick walked away, she stared at his back, her eyes expressing uneasy ambivalence.

When Garick had disappeared out the front door, Sandra's voice brought Ashley back to the matter at hand.

"How much do you really know about zoology, Ashley?" she demanded in a businesslike tone that was completely different from how she'd sounded when Garick had been in the room.

Surprised, Ashley turned to her. She hesitated as she collected her thoughts, then explained the extent of her education in zoology before she'd gone on to study history.

"Well, that's better than I expected," Sandra responded, relieved. "I was afraid Garick was only taking you along because he's so obviously besotted with you."

Ashley opened her mouth to dispel Sandra's opinion but then she remembered she was supposed to maintain the fiction that she and Garick loved one another. She closed her lips against the truth.

Sandra was now staring at her in a penetrating way that made Ashley uncomfortable.

"And what sort of character do you have, I wonder," the woman muttered more to herself than to Ashley. "Can you be trusted to keep your word?"

She stopped speaking and continued to stare at Ashley, trying to make up her mind about that last question.

Since Ashley didn't imagine that vouching for her own character would cut much ice with Sandra, she remained silent.

"Ah, well," the older woman said with weary finality, "I have no choice but to trust you." Then she fixed Ashley with a stern dark gaze and added, "I insist that you vow you will not tell anyone what I'm about to say, most especially Garick."

Ashley frowned. She didn't want to keep anything important from him other than her personal feelings, of course, and he didn't need to know those.

"Now wait a minute—" she started to say.

"You *must* vow to keep silent!" Sandra interrupted.

"If you won't, I'll tell Garick he mustn't take you, that you don't know enough to be of any use!"

It was only then that Ashley realized she wanted to accompany Garick. But before she had time to protest, Sandra tried to struggle up from her chair. She fell back, however, and gasped and moaned in such distress, that Ashley rushed over to kneel beside her, fearing the woman was dying.

"Sandra, stay still!" she urged. "I'll get Garick and . . ."

But Sandra reached out and grabbed Ashley's arm, her nails digging painfully into the flesh. "Vow to me!" she gasped, her dark eyes boring fiercely into Ashley's. "Vow that you'll keep what I tell you secret! Otherwise, my life's work may all have been for nothing!"

She looked so ill and sounded so desperate that Ashley, in an attempt to calm her, automatically said, "All right! I vow! But please, let me help you now. Do you have medicine to take? Let me get it for you."

Sandra nodded weakly. "There's a box of tablets on the kitchen table. Get them for me. And bring me a glass of water."

Ashley quickly stood and went to the kitchen. When Ashley returned, Sandra swallowed a tablet and drank some water. The zoologist began to look so much better so quickly that Ashley wondered if she'd been tricked. Had Sandra actually been experiencing as much pain as it had appeared she was? Surely, the medicine couldn't have worked that fast.

But Sandra's dark eyes disclosed nothing and as she handed Ashley the empty glass and thanked her, she sounded so grateful that Ashley's suspicions dissipated.

"Now," Sandra said, her tone suddenly calm and professional, "I'll tell you what it is you just vowed to keep secret."

As Garick watered and fed Sandra's animals, he wondered how much longer he could keep from Ashley that his special status would have allowed him to refuse her marriage proposal. When she did find out the truth, she would naturally ask him why he hadn't. He dreaded facing her reaction to hearing that pity and lust had figured largely in his decision.

But had those reasons really been the main ones for his acceptance? Garick wondered thoughtfully. All along, he'd thought he wanted only a short-term affair with her. But when they'd been on the *Mayflower VII*, for some reason he had concealed his exemption from having to accept marriage proposals and instead implied that he'd simply convinced women not to propose to him. Now, he wondered if he had subconsciously been insuring that Ashley would expect a yes if she ever decided to propose to him, because if she knew he could say no, she would never have asked.

Hell, he thought, smiling ruefully. *Maybe I trapped myself.*

Chapter Ten

Pointing to a crudely constructed desk placed against one wall, Sandra said, "Go to that desk and look in the middle drawer. There are some drawings I want you to see."

Ashley walked to the desk, opened the drawer, and extracted a sheaf of drawings lying face down. She carried them back to Sandra, who waved her toward a nearby wooden chair.

"Sit down and look those over," she instructed.

Ashley seated herself across from Sandra and turned the drawings so that she could inspect them. The first drawing was a deftly drawn print of an animal's track. Extending from the flat surface of the animal's foot pad were three deep impressions that must have been made by sharp talons. Shifting quickly through the rest of the drawings, Ashley saw they were all the same, possibly made by several different animals at several different locations.

Looking up at Sandra, she asked, "What made these tracks?"

Sandra shrugged. "I don't know. I've only seen the tracks."

"And how old are they?"

"They're recent," Sandra answered. "And whatever made them is much different than anything I've found on New Frontier. In fact, I'm fairly certain it's the missing predator I've suspected all along had to be here."

"Where did you find them?" Ashley asked.

"On our last trip south," Sandra answered, "I went ahead of the others for some distance to just north of the jungle. We haven't explored the jungle yet. You'll do that on this trip. Anyway, I found these tracks leading into the jungle, which I think is the animal's natural habitat. That would explain why no one has seen any of them yet. And that's really all I know so far. I didn't have time to do anything other than make the drawings before I had to rejoin the others."

Ashley hesitated, then asked the question uppermost in her mind. "Do you think these animals are dangerous to humans? The talon imprints look pretty lethal."

Sandra looked directly into Ashley's eyes and said, "No more so than a mountain lion or a bear might have been to early settlers on earth. In any case, I might be wrong. They could feed on jungle foliage, not on other animals, and those talons may only be used to climb trees. But if they are carnivorous, it doesn't mean they're dangerous to humans as long as proper precautions are taken. You'll have a tranquillizer gun and darts and you'll also have my laser. And you don't need to worry about the rest of the team. They all carry lasers and have been trained to take nothing for granted—to be alert to any threat. They can take care of themselves. It's part of their job to face the possibility of danger."

Sandra couldn't have looked nor sounded more honest and straightforward, but Ashley still didn't know why Sandra had wrung a vow of silence from her.

"Well, I admit, I've been puzzled by the seeming lack of carnivores here myself. It doesn't seem natural, unless, of course, nature on New Frontier operates differently from nature on earth. But it doesn't seem to be all that different in other ways." Then Ashley looked at Sandra and asked, "Tell me exactly what is it you want me to do if I find any of these animals."

Sandra leaned forward in her chair, and now her gaze was not only intent, to Ashley's surprise, it was also hostile.

"You must find one of these animals, tranquillize it, make a drawing of it, take blood and tissue samples from it, and bring everything back to me. I'm writing a textbook about the animal life on New Frontier. I'm like a modern-day Adam, naming what I find, creating a whole new scientific lexicon of terms, and I intend for posterity to give credit where credit is due—to me! After all, you're not even a qualified zoologist, so though you may see this animal first, I doubt you'll even know how to classify it properly. Besides, I'm the one who discovered the tracks in the first place, and if it weren't for this cursed illness, I'd be the first one to lay eyes on these animals!"

Ashley understood perfectly. She had run across people like Sandra at the university many times. Their egos were so wrapped up in their work, they would go to almost any lengths to further their professional reputations and perhaps gain an exalted place in the historical annals of their particular discipline.

"Sandra," she said calmly, "I assure you, I have no desire to steal your thunder. As you pointed out, I'm not a zoologist. I'm an historian. So why not just wait until you recover and then go find this animal yourself?"

"Because I don't know how long I'm going to be ill, or if I'll even recover completely enough to go on exploration trips again. Besides, the team is heading for the jungle this time, which is where these animals must make their home. So the chances are they'll be found on this trip."

She hesitated, then added, "And I might as well tell you this now. I'm not going to mention your help in my book. I'm going to write that *I* found, classified, and named this animal!"

Ashley had taken that for granted. She knew scientists like Sandra often took credit for their assistants' contributions. And Sandra might be even more caught up in her fear of having credit stolen from her than was usual if she feared her illness might result in her early death. The New Frontier animal textbook was going to be her only chance for immortality unless. . . .

"Do you have children, Sandra?"

Sandra shook her head. "No. My husband was killed in an accident shortly after we married, before I could get pregnant. And because of my work with the exploration team, I've so far been exempted from having to remarry."

"Exempted?" Ashley frowned.

Sandra looked at her as though surprised she'd had to ask. "You don't think the community would let a woman remain single unless there were compelling reasons to exempt her, do you? Once the planet is thoroughly explored, I'll have to choose a new husband . . . if I recover from this illness," she added, bitter frustration in her voice now.

Ashley's stomach tightened, dismayed by what she'd just learned. It meant that if anything happened to Garick, she would end up in exactly the same situation that had compelled her to propose to Garick in the first place!

Praying Garick would live to a ripe old age, she turned her attention to Sandra. If Sandra didn't recover from her illness, Ashley thought compassionately, the textbook would be her entire legacy to succeeding generations. Ashley then decided to do exactly as Sandra wanted.

"Do you think I will only spot one of them?" she asked. "Or do you think they might live in groups, like wolves?"

"It's entirely possible they do, and if you find that to be true, I want you to observe them and try to get some idea of their group behavior. Take good notes," Sandra instructed sternly. And then she slammed her hand down on the arm of her chair. "Damn this illness! I want so badly to do myself what I have no choice but to allow you to do for me. You don't even look as if you realize how important this assignment I'm giving you is!"

"Yes, I do," Ashley said quietly. "I promise I do. And I also promise I'll do my very best for you, Sandra."

At the sincerity in Ashley's voice, Sandra eyed her uncertainly. "And you will keep your vow of secrecy?" she half asked, half demanded.

"Yes. But the possibility of my taking credit for the discovery of these animals isn't the only reason you made me give you a vow of silence, Sandra. What if I'm not the first or the only one on the team to spot them? Are you worried about someone else on the team taking credit from you? That doesn't seem to me to be likely. They're probably only interested in their own disciplines. And in any case, I'll tell everyone you were the first to find the tracks and that you deserve the cre—"

"You'll do no such thing!" Sandra interrupted, her eyes flashing. "No one must know I found those tracks on an earlier trip. Don't you realize that information could ruin my standing in the community?"

"What?" Ashley was confused.

"Hasn't Garick told you how things operate here? How it's all for one and one for all? If those tracks prove to be made by animals that are predators—especially ones that feed only on caldera which are vital to New Frontier's economy—I'll be viewed as having been disloyal to the interests of the community. That's the ultimate sin here—especially to Garick. He values loyalty above all else. If he thinks

I've been disloyal, I doubt he'll forgive me, and his attitude will influence the others."

Ashley was alarmed. If Sandra thought Garick wouldn't forgive *her,* how much more unforgiving would he be toward a wife who kept secrets from him?

"But . . ." she said slowly, ". . . if there's any chance these animals could be a threat to the community's interests, then you are being disloyal, Sandra."

"That depends on how you look at things!" Sandra snapped. "Do you want to see the wholesale extermination of predators on New Frontier as happened on earth when farmers and ranchers began to move west? If these animals are predators, they may be a vital link in the chain of life on this planet! But try telling that to the ranchers if it turns out the animals prey on caldera. No rancher has lost a single caldera from one of the fenced herds yet, and millions of caldera still roam free. But none of that will matter to the ranchers. And try telling it to the merchants who make a profit off the caldera skins sold on earth."

She paused to take a breath, and she looked so distraught that Ashley didn't want to say anything to upset her further.

"No," Sandra said firmly as she continued. "If these animals are predators, the longer we keep their existence secret, the better. Once you've brought me back some hard facts, and if they warrant it, I'll contact earth to ask that representatives from the Council for the Preservation of Alien Animal Species be sent here to do a more thorough study and if necessary, put the animals under protected status."

"But there's no guarantee I'm the only one who will see them, Sandra," Ashley pointed out. "And if I'm not, the secret *can't* be kept."

"I realize that." Sandra nodded grimly. "But I'm hoping, on the basis that the animals haven't been spotted so far, that they shy away from humans. The team is used to my going off on my own, and you can do the same so that you can search for them. And if it's true that they hide from humans, there's at least a *chance* that none of the others will learn they exist—at least not yet. I wish I could do more than hope that's what will happen, but I can't. I just have to live with the risk that someone besides you will also discover the animals."

She inhaled deeply, then went on. "But if someone else does spot them, you mustn't say a word about my finding their tracks earlier. This illness has made me helpless, and for the present, I have to depend on the good will of the community for my very survival. And in any case, if I recover, I'll be spending the rest of my life here, and I don't want to be ostracized and denied the chance to marry again and have children."

Ashley could relate to the threat of being ostracized, and her sympathy for Sandra was rearoused.

"Therefore," Sandra said grimly, "you might as well know that if you do break your vow, I'll deny the whole thing. Since my standing in the community is already established and yours is not, I'm the one who will be believed, and you'll be labeled a lying troublemaker and lose your chance to make a place of your own in the community."

At seeing Ashley's shocked reaction to her threat, Sandra responded with a spurt of irritability.

"Oh, don't be such a naive child!" she snapped. "Here I am offering you the chance to help save the ecology of a whole planet, and all you can think of is your own mundane, short-term well-being."

"But isn't that exactly what you're doing?" Ashley said indignantly.

"Not at all. I'm acting in New Frontier's best interests whether its present citizens might like what I'm doing or not. Besides," Sandra added with a shrug, "while I agree with the community's all-for-one policy up to a point, they take things to ridiculous lengths sometimes. Why should I be punished simply because I found those tracks and didn't mention them because I hoped to find the animal myself on the very next trip? I only wanted to establish whether the species is carnivorous and take steps to protect it if it is. If I hadn't fallen ill, that's exactly what *would* have happened. But now that I've kept the secret, I have to continue to keep it, and I have to rely on you to keep it as well—as you vowed you would."

Ashley was now sure that Sandra had tricked her into making the vow, and she didn't appreciate the pointed reminder that she was bound by it.

"But what about when your textbook is published?" she pointed out. "Do you plan to leave out when you found the tracks?"

"Of course," Sandra said. "I wouldn't even have told *you* the truth if I hadn't needed to make sure you would search for the animals. I needed to make you understand that if you do find them, their existence must, if possible, be kept secret to avoid the risk of their being exterminated before we can find out if they're vital to New Frontier's ecology."

"Not to mention," Ashley said wryly, "that you

wanted to make clear to me that any credit for finding them goes strictly to you."

"Which is only fair," Sandra said, her eyes flashing with angry self-justification.

Ashley sighed, feeling trapped. For while she saw Sandra's point about protecting the predators, and even agreed with it, she was very uneasy about the whole situation. But even if Sandra had tricked her into keeping silent, a vow was a vow, and Ashley couldn't easily break her word.

She also remembered that she'd made a lot of vows to Garick on their wedding day. She frowned as she realized she hadn't been very honorable in taking those vows as she had made them for selfish reasons and with the hope that a way could eventually be found to break them.

Along the same lines, she wondered if keeping this secret from Garick was, in a sense, breaking her marriage vows. And even if that wasn't technically true, from what Sandra had said about Garick's valuing loyalty, would he be all that interested in technicalities? Wouldn't he see it as a form of betrayal whether it actually was or not? And if he did, would that make him disregard his concern for the community's well-being and decide to test the rules concerning divorce?

Where once that possibility would have filled Ashley with joy, now it filled her with dread. For several different reasons, some of them purely selfish, some too complicated to contemplate now, she no longer wanted to be divorced from Garick.

"Sandra," she said uneasily, "please let me at least tell Garick. I can't believe he would condemn you for keeping your discovery of the tracks secret. And in any case, he would be a lot more forgiving if you told him now, before the team leaves, than he would be if we find those animals and one of them hurts someone. After all, the team may have become complacent, lax. What if a situation arose where a split second gained from being forewarned could make all the difference?"

At that, Sandra stared at Ashley thoughtfully for a few seconds, during which time Ashley hoped she was reconsidering her position. But it turned out she was considering something else entirely.

"How far would you go to protect Garick?" she asked Ashley curiously.

"What?" Ashley asked, not understanding.

"For instance," Sandra continued, "if you were to tell Garick this secret and he told everyone else so that I was forced to defend myself, what if I were to say that it was Garick who had first found the tracks and pointed them out to me to draw, then swore me to secrecy?"

"But why would he do that?" Ashley scoffed. "And why would anyone believe he would?"

"Oh, he wouldn't do it. Garick takes this all-for-one business more seriously than almost anyone. But that's not the point. The point is I would have a good chance of being believed, or at least of creating doubt, because Garick's parents were ardent ecologists. That's one of the reasons they became space explorers in the first place. They saw what was happening to earth and it sickened them. And they vowed if they did find another planet, they would work to make sure nothing similar ever happened again. In fact, if they hadn't been killed, they would have been the first people I would have asked to help me in this matter. So people, especially the ranchers and merchants, would at least start to wonder if Garick wasn't following in his parents' footsteps, willing to save the predators at the community's expense."

"Maybe he *would* help if you'd give him a chance," Ashley pointed out.

But Sandra shook her head. "If you believe that, then you don't know your husband as well as I do," she said drily. "He's like his parents in some ways, but not in every way. He'll always put loyalty to the people here above every other consideration."

Since Ashley didn't know Garick all that well, she had to accept Sandra's evaluation of his priorities.

Sandra saw the doubt in Ashley's eyes and pressed her advantage. "Trust me on this, Ashley," she said firmly. "Telling Garick would risk everything I want to accomplish. And I won't sit back and see that happen without retaliating. Think about the large picture, Ashley. Think about all the cumulative short-term thinking that got earth in the mess it's in today, then tell me I'm wrong to want to prevent the same thing from happening here, at least in the one area in which I'm qualified to make a difference. There will be other areas, of course, where people will make the same sort of mistakes here they've made on earth, and I can't do anything about that except with my vote. But in this one thing, I can do more than that and I intend to. And since you just left earth where you lived every day with the consequences of short-term thinking, I should think you would feel as I do."

Ashley did share Sandra's concerns about the

predators. She just didn't approve of Sandra's methods to ensure their survival. But maybe Sandra was right, Ashley thought with discouraged realism. After all, Sandra knew the people on New Frontier better than Ashley did; she even knew Garick better than Ashley did. So she was in a better position to judge the best way to accomplish her objective as well as to judge Garick's reaction to hearing the truth.

"You gave me your vow, Ashley," Sandra said in a challenging tone. "And I need to know if you're going to keep your word. Are you?"

Ashley hesitated, but in the end, she didn't consider she had any choice in the matter. She'd given her word and she agreed with Sandra's basic objective and didn't want to be the cause of Sandra's ostracism if the truth came out. She didn't know Garick well enough to judge his reaction to the truth if she broke her vow to Sandra and told him what she'd just learned; and most especially not when telling Garick the truth might result in endangering his status in the community. She'd already cost him his freedom, and she didn't want to cost him anything else.

"I'll keep my word, Sandra," she said unenthusiastically.

At that, Sandra's expression slowly began to relax from hostile suspicion to satisfaction, and she leaned wearily back in her chair.

"Good," she said, nodding. "Then let's discuss practicalities. As I said, you'll need animal tranquillizers and my laser gun. Not that you'll necessarily need the laser gun, but it's just as well to be prepared. There's also a map in my desk which is marked to show where I found the tracks. Take it so you'll have an idea of where to start looking for the animals, but keep it out of sight. We don't want anyone to start asking questions about the markings on it. The laser gun, tranquillizer gun and darts, specimen bottles, and surgical scalpel are in my laboratory at the back of the house. There's a knapsack on a table there. Pack it with everything you'll need."

Since Sandra looked as if she needed a rest, Ashley went to collect everything and put it in the knapsack. When she returned, Sandra inspected the equipment, then actually smiled at Ashley for the first time.

"Since you're an historian, you should be thinking about writing the definitive history of New Frontier as far as it's developed," she suggested. "No one's done it yet. There are only dry official reports and papers thus far. You could use them as research as well as talk to people and get their personal accounts. And, of course, Garick can tell you a lot."

"I may do that," Ashley agreed.

Since Sandra still looked drained, Ashley then asked, "Would you like to lie down, Sandra? I'll help you to your bedroom if you do."

"No." Sandra dismissed the idea with a grimace. "I have to spend too much time in bed these days as it is. I'll sleep when you and Garick leave. But I do want you to go out and look at my menagerie. I have two sets of the notes and drawings I've made on the animals I've collected and you can take one set with you so you won't duplicate what I've already done. They will also help you get an idea of what I focus on. I'll sit here and rest until you and Garick return."

"All right." When Sandra leaned her head back and closed her eyes, Ashley quietly left the house.

It felt good to be out in the open air again, and Ashley looked curiously around her as she joined Garick, who was just finishing feeding and watering the animals.

"Are you and Sandra through with your briefing?" he asked as she came to stand beside him and gaze into a pen that contained femuras, calderas, garellas, and a few animals she'd only seen pictures of.

"Yes. She sent me out here to look at these." She gestured at the various animals milling in the pen.

"That's a good idea. No sense duplicating what she's already done."

Ashley nodded absently, but she didn't like seeing the animals penned, even though she knew the necessity for observing them at close range, and for preserving them. Indeed, if it weren't for the zoos on earth, almost every animal that still existed would long since have been extinct.

Garick took her around the outdoor pens, identifying the animals so that she could compare them to Sandra's notes.

Finally, he looked up at the sun and said, "Did I tell you we're dining with Mary and Jim tonight? We'd better leave soon, or we'll be late."

"No, you didn't tell me," Ashley said. "But it will be nice to see them again. And we can leave now if you like. Sandra and I are finished talking and I've seen everything out here I need to."

She was quiet as she and Garick took their leave of Sandra, who gave Ashley one last warning look before their departure, and she remained quiet as she and Garick rode on to Jim and Mary's farm. Sandra's secret had robbed her of much of her earlier joy of being a resident of New Frontier, for it had reminded her that whatever the environment, people stayed pretty much the same.

A neat wooden fence surrounded Jim and Mary's farmhouse, and as Ashley and Garick rode toward the gate, their host and hostess stood waiting for them on their porch. They weren't alone, however. A small, dark-headed boy stood between them.

"Who's the child?" Ashley asked. "I thought Jim said he and Mary had no children."

"That's Jason Bready," Garick said, smiling as the boy began running toward them. "I imagine he's staying with Jim and Mary while his parents are in town to get supplies." Then, as the boy raced through the gate and almost ran under the hooves of Garick's femura, he laughingly said, "Whoa, Jason! Stand back before you get trampled."

Ashley had never heard Garick laugh before, and she found the sound charming. Also, as she stared at him in surprise, she realized she had never seen him look quite so relaxed either and the contrast to his normally fierce-looking visage was enormously appealing.

And then, as he dismounted and Jason threw himself on him, the sight of him hugging the small boy brought a lump to Ashley's throat. Suddenly, she pictured him hugging their own son—a small, dark-haired carbon copy of his father. She was so enchanted with the fantasy that she didn't want to come back to reality. But after a long moment, the fantasy faded, leaving Ashley stunned with the realization that Garick had been as important a part in her fantasy as the imaginary child had been. She didn't just want a child. She wanted *Garick's* child!

That realization not only confused Ashley, it frightened her a little. Coupled with the odd longing she had felt from time to time that day for something more in her marriage than sexual compatibility, it would seem that her feelings for Garick were deepening in a way she had never expected they would. But surely it was much too soon for anything like that to happen, especially when she didn't even know Garick very well yet. In fact, practically everyone on New Frontier knew her husband better than she did!

Shaken by her thoughts, Ashley nevertheless realized how wonderful it would be if she did come to love Garick—so long as he came to love her as well. But what if he didn't? What if she gave him her heart and he didn't want it?

Ashley had never experienced unrequited love, but if all the books and films were right, it was very painful and to be avoided at all costs. She eyed Garick warily, suddenly very much on guard.

"What have you been up to, Jason?" Garick was saying to the boy he now held in his arms. "Nothing but trouble, I expect," he added as he ruffled the boy's hair.

The child was positively beaming at the attention he was getting from Garick, who was obviously one of his heroes.

"I been good, Uncle Garick," Jason responded innocently. "Mama ain't had to scold me in a whole week!"

Mary came up then, laughing. "You little imp," she said to Jason. "You know your mother almost never scolds you, so don't pretend to be abused."

Jason grinned unrepentantly, and after the greetings, everyone began to walk up the path to the farmhouse, which Ashley noted was constructed very similarly to Garick's house.

My house, she reminded herself an instant later. But despite the reminder, it was difficult for her to think of Garick's house as hers. She wondered if that was because Garick had such a strong personality that anything he put his particular stamp on stayed his forever. And if that were so, did these emotions he was starting to arouse in her mean that he was already putting his stamp on her after only one day of marriage? Was she already becoming more a wife than an independent personality? God forbid!

Ashley was in an uneasy frame of mind as everybody sat down in the main room of the farmhouse, where Jason promptly crawled into Garick's lap, and Mary served wine.

"This is very good, Mary," Ashley praised the drink. "Did you make it yourself?"

"Thank you, Ashley," Mary responded, pleased, "and, yes, I made it. Almost everybody here does. One of these days, you will, too."

Given the fiasco of her attempt to make breakfast that morning, Ashley wasn't so sure about Mary's prediction.

After a few minutes spent chatting, Mary got to her feet and asked Ashley to help her put the finishing touches to dinner.

Ashley stood, but her expression was rueful. "I'll be glad to help, Mary," she said, "but I think you should know that I can't cook yet." She glanced at Garick, whose face was unrevealing, and added, wryly, "Just ask Garick. I expect he thinks my attempt to fix breakfast this morning was more an attempt to poison him than feed him."

Garick loyally said, "You'll learn."

"Of course, you will," Mary echoed his assurance. "I didn't know how to cook when I got here either."

"And now she's the finest chef on the planet," Jim boasted.

Mary beamed fondly at her husband, then headed for the kitchen.

Ashley followed her and watched as Mary tied an apron around her waist. Then Ashley joined her at the stove, where Mary stirred the steaming contents of a large pot.

"What is that, Mary? It smells wonderful."

"Caldera stew," Mary said. "And it tastes as good as it smells. Our food is one of the best things about New Frontier, Ashley. It's nothing like the revolting synthetic glop we were all used to eating on earth."

She winked at Ashley mischievously then and added, "I admit, when I first got here, I wasn't thrilled by the sociologists' decision to implement the traditional, conservative family unit that was once prevalent on earth. I thought it would mean we women would lose many of the rights we had fought long and hard to obtain."

She replaced the lid on the pot, moved to lean comfortably against the counter, and continued her discussion.

"But then I discovered it's not all as cut and dried as it may seem on the surface. The family structure of the past may be our model, but the attitudes of the past are gone. Jim doesn't view me as a brainless combination of domestic help, brood mare, and sexual toy. He respects my mind and capabilities as well as my feminine attributes, and all our decisions are joint ones. And when we have children, the parenting won't be all my job. Jim is eager to help. So if you're tempted to judge our society here merely on surface appearances, Ashley, don't. Judge it according to whether the people here are happy and contented, and I assure you, most of us, both male and female, are very happy."

She paused then and gestured at the table. "But I'm talking when we should be getting dinner on the table. Sit down and grate these vegetables for a salad, Ashley, while I slice bread and pour the milk."

Ashley sat down, but was uncertain as to how to use the utensil Mary gave her. Without commenting on Ashley's ignorance, Mary showed her what to do, then bustled about her own tasks.

As Ashley awkwardly grated a large white vegetable, she said, "Jim talked about you a lot on the trip here. You couldn't ask for a more devoted husband."

Mary smiled with satisfaction. "You'll find that all of our married men appreciate their wives," she responded. "There's nothing like a little scarcity to make people value what they might otherwise take for granted."

"Not to mention that they've all been psycho-programmed," Ashley commented unthinkingly. Then she bit her lip, afraid she might have offended Mary.

"Yes, there's that to thank for the happy state of marriages here as well," she agreed with cheerful satisfaction.

Since Mary seemed to feel no discomfort about the

topic, Ashley then said, "Well, if you're so happy about it, I'm happy for you, Mary. But I'm glad Garick isn't psycho-programmed. I want his devotion to me to be absolutely sincere, not imposed by brainwashing."

Hearing her own words, Ashley felt a small jolt of consternation. There it was again—another indication that she was starting to want more from her marriage than she might ever get!

Mary sat down beside Ashley and reached over and patted her hand. It was obviously a gesture of comfort, and when Ashley looked at her in confusion, Mary's expression was kind and understanding.

"Ashley, since you're so recently from earth, I understand your attitude toward psycho-programming," she said. "But I assure you, it isn't nearly as bad as you think. You surely understand the practical reasons for implementing it, don't you?"

Ashley nodded, albeit reluctantly.

"Well, in addition to the practical reasons, I can tell you from my observation of the other couples here, and from my own experience, that it has many advantages aside from being practical. There's an enormous sense of peace in knowing your family will never be threatened by a failure of love, a resulting betrayal, and finally divorce. And it isn't at all phony. I loved Jim before I chose to marry him, but I also made sure he genuinely loved me before I chose him. I didn't want his phony devotion any more than you want Garick's. So the psycho-programming is merely assurance that our love will withstand outside pressures. And since Garick has always scrupulously observed the rules against adultery here in the past,

I'd say that bodes well for the two of you as well, even though he isn't psycho-programmed."

But I didn't love Garick when I asked him to marry me, Mary, Ashley thought with an unsettling sense of bleak regret. *And he didn't accept my proposal out of love.*

Mary then frowned and added, "However, I must confess I don't envy the two of you if another planet is found and it turns out to be one that isn't suitable for married life and children."

Ashley stopped grating and looked at Mary in confusion. "What are you talking about, Mary?"

Now it was Mary's turn to look confused. "But you know what I'm talking about, Ashley," she said in a puzzled way. "Remember how, after you proposed to Garick, I asked you how you'd ever gotten the courage to do it? I meant that I wondered how you could stand to think about the possibility that if a new planet is ever found and it isn't one he can take you to, both of you might be separated for years."

Ashley froze. She said nothing, merely stared at Mary in numbed shock.

Mary didn't notice Ashley's expression. She was continuing to speculate. "But when you said he hadn't had any choice about accepting your proposal, I assumed you meant the two of you loved one another so much, you were both willing to take whatever time together you might have before he had to leave. I thought too that you were hoping another planet is never discovered, or that if one is, it will be one where he can take you with him. And I thought you were a very lucky girl because a love that will accept that kind of risk is extremely rare. As I told you on your wedding night, many women had wanted to propose to Garick before, but he'd never loved anyone enough to marry under those circumstances until you came along."

No, Ashley thought numbly, *and he doesn't love me enough either. But he never thought I'd propose to him in the first place. Even if he'd thought there was any danger of my doing it, he'd told me aboard ship that he'd warned off all the other women who wanted to propose to him. So why would he think I'd have the courage to ignore his warning when no other woman ever had? And since he had to accept my proposal, but doesn't love me, I don't imagine the prospect of leaving me behind one day worries him at all.*

Mary's brow furrowed in confusion as she added, "But I must confess, the fact that you two were in love surprised me, because you certainly didn't act as though you were in love with anyone when you first came off the shuttle. And why did you ask me if any man had to accept your proposal if you already knew you were going to propose to Garick?"

Ashley knew Garick wouldn't want her to tell the truth, so she thought fast. "Ah . . . I didn't know for sure myself that I loved him as much as I do until I realized I couldn't stand the thought of sleeping with anyone besides him."

Mary's expression cleared. "So that's why I had the vague feeling you were only marrying Garick to get out of sleeping with the other men," she declared, looking satisfied that the mystery was cleared up. "Of course, I had it wrong in a sense. But at the time, I only had a strong feeling I'd better warn you about the consequences of letting anyone suspect you were only trying to get out of sleeping with the other men. I didn't know you didn't want to sleep with them because you were in love with Garick."

Ashley smiled faintly, thinking, *And it's best if you never find out your instincts were truer than you realize, Mary.*

Then, because she desperately wanted to know more about Garick's situation, she took a small risk and said aloud, "Mary, Garick doesn't talk much about himself or his life. He's the strong, silent type. So would you do me a favor and tell me all you know about him?" She paused, smiling in a way she hoped was fatuous and added, "You know how newlyweds always like to know every little detail about one another."

Mary smiled fondly. "Yes, I remember what it's like." She settled herself more comfortably in her chair. "Well, you surely must know that Garick's status is special because he was the first person born here, New Frontier's first native citizen. So some of the rules that apply to the rest of us don't apply to him."

Ashley nodded. Garick had told her he'd been born on New Frontier. He just hadn't bothered to mention that he was the *first* person born here just as he hadn't bothered to mention that he might one day leave his native planet, or that he might have to leave her behind when he did. That prospect, much to Ashley's dismay, didn't fill her with nearly as much joy as it would have only twenty-four hours earlier.

"And you know," Mary went on, "that he wasn't psycho-programmed. It wouldn't have been wise for him to undergo the type of psycho-programming suitable only to New Frontier when it might not fit with whatever type of society the sociologists decide to impose on a new planet. Our type of psycho-programming is irreversible, you know."

"I'm not sure I understand all that," Ashley said, forcing only mild curiosity into her voice.

"Well," Mary said, "suppose Garick had been psycho-programmed before he married you, and at some point in the future, he is sent to a new planet that isn't suitable for family life. Suppose the planet is only fit for a rough mining community, for instance, where mostly only men go to make their fortunes, with the intent of returning to earth or possibly coming here afterwards. If that's the case, the sociologists would likely implement a system where they'd contract a rotating pool of women to go to that particular planet for a certain length of time and service the single men who work there. But if Garick had been psycho-programmed, he couldn't take advantage of that pool of women and he'd have to go a long time without sex, which is a lot to ask of any man."

She then gave Ashley an apologetic look. "I realize that would be considered adultery here, Ashley, but it wouldn't be considered that on a planet such as I've just described, and you wouldn't want Garick to suffer, would you?"

The hell I wouldn't! Ashley thought sourly.

Aloud and as straightfaced as she could manage, she said, "But if I had to stay here, *I* would be expected to stay celibate, wouldn't I?"

Mary looked startled. Then she nodded, looking rueful. "I see your point," she agreed. "It's not exactly a fair arrangement, is it? But that's just an example I gave to show you why the sociologists decided not to psycho-program Garick. The actual situation, if a new planet is ever found, may be entirely different. There are all types of different social arrangements the sociologists may try, depending on the environment of a particular planet."

Ashley didn't say anything. She was still too disturbed by the thought of Garick having sex with another woman to do anything but sit frozen in her chair. Then the memory of Garick telling her he would stay married to her for as long as he was on New Frontier popped into her head, and she was even more disturbed. What exactly had he meant by that? she wondered. And just how many of the rules on New Frontier did Garick's "special status" exempt him from? For instance, was he exempt from the rule against divorce? Was that what he'd meant when he'd said he'd stay married to her for the duration of his stay here?

Ashley could see why he wouldn't want to upset the community while he was living on New Frontier by applying for a divorce. But would the community be all that upset if he applied for one because he was leaving the planet? Or would he simply leave her behind without going to the trouble of applying for a divorce?

Ashley's mind and emotions were in turmoil and she needed time to think. But one thing was clear. If Garick did divorce her, she would be expected to marry someone else, and she wanted to marry someone else even less now than she had when she'd proposed to Garick. She couldn't imagine kissing another man, letting another man touch her the way

Garick did, having another man father her children.

Her expression must have shown her thoughts because Mary clucked sympathetically and patted Ashley's hand again. "I'm sorry we talked about this," she said regretfully. "It's upset you, hasn't it? But maybe it will never happen, Ashley," she said with forced optimism. "Maybe another planet will never be found. Or if one is, maybe Garick will be able to take you with him."

But will he want to take me? Ashley wondered with a sudden bleak sense of loneliness. *Somehow, I doubt it.*

"Let's just get on with dinner," Mary changed the subject briskly. "I'm sure everyone is starving."

Ashley nodded, and all through the evening, she did her best to behave normally. But as she and Garick rode home, she was subdued and silent. And by the time Garick had taken care of the femuras and climbed in bed beside her, she was so upset at what she had learned from Mary, that she wasn't in the mood to have Garick make love to her—until he turned her into his arms and kissed her.

At the first touch of the bare length of his strong, warm body against hers, at the first taste of his possessive mouth and tongue, all of Ashley's emotions other than arousal faded into the background. She couldn't help kissing him back as fervently as though she'd been waiting for his lovemaking for hours. With an inward sigh of resigned acceptance, she realized she apparently had been, even if the waiting had been on a subconscious level.

But when he released her mouth and moved his lips to her throat, she suddenly asked a question. She badly needed to know something she hadn't really wondered about before.

"Garick?" she murmured against the desire quickening her breath.

"Mmmm?" He didn't stop kissing her throat to answer her, and now his lips were sliding deliciously across her shoulder.

"Did—" She stopped and gulped, almost losing her train of thought when Garick's hand closed over her breast, bringing a surge of desire shuddering through her body. "Did you ever think about me like this before I proposed to you?"

She felt his lips move into a smile against her skin before he lifted his head and moved his mouth to within a breath of hers. She couldn't see his face clearly because of the darkness, but the gray of his eyes was light enough to suggest heated amusement.

"Ashley," he whispered thickly. "No man in existence who hasn't been psycho-programmed could look at you and *fail* to think of you like this."

He then took her mouth in a drugging kiss and renewed his lovemaking with a passion that Ashley gave herself up to wholeheartedly. Her responses were heightened by her relief at learning that Garick had felt desire for her before he'd been forced to accept her proposal. Maybe that meant he hadn't hated having to marry her as much as she'd thought he had.

But later, as Garick slept beside her and Ashley lay pressed against his warm body, she knew that physical desire wasn't enough for either of them. She felt the same longing for more that had plagued her all day, and yet, after what she'd learned from Mary, she had less hope of getting it more than ever. What good was it to want Garick's respect, his friendship, and possibly even his love and his unpsycho-programmed devotion, if he might leave her someday?

In the darkness, Ashley shook her head at her own foolishness. What possible result could she expect from these feelings she had for Garick other than eventual frustration, pain, loss, and grief?

No, she thought with grim determination. *I'm not going to set myself up for pain. From now on, I'll take Garick's attitude as my own. I'll take the sexual pleasure he can give me for as long as it lasts, without hoping for or wanting or needing anything more from him.*

If she was going to hope for anything, she thought a moment later, it would be that when Garick had to leave New Frontier, he would be reluctant to cause the community distress and wouldn't attempt to use his special status as a lever to exempt the two of them from the divorce laws. Instead he would just leave her behind, still married to him, and therefore exempt from having to marry anyone else.

If he did that, it would mean she wouldn't ever be able to have children, and that was a sad prospect. But not so sad a prospect as having to endure marriage and sex with another man.

Upon making her decision about her feelings for Garick, Ashley expected to feel relaxed and at peace. Instead, she was filled with a sense of loss that seemed to grow by the minute.

Dismayed, she set out to ignore what her heart was telling her and concentrate instead on the reality of her situation.

Before she met her goal, however, she fell asleep.

Chapter Eleven

The scouting trip began just in time to save Ashley from abandoning all hope that she could be successful in preventing Garick from seducing her emotions as easily as he had seduced her body. For after spending two days alone with him, she was not only reduced to a state where a certain look from him could make her body flush with sexual heat, but she was dreadfully depressed every time she thought of having to live her life without seeing his smile and hearing his voice.

But fortunately, once they joined the exploration team and flew by hovercraft to a southern caldera ranch to pick up femuras and rode further south, Garick changed into the man Ashley had known aboard the *Mayflower VII*—enigmatic, authoritative, and irritatingly male. He was also often absent from her side, which gave her the distance from him she needed to try to gain a little perspective on their relationship. And she was among other people who distracted her from the difficulty of finding that perspective.

One of the people whose distraction she particularly welcomed was a scout named Blackmun. For some reason which was a mystery to Ashley since he seldom spoke, Blackmun seemed to have adopted the role of teacher/protector toward her. He accomplished both tasks more by example and by a subtle ability to be available to do Ashley the most good when she needed him, rather than through words. Ashley was grateful for his silent support.

He had taught her to build a campfire such as the one she was cooking over on this particular morning. As the newest member of the team, she had been delegated the task of rising early to make breakfast. It wasn't as light a task as she could have hoped for when she inevitably awoke sore from a day's ride on a swaying femura back, and tired from a night of lovemaking with Garick in their caldera-skin tent.

Ashley never found it possible to respond any less fervently to Garick's kisses and caresses in a sleeping bag than she had in their own bed. But she did resent that neither the physical rigors of the trail nor their lovemaking, ever seemed to deplete her husband's energy as much as they did hers. He was always up before her, shaking her awake before he left to check the perimeter of the camp.

Now, Ashley squatted half-asleep before the campfire, stirring strips of caldera meat in a skillet. She was unaware that Blackmun, who moved as silently as a ghost, had joined her until she saw his hand reaching for the coffeepot on the fire.

She didn't greet him as Blackmun wasn't one to indulge in unnecessary conversation. Instead, she glanced up, inspecting his dark American Indian eyes and complexion and his stoic expression. He looked steadily back at her, as usual displaying nothing of what he thought, but projecting an aura of comforting solidity that Ashley had come to depend upon.

She smiled a friendly welcome, then turned to stir the food without waiting for him to smile in response because she knew he wouldn't. Blackmun's smiles were inward. Ashley didn't see them with her eyes, she felt them with her heart. And she was all the more warmed by them because she knew she was the only one who got that sort of smile from him.

"It's ready," he said in his quiet, calm voice that was barely above a whisper and very soothing to the ear.

Ashley nodded, knowing he meant the meat was sufficiently cooked. "Yes. Hand me a plate and I'll give you some."

As she was spearing several strips of meat onto Blackmun's plate, Janet and Tom Newly approached. Tom was the team geologist, Janet their cartographer. Fortunately, Ashley liked them. But even if she didn't, Garick had instructed her that in this atmosphere of enforced intimacy it was imperative to behave with the utmost civility toward every team member. There was no leeway for petty grievances and temper tantrums that might affect their mission.

They were exchanging "Good mornings" when Brisby, the team's botanist/biologist arrived, his manner brisk and hearty as usual.

"Good morning!" he rapped out with the sort of

cheerful energy that always made Ashley, in the morning at least, wish she could tap into its source. As he grabbed a cup and reached for the coffeepot, he launched into a description of finding some wildflowers that morning which he was sure had medicinal properties.

"I almost missed them in the dawn light," he said, "but fortunately, I had my flash torch with me and the beam fell on one of the blossoms. And if I'm right, these flowers may lead me to a cure for Sandra's illness."

"That's wonderful, Clyde," Leslie Warren, the team's medical doctor, said as she joined the group around the fire. "Because nothing Andrew has tried yet has done anything other than alleviate some of Sandra's symptoms, and we're both at our wits' end."

Andrew, Leslie's husband, was also a medical doctor. But he wasn't on the trip. He'd stayed behind to provide medical care to the residents in and around Plymouth. And as Ashley glanced up at Leslie's patrician blond beauty and perfect figure, she wished somewhat sourly that Leslie had stayed behind instead of Andrew.

But as Leslie bent and patted Ashley's shoulder in a friendly greeting, Ashley tried to squelch her unworthy thoughts. After all, just because Garick unbent with Leslie more than he did with anyone else on the expedition, seemingly enjoying her companionship and friendship with more fervor than Ashley thought was necessary, it didn't mean there was any real reason to be suspicious or, God forbid, jealous.

However, as Garick approached the group hard on Leslie's heels, Ashley was not very successful in squelching the emotions she didn't want to feel in the first place. For it seemed to her that wherever Leslie was, Garick seemed never to be far behind.

Coincidence, no doubt. Nevertheless, Ashley's smile went a little awry, and her eyes contained a somewhat mutinous gleam as she noted the warmth of the smile Garick was directing toward Leslie. It was small comfort that Leslie's returning smile was not in the least flirtatious.

Then Bud strolled up with a small jar filled with soil in his hand. As the team chemist, Bud tested the water of any streams and lakes they found, as well as taking soil samples. Ashley gave him a warm greeting, glad to see him as always, and amazed, at his good-natured attitude when she knew he missed Sheila terribly.

The team was now complete—eight disparate, but mutually committed, people alone in a vast territory that was becoming increasingly inhospitable, at least in a geographic sense, the farther south they went.

After breakfast, the team dismantled their four tents and stowed their gear on the pack femuras they'd collected at their departure point, a ranch owned by a man named Jim Blanton.

"How far do you think we'll get today, Garick?" Brisby called from where he was helping to fold the tent he shared with Bud and Blackmun. The Newmans had their own tent, as did Ashley and Garick, and Leslie had a small one.

"I'm hoping we'll be close enough to at least see the edge of the jungle by nightfall," Garick responded.

The other members of the team groaned good-naturedly at his words. It was a long way to the jungle, and if Garick meant to press the pace so hard, there would be little time for the side expeditions they all favored. But no one questioned Garick's decision. Ashley had noticed that they never did, which surprised her a little since they were all professionals and probably possessed the egos that went with their status. Yet they followed Garick's lead without question, which, Ashley supposed, was a testament to her husband's leadership abilities.

"Blackmun, what does the weather look like for today?" Garick then inquired of his fellow scout, whom Ashley had learned had a remarkable ability to predict such things.

"Storm coming," Blackmun replied in his usual succinct style.

"When? And how bad?" Garick asked, frowning.

"Maybe this afternoon . . . more likely tonight. Bad one."

In reaction to Blackmun's prediction, Garick picked up the tempo of breaking camp. When everything was stowed on the pack femuras, they started out, strung in a haphazard line but always remaining in sight of one another.

Garick rode in front and set a fast pace. And Ashley was glad Blackmun had taught her, by example, to ride without experiencing as much bone-jarring discomfort as she had endured at the beginning of the trip. She couldn't match him, of course. No one but Garick could. Both men rode as though they were one with their femuras. But she had an easier time of it because she had had the good sense to copy Blackmun's style.

Turning her attention to the scenery around her, Ashley was filled with awe at the stark beauty of her surroundings. They had left the rolling prairies of the caldera ranches behind the day before and were now into a rugged, semi-arid area of scrubs and ravines. Lizard-like creatures darted away beneath the hooves of Ashley's femura, only to stop and peer at her from the safety of nearby sun-baked rocks.

As a result of reading Sandra's notes, Ashley knew she wouldn't see many animals larger than the small lizards in this area during the day. This was a territory for night creatures that came out when the sun wasn't scorching. But she did occasionally spot the distinctive white tail of a kirka, which resembled earth's now extinct prairie dog, disappearing into groundholes.

Though Sandra had already studied the kirkas, they were so cute, Ashley would have liked to capture one for a closer look before letting it go again. But Blackmun, who rode beside her, vetoed the idea when she voiced it.

"Too fast to catch," he said. "No time to make a trap."

So Ashley contented herself with enjoying the sense of freedom she derived from riding through such a vast, uninhabited territory. Idly, she wondered how long it would be before new settlers, and the descendants of the ones who were already on New Frontier, would populate the land around her. Fifty years . . . a hundred? She didn't know, but she was grateful for being permitted to see things as they were now, before mankind crowded these wide open spaces with cities and vehicles and their own presence.

The team halted for lunch at a small, secluded pool of clear green water surrounded by huge boulders. After dismounting, the rest of the members of the team wandered off, too curious as usual to rest.

Ordinarily, Ashley would have joined them, but the sun's heat and the accelerated pace of their morning ride had sapped her energy. So she dipped the cloth she wore around her neck to protect it from the sun into the pool, and bathed her hot face. Then she lay down in the shade of an overhanging rock with the damp cloth covering her face.

She was almost asleep when her skin began to itch, first in one place, then in another. At first, it was a minor annoyance, but when the itches began to sting, Ashley quickly sat up.

An instant later, she screamed as she jumped to her feet and frantically tried to brush off the hundreds of small black insects crawling on her.

Blackmun and Leslie came running toward her. Blackmun was ahead and Leslie yelled at him, "Get her clothes off, Blackmun! Quickly . . . quickly!"

Blackmun began ripping at Ashley's clothing, but she was too panicked to help. Indeed, when she was naked, she struggled against Leslie's and Blackmun's efforts to drag her toward the edge of the pool.

"Throw her in!" Leslie shouted.

Ashley felt herself being lifted in Blackmun's arms, and the next thing she knew, she was sailing through the air. She took a deep breath just before the green water closed over her head and she began sinking to the bottom of the pool.

As her feet touched a submerged boulder, bringing her descent to a halt, Ashley controlled her panic, and even recovered enough presence of mind to be grateful for the ease the cool water brought to the stings dotting her skin. However, when she looked down at her feet, some of her panic returned. Imprinted in the surface of the boulder was a shape that was an exact duplicate of the tracks Sandra had drawn. But this shape suggested its owner was huge and the talon imprints looked so viciously deadly that Ashley bent her knees and pushed upward with all her might.

When she broke through the surface of the water, gasping for air, the first thing she saw was a circle of the black insects drifting away from the spot where she had entered the water. Shuddering, she struck out for the bank, but then remembered she was naked. She stopped, treading water as she looked at the team gathered to watch her.

Garick sat on the bank, and it was obvious he had been discarding his boots in order to dive in after her. But it was just as obvious, now that he was aware she was all right, that he was angry. His gray eyes were pinning Ashley fiercely.

"Could someone get me a shirt or something?" she called out. "And would you all give me some privacy?"

At that, everyone looked relieved and even began grinning and joking as they walked away. But Leslie came back in a second, holding a caldera blanket, to stand beside Garick on the bank.

Ashley swam toward them, and Garick reached down to haul her out of the water. When she stood, he grabbed her shoulders and shook her, his tone as angry as his face.

"What the hell did you think you were doing?" he demanded. "Were you trying to drown yourself or what?"

Ashley, now emotionally reacting to the situation, couldn't answer without bursting into tears. So she glared at Garick's chest, blinking moisture from her eyes.

"You don't understand, Garick," Leslie said soothingly. She wrapped the caldera blanket around Ashley's shoulders. "Ashley was resting, and unfortunately, she picked a pincers' nest to lie down on. Blackmun and I pulled her clothes off and then he threw her into the water to wash the insects away."

Ashley tried to push away from Garick so she could hold on to the blanket, but he reached down and picked her up in his arms.

"Take her over there." Leslie pointed toward a patch of grass. "I'll get some ointment from my bag and some dry clothing for her and be back in a minute."

When Garick reached the grass, he sat down with Ashley in his lap. But she wouldn't look at him until he cupped her face in his hand and tilted it so that she couldn't avoid his eyes. He no longer looked angry, but Ashley still felt resentful and distraught.

"Sorry I yelled at you, honey," Garick murmured as he kissed her forehead. "But you scared me."

Ashley frowned, puzzled. "Scared you?"

"The way everyone was acting, I was afraid you'd gone for a swim and gotten yourself in trouble. Then, when I found out you were all right, I was angry with you for scaring me."

Ashley blinked at him thoughtfully. His reaction was that of someone who cared if she got hurt. But maybe he would feel the same way if any of his team were injured? He took his responsibilities as the leader pretty seriously, so she told herself she shouldn't jump to conclusions about his reaction.

Leslie returned with a tube of ointment and clothes. "Let's take the blanket away so we can get at those bites," she suggested.

Garick lifted Ashley off his lap and sat her down beside him.

Leslie inspected her skin. "You don't have as many bites as I feared," she commented absently as she smeared medicine on the welts. "Your clothes must have protected you quite a bit. And though I know the bites sting, they're not dangerous, Ashley. You'll just experience some discomfort for a while until they heal."

When she was done, she sat back on her heels and recapped the ointment. "I'll go wash out your clothes to make sure none of the insects is still in them, then help with lunch. You just sit and rest, Ashley. You've had a shock."

Leslie's kindness made Ashley's emotions rise to the surface again.

"I feel foolish," she said shakily, staring at her bare feet where several welts were visible.

"Why?" Leslie responded matter-of-factly. "We've all been bitten by pincers, and I'm sure we'll all get bitten again. We should have warned you about them, but I guess none of us thought of it. So it's not your fault you didn't know to look for them before you picked a spot to rest."

She patted Ashley's cheek as she got to her feet, then walked away.

Ashley glanced at Garick and discovered he was now looking at her nude body in a way that made a glow of warm pleasure heat her skin. But since now was not the time for physical intimacies, she regretfully pulled the blanket closer around her body.

He chuckled as he put his arm around her shoulders and pulled her against him. "Don't worry," he whispered huskily. "I'll save acting on what I'm thinking for tonight."

Wanting comfort more than anything else at the moment, Ashley turned her face into his neck, and he put his other arm around her, lying back on the grass to cuddle her for a few moments. It felt wonderful, and Ashley curved closer to him and slipped her fingers under his shirt to stroke his warm bare skin.

Immediately, she felt him begin to harden against her thighs and then he whispered, "Look at me."

She raised her head and he slanted his mouth over hers for a kiss. But the kiss was only a promise of what was to come, and it didn't last long. As he drew back, he said, "Time to get you dressed."

Hearing the desire in his voice, and seeing the heavy-lidded look in his eyes, Ashley didn't feel resentful that he'd stopped kissing her. She was pleased by her effect on him. But then Leslie returned with some food for Ashley. After Garick got to his feet, he pressed Leslie's shoulder with his hand in a demonstration of affection and smiled warmly at her before he walked away, leaving Ashley a little less complacent about her appeal where her husband was concerned.

Somewhat glumly, she dressed herself, then sat by Leslie as they ate their lunch. While she sat silent as Leslie chatted pleasantly about mundane things, she remembered the imprint of the animal track in the boulder under the pool and shuddered. The track must have been made after a volcanic eruption when the boulder was still cooling, but whenever or however it had been made, its owner had been huge.

Frowning as she recalled the skillfully drawn sketch Sandra had made, which gave no indication of the creature's size, Ashley wondered if Sandra had seen the tracks of a younger animal, one that hadn't reached its full growth. Or if she had deliberately concealed the fact that the animal was as big as it was. In any case, coming face to face with a creature of that size and trying to tranquilize it and study it was a far different prospect than Ashley had anticipated, and she didn't look forward to the task at all.

She had told Sandra she wouldn't let her down. But now, Ashley thought uneasily, if, instead of behaving like a cool-headed scientist when she finally found the animal, she would panic and run at her first glimpse of it.

"Mount up, people!"

Garick's call to get back on the trail interrupted Ashley's thoughts. But later, as she rode smarting from her insect bites, and then finally saw a smudge of green on the horizon that signalled they were nearing the jungle, her sense of dread returned.

Automatically, she turned her head to look at Blackmun, who rode beside her, needing the comfort of his calm, stoic strength. She was surprised to find him staring at her, and even more surprised at something new she saw in his normally enigmatic dark gaze—something more personal, more intimate.

Quickly, she looked straight ahead again, telling herself firmly that she had imagined what she thought she'd seen because it wasn't possible for any man on New Frontier to look at a married woman in that way. Her nerves were simply on edge as a result of thinking about what might lie ahead of her, and she cursed Garick's insistence that she come on this trip in the first place. If he hadn't, she could have stayed near civilization and learned some tame, mundane skills necessary for survival on New Frontier, rather than perhaps having to learn how to defend her very life against a creature she had a feeling was going to turn out to be anything but mundane. Too, separated from Garick for a while, she might also have been able to start loosening the emotional bonds he seemed to be wrapping ever more tightly around her heart the longer they were together.

Thereafter, whenever Ashley's eyes fell on her husband's broad back as he rode ahead of her, the expression in those golden-hazel depths was more disgruntled than admiring.

As Garick rode at the head of the team, he maintained his customary vigilance, even though his mind was preoccupied.

The intensity of the fear he'd felt when he'd thought Ashley was in danger had shaken him. It hadn't been at all the sort of fear he knew he would have felt had any other member of the team been at risk. It had been the sort of fear a person only felt when faced with the loss of a loved one.

It's come to that already, then, he told himself with thoughtful acceptance. *So what happens if I have to leave New Frontier? Will she want to go with me? And if she does, does she have what it takes to survive on a new planet considering what conditions are like at the beginning of settlement, and considering that the new planet may be a great deal more dangerous than New Frontier?*

Garick had never expected to have to ask himself such questions. He'd never expected to marry at all, had never expected even to fall in love. And perhaps one of the reasons he hadn't been in love was because he hadn't wanted to have to deal with the questions he was now facing, questions he couldn't answer because he didn't know how Ashley really felt about him other than that she liked their lovemaking. True, he thought her feelings were beginning to deepen beyond that, but he wasn't positive.

But even assuming she did come to love him, he still didn't know if she would love him enough to want to leave New Frontier for his sake and face life on a new planet without any of the amenities of New Frontier and far fewer people. That would take a degree of sacrificial love and an intensity of loyalty and courage that were highly unusual.

Frowning, Garick shook his head. Would he eventually regret accepting Ashley's proposal far more than had seemed possible at the time he'd persuaded himself he could marry her without suffering any long-term negative consequences?

God help you if she doesn't come to love you, or doesn't love you enough, he told himself grimly. It's going to take more than lust to make her give up what she can have on New Frontier without you, especially if you don't divorce her when you leave, for the kind of life she'd have with you somewhere else. And God help you if a new planet is a place where you can't take her even if she wants to go. Because if you have to go alone now, being alone won't be the same as it used to be. Instead, it will be sheer hell.

Chapter Twelve

The team set up camp barely in time to take shelter from the storm Blackmun had predicted. While Garick made some last checks to make sure everything was secure, Ashley stood alone in their tent, watching through the flap a fierce display of nature gone wild. Somehow, the lightning seemed to flash with more intensity, the thunder to reverberate with a more frightening crack here than on earth, and Ashley's nerves were responding unfavorably to the phenomena.

Besides her emotional reaction to the weather, Ashley was trembling with cold from the chill in the air, and her insect bites stung so painfully that she considered risking being incinerated by a streak of lightning in order to go in search of some of Leslie's ointment. But hard on the heels of her thought came such a tremendous flash of white lightning and such a deafening crack of thunder that Ashley quickly abandoned the idea and retreated further inside the tent. She huddled miserably on her sleeping bag with a caldera blanket over her shoulders.

Soon after, she heard Garick shouting something to Bud, and then he dived through the opening of the tent, splattering water everywhere. He was soaked to the skin, and his face indicated that he wasn't in the best of moods.

Since Ashley's own mood was at a particularly low point, she said nothing but merely watched irritably as Garick stripped down and began to dry off. Though she couldn't remain immune to the sight of her husband's hard, tanned body, she was still angry with him for dragging her on this trip. She also didn't appreciate that he hadn't even bothered to greet her yet.

A gust of wind shook the tent, and a violent shiver went through Ashley's body, drawing Garick's attention.

"Why don't you crawl into your sleeping bag?" he asked impatiently. "There's no sense in risking becoming ill because you're cold."

Ashley's irritation turned to hostility, and without answering, she glared at Garick as she hitched her blanket closer around her shoulders.

Frowning, Garick shrugged, then busied himself sorting out dry rations from a leather pouch. Tossing a packet of dry biscuits onto Ashley's lap, he took his own biscuits and crawled naked into his adjacent sleeping bag. He lay munching his unappetizing dinner and stared thoughtfully up at the ceiling of the tent.

Ashley had no appetite so she set the packet of

biscuits aside. She crawled into her own sleeping bag—because she wanted to, not because her husband had suggested it.

"You'd better eat," Garick said.

Ashley turned her back to him and curled into a ball. "I'm tired," she grated. "I'll eat in the morning."

Garick remained silent, and Ashley closed her eyes, willing her mind to ignore the cold and the discomfort of her bites and to go to sleep. It took a long while, but eventually, she drifted off. Sometime later, however, she began to dream that giant monsters with insane ferocity in their beady eyes and blood dripping from their jagged teeth were chasing her through the jungle. Garick stood off to the side, not making the slightest effort to help her.

Terrified, panting from her struggle to fight her way to safety through choked jungle greenery, Ashley heard the monsters behind her getting closer, and she screamed for Garick to help! Then she felt one of the monster's talons descend onto her shoulder, and she went completely wild, fighting frantically to free herself.

In the midst of her struggle, she heard Garick say, "Ashley, wake up! You're having a bad dream. Wake up!"

But she only came fully awake when he pulled her around to face him, then wrapped her in his arms. Her eyes flew open. As she realized she'd been dreaming, tears came to her eyes and she flung her arms around Garick's shoulders, clinging to him so tightly, her fingernails dug into his skin.

"Shh . . ." he murmured as he stroked her back. "You're safe, honey. Relax. It was only a dream."

As Garick continued to stroke her and to murmur comforting words in a soft voice, Ashley's tears gradually subsided and her grip relaxed enough to allow Garick to draw back slightly. He wiped her tears from her cheeks with his fingers and looked at her. His gaze was as warm and as concerned as his mutterings of comfort had been.

"Do you want to tell me what you were dreaming?" he asked quietly. "Sometimes it helps."

Ashley almost did as he had suggested, but then realized that it would be wiser not to. It made her angry that she couldn't speak freely, and remembering that Garick hadn't helped her in her dream, she turned her anger on him.

"It was just a nightmare!" she snapped, pushing at him now to release her.

He looked surprised before his gaze turned thoughtful. "Was I in the nightmare?"

Ashley glared at him resentfully and decided it wouldn't hurt to tell him that much. Besides, she was tired of repressing her feelings.

"Yes, you were," she said hostilely, "and you didn't do a thing to help me! It was like you wanted me to die!"

Garick grimaced and shook his head. But he didn't move away. Instead, he said, very gently, "Ashley, I've never wanted to hurt you. In fact, it made so little sense when you behaved like you thought I wanted to kill you just because you asked me to marry you, that I couldn't take it seriously. But if you're starting to dream that I want you dead, maybe we'd better get this out in the open. Where did you ever get the idea that I wanted to harm you?"

It was hard to maintain her anger in the face of Garick's tone and what he was saying, but Ashley tried. "Well, the first time I saw you, you looked so dangerous, I figured you were a barbarian like in the old days on earth. And I'm still not sure you're not!"

Garick shook his head again, his gaze drily sardonic. "I can't help the way I look, Ashley," he pointed out. "But I don't think I've ever done anything that would make you view me as a barbarian."

"You pointed your laser at me," Ashley muttered, aware, even as she said it, that she was grasping at straws.

"I was cleaning my laser and you walked toward me," Garick drawled.

Unable to think of anything to say, Ashley looked away and remained silent.

"Do you want me to spell it out for you?" Garick then asked.

Ashley said nothing, but her heart leapt as she wondered what exactly he meant.

"I will never shoot you, beat you, or harm you physically in any way, Ashley," he said with dry firmness. "And if anyone or anything else threatens you, I will do my best to protect you. Is that clear?"

It was clear, but it just wasn't enough. It wasn't all that Ashley wanted to hear. However, she nodded grudgingly, but firmly.

"All right. Now, we'd better get some sleep. If it will make you feel better, I'll crawl into your sleeping bag—" Garick stopped as Ashley raised her hand to wipe away the last of her tears and he spotted the welts on her skin. "Have you put anything on those bites since Leslie treated you this afternoon?"

Ashley shook her head.

"Do they hurt?"

Ashley nodded.

"Then slip off your shirt and I'll put some ointment on you."

"You have some here in the tent?"

"Most of us carry it in our packs," Garick said, smiling as he moved to get the ointment. "We've all been bitten."

"Well, you could have given me some to put in my pack," Ashley responded with sullenness as she began to pull her shirt over her head.

"Why? You're my wife. You can use mine."

Ashley knew it was a silly way to react, but Garick's words, and his earlier explanation that he'd never intended to hurt her, that indeed he would protect her, mellowed her mood considerably. Then Garick's warm hands were sliding over her skin, applying ointment, and her irritation melted away completely. In its place came comfort, security, and contentment —all of which were inevitably followed by a growing sexual arousal.

She tried to control her breathing as Garick stripped the rest of her clothing away and began to sooth the ointment over her hips, stomach, thighs, and legs. Their eyes met from time to time, and gradually, his hands administered a more sensuous massage. Then from his tone when he finally murmured, "Turn over," Ashley knew he was as aroused as she.

She turned onto her stomach, but after a moment's inspection, Garick murmured, "I don't see any bites on your back."

She started to turn over again, but Garick murmured, "No," and he put his hand on her shoulder, pressing her down slightly. Then he tossed the tube of ointment aside, and straddled her body with his legs. Leaning down with his hands on either side of her, he began to kiss her shoulders and her back.

Ashley's breath caught in her throat as he moved lower and lower, interspersing the kisses with gentle nips that sent shocks of heat through her veins.

Finally, he gathered her arms close to her sides, and then, supporting most of his weight with his elbows, he lay on top of her back, enveloping her with his hard, warm body. It was the safest Ashley had ever felt in her life. It was also, due to Garick's male hardness against her buttocks and the heat of his skin against hers, the most erotic she'd ever felt.

He kissed her neck, then her cheek, and she turned her head so that he could find her mouth. And for what seemed a long time to Ashley, his kisses displayed only a hint of the possessive fierceness she knew would come later.

The rain beat steadily on the tent, adding to Ashley's sense of being enclosed in a warm, safe, utterly sensual environment. She was erotically aware of every movement Garick made, and when he slipped a hand under her stomach, lifting her slightly, she parted her legs before he rasped his husky request.

She was more than ready for him, and he slipped inside her easily, after which she gently closed her legs again to hold him there. She didn't want him to begin the movements that would make their lovemaking end too soon. She wanted to savor the feeling that he was part of her now, that they would never be separate individuals again.

Garick allowed her time, whispering things she wanted to hear, kissing her, increasing her excitement until at last, she began to move. Then he joined her, matching her rhythm, and slipped the hand that supported her stomach lower, touching her in a way that made her forget that she didn't want his lovemaking to end too soon.

Before it was too late, he abruptly withdrew, wringing a cry of protest from her lips. The protest died away as he almost roughly turned her over, spread her legs, and entered her again.

Her breasts brushed his bare chest as he began the movements she craved, heating her senses further. She raised her hands to his head, twining her fingers in his thick black hair, and raised her mouth to seize his, meeting his tongue with her own.

The rest of it was too wild for Ashley to remember clearly later. She was left only with an impression of having been wrung dry of every emotion, every sensation, it was possible to feel. And when she rested in the cradle of Garick's arms after their lovemaking, she was filled with a sense of wonder and muted apprehension, unable to deny any longer that what she felt when the two of them were together like this was not lust. It was love.

"Sleep now, Ashley," Garick murmured with drowsy humor. "You're going to be tired tomorrow. And so am I."

Those last four words of Garick's should have been too simple, too mundane, to invoke a happy jolt in a sensible woman's heart. But Ashley, with a sense of fatalistic contentment, realized she was no longer sensible. She was in love.

This time when she slept, she did so with a smile curving her lips. And her dreams were no longer frightening, but rather hopeful . . . anticipatory . . . optimistic.

Garick didn't shake her awake the next morning, and when Ashley awoke, she was alone in the tent. From the slant of the sun outside the tent flap, she knew it was later than she usually rose. Smiling at her husband's consideration in letting her sleep late, she got up, threw a caldera robe around her, and grabbed some soap. She wanted to bathe before she made breakfast.

When she stepped outside the tent, she took a deep breath of the sweet, clean air and lifted her face to the sun, feeling a sense of well-being that infused her like an intoxicating drug. Jane emerged from her own tent and called out a cheerful "Good morning." Ashley started to ask if Jane knew where she could bathe, when Blackmun appeared. Since his hair was damp and he had a towel slung over his bare shoulder, Ashley asked him instead.

"I'll show you," he offered, turning back the way he'd come.

Ashley fell in step beside him, saying, "It's a beautiful morning, isn't it?"

Blackmun nodded.

"Where is everyone?" she asked next.

"Around."

Ashley gave up trying to make conversation and simply enjoyed the morning, her surroundings, and her own good mood until they walked through a stand of trees and she saw a small, clear pond that was fed by a gentle waterfall. Fronds and flowers ringed the water except for one area, where there was a natural decline giving access to the pond.

"Oh, how pretty!" she exclaimed as she hurried forward.

When she reached the edge of the pond, she started to shrug out of her robe, then paused. She realized that Blackmun was settling himself comfortably atop a rock nearby.

Ashley hesitated. Of course, Blackmun had seen her naked the day before, but that was an emergency. Was he afraid she might get in trouble again? Was that why he wasn't leaving? He'd always been unobtrusively protective toward her, and yesterday's experience might have made him even more so. Besides, he had to be psycho-programmed, and if she asked him to turn away or leave, it would probably insult him. Ashley was too fond of him to hurt his feelings.

Stoically stifling her modesty, she flung off her robe and ran as quickly as possible into the concealing water, squealing with shock when the coolness enveloped her skin.

Within a few minutes, she had adjusted to the temperature and felt warm again. Before bathing with the soap she carried, she swam a little, floated, splashed, dived for pebbles, and reverted to childlike playfulness before she realized she'd better get serious. The others would be waiting for her to cook breakfast.

As she scrubbed her body, she realized that Blackmun was no longer sitting on the rock. Instead, he was standing at the edge of the pool, focusing on her with an intensity she could clearly feel across the yards separating them.

Puzzled, she called out, "Is everything all right?"

He said nothing, merely nodded.

Still puzzled, Ashley finished scrubbing herself and washing her hair, then hesitated. It was time to leave the pool, but Blackmun was standing where she had to walk out, her towel in his hand. Obviously, he was waiting for her. Again, despite her nervousness and embarrassment at being nude and having to collect her towel from him, she didn't want to offend him.

Left with no choice, she kept her expression pleasantly neutral as she walked toward Blackmun. When she was close, she held out her hand for the towel, saying, "Thank you."

But Blackmun didn't extend the towel, and he was looking at her body with an expression that no psycho-programmed male on New Frontier should have borne. Furthermore, he startled her by launching into what was for him, a lengthy speech.

"You are beautiful, Ashley," he said huskily. "You look like a picture in this setting. All the colors, yours and nature's, complement one another."

"Well . . . thank you . . ." Ashley responded, feeling terribly awkward and shy. "Hand me the towel, will you? I'm cold."

That was a lie but she wanted to cover herself from Blackmun's intent stare. He didn't look as though his psycho-programming was going to hold much longer if she didn't.

It seemed to her that Blackmun handed her the towel with reluctance. She turned away from him and tried to use the towel to conceal as much of her body as she could as she dried off. She held it in front of her as she reached for her robe, which Blackmun had retrieved from the bank while she was drying herself.

"I'll hold it for you," he said, his tone quiet, but containing a definite sensuality that heightened Ashley's nervousness.

Her smile of thanks was slightly strained, but she slipped one arm into the sleeve of the robe without, she hoped, showing how much she wished he would just go back to camp and leave her alone. She was drawing the robe over her shoulders, her back to Blackmun now, when she felt his hands helping her, then instead of moving away, resting on her shoulders.

She was about to move out of his grip as naturally as she could manage when Garick's voice echoed in the silent clearing.

"Well, now," he drawled with a hint of sarcasm. "It must be nice to have one's own private valet on a trip like this."

Ashley stiffened. Blackmun stepped back. Then Ashley turned in the direction of Garick's voice and saw him standing a few feet away, hands on his lean hips, a hard look in his gray eyes.

"Don't you have something to do, Blackmun?" he asked, his tone containing a distinct note of male challenge.

Ashley glanced at Blackmun, but it was impossible to tell what he was thinking. He merely shrugged and walked away in the direction of the camp.

Ashley turned back to Garick. "I was just bathing," she said, trying her best not to make it sound like an excuse, but rather a calm explanation. "Blackmun showed me the pool, and I guess he stuck around to protect me. He must think I need protection after what happened yesterday."

Garick's eyes studied her coolly, his expression still hard.

"You think he stayed to *protect* you?" he asked disbelievingly.

"Well, what else?" she asked, her puzzlement in her voice. "After all, he's psycho-programmed, and, for all I know, he's married, though he's never said one way or the other. But surely you don't think—"

"Blackmun's not psycho-programmed," Garick interrupted, his tone grim. "Nor is he married."

Ashley was stunned. "He's not psycho-programmed?" she asked, bewildered. "But I thought all the men other than you were."

Garick shook his head. "Blackmun's a scout. He'll go on to other planets one day if any are found. That's why he's exempted. And until now, there's never been any problem with his lack of programming. He's never caused anyone any problems."

It was the first time Garick had mentioned the expectation that New Frontier's scouts might someday go to other planets, and Ashley hadn't wanted to bring it up herself. Nor did she want to get into a discussion about it now.

She eyed Garick warily. "Until now?" she repeated.

Garick didn't go into details. "Stay away from him, Ashley," he said in a tight, autocratic tone. "And don't mention his behavior toward you today to anyone. I don't want Tom or Leslie's husband to start worrying about him."

If Garick had asked her to stay away from Blackmun because *he* was jealous, Ashley would have been delighted to comply. But he didn't sound as though he cared about anything other than keeping the other husbands from becoming jealous. And the slight accusatory note Ashley thought she heard in his voice made it sound as though he were blaming *her* for Blackmun's behavior, which made her angry.

"I can't start avoiding him now," she said stiffly. "Not when we're all thrown together the way we are. It would be noticed. Besides, he's always been very kind to me, and I don't think he'd do anything to—"

She stopped because Garick grabbed her wrist, his eyes expressing a degree of anger she'd never seen there before.

"Hear me, Ashley," he ordered. "I didn't ask for your opinion. I said stay away from him and I expect you to do just that. Now get back to camp and fix breakfast."

Ashley jerked her wrist away. "Yes, master," she mocked scathingly as she pivoted on her heel and strode angrily away.

But even before she'd taken a few steps, her anger had turned to pain because the promise of the night before seemed to be fading to ashes with the light of day. It was stupid of her ever to have hoped that Garick might come to feel more for her than lust. But just because she knew her hope was stupid didn't make it any easier to feel it begin to die.

Garick fought the anger he knew was a result of sheer jealousy, as he watched Ashley walk away.

Damn it, he thought heatedly, *if she had to start getting interested in another man, she could have chosen better than someone who's in exactly the same position I am.*

But after calming down a bit, Garick realized Ashley hadn't exactly behaved as though she were interested in Blackmun. She had thought Blackmun was psycho-programmed. It was Blackmun who'd been showing the interest that had made Garick seethe with jealousy, and Ashley's reaction to his order to stay away from the other scout was more likely a result of sheer temper over his highhanded manner rather than anything else.

But it was the intensity of his jealousy that occupied Garick's thoughts as he headed back to camp. It was just one more indication that he had come to love the wife he'd only meant to protect and to seduce.

Chapter Thirteen

They were close enough to the jungle to hike to the outskirts for some preliminary exploration, leaving the camp intact. Each team member, as usual, would go his or her separate way.

After breakfast, as everyone went to their tents to gather supplies, so did Ashley. And since Garick wasn't with her, she took the opportunity to study the map Sandra had given her. Then she collected some rations and a flask of tea and added them to the knapsack she'd packed at Sandra's.

As she came out of the tent, Garick arrived at the entrance.

"I see you're ready," he said, glancing at the knapsack on her shoulders. "Give me a minute to collect a few things of my own and we'll be off."

"We?" Ashley repeated warily. It hadn't occurred to her that Garick would want to accompany her, and because she feared what she might find, she wished he could. But considering the secret nature of her mission, she couldn't let him. "Ah . . . it's better if I go alone, Garick. Too many people might spook the animals I hope to find, and—"

"Ashley," Garick interrupted with dry reasonableness, "considering your lack of experience, I'm not about to let you go off into the jungle alone. Besides, I've tracked more animals than you've probably ever even seen. You don't have to worry about me spooking them. It's more likely it will be the other way around."

Before she could make any further protest, he turned to duck into the tent, but just then Brisby called to him, and he stopped.

"I'd better see what he wants," he said to Ashley. "You pack my knapsack. I'll be back in a few minutes and then we'll get started."

Left with no choice, Ashley ducked into the tent and half irritably, half gratefully, packed his knapsack. It wasn't that she wanted to go into the jungle alone. But she would be letting Sandra down if Garick or anybody else was with her when she spotted the creatures the veteran zoologist had instructed her to find.

But maybe they wouldn't see the animals today, she thought as she reemerged from the tent. And Garick was right. She wasn't experienced. So it probably was just as well for him to be with her. She would watch and listen carefully, and once she had gained some experience, perhaps he would let her go off on her own another day.

"Thanks," Garick said as he approached and took

his knapsack out of her hand. "Come on. Let's go."

Garick set a fast pace and Ashley had her work cut out for her to keep up. Vegetation had been sparse around the camp, but now, as they approached the jungle, there were more plants of such a bewildering variety and strangeness that Ashley didn't even try to equate them to what grew on earth. That was Brisby's job.

There wasn't much animal life around, however. Just the lizards, and the kirkas, and in the sky, an occasional bird with an impressive wingspread.

"There's a ravine coming up," Garick said over his shoulder.

A moment later, Ashley joined him at the edge of a fairly deep gash in the orange-colored earth. The sides of the gash were dotted with stones and boulders.

"Follow my steps," Garick instructed. "This could slide if we aren't careful."

Ashley followed him over the edge, placing her feet where he had. They had made it about halfway to the bottom when she felt the ground shift under her, slowly at first, then with gathering momentum.

"Garick!" she yelled, and he reached back and took her hand just as the soil gave way and they went tumbling to the bottom amidst a shower of dirt and rocks. Ashley somehow ended up ahead of Garick, and he landed on top of her, knocking the breath from her lungs.

She was struggling to breathe as he lifted himself on his elbows and gazed with alarm at her face.

"Are you all right?" he demanded.

Even in her present state, Ashley couldn't help but

be pleased by his sincere concern for her.

"I think I'm all right . . ." she panted. "Just the breath knocked out of me."

He slid to her side, but his eyes remained anxiously on her face. And when her breathing became more normal, he said, "Lie still. I want to check you over . . . See if anything's broken."

His examination was not at all unpleasant and by the time Garick was convinced she was fine and helped her sit up, Ashley was smiling.

Garick smiled back, then dipped his head to kiss her. But the kiss was interrupted by a roar the like of which Ashley had never heard before in her life and which raised the hair on her nape. Garick was on his feet in an instant, looking around him.

Ashley scrambled to her feet and stood by his side. "What was it?" she asked, sounding as shaken as she felt.

"I don't know." Garick shook his head as he took his laser out of its holster. "I've never heard anything like it before. And I don't like hearing it now."

Since the sound obviously hadn't issued from the ravine, he then said, "Stay here, Ashley. I'm going up top to have a look around."

"Not on your life!" Ashley protested, moving with him.

Garick stopped and gave her an impatient look. "Ashley, do as I say!"

"Animals are my job," she reminded him, holding his gaze firmly.

He hesitated a second. "All right. Maybe it's better if you're with me. Just don't get in my way if I have to shoot."

Ashley nodded, then followed as Garick began to

climb the far side of the ravine. Just before they got to the upper edge, Garick lifted a palm to motion Ashley to stop, then cautiously raised his head over the edge.

"I don't see anything," he murmured. "Come on."

They climbed over the lip and once they were standing, Garick strode at a rapid pace toward the jungle. Ashley caught up with him.

"Maybe we should go back to camp," she suggested. "The others . . ."

Garick shook his head. "Not until I find out what we're facing. We need to know what it is, how many of them there are, and how dangerous they might be before we make any decisions at all."

After that, Ashley had to walk so fast to keep up with Garick that she didn't have breath left to ask more questions or to make suggestions.

Once they entered the belt of trees that marked the beginning of the jungle, Garick had to slow down in order to force their way through the heavy vines and ground cover. There was no breeze, and the hot, fetid air soon had both of them wet with perspiration. Ashley was behind Garick, wanting nothing more than to return to camp and to fling herself into the pond, when Garick stopped and she bumped into his back.

"What is it?" she whispered, peering around his body.

"A path."

Ashley moved to his side and saw what he meant. It was a path all right, but not one made by any human. No human would have needed so much room to pass through the jungle. The tunnel through the trees and undergrowth had obviously been formed by an animal of tremendous size forcing its way through, crushing and breaking everything in its path.

Her expression denoting her dread, Ashley could only hope that whatever creature had passed this way fed on vegetation, not flesh. Sandra had said that was possible, but Ashley, remembering the talons the creature possessed, doubted it.

Garick was staring at her face and when she glanced his way, he said, "Maybe I'd better take you back to camp. The rest of the men and I can come back tomorrow and try to find whatever did this."

Ashley wanted to take him up on his offer, but her conscience wouldn't let her. Garick's obvious concern for her well-being swamped her with guilt because of her secret pact with Sandra. But she was bound by the vow she'd made, and she also felt honor bound to try to find the creature herself rather than endanger anyone else. But she knew Garick wouldn't let her continue on her own.

"Let's go on just a little farther," she temporized. "Maybe we'll learn something that will help us be better prepared when we do come back."

To her surprise, her reply brought a smile to Garick's lips and a light of admiration into his gray eyes.

"That's my girl," he said quietly. "Then come on. Let's see where this tunnel leads."

As Garick started down the tunnel, and Ashley followed him, she was far from feeling pleased that she had managed to inspire her husband's admiration for her courage. Instead, she felt like scum for withholding information from him. But she couldn't tell him about her own part in the secret pact without revealing Sandra's part as well. If she did that, Garick, and probably the rest of the community, would likely be furious that their supposedly responsible zoologist had kept information from them. Besides, what would be the point of confession now other than to ease her conscience? Ashley wondered glumly. Garick was already aware that a new animal existed, and now that he knew, he would investigate cautiously, and at this point, that was all anyone could do.

As they continued walking, Ashley became aware of a faint, unpleasant smell. It grew stronger the farther they went, until it became a nauseating miasma that made Ashley's head ache and her stomach roil with nausea. She began to dread taking her next breath. And then she noticed that Garick was no longer holding his laser down. He was pointing it ahead of them. It made sense and his action comforted her, because the stronger the odor, obviously the closer its source. But his action also made her realize she should get the tranquilizer gun and darts out of her backpack.

She was about to when a duplicate of the roar she and Garick had heard reverberated down the tunnel, only now it was heart-stoppingly thunderous and far too close for comfort. Before the first roar died away, an answering roar, delivered as an enraged challenge, sounded and Ashley felt terror rising in her throat. Facing one of the creatures was bad enough, but there was obviously more than just one animal ahead of them.

Garick quickly took Ashley's arm and pulled her to the side of the tunnel. "Stay here," he whispered. "If anything comes into view, duck out of this tunnel and find cover and stay as quiet and still as possible."

To Ashley's horror, he then started down the tunnel by himself. She couldn't let him go alone, and she fought her terror as she began to follow. The roars ahead were now accompanied by sounds that could only mean a battle was taking place.

Garick didn't look back until he reached where the tunnel began to open, and when he saw her, a grimly frustrated expression appeared on his face momentarily. But he didn't order her to go back and motioned her to come closer and join him.

When Ashley reached his side, he took her arm, whispering, "Keep quiet. We'll stay out of sight."

Keeping to the side of the tunnel, they moved forward until the tunnel opened out into a clearing, where Garick, with a sharp intake of his breath, stopped.

The clearing was roughly a mile across and in the center of it was a small, shallow lake. At the edge of the lake, two huge, green-gray beasts were locked in mortal combat.

Ashley, staring open-mouthed and horrified, at first couldn't believe her eyes. The size and appearance of the beasts, as well as their savage brutality, were beyond all of her experience, or even her imagination, for her to accept them as real. True, the creatures vaguely resembled pictures and skeletons of ancient earth dinosaurs she'd seen, but they were also alien in a way that froze her blood.

Their teeth resembled razor-sharp daggers, and it was all too obvious what they were capable of, for both beasts had streams of blood flowing from huge wounds where massive chunks of flesh had been torn away. But teeth weren't these creatures' only weapons. The talons on their relatively short forelegs and on their hind legs upon which they stood were equally deadly and were being used with savage effect.

The effect of watching, hearing, and smelling such butchery was so grotesquely overpowering, Ashley thought for a moment she was going to faint. But she found the strength to fight her body's reaction and to use her eyes and mind to catalog the rest of the beasts' appearance.

The animals had strong hindquarters that tapered into smaller stems below the knee joints. Their powerful, reptilian bodies were the size of small hovercraft, and the short forelegs extended from their shoulders. Their heads were large bony blocks set on sinuous necks, and their jaws looked capable of swallowing a full-grown caldera almost whole.

Bellows of rage shook the trees surrounding the clearing, and the water in the lake was churning into small waves as a result of the fierce battle between the two monsters. It was obvious the struggle would be to the death, but Ashley didn't see how either creature could survive. Their flesh was already so dreadfully mangled that there was scarcely a patch of undamaged skin anywhere she looked. Yet neither seemed to be weakening, and at last, the smaller of the two beasts used its lesser stature to cunning advantage.

First, it raked one sharp-taloned foreleg across the cold, bulbous eyes of its adversary, blinding it. Then it dipped its head under the dripping bloody maw of the larger beast and fastened its teeth into the soft flesh of its throat, hugging the body with its forelegs to protect its own underside. With a tenacity that made Ashley shudder, it held on despite the rips scored in the flesh of its back by the talons of the blinded beast's forelegs.

Finally, the smaller beast's cunning and tenacity paid off. The larger beast's hind legs trembled, buckled, and then gave out beneath its huge body, and the creature landed on its side in the water. But even then, the smaller monster maintained its hold on its adversary's throat, forcing its huge head under the water and keeping it there until the beast drowned, and the last ripple of life left its monstrous body.

The smaller beast's obvious intelligence frightened Ashley almost more than its gruesome appearance and huge size, and she moved closer to Garick and gripped his arm. But what she saw next completely unhinged her.

With its enemy conquered, the victor raised its head, gave a roar of triumph that shattered the air, then immediately began to feed. Slashing its teeth into the soft underbelly of its vanquished foe, it ripped the skin open, then plunged its head into the cavity and began to gorge with a ferocity that brought the taste of bile into Ashley's mouth.

She started to tremble and retch, and Garick turned sharply toward her, grabbing her shoulders.

"Don't, Ashley!" he ordered in a fierce whisper.

But it was too late. She fell to her knees and lost the contents of her stomach. For long, agonizing moments, she was unaware of anything other than her own misery. When she at last gained control of the retching, Garick pulled her to her feet and started dragging her back down the tunnel.

"Move!" he urged in a whisper. "Run!"

But again, it was too late. The monster in the water abruptly stopped feeding and turned its malevolent bulbous eyes in their direction. An instant later, it roared a challenge and started toward them, moving with a speed that belied its bulk.

Garick threw Ashley out of the way, and as she stumbled to the side, he fired his laser. Ashley saw a flash of light explode against the beast's left eye. But though the animal screamed, it didn't stop. Garick fired again, blinding its other eye, but apparently guided by smell and hearing, seemingly impervious to its own pain, the creature advanced.

Garick continued to shoot, yelling at Ashley to run, but none of his shots did more than cause a momentary pause in the attack, and Ashley was too frozen by terror to make her legs move. However, she did find her voice, and she screamed at the top of her lungs, "The throat, Garick! Aim for its throat!"

As if obliging her, the creature raised its head to roar another rage-filled challenge, and Garick with a lightning move of his thumb adjusted his laser to spew a wide beam, then shot straight at the animal's exposed throat. Immediately, an explosion of blood and tissue filled the air, and since the beast was so close to them now, Ashley and Garick were spattered with the gore.

For a moment, Ashley thought it had worked, for the animal stopped its onward rush with an abruptness that was startling. Then her heart rose in her throat and she at last got her legs moving and started stumbling backward, as the animal started forward again.

"Ashley, run!" Garick yelled as he reached to steady and help her. "My laser's empty now!"

But in the next instant, the beast's legs gave out and it crashed onto its side, landing with a force that made the ground shake.

For a long moment, neither Ashley nor Garick moved. Then Ashley collapsed onto her knees and buried her face in her hands, trembling so badly she thought she might fall apart. Garick, on the other hand, walked toward the beast and stood watching until the last twitches of its death throes ceased and it lay still. He kicked its sides a few times, making certain it was dead. Then he headed back to Ashley, pulled her up into his arms, and held her until her tremors subsided to a faint shuddering. He tilted her head up with his hand, inspected her gore-spattered face, and started to smile.

"Well, I've seen you look better," he commented with a calm humor that helped to restore her emotional balance. "But once you've got a clean face again, you'll do."

A short burst of spontaneous, half-hysterical laughter issued from Ashley's throat, surprising her, and more important, further restoring her equilibrium.

"So glad you approve," she stammered out with dry sarcasm through her still-chattering teeth. "My appearance is uppermost on my mind at the moment, of course."

"Then let's go down to the lake and wash you off," Garick said, grinning, as he slipped his arm around her shoulders and turned her toward the lake.

"Are you crazy?" Ashley snapped, hanging back. "I want to get out of here."

"Before you've taken any samples of blood and tissue from that thing on the ground?"

Garick's tone was mild, but firm, and when Ashley looked at his face, she was dismayed when she realized he was serious.

"You can do it, Ashley," Garick added. "After seeing how you've behaved in the last hour or two, I believe you can do anything."

It was a sincere compliment, too sincere and delivered with too much quiet emotion for Ashley to ignore it or to act counter to it. Besides, he was right about getting samples. The more they learned about these creatures, the better.

Nevertheless, a deep shudder went through her body before she was able to reply, much less to act.

"All right," she nodded. "I'll do it."

Garick gave her a smile that made her capitulation almost worth it, then led her to the lake, where they both knelt and washed their faces and hands.

When they stood, Garick lifted Ashley's knapsack from her shoulders and held it out to her. "I'll keep watch while you do what's necessary. But, damn, I wish I had another laser. Mine's drained."

"Sandra's is in my knapsack," Ashley said. Then, as Garick began to rummage inside the sack with a relieved look on his face, she added, "There's also a tranquilizer gun and darts in there. I was about to get them out when we heard the beasts again and it was too late."

"You did fine, Ashley," Garick said. Unfortunately, as he pulled the laser out of the sack, Sandra's map came with it and fell to the ground.

Ashley quickly reached for it, but Garick was faster.

As he picked it up, the part of the map Sandra had marked in red was clearly visible. Garick started to put it back in the knapsack, then frowned, and took a closer look at it while Ashley restrained herself from snatching it out of his hand.

"Did Sandra give you this?" he asked, now openly studying the map.

Ashley cleared her throat. "Yes."

Something in her tone must have alerted Garick and he raised his head to stare at her in a way that made her apprehensive. But to her relief, he didn't say anything. Instead, he shoved the map into the knapsack, along with his now useless laser, put Sandra's in his holster, then handed her the bag.

"Do what you have to do as quickly as possible, Ashley," he said. "We need to get out of here."

Ashley didn't have to be reminded of that fact twice. While Garick paced, studying the surrounding area with a sharp eye, she took the knapsack to the fallen animal and reluctantly knelt beside it.

The carcass stank and Ashley was glad she didn't have anything left in her stomach to throw up. Though covered with blood, the monster's hideous wounds were still visible. Too, one of its empty eye sockets seemed to stare at her with a malevolence that made her shudder. But she stoically blanked her mind as much as possible to everything but the task at hand, extracted a scalpel and specimen bottles from the knapsack, and began to collect blood and tissue samples.

When she was done, she stowed the bottles in the knapsack and got to her feet. "I should make drawings," she said, but Garick shook his head.

"Do it later from memory. I'll help. Right now, let's get out of here."

Ashley never remembered much about the long journey back to camp because shortly after they started walking, shock overcame her. She was so physically weary and emotionally wrung out, it was an effort simply to continue to put one foot in front of the other. She was too numb even to keep an eye out for more beasts.

It was almost dark by the time they arrived at the campsite, and by then she was unable to deal with the questions and curiosity of the other members of the team. Thankfully, Garick turned her over to Leslie, who helped her to the tent while Garick dealt with the questions.

As Leslie stripped away Ashley's filthy clothing, Ashley was docile and uninvolved, and even began to doze while Leslie gave her a sponge bath. She fell asleep when Leslie left to fetch hot sweet tea, and resisted when Leslie came back and woke her.

"I think you're in shock, Ashley," Leslie explained firmly. "You need this. Now drink up."

It seemed easier to comply than to continue to resist, so Ashley obediently drank the cup of tea, then sank back into the warm folds of her caldera sleeping bag, letting Leslie tuck her in.

She awoke only once during the night, in reaction to a movement from Garick, who was sleeping in her bag. But after he pulled her against the warmth of his body and whispered, "Go to sleep. You're safe, and I'm going to keep you that way," she drifted to sleep again, secure in his arms and in his assurances.

* * *

As Garick held Ashley in his arms, his brow was creased with the contradictory feelings he felt far too often where his wife was concerned. On the one hand, he was immensely pleased by the way she had handled herself today. Her behavior gave him hope that if another planet was discovered and he had to leave New Frontier, and Ashley wanted to go with him, she could handle the hardships and danger of being among the first to try to tame a new planet.

On the other hand, what the hell did the markings on that map she had mean?

Garick knew Sandra well enough that he couldn't really believe she would hide anything of importance from the exploration team. But when he looked at the map more thoroughly in the morning, if he discovered she had suspected the existence of those creatures and hadn't told anyone, he would have to accept that she had put the whole team in danger for reasons he couldn't even begin to fathom.

He would also have to accept that Ashley had known too and that she had been disloyal in hiding the truth from him.

Disloyalty was the one thing Garick couldn't tolerate. To him, it was the root of all evil. And the possibility that the woman he had come to love might be guilty of it was more than he could deal with, unless it turned out he had no other choice.

Chapter Fourteen

Ashley awoke to the sounds of activity outside the tent and the smell of food, which meant she had overslept. Hastily, she climbed out of her sleeping bag and reached for her robe. The sponge bath Leslie had given her the night before wasn't enough to make her feel really clean, and she wanted to bathe in the pond before she dressed.

As she was donning the robe, however, she glanced at Garick's sleeping bag and froze. Sandra's map was spread out, which meant Garick must have looked it over. But that didn't mean he had put two and two together and come up with the truth, she told herself anxiously as she picked up the map, folded it, and put it in her knapsack. After all, she hadn't picked the route yesterday. Garick had led the way.

But she still felt guiltily uneasy as she gathered

soap and a towel and stepped out of the tent. She wanted very badly to be honest with Garick, even though telling him her secret wouldn't make any difference now to how things developed as far as the animals they'd found were concerned. Easing her conscience would only subject Sandra—and Garick, if Sandra carried out her threat to lie about his part in all this—to the censure of the community. Therefore, she couldn't justify speaking up unless she was given no choice.

She was walking to the pond when Garick came striding toward her. From the look on his face, Ashley had a sudden premonition that the time when she would have no choice other than to tell the truth had arrived.

"I'll walk with you," he said as he took her arm, and though he spoke quietly, Ashley detected a certain grimness in his tone, while his grip on her arm was not exactly gentle.

Normally, Garick's manner would have angered her. But after what had happened the day before, Ashley felt he had a right to be angry. They both could have been killed, and if any member of the team had come upon the animals unaware, they could have been killed as well.

Garick led her to a boulder near the pool and sat her down. Then he towered over her.

"Tell me about the map, Ashley," he said, his voice softly threatening, his gray eyes angry and disgusted. "Tell me I'm wrong in thinking you knew what we were going to find yesterday and didn't warn me or anyone else."

Ashley shook her head. "I didn't know we'd find what we did," she said with quiet resignation.

"Sandra believed there was a predator, but she thought it would be like a bear or a lion. And I—"

Garick interrupted, his tone hard now. "Sandra thought," he repeated. "Why don't you tell me the rest of what Sandra thought—and especially why you didn't tell me what she thought?"

It wasn't an invitation. It was an order. But for once, Ashley didn't resent Garick's manner. She was ashamed because she realized now she could have told Garick about the track in the boulder under the pond without implicating Sandra. And she *should* have told him because the size of the track wasn't that of a lion or a bear. So she had used bad judgment, especially in not telling Garick about her secret pact with Sandra.

It wasn't easy, but Ashley started at the beginning and told him everything other than the part about Sandra threatening to say Garick had known about the tracks from the beginning. She didn't tell him because she wasn't sure if he would believe her, and because, since their budding relationship was probably now over, she didn't want him to know how much she'd come to care for him. Not that he'd believe that either under the circumstances.

"I was going to go alone yesterday, Garick, remember?" she finished her explanation. "Surely you don't believe I would have been willing to do that, or to put you or anyone else in danger, if I'd known what those monsters are really like."

"Oh, I believe that," Garick said disgustedly. "I saw your face when you got your first glimpse of them. And I'm glad I did go with you or you wouldn't have come back alive," he added, his voice rasping with his anger now. "But you realize it's sheer luck no one else found those animals yesterday. If they had, they might not have hit the creatures in the right spot or there might have been too many of them to fight. And if anyone had been killed, it would have been at least partly your fault."

What Garick said was true and Ashley couldn't deny it. She said, with quiet misery in her voice, "I know. And I'm so very sorry."

Being sorry wasn't enough, and Ashley knew that as well.

Obviously, Garick agreed. "Damn it, Ashley," he grated with raw fury. "I can't believe you kept something like this a secret from me! Do you feel no loyalty toward me at all? Do you have no trust in me at all? And even if you have no regard for me, what about the rest of the team? Did you feel no responsibility toward them?"

Although Ashley actually felt she had no right to a defense, she reacted automatically. "I made a vow!" she protested. "And I didn't know I would be putting anyone at risk! Sandra's the real zoologist, and she told me the team was trained to be ready to face anything! She told me there wouldn't be any risk if proper precautions were taken—"

"And how was anyone supposed to know they needed to take precautions since you didn't tell anyone about the tracks!" Garick interrupted.

Suddenly, he bent forward and grabbed her shoulders, giving her a hard shake that Ashley knew displayed only a portion of the anger he felt. But she wasn't frightened. She was only miserably bereft.

"*Any time* you keep *anything* from me, there's a risk!" he grated. "This is not a zoo or a park, Ashley! This is a new world that hasn't been thoroughly explored yet! If you couldn't trust me, then you should have trusted your own common sense—if you have any, that is!"

As abruptly as he'd seized her shoulders, he let her go and straightened. Then he turned his back on her and ran a hand violently through his thick black hair. Ashley would have felt the tense anger inside him even if he hadn't already made it clear how he felt.

She wanted to tell him she did trust him. The last thing she'd wanted was to be disloyal to him. Though she was guilty of bad judgment, she wouldn't have put him or anyone else in danger deliberately. But she didn't think her words would make any difference, so she apologized again, and then went on to deal with the future, not the past.

"Garick, I'm sorry," she said with sad sincerity. "I'm truly sorry. But I can't change what I did now. And we have to decide what to do about our discovery."

"Oh?" He looked at her over his shoulder, his face and his tone hard. "And what do *you* suggest we do?"

Ashley shook her head. "I'm not a fully trained zoologist, Garick, but I do know enough about the subject to realize those animals, as vicious as they are, as disgusting as they are, might be vital to the overall ecology of the planet. Sandra is sure that they might be, so she kept their tracks secret. She was afraid if the ranchers found out about them, they might react by wanting to wipe the animals out before we know if that would be a terrible mistake. So it seems to me we need to protect them until a full-scale study is done concerning their role in the planet's ecology."

Garick turned around. "If I recall correctly, they

seem perfectly capable of protecting themselves," he pointed out in a tight voice. "And who do you suggest we get to do the study?" he added sarcastically. "You and Sandra? Hell, I'll be lucky to keep you two from being lynched if anybody finds out what you've done, much less turn you loose to conduct a *study*. Besides, Sandra's ill and you aren't qualified to do such a study on your own, even if I'd let you face those glorified lizards again!"

Ashley winced, but kept to the point. "There's an agency on earth that's supposed to oversee such matters here, isn't there?" she insisted. "Surely, there are already provisions in place for an eventuality such as this."

Garick sighed heavily. "There are," he clipped out. "But if you think the people on New Frontier are going to sit still until a message can be taken to earth to send a team from the Agency for the Preservation of Alien Animal Species here, then wait for that team to arrive, and wait even longer while they conduct their study, don't count on it."

"That's what Sandra was afraid of." Ashley nodded. "But the animals haven't caused the ranchers any losses yet, Garick, and if we equip the ranchers who are most likely to be threatened by the animals with tranquilizer guns and darts, they could protect their herds without killing the—the lizards, as you call them. And I guess at this point, that's as good a term as any other."

Garick narrowed his eyes, and Ashley, wishing she could have kept her mouth shut, bit her lip. He was staring at her as though she were even more alien to him than the monsters—and certainly more stupid.

"Garick, I realize the tranquilizers may not work on the lizards," she said. "But neither do lasers unless you hit them in the right place." She hesitated, then made an offer she would have given almost anything not to have to make. But she had a lot to atone for, and it seemed to be the only way to do it. "So if you'll just let me try a tranquilizer on one of them—" she started to say.

Garick cut her off before she could finish her sentence. "No," he said flatly.

"But—"

"No."

There was absolutely no give in his voice and Ashley, half glad that he was adamant, half resentful that he was cutting off the only logical thing to do, tried another tack.

"Then we'll just have to tell the ranchers to try tranquilizers, and if they don't work, where to shoot the animals with lasers to stop them. But since the ranchers haven't so much as even seen one of those creatures yet, it probably won't even come up. There should be plenty of time for a team from earth to get here and do what's necessary before anyone is threatened by one of the lizards."

"Ashley, I can promise you, if one of our ranchers sees one of those things, they aren't going to be interested in tranquilizing it," Garick said, angry again. "All they're going to want to do is kill it. And even if they did tranquilize it, what happens when it wakes up? And what if they have to face several of them at a time?"

"But what if there are only a few of them, Garick?" Ashley countered. "What if the ranchers kill off every one there is, then we later find out that they formed some vital link in the chain of nature here that can't be replaced?"

"Even if that turns out to be the case"—Garick shook his head—"you know from what we felt yesterday that at the moment anyone is faced with one of those monsters, the survival instinct will take over and ecology isn't going to matter. In any event, the whole thing has to be presented to the rest of the community and voted on. It isn't your decision, nor is it mine."

"Not if there's already a regulation in place concerning such matters," she pointed out. "The people here will have to obey the regulation or—"

Garick cut her off again. "Not if the agency never even learns these creatures existed," he said. "The community may decide to handle the matter on their own and keep any knowledge about the creatures and how they dealt with them to themselves."

"But you wouldn't let them do that, would you, Garick?" Ashley asked, frowning at him in disbelief.

He didn't answer. But Ashley thought his expression said his loyalty would stand with his fellow citizens of New Frontier, not with a government agency on earth.

Ashley knew then she faced a choice, and she closed her eyes in despair. But she had lost so much already—her relationship with Garick, her acceptance by the people of New Frontier, and her own self-respect—that she didn't think going with her conscience could cost her anything else. If it had ever been possible that Garick would take her with him when and if he ever left New Frontier, she was sure the possibility had disappeared now. And her standing in the community would be destroyed the instant they learned what she had done at Sandra's insistence. That left only her self-respect to be salvaged, and there was only one way to do that.

She opened her eyes and looked at Garick, her expression disclosing her heartsick regret at what she had to say.

"Then I'll do it, Garick," she said quietly. "The people need to know that they can't kill all the lizards and try to keep it a secret, because I'll tell the agency what they've done. I hope their knowing my intentions will keep them from deciding to act in a way that might turn out to be against their own best long-term interests."

She couldn't tell what Garick's reaction was. His eyes and his face were blank. But she assumed she had just ended their relationship, and the assumption was almost more than she could bear.

When he finally spoke, Garick's tone was flat, displaying none of what he felt. "Take your bath. Then get back to camp. We'll be returning to Blanton's ranch as soon as we pack up."

He turned and walked away. Ashley stared after him with tears in her eyes, drooping shoulders, and an inner certainty that she had just lost a precious, irreplaceable future which, for most of her life, she had never suspected she could ever want as badly as she did.

A little over an hour later, the team started their return journey to the Blanton ranch, and it was obvious that Garick meant to set a hard pace. As

Ashley rode along, she wondered what he intended to do once they reached civilization. After telling everyone about the lizards, and her decision to protect them, would he recommend organizing a hunting party anyway and lead it?

But no matter what Garick or the rest of the community might decide, Ashley didn't contemplate changing her mind. The more she thought about it, the more she realized she would have been obligated to stand up for what was right even if she'd still had something left to lose.

If science had proven anything in the past few decades, it was that the whole ecosystem of a planet was interrelated and interdependent, even if human beings did react with fear, hatred, or disgust to some of the species that had a place in that pattern. It would be worse than bad judgment if Ashley didn't act to prevent the destruction of the lizards. It would be criminal to stay uninvolved if the community's decision proved to be an irrevocable, disastrous mistake, like those which had been made so often on earth, and which the settlers' children would have to cope with later. Even if standing up for the best interests of New Frontier's children meant Ashley would never have any children of her own, then so be it.

Mentally reaffirming her position didn't make Ashley feel any less depressed over what her past mistakes had already cost her and were likely to cost her in the future. But it did strengthen her in some measure and that was all she could ask for under the present circumstances.

After several hours of riding, Garick called a halt

for a short rest beside a stream. But instead of climbing down from her femura, Ashley sat where she was for a few moments, wondering if she had the strength to dismount. She was absolutely exhausted.

"Are you all right?"

Blackmun stood beside her and there was real concern in his dark eyes.

"I'm just tired," Ashley said.

"Let me help you down," he offered. But as he was reaching for her, Garick rode up, his expression cold.

"I want you to ride on to the Blanton ranch, Blackmun," he said. "Tell them to expect us tomorrow around noon. But don't tell them about the lizards yet. I'll do that when the rest of us arrive. Go on. Get moving."

Blackmun, his face blank, moved away, mounted his femura, and headed north. Garick swung down from his femura and came to Ashley's side. She was too tired to speak as he lifted her from her saddle, then took the reins of both femuras, and led them to the stream to drink.

Ashley followed and knelt to bathe her face, then found a spot to lie back and rest. After a few moments, someone sat down beside her, and she opened her eyes. It was Garick.

After making sure no one was within ear shot, she asked, "Do you intend to tell everyone what Sandra and I did?"

He gave her a look she couldn't interpret and shook his head. "No." Then his look turned harder and he added warningly, "And you're not going to tell anyone either, understand?"

Ashley didn't understand for a moment. Then she

realized Garick wanted to protect Sandra, which was ironic when Sandra had been willing to ruin his reputation to get what she wanted. But Garick was right to protect Sandra, Ashley decided. The zoologist was ill, and there was nothing to be gained by revealing that she hadn't disclosed the possibility of a predator's existence on New Frontier.

"All right," she agreed, then asked, "what exactly will you do when we get back, Garick?"

"Call a meeting. But if a decision about what to do isn't made quickly, I won't wait for it. Somebody needs to return to the jungle and make sure those beasts aren't straying in this direction, and I'm going to get a team together to do just that."

Before Ashley could respond, he got to his feet, calling for everyone to mount up.

A few minutes later, they were on the move again. By the time it was dark and they stopped to make a fire and spread out their sleeping bags without bothering to set up the tents, Ashley was numb with fatigue. She fell asleep before she could eat or even wrap the folds of her sleeping bag completely around her.

As he was making a last check around their makeshift camp, Garick found Ashley sprawled uncovered. He knelt beside her, covered her gently with the folds of the sleeping bag, then stared down at her face, thinking she looked like an exhausted child.

But she wasn't a child, he reminded himself. She was an adult woman capable of making adult decisions. And one of the decisions she had made recently was incomprehensible to him. A person owed loyalty to one's teammates, to one's fellow citizens, and most particularly, to one's spouse.

Garick didn't fault Ashley for wanting to protect the lizards until a study determined their role in the ecology of New Frontier. In fact, he agreed with her that that was the most sensible way to proceed as long as the safety of the settlers wasn't compromised. But he also admired her courage to face the whole community's disapproval willingly to do what she thought was right. He'd admired her courage yesterday as well, when they'd found the lizards.

No, it wasn't Ashley's courage Garick faulted. It wasn't even the fact that she was capable of bad judgment that really disturbed him. Everyone was guilty of bad judgment at some time or other. After all, even Sandra, whom Garick would have thought cared enough about her fellow team members to go to great lengths to protect them, had let her judgment be clouded by her obsession with ecology. It was the disloyalty to *him* that Garick not only faulted, but which made him feel sick at heart.

Garick wouldn't have liked Sandra's disloyalty, and irresponsibility toward her fellow teammates and the citizens of New Frontier even if Ashley hadn't been involved. But he almost hated the woman because she *had* involved Ashley in her deception.

Still, it had been Ashley's choice to agree to the deception, and by doing that, she had made it clear that she didn't understand the first thing about marriage—or at least about the kind of marriage Garick thought the only kind worth having.

When he was settled in his own sleeping bag, Garick lay awake thinking, mulling his options. Ashley might not understand the importance of loyalty, but he did. Though he didn't think their marriage could last now, that conclusion didn't release him from his obligation to protect her as long as she was his wife. That, plus Sandra's illness, was why he didn't intend to tell anyone what the two women had done. Besides, there was no point in making such a revelation now. It would only add fuel to the fire that would erupt when Ashley stated clearly her position about the lizards to everybody.

Garick dulled the pain of Ashley's disloyalty and its effect on their marriage by thinking about the best way to handle the situation so that the people of New Frontier would be safe from the lizards, while protecting the lizards from the people of New Frontier.

Chapter Fifteen

Rex Blanton, the owner of several thousand acres of land and uncounted numbers of caldera, was a blond, middle-aged, prickly-tempered man whom Ashley hadn't liked at first meeting him. She thought either the isolation of his ranch and the authority he wielded there had molded him into an insular tyrant, or else it was just his nature to be arrogant and unpleasant. Her heart sank as he greeted them from the porch of his ranch house for he already looked grim and he didn't even know about the lizards yet.

"I'm glad you're back, Deveron," were his first words as they rode up. "I've just lost twenty caldera to some predator that leaves nothing but crushed bones behind, and I want something done about it."

Ashley didn't move, and her eyes on Garick's face were anxious. He gave her a warning look, then glanced back at Blanton.

"We know there's a predator," he said as he dismounted. "That's why we're back early. I need to call for a hover to take me back to Plymouth so the community can figure out what to do about it."

"Hell, I *know* what to *do* about it!" Blanton snorted. "We round up some men and go hunting!"

Garick shook his head. "The decision is not up to you. Besides, you don't know what you're facing yet, and I do. Ashley will draw you a sketch, and we'll tell you what we know so far."

He moved to Ashley's femura to help her down. As he lifted her from the saddle, he held her a moment and whispered, "Not a word about you and Sandra and the tracks, hear?"

She nodded and when she was on her feet, she turned back to her femura to collect her knapsack.

Inside, Blanton's wife, who was a strapping, hearty woman and looked capable of running a ranch on her own, immediately gathered everyone into her kitchen to eat a hot meal while Blanton went to his radio to call for a hover. Garick kept Ashley in the living room.

"I want you to make two drawings of the lizards," he told her. "I'll take one of them with me to Plymouth, and in the other, show where to hit the beasts to kill them. It may be that Blanton and the other ranchers won't come across any of them any time soon, but if they do, they'll be sensible enough to run instead of fight. If they're not sensible, or if they aren't given a choice, I want them to know how to protect themselves. I'll also take the tissue and blood samples to Sandra. I know she's ill, but maybe she'll be able to do some preliminary studies on them at least."

As Ashley got out her sketching materials, she asked, "What do you think the community will decide to do, Garick?"

He shrugged. "I don't know. But I know what I'm going to recommend."

Ashley glanced at him sharply. "Wipe them out?" she responded in a slightly bitter tone.

At that, Garick's gray eyes went cold. "It always seems to come easy for you to think the worst where I'm concerned, doesn't it, Ashley?"

Ashley frowned, realizing that Garick had some justification for his comment.

Before she could say anything, however, he continued, "Those monsters are intelligent as well as savage. That being the case, it won't take them long to figure out that the caldera ranches are an easy source of food. I imagine that wasn't the case until the ranchers started grouping the animals together and fencing them in, but now that some of the caldera no longer roam free, I expect the lizards will take advantage of the situation. So I'm going to recommend that we teach them that the caldera on the ranches are not such easy prey."

"By killing them," Ashley responded, frustrated. "Garick, you're only guessing. We don't yet know how many beasts there are, their normal habits, or anything else about them other than that they fight and eat one another, which is probably only to protect their territory, and that's natural for any species. I told you before, we need to assess the situation and learn some hard facts before we take the chance of slaughtering a whole species."

Garick's stare grew even colder. "If it comes to protecting humans rather than preserving a species, especially as unattractive a species as the lizards," he said flatly, "my choice is easy."

"But you're not talking about protecting humans," Ashley pointed out. "You're talking about protecting calderas."

"It could turn out to be the same thing," Garick said. Then, before Ashley could argue further, he added, "I need to eat before the hover gets here. You spend your time while I'm gone telling Blanton and his men about the lizards. Try to convince them to act sensibly instead of risking their lives."

"But I want to go with you and present my side of the argument to the community!" Ashley protested.

Garick had turned away to go to the kitchen, but he turned back and gave Ashley a look filled with such harsh bleakness, she took a step backward.

"And of course," he said in a flat tone, "it's beyond your capacity to believe that the two of us might be on the same side, isn't it."

It wasn't a question, and he didn't wait for an answer. He turned and walked away.

It was just as well he didn't wait for an answer, because Ashley wouldn't have known what to say. Neither could she find anything to say a short while later when Garick took the rest of the team with him back to Plymouth on the hover, but left her behind at the Blanton ranch.

Garick stared out the window of the hover as it took off. Ashley stood alone, watching everyone leave, and she looked almost as vulnerable and unhappy as the day he'd acted against his better instincts and accepted her proposal of marriage. And, in spite of everything, Garick felt the same mixture of protectiveness and desire toward her he'd felt then. Only now he had to fight as well against the even stronger emotions he'd grown to feel for her during their marriage.

I wish I'd listened to my instincts, he thought bitterly, *and saved myself a lot of grief. Who needs a wife to whom loyalty is just a word. But it's not surprising she can't be loyal when, in spite of living with me and making love with me for several weeks, she's determined to ignore the evidence of who I really am and would rather think of me as a vicious barbarian whose instincts are on the level of those lizards.*

Determinedly, he turned his thoughts away from Ashley and toward the more practical matters on his immediate agenda. But before he could come up with a solid plan to protect both the lizards and the inhabitants of New Frontier, the hover arrived in Plymouth and Garick found not only Jim Jacobs awaiting him, but five of the elected council who had been in town and available to come to a meeting.

"Blanton told us as much as he knew when he called for the hover," Jim said worriedly after greeting Garick. "What's going on?"

"I'll tell you on the way to Sandra's, Jim," Garick said. "We need her help. Let's see what she can learn from the blood and tissue samples Ashley took from the new animal we found. Let's get on the road. There may not be much time to waste."

"Garick, I'm not sure Sandra *can* help." Jim shook his head. "She's here, not at her place. She got worse, and we brought her into town so we could look after her. She's at Leslie and Andrew's home. Come on, we'll go over there. But don't get your hopes up."

At his first glance of Sandra's face, Garick knew she

was not only unable to help; she was near death. But she was conscious, and as Garick explained things to her, as well as to Jim and the other members of the council, she looked horrified, then worried, then resolved. Finally, she gathered enough strength to ask for paper and pen and to speak to Garick alone.

Somewhat puzzled, Garick looked at Jim, who nodded.

"The rest of us will get started discussing what to do," he said, and he and the other council members left the room.

When they were alone, Garick sat quietly beside Sandra's bed, listening as she talked in gasps while she wrote. And at what she said, the pain in Garick's heart began to lift. But when Sandra finished writing and speaking and quietly closed her eyes for the last time, another kind of pain settled in—the pain of watching another human being die.

After a long while, Garick gently took the paper from Sandra's lifeless hands and stood up. He knew what to do now, and there was little time to lose.

Late the next day, Ashley was tired and frustrated from trying to convince Rex Blanton and the other ranchers whom he'd called not to obey their macho instincts and instead to act rationally. She stood slightly apart from the others, watching a hovercraft land near the ranch house.

Garick was the first to alight. Ashley noted how weary he looked and realized he probably hadn't slept since he'd left the day before. She wanted to go to him, put her arms around him, and insist that he rest. But since she supposed he would probably fend her off and make her feel a fool for behaving as though their relationship hadn't changed, she forced her eyes away from his tall, lithe frame and looked to see whom he'd brought with him.

Blackmun, Bud, and Jim were there, along with a tall, confident-looking older man Ashley didn't recognize. But Ashley's heart sank when she saw that Sandra wasn't with them. The zoologist would surely have made the trip if she had been able to. Since she hadn't, Ashley knew she would have no help at all if it turned out she had to fight the decision to kill all the lizards.

Garick came to her side and took her arm. "Let's find some privacy. I want to talk to you."

He led her around the corner of the ranch house to a wooden bench under a whistle tree. When the wind was strong, the curled leaves emitted a gentle whistle that was pleasant to hear, but today there was only a soft breeze, and they only hummed.

After Garick sat down on the bench beside Ashley, he leaned back, stretched out his long legs, and closed his eyes wearily.

"Have you slept at all?" Ashley asked, her eyes gentle as she inspected the fatigue lining his face.

He shook his head, opening red-rimmed eyes to look at her. "Sandra's dead, Ashley."

Ashley stiffened, then shook her head in denial. But Garick's eyes echoed the truth, and she had to accept it.

"She died yesterday . . . after we told her about the lizards." Garick shrugged fatalistically. "But she wrote you a note first."

He withdrew a folded slip of paper from his pocket and handed it to her.

Ashley hesitated, then opened the paper, and read

the scrawled words. "It's up to you now. Save those animals. See that my book gets finished and that credit is given where credit is due."

The rest was indecipherable, but it didn't matter. The note had been unnecessary. Sandra hadn't written anything Ashley didn't already intend to do.

"What did the council decide?" she asked Garick. She knew there hadn't been time to put the matter to a full vote of the entire community.

"To send some of us back to the jungle to assess the situation and let those of us on the spot decide what's best to do," Garick said as he got to his feet.

Ashley stood up as well. "When do we leave?"

"As soon as everyone is ready. Some of the single men from in and around Plymouth and supplies for an extended stay will be flown to meet us where we last camped. The rest of us and Blanton and some of the other ranchers will fly from here."

He hesitated then, looking as though he wanted to say more. His expression wasn't as cold as it had been when he'd left for Plymouth, but neither was it warm. In fact, it was very odd, and Ashley couldn't fathom what he was thinking. Then he shrugged and said, "Let's go to the house, Ashley. I need some sleep."

As they walked, Ashley stifled her desire to have a much more personal conversation with him, not that such a conversation would have done any good. Garick hadn't bothered to kiss her when he'd arrived which indicated that he had no intention of maintaining the fiction that they were happily married even in public now, much less in private.

When they reached the house, Jim was explaining to everyone the course of action the council had decided upon, while the stranger who'd come with the group from Plymouth sat quietly in a corner. Ashley glanced at him, wondering who he was, but then her attention reverted to Garick. He spoke briefly to Mrs. Blanton, then disappeared from the room, heading in the direction of one of the bedrooms.

Soon after, Ashley was asked to relate her version of the incident with the lizards, which she ended with a brief statement of her views on the matter.

"I feel it only fair to tell you, Jim," she directed her final statement to her old friend as the mayor of Plymouth, "that if a decision is made to illegally exterminate the lizards wholesale, I won't remain silent. I'll make sure the Agency for the Preservation of Alien Animal Species on earth learns what's been done. I want everyone to take that into consideration before making a final decision."

Jim frowned, but it was Rex Blanton, predictably, who exploded. "You mean you'd see human beings die rather than those ungodly lizards?" he asked, his tone scathing.

"I don't believe such a choice will have to be made," Ashley replied, holding on to her patience. "Not if we're careful and sensible."

"But if it does come down to such a choice, it's clear whose side you'll be on!" Blanton sneered.

Jim stepped in before Ashley could reply. "Let's leave that kind of discussion until we find out exactly what we're facing," he said with firm authority. "Right now, Blanton, you need to get the supplies ready to take to the jungle!"

Blanton stormed out of the house, and Ashley,

unwilling to say more, quickly left the room and walked to the bedroom she'd used the preceding night, looking for some privacy. But when she opened the door and saw a sleeping Garick sprawled across the crude bed against one wall, she hesitated, then left the house by the back door to take a long walk instead.

Several hours later, Ashley stood alone at the campsite near the jungle, watching as the last load of gear was removed from one of the hovercrafts. Judging from the nature of the glances directed her way, she thought she would likely remain alone for the duration of her life on New Frontier. Blanton had obviously spread the news that she was a traitor to humanity. And from the amount of weapons that had been brought to the site, it was just as obvious that the prevailing view echoed Blanton's: Shoot first and worry about New Frontier's ecology later.

Ashley knew their fear had provoked bloodlust among them. Primitive and powerful, it would likely only get worse once they saw the creatures, especially if they were engaged in the sort of battle she and Garick had witnessed. Though she couldn't really blame her fellow humans for their reaction, she still couldn't agree with it. She would remain firm, she knew. But she also knew that being firm had already cost her dearly and would likely cost her even more before the matter was settled.

The sound of voices raised in an argument drew her attention, and she turned her head to look to her right. Her heart leapt in consternation as she saw Rex Blanton confronting Garick.

"How do we know you're not just as much of a traitor to the people on New Frontier as your wife is, Deveron?" Blanton sneered. "I doubt she'd have the guts to fight us if she didn't have your support!"

Ashley expected Garick to behave with his usual calm control, but to her dismay, he tensed his muscles and directed one of his most dangerous looks at Blanton—a look that presaged violence.

"Watch your mouth, Blanton!" he said, his voice an icy threat. "If you'd use your head for something besides counting caldera, you'd remember that my wife, like every other citizen of New Frontier, is entitled to her own beliefs. Just as I, as her husband, whether I agree with her or not, am obligated to protect her safety. If I were you, I'd keep that in mind. Any man who threatens her will have me to deal with, and dealing with me won't be as easy as trying to bully and intimidate a woman half his size!"

Though Blanton's hostility didn't diminish appreciably, it was clear he wasn't going to risk taking Garick on in a physical confrontation.

"Well, what are we supposed to do here?" he demanded. "Sit around and let your wife play scientist while those lizards make off with every head of caldera on the planet and kill human beings as well?"

"You haven't lost more than a couple of dozen caldera so far, Blanton," Garick said in a hard tone. "And so far, no one other than Ashley and I has even seen one of those beasts. So until somebody is actually threatened, let's keep our heads. We're here to see what we're up against and then decide what to do, not let our imaginations run away with us and act like scared animals ourselves!"

With a final hard stare at Blanton, Garick turned on his heel and strode away, heading toward the hovercraft.

As he disappeared inside, Ashley heard Blanton utter a final shot. "We'll see about that, Deveron. You haven't got any caldera to lose! We do!"

Placing his hand on his holstered laser in a meaningful way, Blanton nodded sharply at the men around him, then walked to his nearby tent, and ducked into it.

Ashley looked at the faces of the remaining men, trying to discern if they were as bloodthirsty as Blanton. To her relief, though some of them obviously agreed with the rancher, many others had impassive expressions, indicating that they would withhold judgment on the matter until they knew more.

Ashley turned her back on them, regretting with all her heart that the hostility she had brought down on her own head was spilling over onto Garick. She knew he hadn't had any real choice in defending her, and she was grateful for his loyalty, despite the fact that it had most likely been given more out of principle than personal desire. But she intended to make clear that far from swaying Garick to her view, she had no influence on him at all.

Ashley then walked to the cooking tent to begin sorting out food supplies. Bud came into the tent as she was working, and though he didn't look hostile, she didn't really expect him to be as friendly as he'd been in the past.

"If you're hungry, Bud," she said in a neutral tone, "it will be awhile before a hot meal can be prepared. But there are some dry biscuits if you don't want to wait."

Bud shook his head, and when he spoke, his words had nothing to do with eating.

"Ashley, do you think it's wise for you to stay here?" he asked worriedly. "I mean, aside from the danger the lizards represent, some of the men are in an ugly frame of mind, and your presence here is going to make it harder than it has to be for Jim and Garick to keep control."

"Bud, I'm not staying because I want to," Ashley replied drily. "I'm staying because I feel it's absolutely necessary that I be here. And in fact, I think my presence may make it easier for Garick and Jim to keep control of the situation. I'm the objective eye, the witness who may make the others think twice before they give in to impulses they might later regret. And surely, you don't think the good citizens of New Frontier would resort to violence to get rid of me?"

In a gesture of frustration, Bud ran his hand through his hair. "Hell, I hope not, Ashley. That would be unforgivable. But knowing how hot some of the men's tempers are getting, I'd watch my step if I were you. If you had an accident, some of them wouldn't be all that unhappy about it."

Ashley considered Bud's opinion, feeling depressed and anxious. But she couldn't really believe anyone would go that far, and she finally shrugged and shook her head.

"I'm sorry, Bud," she said with quiet resignation. "But I'm staying." Then she added, "But I don't want anybody blaming Garick for my position, Bud. So I'd appreciate it if you'd make it clear to people that while he's my husband, he's his own man. My opinion is not his."

Bud shook his head. "To convince anybody completely, Garick would have to stop protecting you, Ashley, and he won't do that. Hell, if it were my wife, I'd do exactly the same as he is. And so would all the other men concerning their own wives. So whether he agrees with you or not isn't the point. He's helping you."

He shrugged and left the tent, leaving Ashley with a decidedly guilty conscience. While she was ready to take the consequences for her own actions, she didn't think it fair that Garick should have to simply because he had the misfortune to be married to her—and not even of his own choice.

Worried, she turned back to work. But after a few moments, she sensed she was being watched, and turned sharply on her heel to look at the tent's entrance. Blackmun stood there, staring at her with an intensity that pricked her already-overwrought nerves.

"What is it, Blackmun?" she asked in a sharper tone than she'd meant to use. "I'm sorry," she apologized quickly. "My nerves are on edge."

Blackmun walked toward her, moving with the gliding grace that made his passage silent and slightly spooky.

"Did you come to ask me to go away from here, too?" she asked as he arrived at her side. "If you did, you might as well save your breath. Bud was just here for the same reason and I turned him down."

"I do want you to leave here," Blackmun said softly. "But not alone. I want you to leave with me."

Ashley stared at him, wondering if he meant what she was afraid he did. When Blackmun reached to take her hands in his own, staring into her eyes in a way that left little doubt of his feelings for her, she felt a great deal more depressed than flattered.

"We can take the hovercraft back to Plymouth and be off New Frontier soon," he said in his soft voice. "When we went back to Plymouth to tell people about the lizards, we found out a couple of new planets have been discovered and will need to be explored. Garick will be asked to go to one of them when he's done here, of course. But I'll be sent to the other, and you and I can go there together."

It was the longest speech Ashley had ever heard from Blackmun, and in a way she was touched. Furthermore, had she cared for him in the way he obviously cared for her, his proposal would have been the perfect answer to the problems she knew she would face when the matter of the beasts had been settled. Because when the time came to resume her normal life on this planet, she doubted she was going to have a life that would be a happy one.

She had ruined her chance to have a good marriage, and she was positive that when Garick did leave New Frontier—a prospect that made a shaft of pain surge through her heart—he wouldn't take her with him. She was also in the process of losing her place as an accepted member of the community and had no chance of returning to earth. So any sane woman would have welcomed Blackmun's chance to start a new life on a new planet with relief.

But Ashley's conscience wouldn't let her accept his offer. She didn't love him. She would never love him. It would be unfair to burden him with a mate who only viewed him as a friend when he might someday find a woman who would truly love him. Besides, whether Garick wanted to be married to her any longer, whether they were ever again together as man and wife, Ashley felt married to him for life.

"I'm sorry, Blackmun," she said gently. "I can't."

Her answer sparked such pain in his dark eyes that Ashley tried to ease it.

"Blackmun, I know Garick won't want me to go with him when he leaves to explore one of the new planets," she said with resignation. And at seeing the look of puzzled surprise in Blackmun's eyes, she added, "Oh, yes, it's true. He thinks I've been disloyal to him, and you must know how he feels about loyalty. And I also know I won't have an easy time of it here after we've settled the question of the lizards. Blanton seems intent on convincing everyone that I'm also guilty of disloyalty to the community. But that doesn't mean it would be fair of me to go with you to another planet, not when I don't love you. Not when you'll eventually find someone who will love you the way you deserve to be loved. But I'll always treasure your offer, Blackmun. And I'll always love you as a friend."

Though the pain was still in his eyes, Blackmun raised one of her hands, gently unfurled her fingers, and pressed his mouth to her palm. It was a tender rather than a passionate gesture and Ashley's eyes welled with tears as he stepped back, gave her one last lingering look, then turned on his heel.

But then he stopped short, and Ashley froze as well. Garick was standing in the tent flap, and it was obvious he had seen Blackmun kiss her hand. Ashley didn't know if he'd heard their conversation, however, and she didn't find out because Garick immediately turned and left.

Blackmun glanced at her over his shoulder and hesitated. But Ashley shook her head at him, and he reluctantly left her alone.

When he was out of sight, Ashley collapsed onto a nearby box, feeling completely drained and dejected. If only it had been Garick who had asked her to go away with him, she would have been ecstatic. But as things were, she felt as if she'd lost everything. She put her face in her hands to press her fingers against her eyelids to stem her tears.

After a few moments, she told herself to stop thinking about what might have been and to deal with reality. Then she made herself get to her feet and continue to sort supplies.

Feeling betrayed by his old friend, wanting to lash out at him, Garick instead made sure he stayed away from Blackmun. With the volatile atmosphere already simmering in the camp, a fight would ignite a fire that would be difficult to put out.

But while his feelings toward Blackmun were violent, his feelings toward Ashley were entirely different. He wanted more than anything to go to her and put things right between them. But again, the atmosphere in the camp made that a bad idea. Though it was a bitter pill to swallow, given Garick's feelings about Ashley and loyalty, there was a limit to the outward support he could safely show her now without sabotaging everything both of them wanted to accomplish.

His willingness to defend her from physical attack

was to be expected and would be accepted by the men. But anything more than that would compromise the facade of objectivity Garick had to maintain to ensure respect and control. The only sensible thing to do was to wait awhile before getting things straight with Ashley.

Knowing that being sensible was the least of what he wanted, it was a testament to his strength of will that he followed his head instead of his heart and stayed away from his wife.

Chapter Sixteen

After the camp was in order and the evening meal consumed, the men sat around a huge campfire, their mood tense and jumpy. There were sporadic bursts of conversation, but for the most part, they stared into the flames or cast worried, speculative glances southward toward the jungle.

Ashley sat apart, nursing a cup of hot tea. And then Garick strode into the center of the circle of men and everyone turned to listen as he outlined the plan of operation for the next day.

"There are about twenty of you," he began without preamble, speaking in a calm, carrying voice, "so tomorrow you'll divide up into teams, five men to a team. The hovers will take one team north, one team south, and so on about ten miles in each direction from the lake and clearing you've all heard about.

You'll spread out and head toward the clearing. But don't get so far from one another that you won't be able to aid any man on your team who gets in trouble. Keep your radios open and sound an alert the instant you see any sign of the beasts. If there's any wind, make sure you place yourselves so your scent isn't carried to them. Don't try to kill them unless you're directly threatened. Send for me. I'll be in a hover, and I'll get there as fast as possible."

Ashley listened to the part about not trying to kill the beasts with wry scepticism. She wondered how many of the men would kill first and lie later that they'd been directly threatened.

Paulus Glignan, the man who had accompanied Jim and Garick from Plymouth, spoke up then. Ashley still didn't know who he was. She had overheard some of the men say he hadn't been on New Frontier long and that no one else knew much about him either, other than that he had not yet filed for land, nor had he indicated that he had other skills needed by the community. But he seemed to have Jim's confidence, so he was accepted as a new emigrant.

"Be more specific, Garick. What exactly happens if anyone sees one of the creatures?"

Garick smiled wryly. "If you are alone at the time and the lizard hasn't spotted you yet, radio the position of the beast to your team and to me. Everyone should keep their radios open to hear the alert. Then hunker down and hide from the beast if possible. If that isn't possible, run like hell until and unless it becomes obvious that you're going to have to kill or be killed. And if you have to shoot, aim for the throat because a hit anywhere else won't stop them."

There was a stirring in the audience, and when it died down, Garick resumed his speech. "Remember," he said. "Our purpose here is to try to find out how many of the beasts there are, where they are, and how much of a threat they represent to our people and our animals. This is not a hunting party. This is a reconnaissance."

"Thanks to your wife," Rex Blanton responded sarcastically. "I'm surprised you don't want us to try to capture one of those monsters so she can study it at close range or keep it for a pet."

Garick's face remained impassive, but Ashley knew him well enough by now to realize he was angry. But she wasn't. She was worried that Garick might respond to Blanton's baiting in a way that would diminish his stature among the men.

"You're welcome to *try* to capture one if you think you're up to it, Blanton," Garick drawled with insulting humor. "But it would be sort of a wasted effort since my wife, after facing one of those beasts more bravely than some men might, has already decided that she doesn't want one of them as a pet, and she's already taken all the blood and tissue samples she needs for scientific study as well."

It wasn't strictly true, of course. A great deal more study of the creatures needed to be done by more qualified scientists than Ashley. But Garick's statement had the effect of winning her a few grudging looks of respect from some of the men. However, as Ashley noted Blanton's flushed and angry face, she didn't feel relieved. She had a feeling Blanton would be a potent enemy, and she didn't want Garick to have enemies—not because of her at any rate.

Paulus Glignan again asked a question, diverting everyone's attention from the hostility shimmering between Garick and Blanton.

"Is it true that there will be legal consequences should we kill the creatures for any reason other than being directly threatened by them?"

Ashley tensed, expecting the reaction that immediately followed Glignan's question. The men stirred and murmured angrily as they looked in her direction.

"No agency on earth can charge us with depleting a whole species if we kill only those animals which threaten us directly," Garick said, "and the speed, intelligence, and savagery of these beasts constitute a direct threat to any human they see. Keep that in mind and try to make sure they don't spot you if you can possibly help it."

Ashley sighed. Garick's statement, though correct, could also be interpreted as an encouragement to kill and excuse the killing later by claiming there had been a direct threat.

"If you see more than one of them at the same time," Garick added, "it goes without saying that you need to be doubly cautious. True, the evidence so far points to the fact that they're as dangerous to one another as to anything else, but we don't know enough yet to be absolutely sure they wouldn't act in concert against another species."

Garick then appointed guards to patrol the outer perimeters of the camp in turns during the night and suggested the rest of the men go to their tents and rest.

As the men headed for their tents, Ashley stayed where she was for another few moments. She was reluctant to go to hers and Garick's tent because she knew the atmosphere there would no longer be one of shared intimacy. Instead, it would likely be tense and hostile.

As she procrastinated, Paulus Glignan approached her. She got to her feet and looked at him inquiringly.

"Your husband's speech sort of took the teeth out of your promise to expose any action that violates the Agency for the Preservation of Alien Species' rules, didn't it, Mrs. Deveron?" he asked, his tone light and noncombative.

Ashley didn't reply because she didn't want to expose Garick to any censure from the agency. Instead, she shrugged and turned to pick up her cup from the boulder where she'd left it.

"So what do you plan to do now?" Glignan persisted.

"Watch, learn, and suggest whatever action seems to fit the situation once we know more about what that situation is," she said in a clipped tone.

She wanted to end the conversation, and she began to walk in the direction of her tent. But Glignan, instead of moving away, accompanied her.

"Of course," he went on in a conversational tone, "if you look at things objectively, it makes sense to discourage the lizards from preying on the ranches for food because if they get spoiled by easy pickings, there's a bigger chance of people as well as caldera getting hurt. But if the lizards are intelligent as well as savage as you and Garick claim, then they will realize those 'easy pickings' represent a threat to them, and perhaps they'll move farther south to safety. That will not only preserve them as a species until a team from earth can get here to study them, but will make the population of New Frontier breathe a lot easier."

"I agree," Ashley said. "Unless, of course, they aren't as intelligent as Garick and I presume. Or unless there are so few of them that by the time they learn their lesson, it's too late because they've all been slaughtered."

Glignan gave her an understanding smile. "That's a worst case scenario, Mrs. Deveron. Let's hope it doesn't come to that. Meanwhile," he added, as they came to the tent and Ashley stopped walking, "let's all get a good night's sleep. It promises to be a long, hard day tomorrow, and in any case, sleep will ease your worries. Good night."

With a wink and a wave, he strode away in the direction of his own tent, leaving Ashley to stare after him in thoughtful puzzlement. Her conversation with Glignan had left her with the definite impression that he was on her side. But she wasn't sure, just as she wasn't sure what good it would do her if he was on her side, to put much hope in his attitude.

Ashley ducked inside the empty tent, and decided the best way to avoid a very uncomfortable situation was to pretend to be asleep when Garick came into the tent. This time, she would do a better job of it than she had on their wedding night.

As it turned out, she didn't have to pretend. She hadn't slept well the night before. She was so physically and emotionally exhausted, she had barely closed her eyes before she was practically comatose.

* * *

Garick slipped inside the tent with a lantern in his hand. He could see that Ashley was lying very still in her sleeping bag, and he frowned. He hadn't counted on her being asleep. But maybe she was just pretending, the way she had on their wedding night.

He stooped beside her, holding the lantern so he could see her face. She certainly didn't look like she was pretending. In fact, she looked so exhausted, he felt guilty about what he did next.

"Ashley?" He gently shook her shoulder.

Ashley didn't respond at all.

Sitting back on his heels, Garick shook his head. "Hell," he murmured impatiently. Then he stood up, undressed, blew out the lantern, and without bothering to be quiet or careful about his movements, crawled into Ashley's sleeping bag beside her. She didn't wake, however, not even when he cradled her in his arms, kissed her, and stroked her breast.

Garick finally gave up and went to sleep, frustrated.

Chapter Seventeen

Garick didn't approach Ashley the next morning until after everyone had eaten and the men were beginning to form into teams.

"You'll come with me in the hover," he said, holding her gaze in a way that meant she wasn't to argue.

"But I could guide—"

"Ashley," he cut her off, unyielding, "you'll come with me in the hover."

It made sense when Ashley remembered what Bud had said about how some of the men wouldn't mind if she had an accident. Accidents would be easy to arrange in the jungle.

After the hovers had taken the four teams to their designated locations, she made no protest and climbed aboard a hover with Garick when one of them returned to pick them up.

The pilot flew the hover back and forth over the jungle. They saw nothing but an unending spread of green and the now deserted clearing and lake where Ashley and Garick had witnessed the savage battle between two of the beasts. As the time passed, there was no word from any of the men on the ground.

Finally, as they were passing over the clearing once again, Ashley spotted the small figure of a man break through the foliage surrounding the clearing and walk toward the lake.

Garick saw the man as well. "I think that's Bud," he said to the pilot. "I'll see if I can raise him on the radio."

A few seconds later, Ashley heard Bud's voice crackling over the radio.

"Not a sign of them, Garick," he declared. "The others should be reaching the clearing any minute, but they haven't made radio contact, so I assume they haven't seen anything either."

"Roger, Bud," Garick responded. "But keep an eye out anyway. Don't get careless."

Gradually, the clearing filled with the other men until all twenty were in sight. None had seen any sign of the lizards. Ashley was both relieved and puzzled.

"Bud, you and Blackmun lead the teams back to camp," Garick was saying over the radio. "I'm going to fly further south and see if the lizards might be heading in that direction. If you see anything on your way back to camp, call me on the radio."

He clicked off the radio and instructed the pilot to head south. Then he picked up a map and studied it.

Ashley knew the map showed the jungle extending southward before it ended and the desolate area separating the jungle and the southern pole area began. Since the green below her was mostly impenetrable, she stopped trying to see, and waited until they passed over it. When the green gave way to areas of barren, rocky, recently volcanic territory, she sat forward again, her gaze more intense.

The pilot reduced his speed now that the view was better, and as Ashley gazed downward, it was like seeing an empty moonscape. Black dust and rocks, with only an occasional hardy thorn bush or a deep gully to break the monotony, composed the landscape for miles—until she caught a flash of movement down below that made her straighten abruptly.

"Garick . . ." she said hesitantly, straining her eyes.

"What is it?"

He turned toward her, but before she could say more, the pilot uttered a whistle of astonishment. "Look at that! God, they look like something out of prehistoric earth!"

Ashley, Garick, and the pilot gazed with fascination as a whole string of the beasts appeared out of a gully that had previously hidden them. They were moving as a herd, not as individuals, and Garick echoed Ashley's thoughts as he noted the fact.

"They look like one big happy family now, don't they?" he commented with puzzlement.

"Maybe they're all females," Ashley suggested. "Maybe the two we saw were males. Perhaps it's mating season and the males fight over the females."

"Maybe so," Garick responded drily, "but from where I sit, it looks like the larger beasts down there are male and the smaller ones female. So if your theory's right, then the mating season and the fighting must be over and everybody's getting along again."

"I wonder where they're heading," Ashley said, perplexed. "Why would they leave the jungle and head for a desolate area where there isn't any food?"

"There may be at the pole area," Garick responded. "I flew down there once briefly, and where the volcanoes are dormant, it's hot, steamy swamp. There may be animals there they can feed on."

"And maybe it's time for the females to have their young," Ashley added. "I don't know if they lay eggs or produce live offspring, but if they do lay eggs, maybe they need the heat for the eggs to hatch."

As Ashley became aware of all the possibilities, she lifted her shoulders in an expression of frustrated helplessness.

"But who knows anything for sure at this point," she said, looking at Garick with an unconscious plea in her eyes. "All even a fully qualified zoologist could do right now is make educated guesses until a complete study of the animals and the way they function is undertaken."

Garick nodded and Ashley saw a slight smile in his gray eyes as he said, "Yes, but one thing seems clear. If all the members of this species are migrating to the south pole right now, and if they stay there long enough for some specialists to arrive from earth, our immediate problem is over."

It took Ashley a moment to realize that what Garick had said, and the way he looked, meant he was on her side, that he had been all along. He favored studying the beasts instead of killing them just as she did! And then a stunning thought hit her all at once and her eyes opened wide.

"Garick . . ." she said slowly, ". . . tell me something."

He raised his eyebrows.

"How did you get that scar at the corner of your mouth?"

Garick looked puzzled, and then shrugged. "I got it when I was a boy. I was playing catch with a friend and I jumped up to get a high ball, lost my balance, and when I fell, I hit my face on a jagged rock. It took plastic surgery to get it to look as good as it does now. You should have seen it when it happened."

Ashley closed her eyes and let out a long, bitter sigh. When she opened her eyes, she stared at Garick sadly and shook her head. "I've misjudged you all along, haven't I?" she said quietly. "And not just about the lizards."

He obviously knew what she meant, and for an instant, a cool, distant look came into his eyes. But there was also a faint hint of pain which cut Ashley to the heart.

"We'll talk about it later, Ashley," he said with a quiet dismissiveness that made the pain in her heart sharpen.

The pilot broke in before Ashley could reply. "We'd better head back to camp. We're running low on fuel. We can come back later."

Garick nodded, and the pilot made a sweeping turn and headed north.

For the rest of the return trip, Ashley was silent, sunk in a numbing sense of dismay. She'd let circumstances, surface appearances, her own imagination, and her mother's biases blind her to the real nature of the man she loved.

In fact, she had twisted reality where Garick was concerned, and it was a wonder she loved him at all.

She actually loved an illusion of her own making. And since she was now almost positive that the real Garick Deveron was twice as lovable as the one who had managed to snare her heart, her impending loss was almost more than she could bear.

Back at camp, as the pilot refueled the hover, Garick collected Jim, Bud, and for some reason Ashley couldn't comprehend, Paulus Glignan, to make the return trip with him. He obviously expected her to go along as well, but Ashley couldn't face it. She needed some time alone to try to come to terms with the bleak future she faced. Shaking her head, she walked to their tent and disappeared inside, where she flung herself down on her sleeping bag and burst into tears.

Garick watched Ashley walk away, noting the discouraged slump of her shoulders, her general air of defeated hopelessness. He'd never seen her look like that before, and it worried him. Since he'd known her, she'd always met each new crisis in her life with courage and creativity. And now that she knew he was on her side about the lizards, why was she acting as though the world was coming to an end instead of being delighted to find he was her ally, not her enemy?

Unless. . . .

As a likely answer to his question occurred to him, Garick's worry turned to thoughtful hesitation. Did he have time to speak to her before leaving again?

Just then the pilot announced the hover was ready, and the other men started climbing aboard. And after deciding the conversation he and Ashley needed to have soon required time and privacy, Garick joined them.

Cried out, worn out, and depressed beyond measure, Ashley lay on her sleeping bag wondering if she should, after all, accept Blackmun's offer to go away with him. The thought of facing the rest of her life without love or even friendship on New Frontier after Garick left made even the prospect of being married to a man she didn't love seem desirable. That way, she would at least be able to have children eventually. And she *liked* Blackmun.

As if her thoughts of him had brought him to her side, Blackmun ducked through the tent flap and squatted beside the sleeping bag.

Gazing dully at his face, Ashley sat up. "What is it?"

He shrugged. "Just thought it might be a good idea to stay close to you."

Uncomprehending, Ashley frowned. Then she realized that with Garick gone, Blackmun was concerned for her safety.

At the moment, Ashley could have cared less for her safety. But realizing that Blackmun wouldn't listen if she tried to send him away, she said, "Do you really think anybody would go so far as to harm me when they'd have to face Garick later?"

Blackmun shook his head. "Not really," he admitted. "But it's still not a bad idea to let them know you're not completely on your own here."

"If you say so," Ashley responded, off-handed.

"What did you see further south?" Blackmun asked.

Though Ashley wasn't in the mood to talk, she told him, and was too immersed in her own misery to notice that he coaxed her to talk, to speculate about the lizards.

When she had speculated all she cared to, a comfortable silence fell between them, during which time Ashley went back to wondering whether she should accept Blackmun's proposal. He was easy to be with, undemanding, kind, a good friend, even attractive.

But actually, all those qualities and the fact that she didn't love him, made her conclusion inevitable. Had he meant nothing to her at all, or had he been undeserving of consideration, she might have condemned him to a life with a mate who didn't love him. But Blackmun deserved better, especially from her. They were friends.

As she sat on her sleeping bag, with Blackmun sitting silently beside her, Ashley was unaware of the passage of time. All she was really aware of was that, without Garick in her life, nothing much else mattered.

Ashley was still sunk in her thoughts when Garick ducked into the tent. She blinked in confusion because she hadn't heard the hover return. And then as Garick's gray eyes, the expression in them growing harder by the second, swung from her to Blackmun and back again, she realized Blackmun must have heard it. Blackmun heard and saw everything. He must have realized what Garick's reaction to finding him with Ashley would be. But Blackmun didn't explain, and Ashley, thinking it would do no good, didn't either.

"We're about to have a meeting," Garick said flatly. "If you're interested in what we've decided to do about the lizards, Ashley, I suggest you attend."

An instant later, he was gone, and Ashley looked at Blackmun, her gaze sadly chastising. Blackmun stared back at her with no hint of remorse in his black eyes. Ashley wondered if, far from giving up on her, he was intent on driving the wedge between Garick and her even deeper in hopes of gaining from the rift.

Since Ashley thought the gap was already too wide to be healed, and she'd already made up her mind she couldn't use Blackmun as an escape from her unpromising future, she couldn't find it in her heart to berate him for what he'd done. She shook her head at him slightly, then got to her feet and left the tent.

Outside, the men were gathered around Garick and Jim, and Garick explained that the beasts were apparently migrating to the south pole, possibly to lay eggs, or to birth their young, and no longer represented a direct threat to anyone for the time being. He added that it had been decided to send to earth for a team from the Agency for the Protection of Alien Animal Species and hope the lizards didn't come north again before the team arrived.

"I say we don't wait for anybody!" Rex Blanton challenged the decision. "I say we go down there by hover and pick them off one by one from the air while they're in barren territory and easy to spot before we've got a whole new crop of them to deal with!"

Garick shook his head. "We couldn't justify doing that now that they no longer represent a direct threat to us," he said firmly. "Besides, it wouldn't be as easy as you make it sound, Blanton. There's a whole herd of them, and from the air, we'd likely end up only wounding them rather than killing them. You haven't seen how much physical injury they can sustain and still function, and how hard they are to kill. I have. Besides, if the agency ever found out what we'd done, we'd be in very hot water."

Blanton's face flushed angrily. "That's about what I expected you'd say, Deveron," he sneered. "You're dragging your feet because of that woman of yours! But we don't have to do what he says," he raised his voice and swung his head to talk to the other men now. "If Deveron won't lead us to wipe out those lizards, I will! What do you say, men? Do you want to see those killing machines come up from the south in a few days, or a few weeks, or a few months from now—however long it takes for them to hatch a whole new crop of lizards—and threaten your wives and children?"

Ashley glanced uneasily at Garick to see how he was taking this challenge to his leadership, and saw that he wasn't taking it well at all. His eyes were lit with gray fire, and his face looked more threatening than she had ever seen it look. The scar at the corner of his mouth was a white blaze against the tan of his skin, his fists were doubled, and he held his body with a taut readiness that spelled out his desire for a physical confrontation with Blanton.

"I've told you before to watch your mouth, Blanton!" he said with a lethal quietness that made everyone tense and go still. "I won't tell you again."

This time Rex Blanton was apparently too angry to behave wisely. "We're going after those lizards whether you like it or not, Deveron!" he snarled. "So just make up your mind to—"

"Hold it!" Jim Jacobs roared, at last exerting his authority as part of the governing body of New Plymouth. "You're not in charge here, Blanton.

That's not the way it works on New Frontier and you know it!"

"It's the way it works if the rest of these men agree with me!" Blanton yelled back.

He half-turned away from Garick and Jim, obviously intending to exhort the rest of the men to back him up. But before he could say a word, Garick moved forward, put a hand on Blanton's shoulder, spun him around, and cracked a fist against the rancher's jaw. Blanton fell to the ground.

Ashley was appalled at the display of violence. And then she was afraid for Garick as Blanton, bellowing his rage, grabbed a hefty dead tree branch from the ground near his hand. He jumped to his feet, and raising the tree branch in his hand, headed for Garick.

With an ease that left Ashley blinking in astonishment, Garick neatly sidestepped the first descending blow. He reached out with blinding speed, grabbed the branch, twisted it out of Blanton's hand, and tossed it aside. When Blanton then came at him swinging his fists, Garick parried those blows as well, then crashed another fist into Blanton's jaw. When Blanton fell this time, he didn't get up again.

Garick then fixed the crowd of men with a cold look and asked, "Anyone else in the mood for a fight?"

To Ashley's relief, no one took up the challenge. Indeed, as she glanced around anxiously, she saw that the other men were gazing at Garick with wary respect rather than with hostility.

It was at that point that Paulus Glignan came forward. Though his palms were upraised in a peaceful gesture to show that he wasn't challenging Garick, his manner was not the least subservient. His brown eyes were steady, his carriage self-assured.

"I think perhaps," he said in a carrying voice that was tinged with relaxed authority, "it's time to introduce myself more fully than I have since I arrived on New Frontier." He reached into a pocket and withdrew an official-looking piece of paper and extended it to Jim.

From the benefit of having spent weeks sharing a cabin aboard the *Mayflower VII* with Jim, Ashley had the distinct impression he'd known all along that Glignan wasn't what he seemed to be—an innocent emigrant. Furthermore, when she glanced at Garick, she decided he wasn't surprised by Glignan's actions either. Nevertheless, both Jim and Garick behaved as though Glignan had taken them by surprise. Jim read the paper with interest, then looked up and gave the men a subtle warning look.

"This says that Paulus Glignan is a representative of the agency on earth which oversees New Frontier affairs," he told them.

Ashley supposed she was the only one there who greeted the news with uncomplicated relief. All the others looked warily at one another, and a murmur of surprise, tinged with resentment, ran briefly through the crowd. Ashley heard one man who was behind her mutter to someone else, "See, I told you they sent people here to spy on us."

Glignan waited with calm dignity until the murmurs stopped, and then he addressed them in a tone of authority. "I'm sure you'll all be interested to know that I've already alerted the Agency for the

Preservation of Alien Animal Species to send a team here to study the lizards," he said. "I did it as soon as Mr. Deveron brought the news to Plymouth that the creatures existed."

Another murmur ran through the crowd, this time one of resigned acceptance. They knew what Glignan's words meant. Anyone who killed one of the lizards now for any reason other than self-defense would be prosecuted.

Ashley glanced at where Blanton had been lying on the ground. He was now sitting up, his face turned toward Glignan. To Ashley's relief, his face showed resigned acceptance as well, even if it was still tinged with anger.

"Of course," Glignan went on, "you are all entitled to protect yourselves and your families. But none of the animals apparently is a direct threat to anyone for the time being, and I'm hoping the team will arrive before the animals come back this way. Meanwhile, it would seem prudent to post lookouts in case the animals do come north before the team gets here. But even if some of the animals do return, they still must pose a direct threat to human life before any killing takes place. I hope that's clearly understood. Any questions?"

There were no questions, not even from Blanton.

"Very well," Glignan said. "Then I'm turning this meeting over to the competent supervision of Mr. Jacobs and Mr. Deveron." He touched his hand to his forehead in a casual salute, then walked toward Ashley.

Ashley stared at him with gratitude. His brown eyes were twinkling with mischief as, after reaching her side, he bent toward her and whispered, "See, I told you things would work out for the best. I do hope, though, in the interest of getting out of here alive, that no one overly resents the fact that I've been spying on them."

He then stepped to her side and faced Garick and Jim, as everyone else was doing.

Smiling faintly, Ashley glanced around. After deciding that no one was going to express their resentment of Glignan's spying with anything other than sidelong glances of suspicion and disapproval, she turned her eyes toward Garick. She wished Glignan could make everything turn out for the best where her marriage was concerned as he had for the lizards.

"I'll stay behind while the rest of you return home," Garick was saying, much to Ashley's consternation. "The other members of the exploration team will fly down to join me in about a week so we can finish our job in the jungle. Thanks for coming. Now go pack up and be on your way."

That was the end of the meeting, and as the crowd dispersed to gather up their tents and gear, Glignan turned to Ashley. There was still a twinkle in his eye.

"Well, it's been a pleasure meeting you, my dear," he said, "even if our acquaintance will be all too short. Now that my cover is blown, I'll be departing for earth. But don't worry. I'll brief my successor that he can count on you to keep a cool head when others lose their perspective, and to back up your principles with courage."

At that, Ashley fixed him with a steady look and shook her head. "So long as you don't tell your successor to expect me to become a government spy against my fellow citizens," she said firmly. "That wasn't what this was all about. I didn't act against them. I acted in their best interests in spite of what they may think now. Or rather perhaps in the best interests of their grandchildren, since whatever role the lizards play in the planet's ecology may not be evident for a while."

"Oh, I'm aware of that." Glignan nodded, his smile resigned. "And I shall make that clear in my report. But I wish you didn't make it sound as though the agency that employs me *doesn't* have the best interests of these people in mind. I assure you the truth is quite the opposite. The government didn't bring these people here in order to hamper their survival, but rather to assure it."

"Maybe so," Ashley said, "but I'm a history major, and I've read of many instances where a government's actions didn't always coincide with its stated objectives. Besides, what one government decides, the next one can undo—or else tamper with to a disastrous extent."

"True," Glignan agreed mildly, "but the objective to save humankind from extinction has so far survived intact through several succeeding governments on earth, and I have hopes that it will continue to do so."

"So do I," Ashley retorted absently, her eyes searching for Garick now. But he was nowhere to be seen.

"Well, I suppose I should begin packing," Glignan said. "Thank you for your help in this matter, Ashley, even if the help was given as a result of your own beliefs rather than a desire to make my job easier."

He took her hand, bent over it and kissed it, and then, with a charming smile, he walked away.

Ashley hesitated, then started walking with slow reluctance toward her tent to begin her own packing. She felt someone come up beside her and she turned her head. It was Blackmun who looked at her in a way she knew meant he was wondering if this was the last time he'd ever see her.

"We don't have to say our final good-byes yet, Blackmun," she said with a faint smile. "I'll be going back to Plymouth on one of the hovers."

She could see that what she'd said conflicted with the hope he felt at the fact that she wasn't staying at the campsite with Garick. So she turned to face him, stepped into his arms for a hug, and whispered gently against his ear, "Yes . . . we'll be saying a final good-bye then. Don't hope I'm going to change my mind. I can't."

Then she kissed his cheek, moved out of his arms, and hurried the rest of the way to her tent, leaving him staring for a long, lonely moment after her before he headed in the direction of his own tent.

Garick caught up with Rex Blanton just before Blanton reached his tent. He didn't particularly look forward to what he had to say, but the friction between them needed to be eased for the good of the community. Besides, he knew Blanton had been his substitute for Blackmun in their fight. It was the old friend who had betrayed him whom he really wanted to punch, not the rancher who was only concerned for his livelihood.

Blanton eyed him with angry wariness at first, until

Garick said, "My temper got the better of me back there, Blanton. It shouldn't have happened. No hard feelings, I hope?"

Blanton hesitated, then relaxed somewhat and shrugged. "Well, I guess if you'd been talking about my wife the way I'd been talking about yours," he admitted, "I wouldn't have taken it lightly either. And," he added a little sheepishly, "I pushed you pretty hard about going after the lizards as well."

"We all have our buttons that set off the fireworks when they get pushed," Garick said with a wry smile.

The two men shook hands, Blanton ducked into his tent, and Garick turned away and hesitated. He still wanted to find Blackmun and have it out with him. But having already behaved in a way that might make Ashley think of him as a barbarian again, he decided it wasn't worth it. Blackmun's betrayal of their friendship hadn't gained the bastard anything anyway. Ashley had turned him down.

At least she had turned Blackmun down last night, Garick thought, frowning. But had Blackmun really given up? If so, why had he been with Ashley again just before the meeting?

It was then that Garick looked to his right and saw Ashley a few yards away—wrapped in Blackmun's arms.

Chapter Eighteen

Seething with cold rage, Garick started toward Ashley and Blackmun. But before he reached them, they broke apart and Ashley walked away.

Garick didn't follow her. He followed Blackmun. And in the privacy of Blackmun's tent, there was a short, rather violent altercation. When it was over, Blackmun, his dark eyes resigned, stroked a tender jaw with one hand while dragging his knapsack with the other, and headed for one of the hovers. He boarded it without looking back.

As Ashley packed her things, but not Garick's, tears streamed down her cheeks. They were separate now, each going a different way. For a long time, she had accepted being alone as natural. She had never even suspected what it was like to be so entwined—heart, mind, body and soul—with another human being that even their separate identities had somehow merged to encompass a new, whole one. But being alone was no longer natural to her; in fact, it was the last thing she wanted.

But if she and Garick had truly become one, she thought an instant later with sad puzzlement, then why hadn't she ever seen him clearly until today? How could she have maintained an illusion of him that was so far off the mark? Or had her subconscious recognized his true nature, she wondered, allowing her to love him despite what her conscious mind thought about him?

She shook her head. Her mind had been awake and aware the entire time she'd known him. She had seen that he wasn't barbarous, but merely different from what she was used to; that he wasn't ruthless, but strong; that he wasn't vicious, but was more often kind than not. So it must have been the other way around. Her subconscious, which she had thought knowledge and experience had purged of her mother's early messages, must have been running the old tapes of fear and distrust all along, subverting her logic.

But what difference does it make now? she asked herself sadly as she closed her knapsack. *The result is the same. I've lost the only man I'll ever love.*

"What the hell do you think you're doing?"

Garick stood at the tent flap, and his harsh tone of voice made Ashley automatically spin around before she could brush away the tears on her cheeks. When she realized he had seen that she'd been crying, she quickly turned away from him. She began surreptitiously to wipe her eyes and cheeks as she answered, "I'm packing, of course."

"Why?"

Why? Ashley thought with a sudden irate incredulity that replaced her former misery with anger. *He knows why! Does he want a pound of my flesh to go along with my broken heart for his dinner tonight?*

Then she realized that last thought came straight out of her old perception of Garick as a barbarian and she quickly pushed it away.

"You know why, Garick," she answered as calmly as she could, but without turning around to face him.

"Do I?" There was still an edge to his voice, but he didn't sound quite as harsh as he had earlier. Instead, there was a certain bleakness to his tone now. "Are you telling me you've changed your mind about going with Blackmun to one of the new planets?"

Forgetting that her recent tears were still probably visible on her face, Ashley turned quickly to look at Garick, astonished.

"No, of course not!" she protested. Then she added, "So you did hear what he said to me last night?"

"I heard." Garick nodded, his expression thunderous.

"Then you must have heard me refuse him," Ashley said, scowling. "So why ask me if I've changed my mind?"

"Because you're packing."

Ashley shrugged, the gesture denoting her helpless bewilderment. "Well, what else should I do? I knew you wouldn't want me to stay here with you, so—"

"Oh, for God's sake!" Garick interrupted, sounding

thoroughly disgusted, yet relieved, at the same time. "Are you completely hopeless at reading what's on my mind?"

Despite her love, the pain of losing him, and her common sense telling her this was the time to be calm and have a meaningful, honest conversation with him, Ashley's temper rose.

"Well, you needn't sound like I'm stupid!" she snapped. "I never claimed to be telepathic!"

"Why *not* imply you're stupid, when you're behaving stupidly?" Garick shot back.

Ashley's temper rose higher. "Oh—stuff it!" she bit out. "I should have known you wouldn't be gentleman enough to let me leave without picking a fight! Just get out of the way and let me go!"

"Be my guest," Garick grated, turning his body to give her room to pass him.

Ashley snatched up her knapsack and stomped toward him. But her temper wasn't quite out of control. She hoped he would reach out and stop her before it was too late.

He didn't so much as twitch an eyebrow, much less reach out and try to stop her from leaving, however, and as Ashley neared the tent flap, she was already calling herself every kind of fool in the book. If she had only kept calm, perhaps they could have patched things up. Or, if that wasn't possible, at least they could have parted in a way she wouldn't ever afterward remember with crushing regret.

She hesitated. Then she stopped. And finally, she turned slowly back toward Garick. Her temper was gone now, but she was fighting her pride. She struggled to behave like a mature adult instead of a sulky child.

Garick had a peculiarly intent look in his gray eyes, and he seemed to be holding his body taut. As Ashley looked at him, her love at last overcame her pride.

"I can't go without saying . . ." She paused to control the quavering emotion in her voice, took a deep breath, then began again. "I—I haven't thanked you properly, Garick, for defending me the way you would a wife you'd chosen yourself. And I haven't thanked you for teaching me about love."

When she paused to take another breath, Garick asked, "What kind of love are you talking about?"

Ashley shrugged helplessly. "All kinds," she said simply. "Anyway . . . thank you, Garick. With all my heart, I thank you. And I hope your future holds all the happiness you deserve." She hesitated, then forced the last word she had to say out of her mouth. "Good-bye."

The word came out sounding so strangled with tears that Ashley couldn't look at him. Nor could she stand there any longer. She quickly spun on her heel, dived through the tent opening, and started at a fast walk toward where the hovers were parked.

She was so blinded with tears, it took her a moment to realize the hovers were no longer on the ground. One was already in the air and the other was just lifting off.

Ashley stopped short for an instant, then broke into a run, yelling, "Wait! Wait! You forgot—"

The "me" she'd meant to say turned into a gasp as her boot snagged on a half-hidden rock in the ground and she went flying. She lay flat on her stomach with the breath knocked out of her. As she tried to struggle to her knees, Garick's two strong hands lifted her from behind and set her on her feet. She still couldn't talk, but she tried to gasp the words she wanted to say as she lifted an urgent hand to point at the departing hovercraft.

Garick ignored her wheezing protests, as well as her pointing finger. He looked at her, shaking his head in the way he had that Ashley always interpreted as meaning he thought she was beyond help.

Angry again, she stamped her foot and found her voice. "Make them . . . come back!" she gasped.

He shook his head again, then stood watching her, his hands on his hips, his gray eyes steady on her face.

Ashley glared angrily for another couple of minutes before it occurred to her to wonder *why* Garick wasn't attempting to call one of the hovers back by radio. It couldn't be that he wanted the two of them to be left here alone together—could it?

Garick was obviously reading her like a book. He nodded a bare instant after the thought crossed Ashley's mind.

"But why?" she asked.

"Think about it," he said. Then he turned on his heel to go make a fire so they could have dinner.

Ashley wasn't in the mood to "think" about it. She was in the mood for straight, honest talk. She caught up with Garick, grabbed his arm, and tried to swing him around. He wouldn't budge, so she darted in front of him and wouldn't let him pass her.

"Not this time!" she wheezed at him furiously, still somewhat breathless. "You tell me, Garick, and you tell me now! In detail! At length! Starting this minute!"

Garick sighed.

* * *

As he looked down at Ashley's flushed, tear-streaked face, at her tangled auburn hair, at the anger and puzzlement evident in her beautiful golden-hazel eyes, and at the tension in her small, shapely body, he found it hard to believe that she really needed explanations.

He had married her. He had made love to her. He had shown jealousy when it became evident that Blackmun wanted her. He had defended her. She knew now that he was on her side about the lizards. And finally, he had kept her here with him when everyone else had left, which should have made it obvious to her that he wanted their marriage to continue.

But if explanations were what Ashley wanted, he was perfectly willing to make her happy, so he took her shoulders in his hands, looked her straight in the eye, and spelled things out with perfect clarity—or so he thought.

"I kept you here because I forgive you," he said. Then he let her go and walked to the fire pit. He was hungry.

Ashley stared at her husband, her fury rapidly sliding toward smoldering resentment at his self-righteousness. But underneath the resentment was pure joy, rising in a tide so intense it nearly swamped her ability to think. Nearly, but not quite.

"You *what?*" she asked Garick's back.

He went on placing wood on the fire.

"You heard me," he said. "I forgive you for your disloyalty."

"You forgive me," Ashley repeated as she walked to

a nearby boulder and sat down on it with a thump as her legs gave out on her.

Garick nodded.

"When did you decide to forgive me?" she asked.

"When Sandra told me she clinched getting you to agree to keep her secret when she threatened me. That cancelled out your disloyalty in keeping secrets from me because you were being loyal in another way."

"Then what is there to forgive?" Ashley's resentment rose a notch above her joy.

Garick shrugged, and a small smile twitched his mouth briefly before it disappeared.

Ashley stayed silent for a few minutes, during which time Garick put a skillet of caldera meat and a coffeepot on the fire and settled back on his heels.

"I wonder," Ashley said, her golden-hazel eyes steady on Garick's face, "if besides forgiving me, you also love me."

Garick quickly lifted his head, amusement now shimmering in his gray eyes like sunlight shining through storm clouds.

"Of course," he admitted matter-of-factly. "Just like you love me."

Though another rush of joy filled Ashley's heart, she ignored Garick's last statement. "And when did you decide you love me?" she asked. "When you thought I might run off to another planet with Blackmun?"

"No. I knew I loved you before that. But I wasn't sure how you felt—until you refused Blackmun's offer."

Ashley was silent for a while again. Then she asked, "And does your forgiveness and your love mean you want to take me with you when you go to scout the new planet?"

Garick looked at her again, his gaze steady and serious now. "Yes."

Ashley's joy leapt inside her like a flash of lightning.

"So long as you promise I'm not ever going to have to forgive you for disloyalty again," Garick added.

Ashley's joy was still there, but she bristled immediately. "And what if your idea of what constitutes disloyalty is so complex and overdeveloped, I inadvertently step over the line without even knowing it?" she asked a little snappishly.

"Don't worry," Garick responded with dry humor. "I'm beginning to understand I have to spell everything out for you, so I'll make the boundaries clear."

Ashley bristled again. But she kept a tight hold on her temper in the interest of drawing some boundaries of her own.

"Well," she said firmly, "that brings up a promise I'd like to have from you before I accompany you to some Godforsaken wilderness that's likely to make an old woman of me or kill me before I'm forty."

Garick raised a dark eyebrow.

"You're right," Ashley said. "I do like to have things spelled out for me. So let's start from the beginning, and you tell me everything you've ever felt or thought about me since the first moment you laid eyes on me right up to now. And you promise that you'll continue to tell me what you're thinking and feeling about me from now on."

Now Garick was silent. Then he shrugged and began to talk. He talked while he cooked, talked while they ate, and talked as they got ready for bed. He didn't finish talking until they were lying naked together in Ashley's sleeping bag. By then, he was fiercely hungry again, but not for food. However, Ashley was stiff as a board and seething with anger.

"So you wanted me the first time you saw me," she said ominously, "and you read my file and learned everything about me."

"Yes."

"And you kindly decided it was in my best interests to let you deprive me of my virginity aboard ship so I would be ready for what awaited me when I arrived on New Frontier."

"Yes. But of course," Garick added, "my decision wasn't entirely based on kindness. I wanted you pretty badly. As a matter of fact, after we married, I began to realize that I must have felt more than—"

Ashley interrupted. "And you could have refused my marriage proposal, but you married me because you felt sorry for me."

"Yes. And because I wanted you. And because—"

Ashley broke in, "And you didn't want me to know you could have refused my proposal because then I would have wondered why you accepted. And you didn't want to have to confess that you'd pitied me and lusted after me, much less that you intended to leave me behind when you left New Frontier to explore a new planet if I didn't measure up as a wife!"

"Well . . ." Garick hesitated. "I wouldn't put the last part exactly like that. I just wasn't sure the marriage would work because it was possible you were frigid, and because you seemed determined to think of me as a barbarian. I mean, when I realized you were serious about thinking I'd actually kill you for proposing to me, I realized you had me mixed up with some character out of history—Genghis Khan maybe. But like I started to say before, Ashley—"

Ashley interrupted again. "And when you thought I'd been disloyal, you decided to leave me behind."

"I didn't *think* you were disloyal, Ashley. You were disloyal."

"But there were extenuating circumstances surrounding my disloyalty, right?"

"Yes. And don't forget, I didn't defend you against Blanton and the men who felt as he did about the lizards with other than the expected degree of husbandly loyalty. If I had, my objectivity would have been compromised, and I wouldn't have been able to help you get the agreement you wanted to study the lizards instead of killing them. I might have been deposed as leader of the expedition. It was sheer luck that the beasts started migrating. If they hadn't, I planned to argue for their protection in some way that would make it seem that, while I didn't necessarily agree with you wholeheartedly, your arguments had some merit."

"Bully for you," Ashley said, her voice rising. "But what kind of loyalty is it," she went on acidly, "that allows a man to marry a woman with the intention of leaving her one day! If your brand of loyalty doesn't kick in until you've decided you want the marriage to last, then why should mine have kicked in after only one day of a marriage to a man I thought hated me for forcing him to marry me in the first place!"

The logic of Ashley's words was undeniable, and after a moment of reflection, Garick admitted as much. "You're right. I seem to have been operating from a double standard in the matter."

Ashley raised herself on her elbow and glared down at him. "You've not only been operating from a double standard, you've been lying like a dog to both of us!" she bit out.

"Now, hold on a minute." Garick shook his head. "I—"

"You think you married me because you felt sorry for me?" Ashley cut him off again. "How far do you think your *pity* for me would have stretched if I'd been seven feet tall, weighed 300 pounds, had a face like a lizard, and a personality to match? You liar! You may have told yourself you married me out of pity, or even lust, but there had to have been more to it than that!"

Garick smiled. For the past few minutes, he'd been trying to tell Ashley exactly what she'd just concluded on her own.

"Well," he said mildly, "occasionally your temper does *approach* lizard-like proportions. Let me see your teeth."

"What?" Taken off guard, Ashley frowned at him.

"I want to see if they're razor-sharp. If they are, I think I'll sleep a little further north from here."

Ashley gritted her teeth and flopped onto her back.

Grinning now, Garick came up on his elbow and leaned over her. "Okay, sweetheart," he said, his eyes dancing with humor, "so neither of us is perfect. We sometimes lie to ourselves, and the lies are passed on to one another. But I love you and you love me. And I'd bet my best femura you'd rather come with me to a godforsaken wild planet than stay here on New Frontier without me. So what do you say we let bygones be bygones and start fresh together. No lies this time. No hidden agendas. We admit we stay together because that's where each of us wants to be."

Ashley eyed him gloomily. "How did loyalty get to be so important to you anyway?"

"I was born to parents who spent most of their lives in dangerous situations. Loyalty could mean the difference between life and death. If you couldn't count on the people on your team, you could be in real trouble. It was the same when I came back to New Frontier with the first settlers. That's why we emphasized the all-for-one philosophy from the start and the understanding that the every-man-for-himself philosophy was why earth was dying. We wanted a different way of looking at things here on our new world."

He raised a hand and gently stroked a strand of Ashley's auburn hair back from her forehead. "We're all the product of our upbringing, Ashley," he said, his voice deepening. "You were taught that men were scum. I was taught that disloyalty should never be forgiven. But if we have a son, I can't believe you'll hold on to any vestige of your mother's opinions about men, will you? And from now on, I'll make certain I have all the facts before I decide you've been disloyal to me. And even if you ever are disloyal, which I doubt, I can't imagine not forgiving you almost anything."

His manner and words soothed Ashley's temper. She blinked at him, the tension inside her eased.

"How many children do you want, Garick?" she asked.

"However many we have."

He bent lower to kiss her, but Ashley held him off, shaking her head. "We can't do that, Garick," she said, seriously.

He frowned. "Can't do what? Make love? Hell, if you thought I was a barbarian before, wait and see what I'm like when I'm sexually frustrated, and the way I'm feeling now, you won't have to wait long."

He reached for her again, but Ashley, smiling now, still held him at bay. "No, no"—she shook her head—"that's not what I meant. I meant we can't have more than two or three children."

Garick frowned again. "Why not?"

"It's a matter of principle," Ashley explained, gazing at him solemnly. "Overpopulation is one of the reasons earth is in its present mess. And though I realize there's plenty of room and resources on New Frontier right now so that we could have as many children as we like, and that that will be even truer on a new planet, it doesn't matter. You said your parents wanted a different way of looking at things here and that's why there's an all-for-one policy. But there are other things we need to look at differently on the new worlds, too. And it seems to me that voluntarily restricting the population to as many people as the new worlds can reasonably support is important. Though we are in the beginning stages of a developing society, a principle is a principle."

Garick shook his head. "There are counter arguments to your way of thinking, Ashley. As you said, we're in the beginning stages here. And there are things to consider like the improved quality and diversity of life that can come with the skills, the talents, and the different outlooks a larger population will bring. And we may never get to the point where we can bring enough people from earth to make up that larger population. It may be that at some point, the people who are already here and the ones who will be brought to the new planets are all there are and it will be entirely up to them to populate our new homes. Sure, at some point, the population may have to be restricted. But right now, the problem is just the opposite. We need a larger population than we have."

Ashley sighed. "I see what you mean, but it's hard to turn off years of thinking one way and adopt a completely opposite position."

Garick smiled. "We can't anticipate and solve all the problems that go with being human," he said, "no matter what the experience of mankind on earth may have taught us. And we don't have to think about them all the time either," he added pointedly. "Otherwise, there's no time for just enjoying living."

Ashley looked at him, smiled, and reached up to place her palm on his cheek. "So you want to enjoy living?" she asked innocently.

"If you'll ever stop talking," he said drily.

"Then why aren't you kissing me?"

Garick sighed in a long-suffering manner.

Chuckling, Ashley raised her head and placed her mouth on his, her lips soft and coaxing.

Garick let her tease him for a while before he gave in. But once he did, Ashley's body was soon as soft as her lips, almost rippling in response to the touch of his hand gliding over her skin.

He drew back slightly and smiled. "There were times before our wedding night," he said huskily, "when I wasn't sure I could get through all your defenses and make you respond to me like this. But God, I wanted to. I hoped like hell I could. And then, when the reality was much better than the fantasies I'd had about our lovemaking, I was on my way to right where I am now."

"What makes you think I like this?" Ashley responded, deadpan.

"If you don't, you're a hell of an actress," Garick answered.

"No, I'm not. I'm as transparent as glass," Ashley retorted. "Are you completely hopeless at reading what's on my mind?"

Garick took having his own words thrown back at him with good grace. "So what you mean is," he suggested slowly, "you don't *like* this, you love it?"

"Do I?" Ashley was the soul of innocence.

"Yes, you do." Garick was now the soul of firm certainty.

Ashley laughed and scratched the skin of his shoulder with her nails a little harder than necessary. "Good for you," she murmured seductively. "You're reading me clearly now."

"But you want me to check my readings with questions from time to time, and you want to be able to question me?" Garick asked.

"It would save trouble." Ashley nodded contentedly.

"All right then. Do you love me, Ashley?"

Ashley's eyes widened. "You know I do," she avowed, puzzled that he'd had to ask.

"Do I? You haven't said it yet. I've said it to you, but you haven't said it to me."

Ashley hit him with the heel of her palm on his shoulder.

Laughing, Garick slid on top of her. "Say it," he

ordered, looking down at her with heat growing in his eyes.

"I love you, Garick."

Ashley said it convincingly so that he wouldn't have to ask again. But then, it wasn't hard to be convincing when she was telling the absolute truth.

Garick was satisfied. "I love you back," he murmured as he lowered his head to kiss her.

Before he found her mouth, however, Ashley spoke again, "I love you more."

Rather than contest her assertion, Garick was wise enough to let her prove it—to the total, exhausted satisfaction of each of them.

Ashley lay with her head on Garick's shoulder when a deliciously mischievous thought occurred to her.

"Garick?" she whispered.

"What?" he mumbled sleepily.

"If I asked you to, would you be psycho-programmed for me?"

Silence. Then, "If you asked me *really* persuasively, I'd give it some thought anyway."

"Didn't I just do that?"

Silence again. Then, he said more seriously, "I don't see how I could be any more devoted to you than I already am, Ashley, but if you need it, I'll do it."

Ashley happily snuggled closer. "No, I don't need it, Garick," she said, laughing. "I just wanted to know if you'd do it for me."

"Then you really don't want it?"

"Not in the least. In fact, I'd go to great lengths to

prevent it. I want you just as you are forever."

"Forever's a long time."

"Not when I'm with you. It's not half long enough."

"Your mother would turn over in her grave if she heard you say that," Garick responded, sounding pleased, very pleased.

"My mother must never have met a man like you."

"Remember all this when we're on the new planet and you want to kill me for taking you away from civilization on New Frontier. We may not have much here, but it's a hell of a lot more than we'll have where we're going."

"Will we stay on the new planet for the rest of our lives?" Ashley asked.

Garick chuckled. Then he gave in to his more merciful instincts. "No," he assured her. "New Frontier is my home. I was born here. I want to raise our children—however many of them there turn out to be—here. And I want to be buried here. We'll only be on the new planet until we've scouted it, then we'll come back."

"You're sure it's the sort of place the authorities will let you take me?"

"Absolutely. From what I've been told, it's like Eden. We'll make an extended honeymoon out of our first weeks there—unless the place happens to be home to a snake like the one that messed things up in the original Eden."

Ashley groaned. Then she sighed. And finally, she said, "Well . . . whither thou goest and all that . . ."

"Thank God," Garick said in a softer, more serious tone as he cuddled her closer. "I never knew being alone was all that bad until you showed me how much better it is to be with someone I love. And I don't ever want to be alone again."

"Exactly," Ashley agreed, so moved by Garick's words that tears began to cloud her eyes.

Garick looked at her moist eyes and smiled. "What happened to the Ashley who claimed she never cried?" he teased. "It seems to me that every time I look at you lately, you've either just finished crying or you're about to start. In fact, you've turned into a regular crybaby."

Ashley brushed her tears away, thought a moment, then smiled seductively. "You taught me to cry, Garick. And there are a lot of other things you've taught me since I met you. Want me to show you something else you taught me that I've wanted to do a lot since I met you?"

Anticipating more lovemaking, Garick grinned and stretched sensuously. Putting his hands behind his head, he left himself completely vulnerable to whatever delicious attentions Ashley wanted to bestow upon him and nodded.

Still smiling, Ashley hit him—right on his rock solid jaw.

The blow wasn't all that hard and since Ashley collapsed beside him, laughing so hard tears welled in her eyes again, Garick recovered from the shock fairly quickly and rolled over on top of her.

"Sorry . . ." she gasped through her laughter. "But I *have* wanted to do that a lot since I met you."

"And now it's my turn to do something *I've* always wanted to do since I met you. But I couldn't until now because you were so inexperienced and because it's the sort of thing people don't usually do until they're sure they love one another," Garick responded silkily.

Ashley's eyes opened wide and her laughter died away. But she didn't protest as Garick began to teach her another lesson in the art of love. As usual, she enjoyed the tutoring immensely.